Caroline Hulse spends most of her days writing, having fulfilled her dream of having a job she could do in pyjamas. She also works in Human Resources sometimes. She is openly competitive and loves playing board and card games. She can often be found in casino poker rooms, and wishes other people would want to play Cluedo for money.

Caroline's debut novel *The Adults* will be published in fifteen countries around the world. She lives with her husband in Manchester where the two are captive to the whims of a small, controlling dog.

Find Caroline on Twitter at @CarolineHulse1 or send her an email at carolinehulsewrites@gmail.com

'I loved *The Adults*! Funny, dry and beautifully observed. Highly recommended for anyone whose Perfect Christmases never quite go according to plan!'

Gill Simms, author of *Why Mummy Swears*

'I took this book on holiday and couldn't put it down! I found myself feeling tense as I became more and more invested in the unfolding drama of the weekend away. I've never read anything quite like it and Posey was a highlight'

The Unmumsy Mum

'Such a breath of fresh air! Witty, intensely human and (dare I say it) relatable . . . This novel is the perfect comedy of errors'   Katie Khan, author of *Hold Back the Stars*

'I have a feeling Caroline Hulse might be a genius, this book is so brilliant. It's funny, clever and original. I loved every minute of reading it'

Lucy Vine, author of *Hot Mess*

'Genuinely unputdownable books are rare in my experience. This is one. A brilliant, original comedy'

Daily Mail

'Brilliantly funny – will have you wincing in recognition'

Good Housekeeping

The 'Adults'

Caroline Hulse

ORION

An Orion paperback

First published in Great Britain in 2018
by Orion
This paperback edition published in 2018
by Orion Books,
an imprint of The Orion Publishing Group Ltd
Carmelite House, 50 Victoria Embankment
London EC4Y 0DZ

An Hachette UK Company

1 3 5 7 9 10 8 6 4 2

A CIP catalogue record for this book is
available from the British Library.

ISBN 978 1 4091 7831 6

Typeset by Input Data Services Ltd, Somerset

Printed and bound by CPI Group (UK) Ltd, Croydon, CR0 4YY

MIX
Paper from
responsible sources
FSC® C104740
www.fsc.org

www.orionbooks.co.uk

Adult

/ˈadʌlt,əˈdʌlt/

*noun: **adult**; plural noun: **adults***

1. a person who is fully grown or developed.

adjective

2. to be full-grown, perfected and mature.

Synonyms: ripened, grown-up, in one's prime

||||||||||||||||||||||||||||||||||||||||||||||||||||||||||||||||||||||||||||||||||||||||

Extract from the Happy Forest brochure:

The Happy Forest is the ideal place to unwind. Open the patio doors of your fully equipped lodge and breathe in the fresh air, away from the stresses and strains of everyday life.

The perfect trip for your loved ones is just a click away. Here, at the Happy Forest, you'll make the memories that last a lifetime.

||||||||||||||||||||||||||||||||||||||||||||||||||||||||||||||||||||||||||||||||||||||||

Christmas Eve, 14.06 p.m.

Operator: Emergency, which service?
Woman: We need an ambulance at the Happy Forest Holiday Park.
Operator: Are you in danger?
Woman: Please hurry. We're in the archery field near Santa's grotto, opposite the elves' smoking shelter.
Operator: It's important I understand whether you're in danger now.
Woman: I'm not in danger but we need an ambulance. He's been shot. It was an accident.
Operator: I've got help on the way. I need to go through some questions with you but it's not delaying us, OK?
Woman: Get them to hurry. There's so much blood.
Operator: OK, when you say he's been shot, what has he been shot by? What can you see?
Woman: An arrow. An archery arrow.
Operator: What's your name?
Woman: Alex.
Operator: OK, Alex. Is he conscious?
Woman: Yes. And no.
Operator: Is he breathing?
Woman: Yes, for now. Please come quickly.
Operator: Like I say, the whole time you're talking to me, they're coming with lights and sirens, OK?
(Wind sounds and background noise cut out suddenly)
Operator: When did this happen?

3

Hello?
Does he appear to be completely awake and alert, Alex?
Hello?
Hello?
Are you still there? Alex, are you still there?

I

Matt had known about the trip for months before he dropped it into conversation.

Matt didn't deliberately keep things from Alex; he just dealt with complicated thoughts like he dealt with his post.

When letters landed in the hallway, Matt stepped over them or, when they could no longer be ignored, crammed them into any nook he could find. Next to the cooker, on the bookshelf; the letters went anywhere that was easy-reach and tucked away and – most importantly – had no established retrieval system.

Hence, Matt absolved himself from any sense of urgency and, if the sender tried to contact him again, Matt seemed (and, Alex came to realise, actually *was*) genuinely surprised the issue hadn't just gone away.

Within weeks of Matt moving in, Alex had piles of envelopes in places in her house where there had never been piles before.

After the first few times she spent pulling letters out of what had once been – unappreciated at the time – empty nooks, Alex gathered the letters all together one afternoon.

She laid them out in a Hansel-and-Gretel trail from the front door to the kitchen table.

Matt came to find her in the bedroom, cradling the letters in his arms. 'All this post is mine, Al? Really?'

'I thought I'd put the letters in one place. Make it easy for you.'

Matt shrugged, the letters lifting with him. 'I don't get the point of post. Who do they expect to read post nowadays?'

Weeks later, the nooks had filled up again.

The night Matt told her about the trip, Alex had made a pie – everything from scratch. Except the pastry: Alex wasn't *made* of time. At the age of thirty-seven, she still felt like whenever she cooked an actual meal, it was a notable event: that she deserved some kind of award for not just pouring milk onto cereal.

Alex was washing up after tea when Matt came to find her. He loitered in the doorway, like it had occurred to him to come downstairs on a whim and he hadn't yet decided whether he was staying.

'So. You know what I said about Claire's idea for Christmas?'

Alex glanced round. 'No.'

He widened his eyes. 'I definitely haven't mentioned it?'

'You definitely haven't.'

Matt blew his dark fringe out of his eyes, as he did twenty times each day. His hairline was impressively youthful for thirty-eight and Alex suspected he might have cultivated the habit to accentuate it. He might have, he might not. Alex meant to ask someone who'd known him longer. Not that it mattered – but Alex was a scientist. Once she'd developed a hypothesis, she wanted to test it. Alex liked her facts clean, boxed.

'God, I'm useless, Al.'

Alex peered at the glass in her hand, checking for soap suds so she didn't have to reply.

Matt stayed in the doorway behind her, but reached out to stroke her arm. 'I suppose I didn't know how to bring it up. I thought you might get mad.'

Noting the seamless change of approach from 'I thought I'd mentioned it' to 'I didn't know how to bring it up', Alex unpeeled her washing-up gloves and flopped them over the drainer. She turned to face Matt. 'Am I about to get mad?'

Matt gestured for her to step towards him. He put his arms around her waist. 'Understandably mad, of course.' He kissed her forehead. 'Completely justifiably mad. Not *crazy psycho* mad.'

This did not bode well. 'Go on.'

'So you know I haven't spent Christmas with Scarlett since Claire and I split up.'

Alex nodded. 'Have we got Scarlett this year? I'd like that.'

'No, it's ... Claire wants us to go on a weekend away together.'

Alex took a beat to process this. '*Us?*'

'*Us.* All of us. You and me. Her and Patrick. With Scarlett as the guest of honour.'

Alex stared at Matt. She gestured towards the kitchen table. This was not the kind of conversation Alex wanted to be having with someone who was standing in a doorway. She didn't want to be having this conversation at all, but if

7

she was going to have to do so, it would be with someone who was actually in the same room as her.

'At the Happy Forest holiday park in North Yorkshire.' Matt leaned on the back of a chair, palms down, like he was too excited to sit. 'They pull out all the stops at Christmas, festive magic everywhere. Light-up reindeers and fake snow. Santa's elves wander round the forest singing carols.'

Alex glanced at the wine rack but made herself look away. She refused to get annoyed. Annoyance led to irrationality, and irrationality was a personal – and professional – failure.

She lowered herself into a kitchen chair; it creaked. '*This* Christmas? You mean *one month's time* Christmas?'

Matt sank into the chair next to Alex. He leaned forward and picked up one of her spotty-socked feet and placed it on his knee. 'We've talked about it before, haven't we?' He stroked her foot. 'How magical it would be for Scarlett to spend Christmas with both me and Claire.'

'But we didn't discuss it in *that* way. Not like we were really going to do it.'

Matt looked down at her foot. 'But what other way is there?'

'We were just being smug about how grown-up and classy we are. It wasn't a serious conversation.'

'It was to me.'

Alex felt a softening in her chest. Lovely Matt, who thought this kind of thing was a good idea. Who had accepted he would never be a superstar DJ, two years off his fortieth birthday. Who had recently bought a skateboard again, and who was planning to build a half-pipe in the garden – a prospect Alex hadn't even objected to, knowing there was no chance he would ever get round to it.

Who thought stroking Alex's socked foot would make this conversation easier.

Alex looked down at her lap. 'Or maybe we meant go for a meal sometime. I'm sure no one meant a holiday.' She flicked one fingernail against another. 'Claire can't possibly think it's a good idea. She's a sensible woman.'

'She says we all get on fine. She likes you.'

'I like her too,' Alex said in a rush. She tried to get those words in first, when possible. 'Did you tell her I'd agreed?'

Matt appeared to concentrate hard on Alex's foot. He tipped his head forward; his fringe followed.

Curtains, Alex thought. That's what they used to call that haircut in the early nineties. When it was worn by more age- and era-appropriate people.

'I thought I'd mentioned it, I'm sorry. But we can still make an excuse. Workload. Family clash.' Matt lifted his head in a question. 'Dead grandparent?'

'I'm trying to understand if you've told her I'd agreed.'

Matt gave an *oops* smile.

'What does Patrick think about not getting to spend Christmas in Nottingham? Won't he want to be near his own kids?'

'They're teenagers. Claire said they never want to see him anyway.'

Alex took a deep breath. 'So. Is the trip actually booked?'

'I'm sure we could get a refund. But you know Claire, she's just so organised. Once she's got an idea in her head, that's it.' Matt shook his head tolerantly. 'She's probably packed her case already.'

Alex pressed her lips together. 'Do other people do this? Go on holiday with their exes and their new partners?'

Matt shrugged. 'Does it matter?'

'If we pull out now, I'll be the bad guy.'

'I'm not going to drag you there by the hair, Al.' Matt lifted her foot up and placed it down on the floor with a pat, as if dismissing an eager pet. 'If you really don't want to go, we won't go.' He paused. 'I wouldn't want to go without you – that would be weird.'

'Super-weird.'

'But you always said if you'd met Claire in a different way you might be mates.'

I did, Alex reflected. *I said that.* But it wasn't fair of Matt to quote her out of context. Mixing up real, solid conversations and fluffy-cloud, Vaseline-on-the-lens conversations.

Matt put his hands on the table. 'I just don't want to miss another Christmas with Scarlett. She's *seven*, Al. She was four the last time I watched her open her stocking.'

'Scarlett comes first, of course. But can't we just have her here one year?'

'Claire's her mum. I can't take Scarlett away from her at Christmas. It's not right.'

Alex closed her eyes. That was Matt all over, in one illogical sentence. So irritatingly respectful and chivalrous.

She opened her eyes and saw the washing up in the sink. Perhaps not always that chivalrous. But about this kind of thing, he was chivalrous. About what felt, tonight, like exactly the wrong kind of thing.

Alex watched Matt carefully. 'Are you sure you've thought it through?'

He gave his mouth a side-twist of thought. 'What's to think through?'

'Oh, I don't know. There's nothing complicated? At all? Nothing that might be awkward?'

'Why would there be?'

Alex looked out of the window. In her garden, the security light flickered, flashing her garden into focus in strobe-like images.

Flash. Grimy washing line. *Flash.* Rusty garden chair with the wonky leg. *Flash.* Tiger-in-a-cape hand puppet strewn across the gravel, the cloth sodden and aged with grime, left over from a friend's visit with her baby.

Alex turned back to Matt. She'd always been determined not to infantilise her boyfriend like so many of her friends did, treating their partners like the cack-handed get-nothing-right males who flailed through TV adverts for household products. But he didn't make it easy for her sometimes. She hated it when he pushed her into this position: making her into the wife from TV adverts, her hands on her aproned hips, lecturing him about brands of kitchen roll.

Alex leaned forward in her chair, maintaining eye contact. 'How do you feel – really feel – about spending Christmas with your ex?'

'These things are only complicated if you make them that way, Al. It's all in the mind.'

'No lingering emotion or resentment?'

Matt put his head to one side. 'I don't think so.'

'Nothing, however small, left unsaid? Your history's all empty and wipe-clean? The needle's back on the start of the record and everything's peachy?'

Matt sat back in his chair.

'I'm just thinking of you,' Alex added. 'A lot of people would find the situation hard.'

Me, she thought. *I'd find it hard.*

Matt took a while, visibly giving it some thought. 'I don't dislike Claire. I don't love her and I don't hate her,' he said eventually. 'She's just . . . Scarlett's mum now. And we have to find a way to make it work, because she'll always be Scarlett's mum.'

'Of course.' Alex jiggled her leg against the table. 'And Patrick? You want to spend a weekend with him?'

'I'm sure he's fine.'

Alex leaned forward. 'He doesn't have "A black hole of an anti-personality?"'

'I was being flippant. Claire likes him anyway, and she always had good taste in men.' Matt glanced at Alex's face and held his palms up in response. 'OK, not today. Sorry, Al. Not funny today.'

He stood up. 'I'll leave you to ponder. I know whatever you decide will be the right thing. Just give me a shout when you're ready.'

He scurried upstairs, leaving Alex with the washing up.

Alex emptied the lukewarm water out of the sink and re-filled the bowl.

The water was too hot but she didn't add any cold to the mix. The discomfort of her sweating hands was preferable to the more nebulous discomfort going on in her stomach.

Alex wished she was at work right now. It was easier to forget in the university lab, where there were readings to take, and cells to study. In the lab, Alex could go hours before she raised her head and looked at the trees out of the window. Only then did she look down at her trainers on the scuffed floor, take in the sound of the tinny radio, and remember there was a world other than studying cells taken from diabetes patients.

But it was different at home. At home, it was just Alex and her thoughts.

She could refuse to go on the trip, of course. But that wasn't satisfactory either.

She didn't want to go – but she couldn't *not go* either. She'd feel petty and churlish, which she definitely, actively – explicitly – wasn't. Alex had always been very reasonable about the fact Matt got on with his ex, a fact which other people – people who were actually churlish – would have found difficult.

Alex had overcompensated, if anything. Kissed Claire on the cheek on the occasions they did the Scarlett drop-off. Always had something nice to say about Claire's skirt, or her hair. Everyone had a past and nothing was personal. And Alex wasn't a personal person.

Alex scrubbed at the burnt pastry on the rim of the pie tin.

Though it was only a month away, Alex hadn't given much thought to the logistics of Christmas Day. She'd thought she'd see her parents, maybe, or see Matt's – it didn't matter. Alex didn't care about Christmas. It was just a day when the lab was shut.

But *this* – this was different.

And Matt had known for ages and not told her.

Alex didn't understand how he did it. Was he able to mentally compartmentalise awkward news? Or was he just putting off the inevitable?

Alex couldn't test either hypothesis, which made the situation even more frustrating. Matt had an amazing ability to wrong-foot her, and she ended up agreeing to things she hadn't meant to. Maybe this was why Matt did well in his job in sales, despite having what Alex considered a questionable work ethic.

Alex rinsed a plate; she stacked it on the drainer. She heard a scraping sound upstairs: a chair being dragged across the floor.

Matt was giving her some space. Ostensibly, busy upstairs. In reality, he was just staying out of her way.

After washing up, Alex looked through the online pictures of what she now thought of as *the enchanted forest*.

Not that it looked enchanted in the pictures. There might have been year-round fairy lights to go with the seasonal fake snow, but there were too many plastic barriers and warning signs for the place to look like a proper woodland wonderland.

Alex pushed her laptop away. She tried again not to look at the wine rack.

Don't be silly, she'd said, when Matt suggested getting rid of all the alcohol at home. *We can't be the people everyone avoids because there's no booze in the house.* But some nights she felt more of a pull from the retained wine rack than others. Like tonight. The wine's subtle pressure was multiplied by the jagged weight of a conversation unfinished.

Matt would be expecting her to talk about his suggestion tonight. Though he'd avoided the conversation for weeks, he would expect her to be decisive. They'd had an unspoken agreement in the two years they'd been together that bringing things to conclusion was Alex's role in their relationship.

So. Should they have a row about the trip? It would take Alex's mind off the wine, at least. But arguing about something to do with Matt's ex-wife didn't fit with Alex's view of herself. It would just make her existentially depressed.

No. There was no way she was going to row with Matt about this. That was a given.

Which meant she had to actually go on this stupid trip.

2

After telling Claire that he had to go into work early to do some papers, Patrick went to the gym at 5.30 a.m. He went to the gym again at lunchtime.

Twice in a day was a nice balance. Weights in the morning, cardio at lunch. He even did a conference call with a solicitor whilst on the treadmill.

Here he was – a successful barrister, a forty-three-year-old father of two-and-an-(inherited) half – and Patrick still wore his shirts slim-fit, bought from boys with groomed eyebrows in shops that were officially too young for him (but the staff couldn't stop him, could they, if the clothes still fitted?).

Patrick had stepped up his training regime that September. He'd been sitting at a high table in a coffee shop, drinking a superjuice in a domed plastic cup, when an ex-colleague's familiar haircut floated past the window.

He hadn't looked away in time.

'Patrick!' Tom put his case down on Patrick's table. 'How's things?'

Patrick made himself smile. 'Hi, Tom. I'm horrendously

busy. The clerks at the new place are unforgiving with my diary.'

'Bastards.'

'And I've moved in with Claire now.' Patrick wondered why he was telling Tom this. 'You know Claire Petersen, the solicitor?'

'Claire Petersen, really?' Tom shook his head. 'Punching above your weight again.'

Patrick knew it was meant to be a compliment, but he didn't appreciate being reminded who he'd last 'punched' with. That Tom saw Lindsay at his chambers every day.

Tom looked at Patrick's superjuice. 'Why are you drinking the contents of a compost heap?'

Patrick stirred the drink with his straw, feeling the satisfying heft of the whizzed-up vegetables. 'I'm doing an Ironman next year.'

Patrick hadn't even known it himself until then. Yet, as he said goodbye to Tom, he found himself taking up more space at the table.

Two months later, Patrick still hadn't worked out how to tell Claire. He knew she thought over-exercising a particularly shallow form of vanity.

He hid it well, until he happened to be doing some research on his tablet one evening, at a time he thought Claire was upstairs. So when she came up behind him, saying, 'Patrick, have you seen the big extension plug?' he flinched.

He clicked the screen off.

She grabbed the tablet. 'What are you hiding?'

'Claire, come on! Have some respect.'

'Let's see what kind of porn floats your boat.'

'Can't we just have *some* privacy?'

Claire switched the tablet on and looked at the screen.

Patrick couldn't help following her – hardening – gaze. The gritted teeth celebrations. The wetsuits; the goggles. The picture of the man in sunglasses, holding up his overly defined arms in self approval.

Claire let the tablet fall against her leg. 'You want to do an Ironman?'

'I'm thinking about it.'

'Dan Smith did an Ironman.' Claire arched an eyebrow like that should resonate.

Patrick knew he wasn't always the best listener. 'So?'

'Don't you remember what Heather said? All day cycling on Saturdays. All day swimming on Sundays. The kids barely saw him, and he was always checking out his torso in shop windows. None of them could stand him by the end.'

Claire left a pause for Patrick to reflect.

Patrick chose not to. 'Everyone's different.'

'Heather said she couldn't sleep with someone who fancied himself more than she did.' Claire held Patrick's gaze. 'Dan ended up taking a six-month holiday, Partridge-style, at the Travel Inn on the ring road.'

'I feel like a change.'

'And what about Amber and Jack?' Claire said. 'Lindsay makes it hard enough for you to see them anyway.'

'It was just an idea.'

A good idea, Patrick thought.

But stealth-exercise would soon be unnecessary. Because a few days ago, as the two stood in puffed-up jackets watching Scarlett play on the climbing frame in the park, Claire gave Patrick the golden ticket.

She wanted a weekend away. With her ex-husband.

Patrick spotted the opportunity right away.

'Really?' Claire turned to face Patrick. 'Really?'

'I said fine, didn't I?'

Claire widened her eyes. 'You *really* don't mind?'

Patrick shoved his hands in his pockets. 'You're not the only one who wants Scarlett to be happy.'

She touched his arm. 'I'm pleased, that's all.'

'What did you expect me to say? It's clearly something you want to do.'

'I thought you'd think it was a terrible idea.'

Patrick did think it was a terrible idea. 'I'll always support you in something you want to do. Even if it means being away from my own kids at Christmas.' He paused. 'And those holiday villages have big swimming pool complexes, right?'

The sex they'd had that night had been particularly enthusiastic.

So Claire might have been lukewarm about Patrick's exercise habits. But if he did this – well. The next discussion about Ironman would have to go more smoothly. And Patrick had to register in the next few weeks if he was going to make the next Ironman.

More pressingly, he needed to find another chair in their lounge. This one was clearly ill-judged: too close to the door. Because here she was again, looking over his shoulder at his tablet.

'Archery lessons? But why . . .?' Claire tailed off.

Patrick straightened the coaster on the side table. 'I want

to learn what it feels like to shoot something.'

'This is about Christmas.'

'I've never shot anything before.'

Claire laughed. 'If you're going to try to get competitive at Christmas, you won't have much luck with Matt.'

Patrick had learnt a lot about Matt over the last two years. The Xbox; the T-shirts. The ridiculous new passion for skateboards. And with each thing he learned, Patrick studied Claire, with her buoyant solicitor's practice and expressive eyebrows, a woman with a *whole wall* of personality. He didn't get it.

'You won't be the best at shooting anyway, even if you have lessons.' Claire grinned. 'Unlucky. I shot loads as a child on the farm.'

Claire squeezed his knee and left the room. Patrick turned back to the screen.

Deliberately not stopping to think, he flicked onto the Ironman website and clicked the *book now* button.

3

Alex decided to call Claire before the trip to understand the plan. There was always a risk of error when plans funnelled through Matt.

Like that time she'd turned up to Matt's family party to find it was a pool party – a fact Matt had forgotten to mention, along with that he had a family posh enough to own a swimming pool: an even bigger surprise for Alex.

Matt, of course, stripped off gamely and dived into the pool in his pants. Alex thought about the underwear she was wearing and decided to stay on land.

Alex rang Claire's number. She looked at her fingernails and flicked at a bit of jagged nail, wondering why she was visually simulating nonchalance in an empty room.

When Claire answered the phone, Alex paused.

'It's Alex. Alex Mount.' She paused. 'Matt's partner.' Then, excruciatingly: 'Matt Cutler.'

'Hey, you! Lovely to hear from you! So how's tricks?'

'Tricks are good. So . . . I'm really looking forward to the trip!'

'Are you?' Claire's voice carried a hint of a laugh. 'You don't think it's a bit much?'

'I'm sure it'll be fine.'

'Well, I thought about it, after Matt suggested the Happy Forest. And if barking royals like Prince Andrew and Fergie can manage it, we should be OK. We're all normal, right?'

'Right.'

Claire paused. 'And if it's a disaster, we never speak of it again.'

Alex forced her voice upbeat. 'It will be lovely, I'm sure.'

'I know,' Claire said. 'I shouldn't be so sceptical.'

'Will Posey be joining us for the trip?'

Claire paused. 'It's inevitable, I'm afraid. If you'd told me before how much effort it would take to accommodate an imaginary rabbit, I wouldn't have believed you.'

'I have noticed.'

'Do you think we should shut it down?'

'I think . . . you know best.' Alex had learnt that imaginary rabbits required a surprising level of diplomacy.

'Patrick thinks we should shut it down,' Claire said. 'But Matt and I have decided we'd be concerned if Scarlett was thirty-five and ordering an extra coffee at Costa, or cueing Posey up to do a double-act in the boardroom. But she's *seven*.'

'Let's hope it doesn't come to that.' Alex deliberately kept her voice neutral. 'Posey does seem to have developed in character in the time since I came on the scene.'

'Hasn't he just.' Claire sighed. 'And he goes way further back than that, you know. He was originally a real soft toy that Scarlett took everywhere – she was devastated when Matt left him in a hire car in Tenerife. But then Posey came back, imaginary. He looks just the same, apparently. Though he's a hundred times bigger. And invisible, of course.'

'Right.' Again, perfectly neutral. 'So, this trip away. Is there a plan? Matt was vague and . . . you know, Matt.'

'No plans, we just chill. We'll have to book a few activities in advance, of course, but Patrick's sorting that. And I'll cook some meals – I love cooking, I find it so relaxing on holiday – but we can go out for other meals. Just chill.'

'Matt said you're super-organised.'

Claire laughed. 'Erm – no. Compared to him I am. But Patrick thinks I'm a slacker. I think it depends on your starting point.'

'Can I do anything to help?'

Help. Alex hadn't meant to say it. She had cast herself in the role of sub-adult, and she wasn't even at the lodge yet. This always happened around parents: like there were proper grown-ups in charge and Alex was an understudy, only a whisker of maturity away from sitting at the children's table, flipping plastic bacon on a thigh-height Fisher Price stove.

'It's all under control, Alex, you just use the trip as a chance to relax. You deserve it.'

Alex looked down at her feet in their slipper socks, both resting on the ottoman. She'd been in her pyjamas since getting in from work at seven. 'If you're sure. I feel a bit pointless.'

'We're all good, Alex. You could make a Christmas cake, if you want? Or not. Whatever.'

'I'll do the cake. If you're sure that's all that's needed?'

'Alex, just chill. You don't need to be bothering yourself with the tedious parenting stuff. You work so hard.'

The two said goodbye, and Alex looked at the games console across the room, the buttons on the controllers worn down from the tennis and bowling games she and Matt played in the evenings.

Did Alex work hard?

Claire was clearly being kind, but Alex wasn't sure that phrase applied to her. Was it just one of those things people say to get others onside? Like politicians always referring to hard-working families, because everyone in the world felt they needed more sleep?

Was Claire *over-nicing* Alex?

Alex found Matt in front of the TV in the bedroom. 'Matt, do you see yourself as hard-working?'

'That's a loaded question.' He looked up from what he was watching: an endurance-based competitive eating programme. 'What did I forget to do?'

'It's just what they say, isn't it?' Alex said. 'Everyone thinks they work hard.'

Matt rolled onto his side on the bed. He looked up at Alex, eyes disarmingly blood-lined from that angle. 'I'm a lazy arse, Al, you know that. If I'm dressed by lunchtime on a weekend, I'm giving myself a high-five.'

'You sound proud. You know that's the wrong way up, right?'

'I don't see what all the fuss is about. Why everyone has to say they are busy all the time. I mean, what are they atoning for?'

And there it was: one of the things Alex most adored about Matt. A comment that made her wonder if he was the only person who had life in perspective, all along.

Matt rolled back into his original position and gestured

at the telly. 'Come and watch, Al. He's eaten two trays of sausages already and he's about to vom.'

Alex sat down next to Matt; he pulled her sideways on the bed in an affectionate chokehold. She watched the man on telly try to force down more sausages, dabbing his mouth with a napkin to stem the outward-flowing juices.

'Claire said if I want to help I can make a Christmas cake.'

'Cool.'

'I don't like Christmas cake.'

'Neither do I. They taste of soil.'

'Does Claire like it?'

'I don't think so. No one does, do they?' Matt gestured at the screen. 'This guy's sweating cobs. I hope they've got the bucket ready.'

Alex didn't say anything. She was still thinking about the conversation with Claire.

You don't need to be bothering yourself with the tedious parenting stuff.

What did *that* mean? Was it a straight-up, generous statement? Or one of those humblebrags people did to make themselves sound important?

Or did Claire think Alex was incapable of doing the *tedious*, actually super-important, *parenting stuff*?

If so, she had a point. Alex wasn't brilliant at it, she knew that. Scarlett didn't hate her – but she definitely *nothing*-ed her. On the times they'd met, Scarlett had either whispered constantly with her imaginary rabbit, or she'd been on Matt's iPhone, playing some inexplicable game that involved building dungeons for chickens.

Two years with Matt, and Alex wasn't sure Scarlett could pick her out of a line-up.

Alex tried to concentrate on the telly. Foodstuffs crossed the screen on a *Generation Game* travellator, showing how much the man had eaten.

After Matt suggested the Happy Forest . . .

'Claire said you suggested it,' Alex said. 'The place where we're going.'

Matt nodded at the telly.

'But the holiday was definitely Claire's idea?' Alex said. 'In the first place?'

'Yep. I was just helping her out. You know me, all-round nice guy.' Matt pointed at the screen. 'It's gonna be game over any second. Ha! Here it comes!'

4

A week before their big Christmas trip, Scarlett sat in the back of the car with Posey. Mum was taking them to the big shopping centre, but it had taken twenty minutes to get from the last roundabout to the first car park. There were too many cars for the roads.

'This is disgusting. *Disgusting*.' Mum banged her hand against the steering wheel. 'Commercialism. Ugh.'

Mum often told Scarlett 'patience is a virtue'. Scarlett sometimes wondered whether she was saying it to herself as well.

Mum twisted in her seat to look at Scarlett. 'This place is everything that's wrong with the world.'

When Mum turned back to face the front, Scarlett turned to Posey and rolled her eyes. Posey rolled his eyes back.

They were both the same height (if you didn't count Posey's ears) but Scarlett looked down at Posey on the back seat. Mum said Posey didn't need a booster seat. Scarlett wanted him to have one, but didn't argue. It was two against one – Posey didn't want a booster seat either. The tips of his long purple ears folded sideways against the car roof as it was.

Mum banged her hand against the steering wheel again. 'Don't people feel they have enough *stuff*?'

Scarlett read between the lines. 'Are we still going in, Mum?'

'I've a good mind to call it a day. But you haven't got Alex a present yet.'

That seemed like a silly reason to Scarlett. She barely knew Alex. But Scarlett wanted to go shopping, so she didn't say anything.

In the shopping centre, Mum walked quickly, holding Scarlett's hand. Scarlett still felt herself getting bumped along by the crowd. She held Posey's hand just as tightly, because people didn't get out of the way for Posey. Today, people barely got out of the way for Scarlett. Or Mum.

'These people are just . . . how can they do this?' Mum's blonde fringe stuck to her forehead when she was flustered. 'How can they be *bothered*?'

Scarlett didn't ask *Why are we bothered then?* She didn't need to. It was about Christmas.

Everything odd at the moment was about Christmas.

'The thing is, you can't just get Alex some gloves or something,' Mum said. 'It has to be something meaningful, to show you really care.'

'But I don't care.'

Mum glared at her.

Scarlett knew she wasn't meant to say that out loud. 'And Alex gets rubbish presents. Remember what she got me last year? A *jumper*, Mum.'

'It was a lovely present.'

'It wasn't even a good jumper. It was *green*. It had a *space-ship* on it.'

'I thought you wanted to get Alex something.' Mum's voice had a warning in it. 'I thought that's why we stayed on in all the traffic past the roundabout.'

Scarlett said nothing.

Posey let go of Scarlett's hand. He tilted his head at a shop. 'I'm just going in there. Don't wait for me.'

'Posey!' Scarlett's stomach twisted up. 'You'll get lost with all the people!'

Posey ignored her. His purple furry body disappeared into the crowd and Scarlett watched his white pom-pom tail jiggle as he went. Posey was nearly all purple, apart from his tail and the white patch on his tummy. The only other bit of colour was the red *Made in China* tag that stuck out of the side of his bum.

'Mum! We need to wait for Posey.'

Mum didn't even slow down. 'I don't have time for this today. He'll be fine.'

'I told Posey to stay with me. He just doesn't listen!'

'He's a big rabbit.'

A second later, Posey was back. 'Like my new gear?'

Scarlett looked down. She'd only ever seen Posey naked, but now he was wearing silver moon boots.

Scarlett's stomach tightened in a different way now. Those were the same boots Scarlett wanted Mum to get her, but Mum said Scarlett was allowed to get them as her main Christmas present or nothing. Scarlett wasn't wasting her main present on *boots*.

Scarlett was sometimes jealous Posey could just *get* things, with his different rules.

Scarlett watched Posey's boots flash as he walked. 'I didn't think you wore clothes.'

Posey shrugged. 'Everyone wears these kind of boots in China.'

'Well, don't run off again.' Scarlett sometimes got sick of hearing how good China was. 'We'll never find you in this crowd.'

Across the pathway, a scruffy man with a woolly hat stood outside a pop-up booth, holding a megaphone. The booth was all black and white and covered in photographs.

Scarlett read the words at the top of the booth. *The Society Against* . . .

She didn't know the last word, so she said it, bit by bit, in her head.

'Mum, what's *viv-i-sect-ion?*'

Mum glanced at the booth. 'It's like tennis. Come on, let's dart down here.' She tried to steer Scarlett down a side street, but Scarlett dawdled. She looked back at the man with the megaphone. He was waving his spare arm around as he shouted.

'*These pharmaceuticals are tested on animals. Scientists torture animals, often without anaesthetic, for drugs we don't need* . . .'

Scarlett peered at one picture, of an unhappy-looking rabbit in a cage. The rabbit had metal spiky bits all round its head.

'What's that?' Posey's voice went all high.

'Nothing.'

'What?' Posey's voice went higher still. 'What's happening to that rabbit in the cage?'

'I don't know. But remember what Mum says, not all

people are good ones.' Scarlett nodded to the side street. 'Come on Posey, let's follow Mum.'

'. . . *Scientists keep animals like monkeys and rabbits in cages. They cause excessive suffering . . .*'

'But why?' Posey whined.

A family in front of them stopped suddenly, pointing at something in a shop window. Mum walked into the back of the woman in the group. The woman scowled at Mum. Mum looked like she wanted to hit the woman.

'Right!' Mum spun to face Scarlett. 'That's it, we'll get something online.'

'But I haven't bought anything,' Scarlett said.

Posey looked down. 'At least I got my boots,' he whispered.

Scarlett shook her head. Posey could be selfish sometimes.

When they got back home, Patrick was in his usual chair in the lounge.

Mum stood behind Patrick, peering at his screen. 'Good afternoon?'

Patrick put his tablet down on the floor in a rush. 'Not bad. You?'

Mum threw her handbag onto the sideboard. 'We were an hour just getting parked up. Then there was a protest going on when we got there, which wasn't particularly helpful. A vivisection protest. You know, *vivisection.*' Mum looked at Patrick hard. 'Like tennis.'

Posey crossed his arms. He sat on the floor with an angry bump.

Scarlett shook her head at him. She didn't want Mum knowing they'd heard the man shouting. Mum liked to do a good job keeping Scarlett from horrible things, and Scarlett wanted her to think she had.

'Do you still need anything for Christmas anyway?' Patrick asked Mum. 'Didn't you say you've already bought too much?'

'I haven't got anything for Alex though.'

'I thought we weren't doing presents with Matt and Alex?'

'I mean, I haven't got anything for Scarlett to give to Alex. I forgot.'

'Can't you just get her some toiletries?'

'I don't think so. Alex is a funny one, Patrick. In a good way, but, you know. I don't think she's a bath salts person. She's a scientist, remember?'

A *scientist*.

Scarlett didn't know she'd been listening to their conversation. But she definitely heard that.

Slowly, she turned round to face Posey.

Posey's wide eyes told Scarlett that he'd heard it too.

Posey and Scarlett ran upstairs. They sat cross-legged on Scarlett's bed, staring at each other.

'Your dad's girlfriend's a *scientist*,' Posey hissed.

Scarlett stroked Posey's paw. The fur on his paw felt thin, like lots of it had worn away. 'I know.'

'You told me she was a doctor.'

'I thought she was. It says *Dr Alex* something on her credit card.'

'Doctors make people well. Scientists *torture rabbits*.'

Scarlett smiled calmly. It was her job to be the brave one. 'She won't do that.'

'The man said so.' Posey paused. 'I didn't realise you could get girl scientists.'

32

'Girls can grow up to be anything they want to be,' Scarlett said quickly. 'Astronauts, prime ministers, chief execs.' Sometimes, words came out Scarlett's mouth in a flow she didn't remember putting together. She didn't even know what a *chief exec* was. 'But girl scientists might be different. Maybe girl scientists don't do the hurting.'

'The man in the woolly hat didn't say anything about girl scientists,' Posey said. 'He just said scientists torture animals *for no reason*. That's what he said.'

Scarlett squeezed Posey's paw. 'I won't let her do anything to you.'

'You promise?'

'I promise.' Scarlett held Posey's hand even tighter. 'But we'll have to be careful. So let's both agree to keep a close eye on Dad's scientist girlfriend this holiday.'

5

Hi Alex,

    I've attached a packing list that I've put together to plan what we're taking to the holiday park – thought you might find it useful? Or not. Whatever!

    I've also made some suggestions of who brings which communal things. But I don't mean to be a packing Nazi. Feel free to ignore me, just let me know either way.

    C x

It was very thoughtful of Claire to send this email, of course. Because Claire was a thoughtful person. (Alex might not know this woman at all, but she was determined her inner monologue would be kind to Claire. That was the way good relations lay.)

Alex clicked on the email attachment and scanned the list.

Swimsuit. Wellies. Swimming towel. Waterproofs. Woolly hat, scarf and gloves. Torch.

Alex looked at the bottom of the list, to the communal things.

Alex and Matt – kitchen roll, cloths, washing-up liquid,

dishwasher tablets, washing powder, tea and coffee and sugar.

Claire and Patrick – Christmas decorations, toilet roll, candles, salt and pepper, oil and butter, herbs and spices, bread and milk.

All very reasonable.

So why did Alex feel so claustrophobic when she read the email? Like she needed to take her jumper off and loosen her hairband and open a window?

Alex pushed her laptop a fraction away and pinched the top of her nose. She felt the start of that pressure headache she got when a thunderstorm was on the way – like something behind her eyes was pushing outwards. Predicting thunderstorms with her sinuses was Alex's special superpower, but as powers went it was an annoying one – definitely not comic-book-notable, and never going to save the planet.

A week before the trip, Matt picked up Alex's phone when she was in the shower.

Alex walked into the bedroom, rubbing her hair with the towel. She smiled at Matt.

'But it's not just for kids,' Matt said into the phone. 'And it's got a half-pipe and everything.'

Matt held the phone out to her. 'It's Ruby. For you.'

Alex looked at the phone, and back at Matt.

'Why haven't you told her about what we're doing at Christmas?' Matt asked.

Alex took the phone. After a long beat, she put the phone to her ear.

'Yes, Al,' the voice on the end of the line was sarcastic, '*why oh-why* haven't you told me about Christmas?'

Alex forced a smile at Matt. 'It must have slipped my mind.'

Matt smiled back encouragingly.

'Yes. Because I'm sure I'd remember *that* little morsel of insanity. You told me you were going to your parents.'

'Did I say that? I don't remember.'

'*Or*' – sarcasm made Ruby's voice sound surprisingly aggressive – 'it could it be that you were too ashamed to tell me because you know this weekend's going to go down in a blaze of shit?'

Alex smiled at Matt again. 'I'll take this call downstairs.'

She hurried down the stairs, listening to the onslaught. *You're clearly not right in the head for agreeing to this, Al,* and *You need to have a word with yourself* and *We will definitely be talking about this tomorrow.*

Alex decided to change the subject. 'Do you know how to make Christmas cake?'

'What?' Ruby's voice rose to a shriek. 'Who *are* you?'

'It was just a question,' Alex said.

At lunchtime the next day, Alex and Ruby walked outside to their usual bench in the park. There was no eating in the wet lab, and they never wanted to stop for long. Occasionally they couldn't eat together – university scientists' lunch schedules weren't a key factor in dictating surgery times – but, otherwise, it was a punctuation of the working day that Alex had enjoyed since Ruby had joined as a post-doc three years before. There was something so reassuringly twee about their routine: the enjoyable, unspoken predictability of it all.

'I can understand why Matt would think it's a good idea' –

Ruby raised her gaze in reference to Alex's boyfriend's *la-la* world – 'but why would you humour him?'

Alex sat next to Ruby on the bench. She stared straight ahead as Ruby opened her bag. 'Demi Moore and Bruce Willis do it.'

Ruby opened her foil-wrapped package. 'You're not Demi Moore. And Matt's no Bruce Willis.'

Alex set her own package on her knee. 'What do you want from me, Ruby?'

'I bet Matt doesn't even *own* a vest.'

Alex pressed her fingertips together. 'I said I'll go. I can't un-agree to go now. Be supportive, please. That's what mates do.'

'It's going to go down in a blaze of shit.'

'Is that a real expression? You seem to be using it a lot.'

'Just you wait. It'll start all "pass the salad" and by the end you'll be lunging for the razor blades.' Ruby bit into her sandwich. 'What's the poor child meant to think?'

Alex took a bite of her sandwich. She swallowed with difficulty.

'I'll remind you I told you so,' Ruby said. 'I'm not an enabler. I'm not that kind of friend.'

'Speaking to your friends when you have things on your mind is meant to make you feel better.'

Ruby shrugged. 'Yeah, well.' *My hands are tied*, her shoulders said.

That wasn't the only conversation about the trip Alex had.

Before her conversation with Walshy, Alex had always thought of a weekend as a two-day, two-night thing.

But apparently, that wasn't the only definition of weekend.

At least, not according to Matt (according to Walshy).

According to Matt (according to Walshy), a weekend was some kind of elastic description to cover any general period of time. And if you asked Matt how long a weekend was, apparently you'd get a shrug and a response like *how long is a piece of string?*

In what had turned into a regular Thursday night routine since Matt had moved his skateboard and trainer collection into Alex's house, Walshy sat on the sofa with Alex while Matt was round the corner, restocking at the expensive emergency off-licence.

Alex watched Walshy eat the leftover nachos from her plate. Alex had been saving those nachos for later, but Walshy was not a man defeated by a mountain of food. More specifically, he was not a man restricted by the boundaries of other people's plates. He was, after all, the one who had introduced Matt to their favourite competitive eating programme, and had even been planning to do his own off-brand version on YouTube, until he realised how much all the sausages and pies would set him back.

'The thing is' – Walshy dangled a nacho over his mouth, positioning the ribbon of cheese – 'Matt's stitched you up good and proper. Because you've agreed to go now. And I bet he hasn't told you it's a five-day trip.'

'Five days?' Alex frowned. 'It's not five days.'

'It is.' Walshy scooped guacamole onto another of Alex's chips. 'I said, "Are you sure Alex knows it's five days, because I'm sure she told me it was just a weekend?" And he said—'

'That he thought he'd told me that already.'

Walshy jabbed an over-salsa-ed nacho at her. *Bingo.* Oil ran down Walshy's chin. 'It's a lot to ask, I told him so.'

'Do you want me to get you a napkin?'

'On the plus side' – Walshy wiped his chin with the back of his hand – 'Claire's a great girl. If I was going to be in a weird situation with anyone, I'd want it to be Claire.'

Alex fixed her mouth in a smile. 'Uh-huh.' She gave a vigorous nod. 'Claire's great.'

'I was sorry when they split up. I liked having her around. She was great value on a night out. You never quite knew where the night would end up. A diamond lass.'

Alex gave a tiny cough. 'How thoughtful of you to say that. To me. Right now.'

Walshy shovelled another nacho into his mouth. 'You're a great girl too, Al.'

'Gee. Really? Little old me?'

6

'What do you mean, they're not here?'

Patrick stared at Lindsay from his position on the front step, the presents slippery in their Christmas paper and weighing down his arms. The boxes pulled on some side-back muscles that he didn't know the name of.

'I *mean*, they've gone out.' In a voice thick with generosity, Lindsay added: 'Amber's at a roller disco and Jack's at Leo's.'

'But I told you I was coming this afternoon! You know I go away for Christmas tomorrow!'

'I thought you'd just be dropping the presents off.' Lindsay folded her arms. 'You should have said if you actually wanted to *see* the kids. I'm not a clairvoyant.'

Patrick shifted the presents in his arms, determined not to put them down. Lindsay clearly wanted him to hand them over and be gone, and Patrick made it a point of principle to do what Lindsay wanted as infrequently as possible.

'What's Jack doing at Leo's?'

'Gaming.'

'Why isn't he gaming at home?' Those kids who stay in all day without opening the curtains, talking into

40

headphones, hunting in packs and mutilating creatures with virtual friends – why couldn't his son be one of those?

'What can I say?' Lindsay shrugged with bored accommodation, her arms still folded. 'Maybe they didn't want to see you. I'm not their fucking jailer.'

'They're kids, Lindsay. You're meant to be their fucking jailer.'

She shrugged again, ignoring the force of his glare. 'You parent them, then. If you can get them to see you.' She held her hands out. 'Now, do you want me to take those, or what?'

Patrick narrowed his eyes. Lindsay's expression didn't change. She seemed to have become completely inured to his glare over the years, and had an air of irritated acceptance when she found him on 'her' doorstep (a doorstep that was two-thirds his – not officially but objectively, if you looked at the direct debit arrangements and who put in the most equity at the start).

Worse, Lindsay looked irritated, with *barely any* hint of guilt – no more than if she'd opened the door to one of those ex-offenders selling household items. Patrick's face on the doorstep was as welcome as a flash of an ID card and a request to guilt-buy an overpriced dishcloth.

'Here, then.' Patrick shoved the presents into Lindsay's arms. 'Tell them their dad wished them a happy *fucking* Christmas.' He glared at her. 'But don't say *fucking*. That's just for you.'

Patrick strode down what had once been his path and beeped the car open. He drove away with a jerk. He held his hand up in a wave to the driver he'd accidentally pulled out in front of.

He'd wrapped those presents himself. *Himself.*

He'd anticipated a warm reunion with the kids: hugs and excited faces – maybe a trip to Starbucks for some gingerbread lattes. He'd pictured it, all laughter and unwrapped presents and, *We'll miss you this Christmas, Daddy!* Though, even in this most idyllic of daydreams, the idea that his teenage kids would still call him *Daddy* jarred with his narrative.

Lindsay should at least look sorry.

As the one who left him, she should be leaping up to accommodate his needs and asking how he was getting on – not acting bored of the whole thing, like he was disrupting their routine and creating unnecessary drama. She acted like his time with them had expired and he was trying to hop back on the team bus with an invalid ticket. A ticket that, *don't forget, Lindsay*, he was still paying through the nose for.

He shouldn't have got so angry.

It was his main parenting fault, he knew: that he got so angry.

Maybe they didn't want to see you.

He almost felt like giving up and reinvesting all his parental love into Scarlett: a virtually clean daughter-sheet, the negative boxes still unticked. One of the points of having kids was creating a better version of yourself – and today, it didn't feel like his kids were better versions of him. Today, they were 100 per cent Lindsay.

Yet Patrick remembered that pull in his chest when he held the kids when they were small. When Amber had looked up at him with those face-filling Disney princess eyes. When Jack had begged to be his ball-boy and run on court at every cry of 'let', and who had said at the end of the game, 'Daddy, I want to be as good at tennis as you.'

There was that mushy feeling Patrick still got in his stomach when he hadn't seen them for a while, like this was what it was all about – all the calls with the solicitors, all the papers at midnight, all the trips to obscure tribunals in places like Bangor, the 5 a.m. starts to pay the mortgage on a house where his keys no longer fitted the lock.

But Lindsay just couldn't let him enjoy any of it.

When Patrick got home, he found Claire and Scarlett baking Christmas biscuits.

Claire looked up. 'I've packed our stuff and got your case down from the attic. Are you OK to set off for the forest about ten tomorrow?'

'That's fine.'

'Did the kids like the presents?'

'They were out,' he said shortly. 'Some mix-up.'

'Oh no.' Claire stood up with a head-tilt. She brushed her floury hands down her apron and took Patrick's hands in hers. 'What happened?'

'Amber was at a roller disco and Jack was at a friend's.'

Claire clucked her teeth. 'That's really unfair of Lindsay.'

'She says she's not their jailer.'

'She's selfish.' Claire gave his arm a gentle squeeze of sympathy. 'It's the kids who lose out.'

Patrick gave her a smile, cheering up already. He and Claire had been arguing a bit lately, but he never found her more lovely than when she was criticising Lindsay.

He looked to Scarlett. She stood up next to the table,

concentrating hard, icing a ribbon onto a pre-stencilled biscuit shaped like a Christmas present.

He was going to get it right with Scarlett. Third time lucky.

And maybe – if they made the decision quickly (because he didn't mean to be ungallant but they didn't have long to decide) – he and Claire could have another, shared child of their own.

Either way, with Claire, he was going to be better at it – at marriage, fatherhood – the lot. He was going to get it right this time, whatever it took.

7

Hi Alex,

Patrick was worried all the activities might get booked up, so here's a spreadsheet he put together of what he's sorted in advance. We can always cancel later, but better to be safe than sorry.

He has left the first day free so we can investigate the complex and get reacquainted.

Please bring a book so we can have family reading time. Apparently you can borrow board games there, which is great. And I should warn you that Christmas karaoke was once a family tradition in our house . . . ☺

C x

Alex took a breath. She clicked the mouse to open the attachment.

Itinerary

Date	Time	Pre-booked activities	Who?
Thu 21st Dec	4 p.m.	Arrive	All
Fri 22nd Dec	2 p.m.	Pony-Trekking	Scarlett
	6 p.m.	Crazy Golf	All
Sat 23rd Dec	10 a.m.	Spa	Claire
	11 a.m.	Fluffy the Squirrel's Woodland Winter Wonderland	Scarlett
	4 p.m.	Pool Table (at the 'Five Bells' on-site pub)	All
	8 p.m.	Santa's Grotto	Scarlett
	9 p.m.	Carol Singing Elves (visiting lodge)	All
Sun 24th Dec	1 p.m.	Archery	All
	8 p.m.	Tennis Lesson	Patrick
Mon 25 Dec	11 a.m.	Badminton	All
	1 p.m.	Christmas Lunch at Chico's Italian Restaurant	All
	4 p.m.	Adventure with Owls	Scarlett
	6 p.m.	Ten Pin Bowling	All
Tue 26 Dec	8 a.m.	Ice Cream House (breakfast)	All
	10 a.m.	Depart	All

Alex gave her neck a forceful scratch.

She tipped her head back and pinched the bridge of her nose.

Alex deliberately didn't buy any new clothes for the trip. There was no one to impress.

The only person to impress was herself – and she could impress herself only by actively not trying to impress anyone else.

She finished her last day of work in the lab (or *breaking up for Christmas*, as she still thought of it) gathering up the armfuls of colleagues' Christmas cards and generic Christmas presents.

Ruby's present, when Alex opened it, was a panic alarm. 'For the trip.'

Alex refused to say thank you.

Only that night before did Alex start to pack. Warm, sensible clothes. No heels, no dresses: nothing fancy.

She packed her hair straighteners and her make-up bag. Then took them both out again. After a beat, she put the make-up bag back in. But she definitely wasn't going to take her straighteners.

And she definitely wasn't going to put on make-up before the first coffee of the day. Or get dressed before breakfast. They could take her as she was, in her four-year-old, elastic-perishing Mr Tickle pyjamas or, holiday or not, they could go fuck themselves.

Shaking a little, Alex folded a pair of jeans and placed them in the case. She looked at her unsteady hand and took a deep breath.

*Post-shooting interview. Jared Parker, 27. Happy Forest
   archery host.*
Face-to-face. Happy Forest adventure centre staffroom.

*The man had already passed out by the time I got to the
field with my first-aid box. The ambulance was just arriving,
so I only got a quick glimpse.*

*I saw the arrow sticking out. He also had cuts and
bruises on his face.*

*Of course, I'll tell you anything I can. It was Alfie who did
the training though, and we've sent him home. Poor kid, he
was devastated.*

*It was hard to tell how badly hurt the man was. Arrows
on human flesh make a mess – it's never a neat puncture
because the arrow flexes on the way in. We were taught
that on our training course.*

I'm happy to listen, if you think it will help?

(Listens to 999 call recording)

*She sounds like a cool customer. And it just cuts off like
that at the end?*

*Really, another five minutes like that? No background
noise at all?*

*The first I knew of it was when the woman came to find
me at the archery lodge – the same woman who made the
call.*

Alex? OK, Alex.

*She was out of breath, she'd been rushing. When I got
to the field, I saw the other three. There was the shot man*

on the floor, the other man kneeling beside him, and the blonde woman watching on.

Yeah, they were calm when I found them. Just kind of . . . waiting. Shock, probably.

Poor Alfie. He'll get sacked for this, but the only thing he did wrong was letting them sign the waiver and go off shooting before they'd all had the training. He's just a kid, and Alfie said the blonde woman was very convincing. She was hard to say no to.

I never met any of them before the shooting. But ask Sheila on reception, she knows everything and everyone.

Sheila Kapur. K – A – P – U – R.

I hear they had a kid with them though. So where was the kid when they were shooting?

Dance class? On her own, when all the grown ups were doing archery? That family gets odder and odder.

Mate, my parents are divorced. It was bad enough at my cousin's wedding, and that was just for a day.

Because – a holiday with exes and new partners? What kind of people would do that?

‖‖

Extract from the Happy Forest brochure:
From the moment you enter our purpose-built village, you'll feel like you've discovered a different world.

Freed from the habits of your daily routine, the outdoor life will stimulate your senses. You may find yourself stopping to smell the flowers, or interacting with the wildlife with childlike wonder.

Even grown ups feel the magic of the Happy Forest. So why not come and join us, and become the person *you* want to be?

‖‖

8

Thursday 21 December

Day 1

'Can you set up the satnav?' Alex asked.

In the passenger seat, Matt blew his hair out of his eyes. 'We don't need it yet, Al. I'll tell you where to go.'

Alex gave him a quick smile and turned back to concentrate on the road. A freaky memory for roads and directions was one of Matt's things.

They each had their own things. Alex's were internal: she always remembered the name of people's parents and children and where they'd been on holiday. She always knew the approximate time without looking at her phone. Whereas, if Matt had been on a road, he never forgot it. It was impressive to Alex, whose brain didn't work that way. She liked it when she discovered something Matt could do that she couldn't.

Alex drove up the M1, watching the signs for Sheffield and Leeds turn into signs for Harrogate and Northallerton.

'You know,' she said, 'practically every time I've met Claire, one of us has been standing in a doorway with a coat on, car keys in hand.'

Matt smiled. 'Well now's a chance to work on that.'

Alex looked back to the road. Would she and Claire get on so well if they were actually in the same room? Without coats?

'What should I talk to Claire about?' Alex glanced at Matt. 'If I get stuck?'

Matt looked up from his phone. 'What do you normally talk to people about?'

'You know what I mean. What are her interests?'

Matt shrugged. 'Work. Scarlett. Normal stuff.'

'What about telly? Books?'

'I don't know. She didn't really do that stuff when we were together.'

'OK, newspapers then. Is she political? What does she think?'

'None of what you're saying is really her. She works long hours. She likes cooking.' Matt glanced at Alex's face. 'She's a normal person, Al. Skin and hair and teeth.'

Alex wondered how Claire could be a normal person if she didn't watch telly *or* read books or newspapers, but she let it go. 'And Patrick?'

'God knows. The history of the cello? Or interest rates or mortgages.' Matt gave a snort. 'Consolidated debt obligations.'

'He plays the cello?'

'The fuck would I know?' Matt gave another snort. 'But that's the kind of thing he *would* do.'

'OK, thanks. That's not particularly helpful. Are they small-talk people?'

'Stop being weird, Al. Don't overplan it. You need to get in the left-hand lane here.'

Alex changed lanes. 'I hope we can get to normal quickly. Skip past the polite stage. So it's not all "You first with the kettle", and "After you, no after you, please go first".'

She thought of how Matt sounded when he was on the phone to Claire. He didn't sound like he was in the polite phase.

'What are you thinking?' Matt said. 'You look thinky.'

Alex paused. 'I was just thinking what you and Claire are like together. Wondering how civil you are.'

'We're civil – these days, anyway.'

'Weren't you always?'

'Er . . . We weren't there, for a while. A few too many conversations when we called each other "A lazy fucking waste of space" and "A psycho control-freak bitch".'

'Who was right? The lazy waste of space or the psycho control freak?'

Matt laughed. 'Neither. Both.' He tapped a tooth in a gesture of thought. 'Neither and both.'

After two hours of driving, Alex pulled over in a service station car park. They grabbed a Burger King meal and swapped driving positions.

Burgers eaten and with Matt behind the wheel, Alex played with her phone. She scrolled through Facebook updates – mainly pictures of artfully twinkling Christmas trees. She stopped scrolling, feeling nauseous – probably from reading in a moving car, though she preferred to think it was from the over-facing images of saccharine Christmas perfection that her friends should really be too self-aware to post by now.

Alex's phone buzzed. It was a text from Ruby.

Are you there yet? Has the Christmas magic begun?

Alex put her phone in the cup holder and closed her eyes. 'So what should I expect to think of Patrick? Will I like him?'

'He's all right.'

Alex kept her eyes closed. 'Then what did you mean when you said to talk to him about mortgages and interest rates?'

'You know exactly what I meant. I meant he's a bit of a straight cunt. Always wears a tie.'

'Lots of people wear ties. *You* wear a tie to work.'

'He wears a tie like he *wants to*. He's harmless, really, just a bit full-on and *blah*.'

Alex's phone buzzed in the cup holder.

Matt nodded at it. 'You getting that?'

Alex sighed. 'It'll be Ruby.'

Eventually, she looked at the phone.

Do I take it from your silence you're having too much fun to respond?

'So.' Alex reached for her handbag at her feet. She put her phone in the bag and zipped the bag shut. 'Patrick is *blah*.'

'It's not his fault – he had kids young. That ages you.'

'What happened to you then? You were thirty-one when you had Scarlett, and you still know your high score on Space Invaders.'

'That's not young, it just feels young.' He glanced at Alex and back at the road. 'And I mean having kids young ages you if you're a certain type of person.'

'Do you mean he's boring?'

'He just tries to do everything properly.'

Alex furrowed her brow. 'And?'

'Well, there is just no such thing as *properly*, is there?'

Alex watched Matt tap his hand on the steering wheel in time to the baseline of the song. They had Matt's phone playing music on random – it was a song Alex recognised but didn't know the name of, a piano house track from the nineties.

'When did they get together?'

Matt tapped his hand on the wheel again. 'I don't know. They've been together a while.'

'Before us, or after us?'

'Before us. He was round there once when I went to pick up Scarlett.'

'Was that when you first noticed his "black hole of an anti-personality"?'

'Stop saying that! It's just stuff Scarlett said that made me think that. He's always on at her to shine her shoes – he wants her to do it every day after school. To teach her responsibility, apparently. He tells her off for bringing worms into the house, and tells her to stay out of the mud. What fun's that for a kid?'

Alex didn't know how to respond to that.

'And Patrick keeps trying to get Scarlett to drop Posey,' Matt continued. 'Patrick thinks she's too old. But, come on! She's *seven*. Some days I wish I had a big arsey rabbit to kick about with.'

Alex felt her phone buzz in her bag at her feet. She ignored it.

'So what did you think when you first met Patrick? Was it strange to see Claire with someone else?'

Matt flicked a glance at Alex. 'You know what? Let's not talk about the past. It's really unhelpful on a weekend like this.'

Alex nodded. 'Fair enough. We'll definitely need the satnav soon.' She opened the glove box. 'I'll get it set up.'

Matt tapped the side of his head: an *it's all in here* gesture. 'We don't need it.'

'Have you gone full-on psychic these days? Got the Knowledge of all the roads in the whole country?'

Matt slowed down for a roundabout. 'No. I've been here before.'

Alex felt herself frown. 'When?'

'I came with Claire and Scarlett, when Scarlett was small. With Claire's sister's family.'

Alex sat forward in her chair; she felt the pressure of the seat belt cut into her chest. 'What?'

'I didn't mention it?' Matt took his hand off the steering wheel and glanced at Alex. 'Sorry.' He rubbed her knee. 'Scarlett wouldn't remember anything of it, of course. She was too young for it. She won't be now.'

Alex stared at the road ahead. Something shifted in her stomach. It was like – something solid had been there till now. And now it had gone.

This changed *everything*.

'Hey, Al. You OK? You've gone weird.'

'Why didn't you tell me you'd been here before?'

Matt stared straight ahead. 'I didn't realise I hadn't told you. I didn't deliberately not tell you, Al. Why would I do that?'

Alex took the thought in and rolled it around.

'Does it make a difference?' Matt asked. 'That I've been here before?'

Alex rolled the thought around some more. She didn't trust herself to articulate what she felt right now. She needed to process the thought before she could discuss it. She needed to label and categorise it.

So she didn't answer Matt's question, and Matt didn't ask again.

9

Posey adjusted his seat belt. 'But I'm scared!'

Scarlett gave him a kind smile. 'Don't be scared.'

Scarlett and Posey had spent most of their three-hour journey to the holiday park whispering about how they were going to deal with Alex.

Mum turned round for the thousandth time. 'Why don't you put a film on?'

'We're fine,' Scarlett said loudly. She turned to Posey. 'Keep your voice down. You're not as good a whisperer as me.'

Mum turned back to face the front.

Patrick kept his eyes on the road. He always did the driving because Mum said he was a bad passenger. He kept jerking back in his seat and jamming his feet down. It was funny to watch, but Mum didn't like it.

'Do we tell Alex we know?' Posey said. 'About the scientist thing?'

'It's safer to just treat her as normal,' Scarlett said. 'And make sure we're never alone with her.'

Posey nodded. His ears flapped against the car roof.

'We have to say hello to her,' Scarlett said. 'But we just

say we're tired and go to bed early. And we have to give her that present today.'

'I don't trust her.'

'Let's just avoid her.' Scarlett still wasn't sure Alex *actually* hurt rabbits for fun, but it was no problem avoiding her. It wasn't like Alex was very interesting anyway.

Mum's voice carried from the front. 'Are you *sure* you don't want a film on?'

'We're fine,' Scarlett said in a normal voice.

'Remember what I said at home,' Mum said. 'This is a human weekend. I do *not* want Posey to be around all the time this weekend.'

'Sorry, mate,' Scarlett whispered.

Posey folded his arms in a huff.

'Now,' Mum said. 'There's a petrol station coming up in a mile, if you need the loo?'

Scarlett realised she was feeling a bit fidgety. 'OK.' It was funny how Mum knew she needed the loo before she did.

Posey looked out of the window. 'I'll be going back to China if that Alex keeps hanging around.'

'Posey, don't say that.'

'For Christ's sake, Scarlett! You are testing me, you know?' Mum turned round and made mean eyes. 'So can you give it a rest with Posey, for five whole minutes? Otherwise I am seriously – *seriously* – going to explode.'

10

At the last petrol station before reaching the holiday park, Patrick pulled over to refuel.

He switched off the ignition and was relieved to see there was other activity at the petrol station. There had been no street lamps for miles, giving the roads a spooky feel, even though it was only four o'clock. He was unsettled by anywhere too rural, which he blamed on watching *Deliverance* at too impressionable an age.

Patrick, Claire and Scarlett got out of the car. Patrick couldn't help frowning as he watched Scarlett open the other back door for 'Posey'. Patrick didn't like it when Scarlett whispered to the air – particularly because any time anyone whispered, his default thought was that they must be talking about him. That thought was bad enough when it was about real people. He *really* objected to feeling self-conscious about what an *imaginary creature* might be saying about him.

'I'll take Scarlett to the loo.' Claire slammed her car door. 'Pick me up a Snickers when you're in there.'

'OK.' Patrick put his hands in the hollow of his spine, stretching. He felt that teeny pain in his back that told him he'd been driving too long.

Patrick felt that Scarlett should be rid of that rabbit by now. Claire thought the rabbit was good for her, but Patrick was sick of having to get an extra chair out and play pretend. Sometimes he felt like Claire enjoyed the whole thing a little too much. Like Claire wanted an imaginary friend too.

Patrick refuelled the car and idly watched a family of four get out of a red Corsa. This was three generations of family: two kids with their mum and grandma, he guessed. The mum looked cold in her denim jacket, hunching up in that way of trying to make herself smaller or the jacket bigger. She looked familiar, Patrick thought.

Car full, he put the nozzle back in the holster and went into the shop. He stood in the queue behind the denim-jacketed mum.

'Should we get more logs?' the woman shouted across the store. 'If it's cold we might rattle through them.'

'Whatever you think, love.' The grandma kept her attention on the two girls who were, rather optimistically, looking at the contents of the ice cream fridge.

Patrick studied the back of the mum's ponytail. A few white hairs at her crown glowed bright against the rest of her dark hair. She was off-duty glamorous in her denim jacket and boots.

Yes, she definitely looked familiar.

Patrick wondered if she was someone he'd seen on TV. A reality star, or someone from a soap.

'What about firelighters, Nicola?' the grandma said to her daughter. 'Have we got enough of those or shall I get more for luck?'

Nicola. Patrick furrowed his brow.

Nicola – Garcia. Of course!

Nicola turned round and shouted something back to her mother.

Patrick studied Nicola, peeling thirty years back from her face, imagining her with hoop earrings and fuller lips, lips bright-wet and reddened from those lollipops she'd always sucked on.

Nicola left the queue with an exasperated sigh, and went over to her mother.

'Pump four?'

Patrick blinked back to the present; he nodded at the petrol station attendant.

'Fifty-four forty-seven.'

A morose Christmas song from the seventies rang out on the radio: a song about being lonely this Christmas.

Patrick sensed a person step behind him. He just *knew* it was Nicola.

Patrick waved her ahead. 'You go ahead. I may get something else.'

'That's kind.' Nicola paid for her petrol.

Patrick picked up some sugar-free gum. 'And this,' he said to the attendant. He handed his card over and glanced at Nicola, who was gathering her kids together. He hadn't said anything, and she was leaving.

And now she was walking out. Right now. Right this second. And he wasn't doing anything about it.

Patrick took his change from the attendant. He took a step towards Nicola.

Nicola turned to her kids. 'I'm not getting you ice creams, girls. You can have some tea when we get to the Happy Forest. It's only five minutes away.'

Patrick stopped. He gave a wave to the attendant, sugar-free gum in hand.

Patrick walked across the forecourt, a spring in his step. He threw his packet of gum in the air and caught it.

His good mood even lasted when, back at the car, Claire called him *useless* and sent him back inside for her forgotten Snickers.

A sign over the holiday park entrance had a speech bubble coming out of a cartoon hedgehog's mouth. *Welcome to the Happy Forest! Where relaxation is a force of nature.*

Patrick drove under the sign. He followed the queue to the entrance huts and pulled up behind the one with the red Corsa.

'I'll get us sorted,' Patrick said. 'Wait here.'

In the entrance hut, Patrick waited in the queue behind Nicola, who was just being handed her keys and a map.

'Have a great time!' the receptionist said.

Patrick watched Nicola walk away. He strode up to the desk. 'Patrick Asher.'

Patrick handed over his credit card. He watched Nicola get back in the car.

'Just wondering – I'm in a party with that lady who's just left – with Nicola.' He gave the receptionist what he hoped was a charming, unfurtive smile. 'Is it possible to get a lodge near Nicola's?'

He held his breath.

The receptionist didn't even look up, she just tapped at her keyboard. 'I'm sure we can sort something out.'

*Post-shooting interview. Sheila Kapur, 57. Happy Forest
    receptionist.*
Face-to-face. Happy Forest entrance lodge.

*Shall I get my coat? I'd be happy to come down to the
station.*

*I know I'm not suspected of anything, it's just nice to get
out and about. I sit on this reception desk in all weathers. I
have a blanket on my knees between September and May.
Do you want a cup of tea? I have my own kettle and fridge
here.*

*If you're sure. I'll make myself one though, if you don't
mind.*

*I suspect Jared told you to come to me because he
knows I know what's going on. Did he tell you that respect-
fully, or like I was a gossip? He's a cheeky one. Always has
something to say about my knee-blanket, calls me 'Gran-
nie', but it's OK for him, he gets to walk about all day. And
I've done him lots of favours over the years. I've long-known
his mother from Weight Watchers, and I got him this job
after he didn't complete his GCSEs. His mother is grateful
to me to this day. Though, thinking about it, we both need
to get back to Weight Watchers.*

*I know quite a lot about the shooting family, and I've got
a few ideas as well. I should have been a psychologist,
because I know what's going on in people's heads before
they do, or I can have a good guess, anyroad. I know who's
about to cry. I know who needs to come into my lodge and*

let it all out to old Sheila and her friendly kettle. I say to myself, Sheila—

Oh.

Of course, officer. Far be it from me to hold you up.
They say it was an accident? Do you believe them?
I ask because there were arguments in that lodge.

I heard it from Ben Oakley, who does the gardening, and heard a man and woman shouting by the lake. Then Richard Crawford, who works behind the bar, heard the two men going at it in the bar. One of the men called the other one a 'bellend'. That's not very festive, is it?

Can I look at the photos? Jared said you had photos.
Yes! I did meet them, after all! That man, at least.

Patrick Asher? Right. He came in to pick up the lodge keys on the first day. I didn't meet the other three. But why aren't you showing me pictures of the others in the group?

Far be it from me to correct you, officer, but there were. That man, Patrick, came to my counter and told me he was in a group with the lady in the car before. I did some juggling and found him a lodge next door. It was no bother.

I can look it up on my system, easy.

Nicola Trevor, that's her. She's still here, according to the system. They haven't mentioned her?

Well that's interesting for a start, isn't it?

Oh really? Nothing else?

But will you tell me when you find out what's going on there?

Of course, I understand. I'll find out on my own though. People tell me things they won't tell the police. I'm here when they drive in and I'm here when they leave, and lots of people like to have a little gossip and a cup of tea with

Sheila on their way past. I have fifteen mugs here, just in case. Fifteen.

Feel free to come back anytime. There's always a mug here with your name on it!

II

Patrick unpacked the milk and yoghurts from the cool bag and placed them in the lodge's empty fridge. He listened to the enthusiastic chatter of Claire and Scarlett in the lodge's garden.

He reached for the bottles of white wine and laid them down in the fridge, wedging the yoghurts next to the bottles so they didn't roll from side to side.

Nicola Garcia. *The* Nicola Garcia.

Just seeing her took him right back, with a jittery echo of teenage energy.

And he'd – on the spur of the moment – accidentally kind of *stalked* her.

No. He definitely hadn't stalked her, not at all. And there was nothing premeditated about it. He was just keen to see Nicola again and it was the only chance he was going to get.

Patrick tried to ignore the way the little hairs on his neck were standing up.

It definitely wasn't stalking.

Patrick needed to unpack and go for a run, he decided. He strode out onto the patio.

Claire and Scarlett were kneeling on the ground, holding out cupped hands of what looked like salted peanuts to squirrels. Patrick didn't think they should be feeding wild animals salt. But there it was.

'I want to unpack my suitcase,' he said to Claire. 'But there's only one double bedroom.'

'That one.' Claire gestured to Scarlett at a particularly plump squirrel. 'It's got the most gullible face.'

Patrick wondered what Claire had planned for those squirrels. With Claire, he could never be quite sure. Outfits? A photo opportunity? Claire just *had* to seize the fun in everything. Patrick had loved that about her at first, but now it made him feel a little on edge.

Claire flicked a glance at Patrick. 'You look all forlorn and pointless, standing there.'

'Thanks.'

'Just pick a room if you want to unpack. Finders keepers.'

'We can't take the only double room before they get here. We'll look selfish.'

Claire stood up. 'You stay here, darling,' she said to Scarlett. She walked back inside, Patrick following.

'Then let's take a twin room,' Claire said quietly.

'But I don't want the twin room.'

'Then take the good room.'

'I told you we can't!'

'Why are you getting so worked up?'

Scarlett walked back through the patio doors. 'It won't eat. So I just left the nuts out there in case it changes its mind.'

'Bring the packet in, Scarlett,' Patrick said automatically. 'Don't litter.'

Scarlett shuffled back outside. She shook the nuts out of the packet and brought it inside. She tugged at the patio door with both hands, leaning back to pull it shut behind her.

'What time are the others getting here?' Patrick asked.

Claire shrugged.

'Have you not had a text or anything?'

But Claire just laughed.

'Surely Alex is polite, even if Matt's not?'

Claire glanced at Scarlett and back. 'Matt is very polite.' She gave Patrick a *remember his daughter's here* look. 'He's just a little more spontaneous than some other people.'

Patrick watched Claire and Scarlett head to the smallest room, Scarlett pulling her ride-on zebra suitcase behind her.

'At least Scarlett gets to unpack,' he said to Claire's back. But she didn't reply.

Then Patrick had an idea. 'Scarlett,' he shouted. 'Come and watch me flip a coin.'

12

In the dark, Alex and Matt pulled up outside the lodge. They saw a man jogging the last few steps home, lit up by the forest's Narnia-style lamps. He was clearly returning from a run, and was wearing what looked like very expensive, very serious Lycra.

'Is that Patrick?' Alex said.

'Yep.' Matt wound down his window. 'Knees up, beetroot!'

Patrick jerked round, startled. After a moment, he formed a smile.

Matt put the handbrake on and hurried out of the car. He patted Patrick on the back. 'All right, mate.' He rushed into the lodge. 'Scarlett!'

Alex stepped out of the car slowly, her legs stiff from the journey. 'Patrick?' She held out her hand. 'I'm Alex.'

Patrick shook Alex's hand with a formality that made her feel like she was at a work conference.

'Did you get stuck in traffic?' Patrick asked. 'We were expecting you here at four.'

'Oh, we didn't leave till about four.' Alex opened the boot and pulled out her suitcase.

Patrick grabbed the suitcase from Alex's hand. 'I've got it.'

'Thanks.' Alex grabbed Matt's suitcase instead. It felt suspiciously light, like he hadn't put as much thought (or content) into his packing as he might have done.

He can borrow my moisturiser, Alex thought, *but he can fucking well go to a shop and buy another toothbrush.*

'Leave it.' Patrick jerked his head at Matt's case. 'I'll bring the heavy stuff in.'

'It's not heavy.'

Patrick looked like he wanted to say more, but didn't.

Alex followed Patrick into the house. The lightness of Matt's case suggested Alex wouldn't be receiving a lavish Christmas present this holiday. But they didn't really go in for that kind of thing. Alex's case only contained a few gesture-items for Matt. A bottle of brandy. A pair of socks embellished with pictures of Liono from *Thundercats* (they'd had a conversation about *Thundercats* not long ago, and it felt funny and cute). Whatever Matt had got her, however small – as long as it was wrapped and not still in the plastic bag with its receipt – would be fine by Alex.

Alex followed Patrick down the corridor. She watched the muscles move in the back of his legs. A messy mole sat like a paint spatter on the high, hairless part of his thigh. In normal-length shorts, that mole would have been covered up.

She'd expected him to look a bit more indoorsy. A bit more Sudoku and good wine, a bit less Putin-y, like he spent his weekends chopping wood and wrestling bears. With his over-exercised torso and too-short shorts, he looked nothing like Matt.

But then . . . why should he?

Claire and Alex weren't exactly the same type. Claire was

polished, super-white, lawyerly, with a full-on, shiny way about her that hit you in one go. To look at Claire was to hear dirty laughter and quick, clickety steps on polished floors. Whereas you just had to look at Alex to know her shoes didn't click, they squeaked.

As they reached the lodge's main room, Patrick turned to her. 'You're downstairs.'

Alex wanted to check out the open-plan lounge and kitchen, but Patrick bustled her down a corridor, like he needed her to get somewhere.

When they reached the bedroom, Alex put her case down. Two twin beds filled up most of the room's floor space.

Patrick turned to her. 'We didn't want to just take the master bedroom upstairs, but we didn't want to just give it to you either.'

Alex laughed. 'Fair enough.'

'So I flipped for it. You lost.'

'OK.'

'I said we should film the flip, but Claire said that was unnecessary.'

'It's fine.'

'Scarlett was there. An impartial adjudicator.' Patrick paused. 'It was tails. I'd said tails.'

'Patrick,' Alex said. 'Don't stress.' She gave him her best relaxed smile.

'I'll take your car keys.' Patrick held out his hand. 'And I'll unload the rest of your stuff.'

'No, we'll be fine, Matt will help.'

'I insist. Car keys.'

Alex had no stamina for competitions of aggressive

generosity so, reluctantly, she handed them over.

Patrick took the keys and whisked out of the room. Alex unzipped her case to get out her phone charger.

'Hi, stranger,' Alex heard Claire say in another room. 'Let me hug you.'

Then Alex heard Matt's voice in reply. 'Your T-shirt smells like home. Like our old house.'

'Same washing powder, probably.'

Alex stopped looking for her phone charger. She stood straight upright.

Home.

Claire appeared in her doorway. 'Knock knock!'

Claire held her arms wide, beaming. Alex leaned down for the hug. Claire was a tight hugger, as Alex knew she would be. The top of her head was up to Alex's nose; Alex smelled the nutty undercurrent of Claire's hair. She also smelt something else, a smell she recognised but couldn't place.

It couldn't be the *home* thing. Because Alex didn't know what *home* smelt like.

Claire rocked Alex from side to side and let her go.

Patrick rounded the corner with an armful of coats and Matt's skateboard. He placed them on the floor and disappeared again without a word.

Alex watched him leave. 'Patrick seems to be bringing in all our stuff.'

Claire gave a wave of the hand. 'It's what he does. It's easier to just let him get on with it. I'll get the kettle on, you must be gasping.'

With Claire gone, Alex sank onto the bed.

Matt stuck his head round the doorway. 'Are you OK

here if I take Scarlett to see the ducks?'

Alex gave him a smile. 'Feed them a crust from me.'

Matt waved and was gone.

'But it's dark!' Alex shouted after him.

Did ducks come out in the dark? She realised she didn't know.

Alex looked around her. The bedroom was poky, with drawers the size of shoeboxes and two coat hangers rattling sadly together in the wardrobe. The room smelled of boxes of matches and pencil sharpenings: the outdoors, tamed and made child-friendly. But that was fine.

But – *home*. *Home* wasn't fine.

Alex walked into the open-plan lounge and kitchen area. She smelt – then saw – the big fish, unwrapped and centred in a mound of plastic sheets.

Claire indicated the fish. 'I'm just sorting it out for tomorrow.'

Alex gave a small smile. She deliberately didn't look at the fish again. She didn't know what type it was, but it was big. A *look-at-me, aren't we having a special event* type of fish.

And Alex hated fish.

She hated the smell – that sour decay of coastal holidays and declining towns. She hated the taste, even though people always told her that fish tasted better than they smelled. In Alex's opinion, from her admittedly small sample size, that was a lie.

And she hated the way fish looked. The way they looked just so completely *dead*, their marble-eyes shining open. Alex knew where her food came from, and she had dealt with any moral uncertainty about that decades ago. But she didn't like to see those eyes. No other food came with marble eyes attached.

And she didn't like to be reminded of her squeamishness. Because she was a *scientist*, for God's sake. This dissonance was a sign of mental weakness.

'It's a lovely piece,' Claire said. 'But Scarlett's kicking off because she doesn't like fish. She thinks they look disgusting. She holds her nose if I make her eat it.'

Alex gave a small smile.

'But I told her, you can't just say you don't like things. I don't want her growing up to be a fussy eater.'

Alex moved from the fish, towards Claire, till the fish smell lessened and she could smell Claire again.

Alex gave Claire a quick smile. 'Just need the loo.'

She hurried back into the bedroom and leaned back against the bed's headboard.

Alex thought about Claire's smell.

Not that she was into perfume. She didn't wear it herself, though Matt had bought her a bottle the previous Christmas. Alex had made sure she wore the perfume a couple of times, just to show willing, and Matt had told her how great she smelled. And since then, the perfume had gone quietly and unceremoniously into a drawer.

Alex sat on the bed. There was no getting away from it.

Claire was wearing that same perfume.

13

Scarlett trudged back from the lake with Posey and Dad. Posey stared at the leaves on the path as he walked, his ears drooping at the top.

Dad ran a hand through his hair. 'I'm really sorry there weren't any ducks out tonight.'

'We'll find some tomorrow, Posey,' Scarlett said.

'I promise, Posey,' Dad added. 'We'll find the biggest, hungriest ducks ever. And you can have a whole loaf of bread to yourself. The ducks will think you're the Bread King. How about that?'

Posey gave Dad his bravest smile.

When the three of them got back to the lodge, Alex was waiting.

'Scarlett!' Alex jumped up off the sofa and brushed herself down. 'Good to see you, mate!'

Posey gave a little growl.

Scarlett gave Posey a warning look. 'We *discussed this* in the car.'

Alex kept her smile fixed. 'I'm really looking forward to spending loads of time with you this holiday.'

'Whatever,' Posey said.

Scarlett shushed him.

Alex's smile wobbled. She stood there a moment, looking lost, then sat back down.

Mum caught Scarlett's gaze and nodded towards the envelope on the table.

Scarlett and Posey exchanged glances.

Scarlett picked up the envelope and placed it on Alex's knee.

Mum gave her another deliberate nod.

Scarlett looked at the carpet. 'Happy Christmas.'

'Oh, thanks so much, Scarlett! But it's not even Christmas yet!'

Scarlett looked at the wall now.

'The thing is,' Mum said to Alex, in a rush, 'this present is time-sensitive, and if you're planning things for this week, it's best Scarlett gives it to you now.'

'I'm not sure there's much time left to plan things in, is there?' Alex switched her smile off in an instant. 'I didn't mean . . .'

Mum waved a hand. 'Don't worry, it's fine. I get it.'

Mum was always so nice to Alex. Nicer than she ever was to Scarlett or Posey.

Alex looked at the envelope. She opened it up and pulled out the piece of card inside. She blinked for a bit at the card.

'Surely she can read,' Posey said to Scarlett. 'She *is* a grown up.'

Scarlett put her hand on Posey's arm to stop him talking.

Dad leaned over Alex's shoulder to look at the card. 'What is it?'

'Spa vouchers.' Alex turned to Scarlett, then to Mum. 'Thanks very much?' Her voice went up at the end, like she was asking a question.

'It's such an amazing spa here,' Mum said. 'So relaxing.'

'Thank you,' Alex said. 'I've never been to a spa before.'

'Really?' Mum laughed. 'Then this is a great place to get converted. I had such a good time in this spa last time.'

'Last time,' Alex said in a strange voice. 'When you came here before.'

'Yes. But obviously, the present's not from me, it's from Scarlett.'

'Of course. Thank you very much, Scarlett.'

Scarlett gave a quick nod. She turned to Mum. 'Can I go to bed now?'

'What?' Mum pulled her face back in surprise, in that way she did so she didn't look pretty any more, but like she'd grown an extra chin. 'Am I hearing things?'

'There's lots of fun things to do tomorrow. We've got a big day ahead.'

Mum and Dad glanced at each other.

'Dad can tuck me in,' Scarlett said. 'Come on, Dad. Come on, Posey.'

Dad tucked the duvet round Scarlett. 'Tight as anything.' He tucked more, moving round her body, tucking and tucking. 'You'll never be able to escape from here.'

Scarlett squealed with laughter as Dad kept tucking her tighter.

'Remind me in the morning to give you that advent

calendar I've bought you,' Dad said. 'Only three weeks late, better late than never.'

'Thanks, Dad.'

'But as we're on the twenty-first of December, I've eaten most of the chocolates already. There are only four choc-olates left.'

'You haven't eaten them *all*!'

Dad wrinkled his nose. 'I suppose I haven't. I suppose the calendar's still in its wrapping. You'll just have to eat all twenty-five chocolates this weekend.'

Scarlett nodded at Posey, who was sitting on the end of the bed. 'Posey will help.'

Dad looked round the room, in the wrong direction. 'Do I need to tuck Posey in too?'

'Posey sleeps in the airing cupboard.'

Posey gave Dad a quick nod. Posey felt it was wrong for boys and girls to sleep in the same room. The airing cup-board was the only spare upstairs room in Scarlett's house, and it didn't look very comfy, but Posey was fine with it. He liked having his own space.

'Right, I forgot Posey's sleeping arrangements,' Dad said. 'You'd think I'd remember something like *that*. Is there an airing cupboard in this place?'

'Yep. But there's no rush to go to sleep.'

'I thought you were tired?'

'I'm not now. So Posey will stay here while you read us a story. Which one, Posey?'

'*Bryan the Lion*.'

'We'd like you to read *Bryan the Lion*,' Scarlett said. 'It's just there, Dad, next to you.'

Posey lay down on the bed. 'I hope your dad does the voices better than Patrick.'

'Don't worry.' Scarlett put her hands under her head. 'He does. And he's specially good at the gorilla.'

14

Patrick kept busy to stop himself thinking about Nicola. He organised drinks, prepared sandwiches, arranged bowls of olives and nuts. He was pleased to note that, by eight-thirty that night, he and Claire were clearly marked out in the capacity of hosts.

Matt had put Scarlett to bed, and now Alex and Matt were on the sofas while Claire was mixing drinks in the kitchen area. Patrick was at the dimmer switch, working on the lighting ambience in the open-plan lounge/kitchen/dining room. A man in control of technology.

It was important to set the right baseline, Patrick thought. Start as you mean to go on.

'Sorry it was just sandwiches,' he said. 'We'll do some proper cooking tomorrow.'

'By *we*, he means me.' Claire brought a drink in each hand through to the lounge. 'I'm doing skate.'

'Alex hates fish,' Matt said simply.

Alex's face flushed. 'Matt!'

Matt turned to her. 'What? Would you rather I hadn't told her? Were you going to just eat it anyway?'

'Stop it.' Alex turned to Claire. 'I'm so sorry, Claire.'

'Don't be silly.' Claire placed a drink on a coaster in front of Alex. 'I made you a watermelon cocktail. Non-alcoholic. I got the recipe from the Sunday supplement.'

Alex shot a look at Matt. 'No secrets here?'

Matt raised his palms. 'I thought you wouldn't want any awkwardness. Get the explanations out of the way before we came. Is that OK?'

Claire handed another drink to Matt. Patrick noticed he didn't thank her, and Claire didn't expect to be thanked.

'It's nothing to be ashamed of. And I'm sorry for drawing attention to it.' Claire grabbed Alex's hands for emphasis. 'I was trying to be nice.'

'I know. Thank you.'

Claire smiled and let go of Alex's hands. She went back to the kitchen for the other drinks.

Alex gave an awkward throat-clearing sound. 'I feel the need to add, for completeness, that while I chose to give up booze, I was never a textbook alcoholic, not the bad kind. I was just the kind of drinker that the newspapers warn you about.' Her face reddened by the second. 'The kind that drinks too much supermarket Rioja and is a ticking time-bomb for the NHS.'

Claire nodded. 'Of course.'

'I never woke up face-first in bushes or fought homeless people on petrol station forecourts.'

Matt turned to Claire. 'The good thing is, she barely ever fights homeless people any more.' He patted Alex on the knee. 'She's done really well.'

Alex pushed his hand away good-naturedly. Patrick thought Matt's comment disrespectful, but Alex didn't seem to mind.

Claire handed a cocktail to Patrick without looking at him. Patrick was going to thank her, but decided it would be odd if he thanked her when Matt hadn't.

Alex scratched her mouth. 'Anyway, I just don't drink now, and it's no big deal anyway. Loads of people don't drink.'

Patrick wondered if Alex always talked so much, and so quickly.

'I'm not saying never again. I may take it up again in a year, maybe – weddings, birthdays. Just not all the time.'

Claire picked up her cocktail. 'Cheers.'

They all did the clinking thing. Claire sat back on the boxy sofa and stretched out. She looked like she was trying to make the sofa look as comfortable and relaxing as possible. 'This is such a nice thing to do. Games and outdoor fun and karaoke. Getting to know each other.'

Everyone gave a kind of acknowledging nod. Alex's nod was slightly delayed, but emphatic when it came.

'Scarlett has never really been exposed to much nature. Living in a city. It's like – when I was a kid, I'd seen twenty cows and four pigs by the time I had my porridge.' Claire adjusted her weight onto one side and curled her feet up next to her. 'And Scarlett shrieks with excitement when she sees so much as a duck.'

Matt gave a snort. 'Not everyone has to grow up surrounded by broken tractors and stinking piles of manure.' He saw the expression on Claire's face. 'I'm not saying there was anything wrong with your childhood. Just that your parents' farm was shit.'

'I wouldn't worry. They don't speak highly of you either.'

Matt laughed. 'I wasn't talking about *them*, just the farm.'

'Whatever.'

'Well, you'd better buck up and get ready – they're coming here on Christmas Day and they've got a lot to say to you.'

Patrick saw Alex freeze, but Matt just laughed. When Matt noticed Alex's expression, he smiled and said, 'Al, she's just joking. She wouldn't invite them here. This weekend's not *that* full-on.'

Claire beamed at Alex.

'I think Claire's right about the countryside,' Patrick said. 'It's good for Scarlett to see more of nature.'

They all sat quietly for a minute.

Matt shifted in his seat and turned to Claire with a grin. 'So what *do* your parents say about me?'

'Nothing.'

'They must say something. For you to have said that.'

'They never mention you at all.' Claire flicked a feather off her sleeve. 'Not without the word *lazy* in front of your name.'

Patrick looked at Claire. It wasn't true.

Patrick wanted to tell Matt they always called him *Scarlett's father* now. That Patrick had a name to these people, and Matt didn't any more.

'Shame. Despite their crap, cold house with all the chickens wandering about like they had house keys, I always had a lot of time for your folks.'

Claire raised her gaze to the ceiling. 'No, you didn't.'

'And your mum always had great hair, the way she did that funky thing with the slide.' Matt did a gesture with his hand, holding a bit of hair to the side.

'Shut up.'

'And a lovely, condescending manner with waitresses,

talking down to them like an aristocrat in a period drama.'
He turned to Alex. 'I called her "the Countess".'

Alex lifted her chin in acknowledgement.

'Not to her face.' Matt turned to Patrick. 'Tell me, Pat, does she still fix you with that look when you do something wrong? Like you disgust her?'

Patrick coughed at the use of *Pat*. 'She only did that to you.'

Claire rose. 'More drinks, I think.'

Matt stood up. 'I'll help. You can show me how to make those watermelon things.'

Patrick watched Matt walk away with the casual gait of a man with no worries. He took a sip of his cocktail and turned to Alex to say something. But she wasn't looking at him.

She was staring out of the patio window into the darkness beyond. There was a tension in the way she held her eyebrows, an expression on her face he couldn't read.

15

Alex felt her step lighten as they shut the door of their bedroom.

'I think this is the earliest anyone's gone to bed on record.' Matt rummaged through his suitcase. 'Looks like I'm going to need to borrow your toothbrush.'

Alex swung her shoulder bag onto her chair.

'You think they're gonna nick your wallet?'

Alex followed Matt's gaze towards her bag on the chair. 'Force of habit. I am in a house with strangers.'

'They're not *stranger*-strangers.'

'Patrick is. I've never met him before.'

Alex helped Matt move the beds, nudging one against the other with the side of her knee. The newly exposed carpet looked newer and scratchier than the rest, a haze of undisturbed dust crowning the tufts.

'Matt?'

He looked up.

'Please don't make me do karaoke.'

He smiled and put his arms round her. 'I'll protect you.'

Alex withdrew from Matt's hug and headed for the en

suite. She kept her arms close to her torso as she cleaned her teeth.

A sound from above made Alex pause. A pulsing from upstairs: a faint, rhythmic creaking.

She stopped mid-brush and listened for a minute, then spat into the sink. She noted the angelic whiteness of the spit-foam compared to the rusty-looking foam of the old days, now she no longer drank a litre of red wine before bed.

Back in the bedroom, Matt sat up in bed, shirt off, phone in hand. 'Did they tell you the Wi-Fi code?'

Alex slipped into bed. She batted Matt's phone with the back of her hand, pushing it gently away. 'Or the internet could wait till morning?'

Matt placed the phone on the bedside table. He shuffled down the bed and kicked his legs hard and fast, flailing with the energy of a child having a tantrum, freeing the tucked-in duvet.

Matt tugged at the duvet on Alex's single bed, holding it next to his own, so there were no gaps for cold air. He slipped an arm round Alex and pulled her into a draughty spoon.

Alex snuggled down into the cosy position her body found naturally in his. 'So – spa vouchers. What's that about?'

Matt rearranged his duvet on top of Alex. 'It's a nice idea.'

'Do you want to use the vouchers? You like sitting about doing fuck-all.'

'I would love to take them, but Claire bought them for you. Now go and have a facial like a lovely lady.'

'It was very thoughtful of her.'

They lay in silence for a minute.

'I meant to say – that was funny.' Alex tucked the duvet under her chin. 'When I was in the bathroom. The upstairs pipes creak in a rhythm.'

'That *is* funny, Al. Right up there with one of your dad's anecdotes.'

'It could have been someone having sex upstairs.'

Matt stretched up and backwards with one arm, trying to reach the switches at the side of the bed without moving away from Alex. Alex felt the pulsing strain in his chest. Around them, the lights dimmed and brightened as Matt tested the switches to find the right one.

'On a freaky weekend like this.' Alex lifted her torso up, freeing Matt's other arm so he could stretch further. 'As if they'd be having sex.'

Eventually Matt found the switch that deadened all the lights. The room turned dark.

Alex had only been making a joke, talking for the sake of talking. Yet Matt hadn't replied.

She shuffled up the bed on her shoulder blades. She strained to look at Matt's face in the moonlight. She couldn't see his expression, just his silhouette and the delicate protrusion of his eyelashes.

'Claire wouldn't be having sex in the enchanted forest with us downstairs, would she?'

'How would I know?'

Alex frowned. 'I just mean you should have an idea.'

Matt didn't answer.

Alex looked at the dark shape where Matt was. 'What are you thinking?'

'You know I hate it when you ask me what I'm thinking. You think I'm having deep thoughts, and I'm actually wondering which would win in a fight, an owl or a badger.'

'Would Claire have sex with us downstairs?'

'An owl, I reckon. Because of the beak. And an owl could flap away to regroup if it got out of breath.'

'Matt. Stop dodging the question.'

'No, *you* stop it. You're getting weird on me.'

Alex shuffled up the bed, slightly more upright now.

'Please don't get weird,' Matt said again.

'Why would I be weird?'

'I can feel it in your back. You have a weird back now.'

'I'm just thinking, that's all. Trying to make sense of things.' Alex sat up. She reached over and flicked on the light switch. 'You know I like making sense of things. It's educational.'

Matt blinked in the sudden brightness; he pulled the duvet over his head.

'They wouldn't be having sex this weekend,' Alex said. 'Not with us down here.'

'It probably was the pipes.' Acclimatised to the light, Matt let the duvet drop down so he could see Alex. 'Hey. Your mouth's gone all twisty.' He reached for her hand.

When Matt didn't move or say anything more, Alex switched the light off. She looked at the curtains, a rectangle of blackness framed by a border of moonlight.

She tried to snuggle back into Matt, but her body didn't fit his so comfortably any more. Where there had been perfect nooks and gaps, there was now ridges and angles and too many arms.

They lay for a minute, Alex waiting for their bodies to soften together again.

'Al?'

'Yeah?'

'You know you're the most logical, most sensible person I ever met? You know you've got a brain like a machine?'

Alex didn't say anything.

'Maybe try to remember that? Because this weekend you're acting a little crazy.'

Alex squeezed her eyes shut. She tensed her body, pressing her thighs together, squeezing her buttocks tightly.

'I know,' she said eventually.

*Post-shooting interview. Ben Oakley, 65. Happy Forest
   gardener.*
Face-to-face. Happy Forest staffroom.

Hello, officers. Sheila told me you'd come looking for me.

*No, there's not much gardening to be done in the dark,
but I'm staying around because I'm being Santa later. It's a
nice change for me, and it saves on the CRB checks.*

Of course, happy to. Have you got the photos with you?

*Yes, I saw a man and a lass arguing. That one and that
one.*

Alex and Matthew? If you say so.

*I noticed because it came from nowhere. I was trimming
the edging by the lake and they were walking across the
lawn quietly. Then I'm not sure what happened, but he was
shouting at her, and she looked like she was going to cry.*

*I didn't listen to their argument, I just got on with my
edging. If Sheila had been there she would have noticed
everything, but I'm more interested in what's rustling in
the bushes, or whether my perennials are showing signs
they're going to survive the winter.*

Show me the photos again.

*I saw that blonde lass as well. She brought a little one
to me when I was Santa this morning. She came with the
bullying man. Matthew.*

*It is a long day. But Christmas Eve is the busiest day of
the year for us Santas.*

A few of us have talked about it. Jared is worried he's

going to get sacked because he slipped away to the bookies when he should have been supervising Alfie on the archery. Jared's a good lad really, and they call it a medical problem, these days, if you keep having to go to the bookies. So go easy on him with the bosses, won't you?

Richard's the only other one who saw something. He saw the two men arguing in the bar. Lots of swear words, apparently. But Richard's not working today, he's got Christmas Eve off.

All I know is that the argument was about crisps.

I suppose you'd have to know the background.

Extract from the Happy Forest brochure:

Our carefully planned world is your oyster, even on the rainiest of days.

The swimming complex has different mood zones and ten pools, and transforms from an oasis of calm to a thrill-seekers' delight. Scream down our Splash Landings ride, or glide down our lazy river – any cares you have will float away.

Alternatively, you can stock up on artisan food from our Happy Forest Market* and whip up gastronomic delights in your very own state-of-the-art kitchen.

With home comforts this good, you'll never want to leave.

*Happy Forest Market closed in December for refurbishment. We apologise for any inconvenience caused.

16

Friday 22 December

Day 2

Patrick woke up at dawn, to the sound of intrusively chattering birds. Seemingly hordes of them, all squawking at his bedroom window.

Obviously this was the birds' territory, so it was fair enough. But how did anyone sleep in the countryside?

Patrick looked down at Claire. She was snoring a little, one arm thrown over her face.

Patrick threw on his gym clothes and went for a run. He ran towards the lake, through a flock of birds, sending them skyward and outward, fluttering and chattering.

He passed the crazy golf course, and looked at the oversized photo by the entrance of a dad showing his daughter how to hit the ball through the windmill.

The look of concentration on the girl's face took Patrick right back. He remembered that wet December afternoon he'd spent five years before, teaching Amber how to do that silly card trick. How she'd watched and listened so carefully. How puffed-up she'd looked when she 'guessed' his card.

He'd never played golf with Amber, he realised now. Was he too late? Would Amber let Patrick teach her how to hit a golf ball through a windmill, or had someone else already taught her that?

Patrick wished he could take Amber and Jack to a place like this. But they were teenagers now. So had he missed the window for that too?

Patrick ran faster now, down the winding path towards the outdoor pursuits area.

As soon as he got back home, he was going to find somewhere local and take his kids to play crazy golf. Or – if they were too old for that now – *actual* golf.

He passed Santa's grotto. He passed a tucked-away shelter, in which short men in elf costumes stood in a haze of billowing cigarette smoke.

He thought about Nicola. Right next door, after all this time.

This was silly. Claire didn't know what he'd done. Nicola didn't even know he was here. Nothing bad had happened. So why was his stomach telling him he'd done something wrong?

He could just avoid Nicola and family for the rest of the trip. Then no one would know.

Yes. That's what he'd do.

Patrick reached the archery enclosure and slowed to a jog. He looked at the field: at the row of circular targets, laid out in a primary-coloured line.

He turned and followed the path for the Teddy Bear Trail.

It had been odd the night before, seeing Claire and Matt

interact so easily. When Patrick first met her, she'd looked like she was sick of Matt.

So why did it look so different now?

Three years before, a year before they started dating, Patrick had met Claire at a legal 'meet and greet' evening in a four-star hotel on the East Midlands airport roundabout.

Patrick hadn't had high expectations for the meal. He was there because Frank, the head of Patrick's chambers, had called a meeting a few days before.

'I know it's crass to talk about money,' Frank had said, 'but the next few years are crucial for our industry. We can't reduce our overheads much more, so we need to think about our margins.'

Margins. It was a new thing, this – barristers talking in corporate-speak. These last few years, people in his profession had been trying to make themselves more real-world accessible. The super-clever, fusty-dusty thing wasn't cutting it with clients any more, and now they had to sell themselves onto *preferred supplier agreements* and agree *fixed commercial rates*, and all that stuff that Patrick thought unseemly and grasping when considering they were talking about the Queen's law.

'And we need to stay agile,' Frank continued. 'We have to keep up with the jackals.'

In trying to 'keep up with the jackals', whatever that meant, Patrick found himself at a speed-dating session for corporate solicitors and barristers, prostituting himself in his free time to meet potential clients. Patrick knew what to expect from this session – he'd be drinking champagne, making small-talk with people he had nothing in common with, and those people would probably stand too close.

But, this particular evening, when Patrick entered the bland hotel reception, the first thing he saw was Claire. More specifically: he saw Claire's rear.

Claire leaned on the desk in the hotel reception, next to an elaborate vase of fresh flowers sprayed artificially black. She stood with one hip pushing out, stretching her skirt and straining her zip, showing the definition in her calf muscles.

This girl must be a runner, Patrick thought. He studied her legs. *Sprinter, probably. Not distance.* (He was wrong, he found out later. Claire hadn't done any formal exercise since school.)

'The thing is,' Claire said to the receptionist, 'you just have to remember he's a knob. Then you can hold your head high and let his comments float over you. Just think: *Whatever, Arseface.*'

Claire stood on one leg and took her shoe off. A miniature piece of gravel flew out, skipping along the shiny floor. She held her shoe up and peered into it. She looked to Patrick and gave him a smile of nothingness – a general smile of acknowledgement of whoever he was, but someone who was nothing to do with her – and put the shoe back on.

Patrick felt himself blush, he wasn't sure why. 'Sorry.'

Claire turned to him. 'Sorry?' There was laughter in her voice.

'I was just going to ask your friend' – it felt rude to say 'the receptionist' – 'the way to the law do.'

The receptionist pointed to the large, stand-up sign next to him. 'It's in the Churchill Suite.'

'That's where I'm going.' Claire looked at her watch. 'I

need to come through too.' She turned to the receptionist. 'Good luck,' she said with a smile. 'And, remember, don't take any more of his shit. You're worth more than that.'

She fell into step beside Patrick. The two walked in the direction the receptionist had indicated.

Say something, Patrick willed himself. 'Is your friend OK?'

'The receptionist? I've just met her.' Claire beamed at him. 'But she'll be OK.'

As they walked, Patrick tried to study this woman who apparently achieved a level of intimacy with strangers in less than a minute. She was taut, with muted blonde hair and a nose that was too small. She walked with a sense of absolute purpose. Patrick knew immediately that, however many people were in any room she was in, she'd be the first person you'd notice.

She was *lovely*.

Claire took a seat at a table in the conference room and, after a breath, Patrick took the seat next to her. She smiled at him and picked up her napkin, laying it daintily across her lap.

She lifted her menu and Patrick took up his own. Patrick tried to concentrate on it while adrenalin coursed through his stomach.

Claire didn't speak to Patrick straight away, but he enjoyed the lilting sound of her voice as she spoke to other people. He even enjoyed listening to her place her order with the waiter.

'No starter for me,' Claire said. 'And the salmon for main.'

Patrick smiled at Claire approvingly. A delicate eater. He used to be proud of how naturally thin Lindsay was, but now he saw it for the death-curse it was. That she had no incentive to eat healthily.

Patrick had been sitting next to Claire for over fifteen minutes and, apart from exchanging names and jobs, they hadn't shared a word of chat the whole time. Claire kept speaking to Angus, a red-faced solicitor, comfortably round-bellied, who was seated to her right. Claire's laugh tinkled out charmingly with a regularity that Patrick found profoundly depressing. A beautiful reminder of his own failure.

Patrick looked down at his napkin. He straightened his cutlery.

He wasn't one of those people who could charm with small talk – he knew that. But he knew he had one of those faces that looked like it was thinking serious things.

Deep. Deep was what he aimed for.

Patrick stirred his soup (deeply), mixing in the basil-flecked swirl of oil. He heard a low buzz from Claire's handbag.

'Excuse me.' Claire pulled her phone from her bag. She stepped away from the table: far enough away to indicate politeness, not far enough for any actual privacy.

She put the phone to her ear. 'Is everything OK? Is Scarlett OK?'

Patrick took a small spoonful of soup. It was too hot, burning the delicate V of his inner top lip.

Claire's voice was quiet, but audible. 'No, of course you can just call. But did she get to sleep OK?'

Pause.

'But what's Walshy doing there anyway?'

Pause.

'The what?' Claire frowned. 'The *blowtorch*?'

Patrick frowned too.

'Not off the top of my head. Have you tried the cupboard under the stairs?'

Pause.

'And what are you making at this time that needs a blowtorch? You can't be cooking crème brûlée on a Tuesday night.'

Claire listened, brow furrowing.

'Hot knives? But . . .'

Claire put her hand on the back of her chair to steady herself.

Patrick made himself take another spoonful of soup carefully, keeping it away from the burnt centre of his top lip.

'I just don't understand why that makes it an occasion.' Claire held up a hand to the air with the firmness of a lollipop lady. 'Yes, I understand that – in your head – that makes it an occasion. But you're looking after Scarlett, so be careful. And make sure you stay alert enough to hear her if she needs you.'

Claire switched the phone off and sat back down. She stared across the room and stroked the napkin on her lap in a gesture of self-soothing. *Penny for your thoughts*, Patrick wanted to say. But that wasn't the sort of thing a deep person said.

Patrick noticed the screensaver on the front of Claire's phone – Claire and a grinning man crouching either side of a pigtailed toddler, the toddler holding a cuddly toy of such a large size and poor quality it could only have been won at a funfair.

'Is that your family?' Patrick asked.

'Yep. Matt and Scarlett.'

Patrick studied the picture. 'Your husband's got a good head of hair.'

He put a hand to his own scalp automatically.

Claire laughed. 'He's too proud of it, you know what I mean? It encourages him in bad ways. I can't wait for him to go bald.'

Patrick smiled.

'What about you?' Claire asked. 'Do you have a family?'

Patrick paused. 'Two kids, Amber and Jack.' He licked his lips. 'Married to Lindsay.' He felt the colour rise in his face and he took a deep breath. But it wasn't a real lie. He was separated, and separated was still married.

He cleared his throat. 'Is Scarlett a good sleeper, Claire?'

Claire didn't appear to hear him. She stared into space, stroking her napkin. Then, with violent speed, she lifted herself from her chair and shifted ninety degrees. She bumped back down, now facing Patrick directly. 'How old are you, Patrick?'

Patrick baulked, surprised. 'Forty.'

'And when you were thirty-five, and your wife went out on a Tuesday night and you were looking after your four-year-old on one of the rare occasions you were babysitting on your own, would you have invited your friend round to do hot knives?'

Patrick gave a hard swallow.

'I mean, even without kids, would you have done that at thirty-five?'

'I—'

Patrick stopped. He cleared his throat.

'Have I made you uncomfortable? Sorry. I know we don't know each other. I'm just trying to make a point. To myself.'

Patrick's face steamed with shame. 'I just don't know what you mean by hot knives.' He pictured a juggler, throwing knives with sizzling red blades into the air.

Claire sighed. 'Exactly.' She patted Patrick on the arm. 'That's *exactly* what I meant.'

Patrick didn't have a clue what was going on in this conversation – though he could tell from the sigh and the pat that it was going well.

Claire took a large gulp of wine. 'I didn't know what hot knives were, either, till I met Matt and his stupid friends.'

Patrick's face cooled, though his heart continued to hammer in his chest. 'Should I know what they are? Do you want to tell me?'

'Absolutely not. But apparently Matt's got hold of some black, as he was keen to tell me' – Patrick was struggling more with this conversation every second – 'and you rarely get black any more, apparently, so it's a red-letter day and they're doing hot knives.' Claire scratched her chin. 'So don't do drugs, kids. When they're done by fathers in their mid-thirties, they're definitely not cool. They're pathetic.'

'Drugs? Oh, right.' The tension in Patrick's shoulders released and he gave a half-smile. 'I don't know anything about those. Even as a student, I cared about my grades and my health too much.' He raised his voice for any potential eavesdroppers. 'And the law, of course.'

Claire laughed. 'Even as a student?'

Patrick adjusted his spoon in his soup bowl. 'Sorry.' Back then, before he went to that New You! seminar, Patrick said sorry when he was embarrassed.

'Don't apologise.'

Patrick managed – just – to stop himself saying it again. 'I was always on sports teams. I looked after myself, even back then.' He paused. 'My wife used to do cocaine at university.'

Too late, Patrick realised what he'd said. Lindsay was a barrister too, she might know these people. He could do without having to have *that* conversation with her.

He glanced around, but no one was listening. Though, admittedly, the idea of landing Lindsay in it with shared colleagues was tempting.

Claire shook her head. 'I used to do stuff too, but I grew out of it. Like people are meant to. I've got a *child*.'

'When Lindsay grew out of it, I was pleased. I never liked it when we went out and she was doing drugs. It made me feel like I should be doing them too. To be sociable.'

'You should never have been made to feel like that. Zammo would be turning in his grave.'

'What?'

'"Just say no"?' When there still wasn't any recognition in his eyes, Claire added, 'You didn't watch *Grange Hill* as a kid?'

'I've heard of it.'

A tinkling laugh of incredulity. 'You've *heard* of it?'

'I hardly watched TV as a child. Only educational things like *Countdown*.'

There was that incredulous laugh again.

And again, it felt like it should have been a criticism. On the surface, Claire was laughing at him. But something on her face told him it was OK – that all the criticisms tonight were reverse, parallel-universe, complimentary criticisms.

Patrick felt less defensive than he could remember feeling in any conversation before – and that included the conversations in which he actually understood what was going on.

He wondered: should he tell Claire about his two-episode stint on *Countdown* as a teenager? About his winner's teapot, still in the attic at his parents' house?

No. No, probably not.

Patrick smiled at the waiter who was removing his barely eaten soup. He turned back to Claire.

She was studying him. 'You're an interesting man, you know that?'

Patrick felt a surge of warmth up his chest and into his throat. He felt dizzy under her gaze. With Claire, he was an interesting man.

Claire looked thoughtful. 'When my daughter Scarlett grows up, I want her to date a man like you.'

The feeling was so delicious, Patrick didn't even mind that the warmth in his face must be obvious. Here, on opposite-day, that might even be OK.

Claire gave her lovely laugh. 'You're blushing.'

'I need to get back out dating sometime. Not with Scarlett, obviously,' he added quickly. 'But I told you I'm married and I'm not. I'm separated. So I have to stop saying I'm married and get on and tell people at some point.'

'I'm sorry to hear it.' Claire reached out and gripped his hand. 'It's a hurdle to get over, letting people know. But you have nothing to be embarrassed about.' The skin around her eyes crinkled. She had the most expressive eye area Patrick had ever seen. Those eyebrows had extra muscles or something. She gripped his hand again. 'I bet you're not single for long. You'd be a catch for any woman.'

Gently, Patrick rubbed his thumb against the soft webbing of hers; the intimacy made his breath catch. He gave her hand a squeeze of appreciation and, with regret, let it go.

Claire sat back in her chair and took another sip of wine. 'Thanks for listening to my crap.'

'It's been a pleasure.'

Claire turned back to the solicitor next to her. She didn't criticise Matt to Patrick any more that night, even though Patrick gave her ample opportunity to elaborate on Matt's failings.

On that magical first evening, when Patrick got home, his chest was bursting with the feelings people wrote poems about. He sat down at the kitchen table with his laptop. He opened the intranet icon and entered *hot knives* in the search box.

He clicked on a definition and leaned forward to read the screen.

> **Hot knives.**
> Method of smoking marijuana where two knives are heated using a blowtorch or stove until red hot, then a ball of hash is sandwiched between them. The resulting smoke is collected in a plastic bottle (which has had the bottom removed) and inhaled.

Patrick shut his laptop with a satisfying click.

Blowtorches. Drugs. Cutting up bottles. At the age of

thirty-five. And not even trying to hide it from his wonderful wife.

He zipped his laptop back into its protective bag.

The man must be some kind of idiot.

17

At 9 a.m., Alex smiled at Claire across the lounge area. Alex sipped her tea and looked around at the blond wood and dated tartan fabrics. She took another sip of tea.

Across the room, a two-foot-high, electronic Christmas tree smiled with its tinsel face as it did a jaunty dance in the middle of the dining table.

Jingle bells, jingle bells, jingle all the way . . .'

The tree wiggled its hip-branches from side to side, the bobble of its hat twitching along to its tinny song.

Alex looked at the tree, trying to work out if it was truly sinister, or if she was just in a bad mood.

'Yes or no?' Claire asked Alex. 'Should we keep the tree up? Or put it away as a bad job?'

'Oh what fun it is to ride on a one-horse open sleigh!'

Alex coughed. 'Whatever works for you.'

'We couldn't just have no Christmas stuff here, that

would be so sad. And the tree was silly and, you know' – Claire shrugged – 'portable.'

Alex smiled.

'It has an off switch,' Claire added.

Alex decided this Stepford stepwife thing had gone far enough. 'Well, that's something.'

'See! I knew you hated it!' Claire grinned. 'I've brought the box if it gets too infuriating. Just say the word.'

The front door slammed. Matt entered the room, pulling his beanie hat off to reveal hair pumped with static, lifting in all directions. He ran his hand through it, an action which made no difference at all.

Scarlett followed Matt into the room, her yellow princess outfit accessorised with squeaky pink wellingtons. 'Thanks, Dad.'

Alex experienced a moment of surreal pause, as she always did when she heard Scarlett say 'Dad'. Matt's behaviour in their real life was so unfatherly, the word sounded jarring to Alex's ears. *I think you'll find there's been some mistake.*

Alex had learnt a few years ago that, now, when friends told her they were pregnant, Alex wasn't meant to say, 'Unlucky. Are you going to keep it?' But still. There were people being grown ups, and then . . . there was Matt.

Alex turned to Scarlett. 'Scarlett!' The pitch of her voice sounded patronising, even to her; she lowered it. 'Morning, mate.'

Scarlett looked at Alex. 'Good morning, Alex.' She turned to Claire. 'Can I have the iPad?'

'Nope.' Claire reached into her handbag and got out a box of cards decorated with princess pictures. 'You can play with these.' She turned to Alex and raised her eyebrows expectantly.

Alex clicked her mouth. 'Good parenting. Impressive.'

'Always.' Claire pushed herself up from the sofa. The white spots on her pyjamas weren't quite opaque enough and Alex could see the dark shadow of a nipple underneath. 'I'll leave you two to get acquainted. Help me clean up the breakfast things, Matt?'

Get acquainted. Alex was determined not to react. All right, so she and Scarlett weren't close, and, admittedly, Scarlett had just greeted her with the formality of someone completing a banking transaction – but the idea they weren't acquainted was taking it too far. Was that what Claire really thought?

Did she think Alex was terrible with children?

Worse, *was* Alex terrible with children?

Scarlett put her princess cards down in a semicircle. She was talking out loud, explaining things like a TV chef.

'Can I play with you?' Alex gave Scarlett her warmest smile. 'Will you teach me your game?'

Scarlett shook her head. 'I'm playing with Posey.'

In the kitchen, Claire pulled an overfull bag out of the rubbish bin. 'Maybe you should ask Posey to do something else so you can join in with us?' Claire tied the top of the bin bag. She glanced at Scarlett.

Scarlett fixed Claire with a glare.

Claire blinked back. 'We've discussed this. This is a special family weekend and we need to concentrate on human family. If you want to do the pony-trekking and the swimming pool, Posey has to stay behind.'

At the sink, Matt splashed an excessive amount of water around. 'There's only room for one person on the pony.' He glanced at Claire, deadpan, then back at the sink. 'It's health and safety.'

Claire turned back to Scarlett. 'You were really excited about pony-trekking. Remember? You get to ride a real, live horse?'

'And they don't make helmets with ear holes for rabbits.' Matt looked up at Claire and Alex for appreciation; Alex gave him an eye-roll.

'It's like living in the film *Harvey*,' Alex said.

Scarlett didn't look at her.

'I think this is a great opportunity for family reading time before we go swimming,' Claire said. 'So why don't you take Posey to your room and leave him there. You can bring a book back on your own.'

Scarlett stared at Claire.

Claire stared back.

'Come on, Posey. You can pick a book for yourself.' Scarlett left the room, hand stretched out behind her, leading her invisible rabbit.

Claire looked down at her spotty pyjamas. 'Time for clothes, I think. Swimming in half an hour, everyone?'

There were murmurs of agreement. Alex watched Claire head up the stairs.

Would Claire put that perfume on now, she wondered?

Alex pressed her lips together in self-disgust. There was too little to do here, that was the problem.

'Matt, pass my bag, would you?'

Matt gave Alex the bag and she got her book out. She leaned back on the sofa and flicked through the pages.

She'd tried to start this book three times already. It was something improving she'd bought at a train station, on the way back from speaking at a conference for healthcare professionals. Something the papers told her she *must* read before she died. Something she'd bought when, for a moment, she'd forgotten she didn't care.

Alex turned back to the start of the book again. One last chance, then it was going to the charity shop.

She stared at the first page and tried to make the words into sentences that stuck. But – no. She was drifting again.

Just be normal. Like all of this – tiny toilets, singing Christmas trees, invisible rabbits, five-day weekends, bald men in too-short shorts walking round aggressively at 9 a.m. – is normal.

18

Patrick sat down on the sofa in the lounge. He got his book out of his rucksack and placed it on his knee.

Across the room, Alex was reading *Ulysses*. Patrick was impressed. He had always wanted to read *Ulysses* himself, but never had. (Or maybe it wasn't that. Maybe it was that he wanted to *have read Ulysses*, which was a little bit – but significantly – different.)

Patrick looked at his own book, a paperback thriller recommended by his personal trainer. On the front of the book, the large writing was the colour of blood. Underneath it, a buff man ran with a gun.

Patrick wished he'd brought something classier, now he'd seen Alex with *Ulysses*. He knew from their sweating conversations that his trainer was well-read. He could have recommended a hardback, at least.

Patrick looked out of the lodge window towards the lodge next door – Nicola's lodge – and quickly looked away. He realised his leg was jiggling; he stopped.

He'd only just been for a run. How could he be needing to do more exercise already?

On the other leg of the L-shaped sofa, Matt laughed into his mobile phone.

'Of course.' Matt had slumped in a supine position, dangling his feet off the edge of the sofa, holding the phone a fair way from his mouth. 'I'll pop down for a visit and we can get it sorted after Christmas. If you'll extend the contract, we can work something out.' He laughed again. 'Don't thank me. Well, I'd like to say it was my idea to get you a thoughtful Christmas present, but we both know it wasn't.'

Patrick wanted to tell Matt to hold the phone closer to his mouth.

'Yeah, I'm useless as shit. My boss's PA got it. What did she get you?' Matt listened to the reply. 'Niii-ce.' He said the word with an extra syllable. 'Don't be flattered. You know how much you spend with us? I get to lord it round our office just because you're too lazy to get off your arse and look for a cheaper supplier. I'm going to buy a jet ski just from the commission I get from your account. Maybe I'll let you sail it as a thank you.'

He laughed and threw his head back. 'OK, ride it.' He picked at something sticky that had attached itself to his jeans. 'Well, maybe not a jet ski. More like a canoe. But if you extend the contract, I'll get myself a nice jet ski.'

Patrick wondered how one man could find so many things as funny as Matt did when he was on the phone.

'Yeah, not much coastline in Nottingham. Perhaps I haven't thought it through. Maybe in the leisure centre? But would a jet ski fit in a locker?' Matt laughed again. 'OK, laters. Have a good break, my friend.'

Matt pressed the *off* button on his phone, still laughing a little.

It was a work call, Patrick realised. Jet skis and lockers, Matt calling his client 'lazy' and admitting his own terrible organisation skills. And that was how Matt spoke on an *actual* work call with an *actual* client.

How he'd ever managed to attract a woman like Alex – a woman like *Claire* – was beyond Patrick. It certainly couldn't have been through good planning. Everything that had come to Matt had clearly come to him through right-place, right-time, dumb luck.

Patrick watched Matt. He was just sitting there on the sofa now, a leftover smile on his face. Doing nothing.

'There are some books in our room if you want to borrow one, Matt.'

'Ah, thanks Pat, but I don't read.'

'You . . . don't read.'

'No.' Matt grinned. 'Life's too short.'

Patrick didn't know what to say to that.

'I do *mean* to read more – I know books can be all right if you get a good one. But they can be an arse to get into, you know?'

Patrick gestured with his paperback in Matt's direction. 'I like reading. I read every time I go on a train journey. I read at least one book a week.' He noticed himself saying this, and tried to ignore the fact it wasn't true.

Matt laughed. 'Good for you, Professor Plum.'

Scarlett came back in the room with felt-tip pens and some paper.

'Did you leave Posey in your room?' Matt asked.

Scarlett flopped onto the floor and lay on her stomach. 'Yes.'

'Good girl.' Matt lay down next to her, also in a prone position. 'Give me some paper. I'll race you to draw a horse. I'm good at horses.'

Patrick watched them draw. So, Matt didn't read. It wasn't so unusual – Claire didn't read. But that was because Claire was always busy with other things. Whereas Matt . . . Matt wasn't. And Matt didn't even *care*.

Patrick put down his book and picked up his laptop. He glanced around to check Claire wasn't there, then pulled up the Ironman web-page. He looked at the homepage, at the picture of the shiny-muscled, self-satisfied man celebrating success in his sunglasses – the image that had repelled Claire so much.

But the image didn't look so bad without Claire looking at it over his shoulder. And while – true – the man looked so slappable, basking in his over-trained success, the image was much less annoying when Patrick transposed it in his mind. When he pictured his own face in that image instead.

Patrick pictured his own biceps, swollen from training; his medal glinting in the sunshine. (Admittedly, there wouldn't be much sun in the Welsh valleys that time of year. And Patrick might look a little bit damper than this man in the photo because of his sweating thing.)

Patrick shut his laptop with a guilty snap.

He picked up his book and opened it. Instead of reading, he watched Matt and Scarlett drawing amiably together. It was so long since Patrick had done something like that with his own daughter. She was a teenager now, but still. It was so long since he'd done *anything* that looked as relaxed as that with Amber.

'The thing is,' Scarlett said to Matt, 'it's hard to draw Blossom limping.'

Matt rolled onto his left side, straining to see her drawing. 'Why's Blossom limping?'

'She's hurt her fetlock. And she's got one eye shut because she's got conjunctivitis.'

Matt laughed. 'Poor Blossom. Shall we get her to the Pritt Stick factory?'

Matt raised his gaze to glance at Alex across the room.

Scarlett wrinkled her eyebrows. 'What do you mean?'

'Your dad's just being silly, Scarlett.' Alex looked up from her book to make eye contact with Matt. 'He says the oddest things. I can barely understand him myself most of the time.'

Patrick felt the crackle of deadpan humour between Alex and Matt. He felt himself tense. He and Claire didn't look at each other like that, like they were sharing secret jokes and didn't even need to speak to make each other laugh. Patrick really wanted them to look at each other like that, but they didn't. He wasn't sure now that they ever had.

But he knew the average British couple had sex once a week. He and Claire had way more than that so must be doing OK, at least statistically.

'Scarlett,' Patrick found himself saying, 'shall we show your daddy our dance?'

And he and Scarlett did the routine they'd developed to that EDM song, their hands on their behinds, jumping backwards like they were in a music video.

Matt stood up. He was smiling as he watched Patrick

dance with his daughter. No sharp comment, no attempt to win Scarlett back to the horse drawings. Nothing.

So when they finished their dance, Patrick went further. 'Scarlett, how about you and me go outside and race to the post box and back?'

Scarlett squealed with excitement.

Matt smiled and patted Patrick on the back, in the style of one who thinks another is a *good sort*.

Patrick was not a good sort, he knew. Not right at that moment. Far from it.

That was when, Patrick realised – *properly* realised – that he couldn't rely on Matt to make this weekend fun. That the sporting events would be friendly and *aren't we all winners here* and *it's the taking part that counts*.

Claire bounced down the steps. 'Everyone got their stuff ready for swimming? Shall we go in five?'

'Ah, Pat.' Matt patted Patrick on the arm in a gesture of sympathy. 'You can do the post-box thing another time.'

Patrick looked down at the hand on his arm, then back up to Matt's smiling face.

He just didn't get this man at all.

19

Alex abandoned her book. She collected together her swimming things, thinking.

How had she let herself get *here*?

It was because of Matt. Infuriating, lovely, patience-defying Matt.

Matt had been Alex's twelfth date in the year since she'd split up with Steve of the Sherlock coat and the neat fingernails and, it turned out, intolerably bad temper.

Alex recorded all her dates on a spreadsheet. You couldn't run experiments like this without some kind of controls. She'd seen, early on, the risk inherent in internet dating – that, with each date, her expectations were required to increase to justify her previous choices. All the while, her dating capital was shrinking, due to her increasing age and the decreasing size of the untested market.

Brutal, but Alex was a realist. Hence she set up the spreadsheet to ensure she was making optimal decisions.

Internet dating, in Alex's opinion, was a lab-condition-equivalent of real life, like growing a relationship in a Petri dish. And when you did things under lab conditions you did it from a place of knowledge, with proper assessment and control samples. There was no room for self-serving bias in Alex's lab.

On their first date, Alex got to the pub before Matt. She found a table in the corner and settled in, moving the chairs an appropriate distance apart, wondering why she was here in her dating jeans on a cold Tuesday night, when she would have a better night with just her laptop and her sofa.

Matt was on the phone as he arrived.

Alex blinked at him as he pulled out the chair across from her and, *still talking*, smiled apologetically and continued his conversation.

Alex had an instant urge to reach for her coat.

This guy must be one of these corporate cocks, out to impress her with loud talk of how *the Geneva office is going to shit when they hear this*, or, *Neil doesn't understand EMEA's growth potential*, or whatever else it was that kind of man wanted other people to overhear him saying.

Instant spreadsheet fail.

Alex reached down for her bag and zipped it up.

'If he didn't have the keys to the lock-up, then what was he playing at putting the synthesiser on eBay?' Matt put his hand over the phone and leaned over to kiss her cheek. 'I'm sorry, Alex,' he whispered. 'I'm really looking forward to meeting you.'

He smelt faintly of shaving foam, and like he'd recently eaten some toast.

After a second's hesitation, Alex put her bag back under her chair.

'Can you believe that guy?' Matt flipped his hair out of his eyes. He made a *wanker* gesture with one hand. 'Some people.' He shook his head. 'Anyway, let me go. I'm making a bad impression on my date and she looks really nice.' He paused. 'Not that looks are all that matters to me. As you know, mate, obviously.'

He smiled at Alex again. He listened into the phone a minute longer. 'I'll call you later. I'm going now, stop talking. Stop talking, I'm not listening. Pff – and like that – I'm gone.'

Matt switched off the phone and put it in his pocket.

He blew his fringe out of his eyes. 'He wouldn't shut up. I told him you were waiting.'

'I heard.'

'I'm not usually this rude.'

'If you say so.'

'It was my mate, Walshy. His life's gone to shit and he is threatening to end it all. But I didn't want to cancel on you. Sorry I was late, I know it's unforgivable.'

'But – you were talking about eBay ...' Alex reordered her thoughts. 'Do you need to go to him?'

'He's just having a bad day. I'll pop round to Jean's later. His mum's.'

'Is it fair to involve his mum?'

'That's where he lives now, he moved back home when his last start-up failed.' Matt paused. 'I'm not explaining it well – he won't kill himself, don't stress. It's not an urgent thing. He's been saying it since we left school.' He saw Alex's face. 'Look, don't worry. He's not even a nice man. Self-absorbed and angry at life. He doesn't stop for elderly gents at zebra crossings. Worst-case scenario, it wouldn't even be a massive loss.'

'Is that a joke?'

Matt smiled. 'Mostly.'

'I thought he was your friend?'

'He is. Old friend.' Matt said it like that explained everything. 'But can we stop talking about Walshy, because it's a waste to depress ourselves with his shit when he's not even here. So, more importantly' – he sat forward in his chair – 'apart from being thirty-five and five foot eight and non-religious and dating men in the thirty-one to forty age bracket, Alex Mount, who and what and how are you?'

Matt waited.

Under the intensity of Matt's gaze, Alex started talking.

She started with her degree in biological sciences, but Matt prompted her back further. So she told him about her childhood moving around because of her parents' jobs in pub management; how she didn't ever stay in a school long enough to fit in. She talked about her work in the lab, about her thesis on stem cell treatment for diabetes, about the post docs she'd done in Sheffield and Cambridge. She told him how you only ever got a three-to-five-year contract in her line of work and how, at some point, she might have to leave Nottingham if she couldn't get the research funding to stay.

Alex felt exposed by how much she'd shared. She brought things back to the standard internet date checklist. 'Couple of serious relationships in the past, non-smoker, no kids, no pets.'

'That's a shame. I like pets.'

'Well, sorry,' Alex said. 'I don't have any.'

'Could you get one?'

'No.'

'OK.' Matt shrugged. 'If you're sure.'

Alex blinked at him. 'So what about you? Who and what are you?'

Matt sat back. 'Now there's a question.' He gave a sleepy smile. 'Which version do you want? The airbrushed first-date version? Or the real one, where I mainly sit on the sofa?'

'The real one.'

'OK.' He rubbed his hands together. 'Careful what you wish for.'

What Matt told Alex that night turned out to be pretty accurate, when she viewed him in outside lab conditions in the non-Petri-dish world. He told her that he liked big, stupid action films and recreational drugs and that he didn't phone his parents enough. He told her he worked in sales, but he was winging it most of the time and wasn't sure what his real job was, but thought as long as he didn't actually ask, no one else would know.

And he mentioned Scarlett quickly and honestly that first night. Alex found out later that Walshy had suggested Matt to get it in quick if he liked someone, because *women fancy dads – fact*. Walshy may have had a life that was universally acknowledged to have turned to shit, but was a man whose dating advice Matt still took a punt on.

'Scarlett's a lovely kid,' Matt told Alex that night, 'but I can't claim too much credit. Claire's a legend, she does all the heavy lifting.' He held up a hand to stem disagreement, though no disagreement was forthcoming – Alex didn't have any evidence either way. 'Seriously. I just make duvet dens and take her to age-inappropriate films, or tell her what to think of the latest Forest defensive line-up.'

Alex found herself listening and nodding. *All men want to be dads, really*, Ruby had once said to her. *None of them would want to be a mum. But everyone wants to be a dad. It's parenthood, but semi-skimmed and pasteurised, not full-fat and straight from the cow.* Matt having a kid, having got that out of his system, could only be a good thing. Because Alex wasn't sure she could be a parent. (A dad, maybe, to Ruby's logic. But not a mum.)

Alex didn't say any of this to Matt, of course. That wasn't first-date lab-condition material. Still, they stayed in the pub way beyond her usual two-drink first-date maximum.

After they'd left, Alex noticed she'd done most of the talking. She still didn't know very much about Matt in any real sense, except that he was a loyal, not-particularly-discerning friend, and that if he knew someone who was going through a life crisis, he talked to the person about synthesisers and eBay.

That night, back at home, Alex sat in front of the spreadsheet on her laptop. In the 'summary' box on her spreadsheet, she typed: *Surprising. Nice.* She paused. *A little bit too happy with himself.*

Alex looked at the cursor blinking over the last sentence. She deleted the full stop and replaced it with a question mark.

She knew, without any discussion, that Matt would be getting in touch again. And she would go out with him.

That night of this twelfth date, Alex didn't fill in her usual assessment criteria, and didn't rate Matt on looks, or humour, or intellectual compatibility.

She typed another sentence, because the spreadsheet required it. *Smells of toast.*

As she closed her laptop, she decided she was looking forward to going out with him again.

20

Scarlett looked around the holiday park from her high-up position. She kept being jiggled around, as Dad was always crouching and trying to bump her further up his back. He wasn't as good at giving piggybacks as he used to be, he was slower and more staggery now, but Scarlett loved looking round from up here. She could see trees and lodges and lakes, and the massive glass magical-looking building where the swimming pool was.

The other grown ups walked next to Scarlett and Dad, all carrying plastic swimming bags. Posey trailed behind, doing his own thing.

'Doing OK?' Alex raised an eyebrow at Dad. 'You're a tad pink of cheek.'

Dad tried to bump Scarlett up his back again. He took a few more paces, then stopped. 'I think that might be it.'

'You used to walk me miles,' Scarlett said.

Posey shook his head. 'That's Alex's fault he stopped.'

'The thing is,' Dad said, 'little girls grow. That's what they don't warn you about. Sorry, Scar.'

'Don't call me Scar. That's the bad lion in *The Lion King*.'

'Ah, come on, Matt,' Mum said. 'You can make it all the

way to the swimming pool, surely? Or are you that out of shape these days?'

Dad gave her a look.

'Perhaps not. Scarlett, why don't you show them all how you can lift me?'

'Can you lift Mum?' Dad dropped Scarlett down. 'You're going to have to show me that right away.'

Mum stood in front of Scarlett and got in the right position.

Legs shaking, Scarlett crouched down. She took a deep breath and lifted Mum. It hurt a bit, but it was nice having all the adults smiling at her.

Alex clapped, pretending she was Scarlett's friend. 'Hats off to your leg muscles, Scarlett. You're a strong little thing, aren't you?'

Scarlett let Mum get off her.

'How about me?' Dad said. 'It's only fair, I lifted you.'

Scarlett looked at Dad. She knew she couldn't lift Patrick – she'd tried loads of times – but Dad was smaller and took up less space in a room. 'OK.'

She moved in front of Dad and crouched down. Dad wasn't as helpful at getting on her as Mum, and giving him a piggyback hurt much more. But Scarlett managed a few paces with Dad on her back, before dropping him.

'What a brilliant party trick,' Alex said.

Dad brushed his coat down. 'Our little Princess, strong as a truck.'

Mum beamed at Scarlett. 'How about you try to lift Alex now?'

'No way.' Posey shook his head firmly. 'Don't let her touch you, Scarlett. *And* she's too heavy.'

There was a pause.

'I'm fine,' Alex said.

'I would do,' Scarlett looked straight at Mum. 'But Posey says Alex is too heavy.'

The adults looked in all directions.

'That's not true,' Dad said quickly.

'Ridiculous.' Mum frowned at Scarlett.

Patrick looked Alex up and down like he was trying to judge how heavy she'd be.

Alex folded her arms across her chest so her plastic bag brushed against her front. 'I'm really excited about going swimming. Can we just hurry up and get there?'

'Great idea,' Mum said in a rush.

As they walked, Dad and Alex stood a little away from the others.

'You weigh seven kilos more than me,' Scarlett heard Alex whisper to Dad.

Dad patted her back. 'I know.'

'My BMI is 22.5. That is – literally – textbook.'

'Don't read too much into what happened there.' Dad reached for Alex's hand. 'She was probably tired from lifting us.'

Scarlett looked at Dad's face, how tired it looked with all that disappointment on it.

She turned to Posey and shook her head. 'Posey. *Be nice.*'

'What?' Posey gave a shrug. 'She just looks heavy to me.'

At the swimming pool entrance, Dad and Patrick went one way, Mum, Scarlett and Alex went the other.

Posey gave a *goodbye* wave of his hand.

'Where are you going?' Scarlett asked.

'Boys' changing rooms.'

'You don't have to.' Scarlett looked around. 'They've got family changing rooms. I could ask if we could go in one of those cubicles?'

'I just prefer the boys'.'

'Are you shy, Posey?'

Posey didn't say anything.

Scarlett smiled at him. Posey could be silly sometimes. Scarlett could be shy too, and she didn't like the thought of getting dressed in front of Alex in the girls' changing rooms.

But she didn't want to embarrass Posey. 'Have you got a pound for the locker then?' Scarlett asked.

Posey nodded.

Scarlett looked at his moon boots. 'You'll definitely have to take those off to go swimming.'

'I don't want to take them off.'

'Why?'

He shrugged. 'I don't like my feet. No biggie.'

'They're just rabbits' feet. And you're a rabbit.' Scarlett was going to add that she'd heard rabbits' feet were lucky, but she wasn't sure whether she'd made it up.

'They're not normal. They're bumpy.'

Scarlett sighed. 'There is no *normal*, Posey. Everybody's different. You're perfect as you are. You're *you*. You should love your bumpy feet because they're yours.'

Posey looked at his feet.

'And if you don't put your boots in the locker, you might lose them in the water.'

Posey shrugged his purple shoulders.

'If you lose them, we're not buying you any more.'

Posey shrugged again. He turned round and headed into the boys' changing room.

Scarlett sighed and gave a shake of her head.

Boys.

21

Alex stepped into the Splash Landings entrance pool, overwhelmed by the intensity of smells around her.

There was that sharp tang of chlorine that sat high up her nose, but it was muddled with lower notes. It was these notes she was trying to dissect and classify.

Talcum powder. Synthetic apple. Wet towel. Chips.

And – naturally – a faint hint of urine.

Alex lowered herself into the cold water. She watched her breasts lifting alarmingly in their cups.

On reflection, packing her holiday bikini was a mistake. Alex *really* didn't want to be flashing her chest at Patrick, or chasing her bikini top down a slide in front of Claire and Scarlett.

Not that Claire and Scarlett were there. The two had gone to *make a base*, as Claire put it, while Matt, Patrick and Alex tested whether the Splash Landings river ride was suitable for Scarlett.

Alex forced her head under the cold water and sank to the bottom of the pool. The water lifted her hair from the roots. Sections drifted in front of her face slowly, like seaweed.

As she emerged, Matt swam up next to her. 'It's fucking Baltic in this water.' He gestured at his swimming trunks, about to say something else.

Alex pushed her sodden hair out of her face. 'Please don't tell me anything about the size of your genitals.'

Alex and Matt swam past a woman in dangling earrings, swimming with her neck elevated, in an ergonomically terrible position. Alex wondered whether Claire would be one of those people who swam awkwardly, to keep her hair dry. Probably not, she decided.

Alex was pleased to note that, despite the weirdness of this weekend, her internal monologue was still being consistently kind to Claire.

Patrick swam up to Matt and Alex. He stood and lowered his goggles onto his eyes, pulling the strap tight with a meaty snap. As the plastic pushed into his skin, his eyeballs boggled outwards, froglike.

The three reached the mouth of the Splash Landings river, where the water rushed and bubbled, criss-crossing in rivulets.

Patrick gestured along the mouth. 'Spread out here. Let the riders ahead get some distance away.'

At the word *riders*, Alex and Matt made eye contact.

Patrick put out his hands on the lip of the mouth. He pressed a button on his massive sports watch, and pushed himself up and plunged into the water.

Alex set off a second later. She paddled towards the interior angle of the first corner, where she could see the river was running fastest. She dipped her head into the water and front-crawled into a slower, wider part of the river.

She turned to look behind.

Matt paddled along, gesturing and talking to an elderly couple, one of whom was carrying a toddler on his shoulders. Matt appeared to be mid-anecdote.

Ahead of Alex, Patrick was twisting his head from side to side in a professional-looking front crawl.

Alex slackened her pace. She dragged herself to the left, to take advantage of the full force of the current. She caught the flow and shot past Patrick.

She neared a smooth iceberg obstacle in the middle of the water. Something slammed into her body, sending her crashing into the iceberg.

Alex lurched and stalled. She took in a mouthful of water.

She looked round. She watched Patrick thrash past her.

Had Patrick pushed her into the iceberg? Surely not.

Alex watched him for a moment. He certainly looked exerted.

Was he trying to *race* her?

If he was trying, he was doing it wrong. He was clearly trying to avoid the other people in the water, but that was an error. It meant he was following the parts of the river with the least pace.

Alex watched Patrick flounder in a shallow section of water, trying to unbeach himself. The man clearly didn't even understand even *basic* fluid dynamics, let alone Bernoulli's principle.

Without wanting to think too much about what she was doing, Alex butterflied her arms. She propelled herself to the side, where the current looked strongest. The current took her into its flow, jolting her up and round in a roller-coaster motion.

Alex flew forward and past Patrick.

Was she really doing this? Racing Patrick down a ride aimed at children?

It appeared she was.

They rounded the river's next corner. Alex was ahead of Patrick and moving faster, propelled along by the current, but out of control. She hit the plastic edge of the river; pain flamed in her thigh.

Alex slowed, gasping. She felt something human fluttering at her ankle. Fingers, trying to snare her foot.

She looked round to see Patrick in her wake.

He couldn't be trying to grab her ankle, surely. The man was *forty-three*.

Alex pushed on. Again, skin brushed against her foot.

This was *incredible*.

Alex thrashed her leg out. She heard a jarring yowl.

'Lily!' A woman shouted. 'Lily, are you OK?'

Alex grabbed a rail at the side of the river and came to a stop. She stood up.

Patrick front-crawled past her, the roping muscles of his arms straining.

Alex turned to look behind.

In her wake, a woman held a blonde toddler closely. The girl was crying, holding her hand to her temple. She wore a rubber ring with a protruding brachiosaurus head, along with *Finding Nemo* armbands.

'Oh, no!' Alex tried to control her breathing. 'I'm so sorry – she came out of nowhere – I didn't see—'

Alex stopped, realising she was doing the full drunk driver's defence.

She reached out to touch the girl's head, where there was an obvious scratch. The girl's mother turned her minutely to the side, so Alex's gesture fell short.

'I haven't cut my toenails for a while. I'm so, so sorry.'

'It's OK,' the mother said.

'No,' Alex said. 'It definitely isn't.'

The mother bent her head in agreement.

'I'm sorry. So sorry. You probably don't want to see me now. I'll just get out of your way.'

Alex turned and swam in the river's current till she was out of their sight. She forced herself down, head immersed, pulling her knees up into a foetal position. She listened to the alien underwater sounds.

Alex held her breath until her ears thumped.

She broke the surface again, panting, and floated slowly down the river until she could see the exit pool. She let the water drag her down the last slope and dunk her under the water.

She stared straight ahead as she climbed the ladder and got out of the pool.

Matt flung himself round the last corner of the river. He held his nose at the top of the last slope and splashed, hip first, into the pool.

'That was fun, hey?' Matt climbed the ladder and made his way over to Alex. 'Not one for Scarlett though. Some racing grown up just kicked a kid in the face.'

Alex forced a smile. There was beeping coming from somewhere; she looked over to see Patrick underneath a palm tree, fiddling with his watch.

'Now, important question. Did you remember your wallet?' Matt patted his belly. 'I know Claire's doing lunch, but I reckon I've got enough room for chips.'

Post-shooting interview. Dr Ayodele Uba, 40.
Face-to-face. St Thomas' Hospital.

He came in via A&E, yes. But because of the extent of his injuries and the embedded arrowhead, he was rushed straight to theatre.

They were concerned about internal bleeding on the way here, but he's stable now.

I can't help you, I'm afraid. We don't give out patient notes without consent.

He's sustained significant injuries. That's the most I can tell you without breaching confidentiality.

As I said, we don't give out notes without the patient's consent. And he's currently unable to give that.

Not a good time. He's been in theatre and he's had a general anaesthetic.

I'd let him sleep for now, and aim for a sensible conversation in the morning.

22

At the dining table back in the lodge, Alex relaxed in her chair after lunch, watching Scarlett chat happily with Claire and Matt. She felt more ashamed of herself with every minute. Her thigh throbbed with a tender pre-bruise from her surprisingly violent journey down the Splash Landings river. The patch on her thigh was solid, waiting to flare into the deepest shades of purple and green.

Adults really shouldn't do that kind of thing, she decided.

Alex reached for more salad and a chlorine smell wafted out from her arm. At least . . . She hoped the chlorine smell was from her arm. You never knew with pre-washed super-market leaves. And Matt had prepared the salad, so there wasn't much hope the leaves would have been washed by hand.

Matt's phone rang. He got up to answer it.

'Mate.' He sank down onto the sofa across the room, nodding. 'Sounds tense. You can't be there with your mum for a week over Christmas doing each other's head in.'

Alex could hear a recognisable outraged voice on the other end of the phone.

'Walshy,' Alex said to Claire.

Claire snorted. 'Walshy's still living with his mum? That's been a long two weeks.'

'You could join us here if you need to get away,' Matt said into the phone. 'If you don't mind the sofa? Claire won't mind.'

Alex strained to hear what Walshy said. She couldn't hear his words, just the incredulity in the tone.

Matt furrowed his brow. 'Oh, OK.'

Alex waved her hand to get Matt's attention. Walshy deserved a reward for understanding how wrong this weekend was. 'He's got keys to our house – maybe tell him he can stay there for a few days?'

'Hear that?' Matt paused to hear the reply, then looked at Alex. 'Walshy says you're a legend. And that he'll change the sheets before he leaves.'

'He won't,' Claire said to Alex.

'I know,' Alex said.

Matt finished his call and came back to the table.

'We need more milk,' Claire said. 'I forgot that Matt drank it for no reason when there are perfectly good other drinks. Anyone fancy a trip to the supermarket?'

'Isn't there a shop on site?' Alex said.

'There was one last time, but it's closed for refurbishment.'

Alex mentally finished the sentence for her. *Last time Matt and I were here.* 'Then I'll go to the supermarket after this.'

She could go out in a car, like a normal person, she decided. Get some air that was more urban, less complicated.

'We need a few other things.' Claire turned to Patrick. 'I'm taking Scarlett pony-trekking – could you go with Alex if I do a list?'

'I'm fine on my own, honestly.' Alex sat up. 'I'll find the supermarket.'

'Patrick knows where it is,' Claire said. 'We passed it on the way in.'

Alex slumped back in her chair.

Coat on, Alex sank gingerly onto a dining room chair, trying to keep the weight off her thigh.

Claire tidied up the lunch things and put the dirty plates on the draining board. Matt filled the sink with water. In his signature washing-up move, he squirted in far too much washing-up liquid.

'Scarlett' – Claire grabbed a tea towel, she leant over the kitchen unit to look at her daughter in the lounge – 'you're not still on the iPad, are you?'

'Is this what goes on when I'm not around, Claire? She's parented by the iPad?'

Claire whipped Matt amiably with the tea towel; he jumped back.

'I'm not the only one parenting today, Matthew, can I point out. You're actually *present*.'

'If you say so, *Claire Jane*,' Matt said with emphasis.

Claire picked up the tea towel and whipped him again. 'What's Alex's middle name?'

Matt looked towards Alex, smiling.

Claire bit her lip. 'Don't say you don't know?'

He thought for a bit. 'She hasn't got one.'

Claire looked at Alex. Alex nodded.

Claire laughed. 'Nice save.'

Alex made herself smile. She wondered if Claire had played the same role as Alex in her relationship with Matt.

The eye-rolling, indulgent straight man. The one who got to lean forward and smell the suspiciously plastic flower; the one who got the bucket of confetti water in the face.

Alex watched the two wash and dry up next to each other, chatting as they went. Claire handed back half the plates Matt washed up, like Alex always did. Matt looked unfazed, like it was perfectly normal to wash every item twice, like he always did.

Alex tried to ignore the creepiness of the situation. She looked down at her phone, checking status updates on Facebook.

Claire handed him a plate. 'That's dirty.'

Matt peered at it. 'No, it's not.'

Alex didn't look up from her phone. 'It is.'

Claire laughed. 'See?'

Patrick walked into the room, jangling his car keys. He glanced at Claire and Matt, then turned to Alex. 'Ready?'

Alex took a last look at Claire and Matt. She looked at Scarlett playing with the iPad on the floor of the lounge in front of them.

Alex cleared her throat. 'Enjoy the pony-trekking, Scarlett,' she said.

Of course, Scarlett didn't look up.

23

Scarlett watched Mum and Dad wash up and laugh in the kitchen together. They found each other funnier than she remembered.

She remembered Mum and Dad arguing about things. About jobs and lists – about Scarlett, even. Often Dad hadn't remembered to do something, or bring something, and Mum was sick of having to think of everything. Mum said that a lot. Scarlett tried to remember things herself for Dad in the end – *Do I have a swimming lesson today? Have you got my packed lunch? Did you remember to bring the shopping list?*

Posey tugged Scarlett's sleeve. 'Let's keep the iPad. She's forgotten she's given it to you.'

Scarlett looked down. 'Mum wouldn't like that. She likes to choose when we have it.'

'She hardly uses it though. You know she always says the internet is for zombies, and the iPad's just a sucking-time machine. She won't miss it. It's wasted on her.'

Scarlett glanced up at Mum and Dad at the sink. Dad wasn't even washing up any more, he was just leaning back on the side, tea towel over one shoulder, nodding at something Mum was saying.

Mum prodded him. He stood up and started washing up again.

'Besides, I want to look up what the scientist said about me yesterday,' Posey said. 'She said being with me was like "living in Harvey". What did she mean?'

'I don't know.'

'I think it was something mean. It's best if we keep the iPad – we need to look things up whenever we want, especially with *her* here. We need to be on our guard.'

Scarlett thought about that.

She stood up and turned to face Mum and Dad, holding the iPad behind her back. 'Posey and I are going upstairs now,' she said. 'We don't want to be disturbed.'

Dad smiled. 'OK, chicken.'

She turned and moved the iPad in front of her, so Mum and Dad couldn't see it. She hurried upstairs with Posey.

In the bedroom, Scarlett and Posey left the door ajar. They flopped onto their fronts on one of the single beds.

Scarlett could hear her Mum's voice coming from downstairs.

'I know he might not be up your street, but I thought he was a good man. No, that's not fair. He *is* a good man. A *very* good man.'

Scarlett pressed the button for the internet and typed the letters into the search box on the screen.

There was a Harvey in her class, but that Harvey was an idiot who kept touching his own eyes to scare people.

Posey hated him. But at least Scarlett knew how to spell the name.

Mum's voice was still going downstairs.

'When I met him, I thought he was different. And he is. Some of the things that get to me aren't bad, exactly, they're just about his own hang-ups. If he could just be happy in his own skin, he wouldn't worry so much what people thought. And Lindsay doesn't treat him very well, so Amber and Jack have no respect for him. And he's a good man.'

'You've said that already. About five times. Just pointing that out in case you hadn't noticed.'

'Pick that one,' Posey said, pointing to an entry on the screen.

Scarlett clicked and read something about a furniture sale. *An extra 10% off dining sets – hurry, ends Tuesday!*

'That's not it.'

'I'll try another,' Scarlett said.

'He was such a grown up. Really polite and respectful. He called me to ask for a date and he'd remembered me from a work thing ages before. And – I just thought it was so attractive to go out with a man that wasn't you. Someone I could rely on.'

'You went out with him because he wasn't me. What a flattering criteria you had, Claire. Any man in the world except me.'

'I can rely on him, though, so I was right.'

'Ouch.'

Scarlett scrolled down the list and clicked on one entry at random.

They tried to read it. A fat man in a suit was saying

what he did in his job. Scarlett read how *he'd maximised his sales targets to deliver strategic advantage in a shrinking marketplace.*

'It's gobbledegook,' Posey said. 'Try something else.'

'Like what?' Scarlett said.

'Try *Harvey Rabbit.*'

Scarlett typed the words in. 'Smart.'

'And he's so good with Scarlett. She loves him. I'm just not sure I can see myself spending the rest of my life with a man who thinks the whole world is something to be scared of. You know?'

Scarlett clicked on the page that said *wiki.*

'I should never have let him move in, but he was just so keen, he did it bit by bit, by stealth. And I was psyching myself up to end it, but then he surprised me by saying he didn't mind coming away on this holiday, so that made me think, maybe? See what I mean? He's a really good man.'

Posey looked at the door.

'Don't eavesdrop,' Scarlett said firmly.

'It's like he wants to know exactly what I want, so he can be that person to me. And it just doesn't work like that, does it? He keeps trying to box me in – always saying what I like or don't like, always trying to learn about me, but I don't always know what I think, you know? I don't like being told what I think when I'm not even sure myself.'

'Your mum always talks really loud.'

'I know. Now keep your voice down before she remembers we've got the iPad.'

'And I look at the next thirty years, or forty or fifty even, and I think – how much fun am I going to have? It's just exhausting to be with him and his hang-ups all the time.

There are things I don't tell him, because it's too much hassle and – why are you doing that flapping thing with your hands? Am I talking too loud?'

'I think this might be it,' Scarlett said.

They both leaned forward to read.

Harvey is a 1950 comedy-drama film based on Mary Chase's play of the same name, directed by Henry Koster, and starring James Stewart and Josephine Hull. The story is about a man whose best friend is a pooka named Harvey in the form of a six foot three and a half inch tall invisible rabbit.

'I'm not that tall.'

'No.'

'And I'm not invisible.'

Scarlett didn't know what to say to that. 'What's a pooka?'

Posey shrugged.

Scarlett typed *pooka* into the search box with one finger.

Pooka

/ˈpuːkə/

Noun: pooka; plural noun: pookas

(In Irish mythology) a hobgoblin or sprite able to take on the form of various animals.

Posey looked at Scarlett.

Scarlett lifted her palms in the air.

'I don't understand the first bit,' Posey said, 'but I'm definitely not a hobgoblin.'

'No.'

'I think she's making fun of me.'

Scarlett patted him between the ears, to make him feel better. 'I'm sorry, Posey.'

'I hate her,' he said.

Scarlett sighed. 'I know.'

'If she does one more thing to upset me, Scarlett – just *one more thing* – I'm gonna make that scientist sorry.'

24

As Patrick drove to the supermarket, Alex found herself staring out of the window, watching the forest blur into a wet montage of cabbagey greens.

It was ridiculous that they were sitting here in awkward silence. Patrick might have tried to race her this morning, but he was her natural ally here. Another one on the outer circle of the family. It was stupid not to be on the same side.

'So.' Alex turned to Patrick with a smile. 'My thigh still hurts from Splash Landings this morning.'

Patrick stared straight ahead.

'If Matt had got a bruise like this, he'd call it a haematoma.'

Patrick changed gear.

'It isn't a haematoma.'

Patrick indicated left.

Alex gave a little laugh. 'I'm not sure adults really should do that kind of thing.' She tried to keep her voice light. 'It was . . . intense.'

Patrick coughed. 'I'm quite competitive when I get going, I'm afraid. I've booked to do an Ironman later this year. In Wales.'

'Did you grab my ankle when we were racing?'

There was a pause. 'Did you kick that kid with the pigtails in the face?'

Alex turned in her seat to study Patrick. He was still staring straight ahead, expressionless.

Was that a joke?

'I won't tell anyone,' Patrick said.

Alex sat back. So it *was* a joke. Maybe they could do this after all. Maybe he thought this whole situation was terrible too?

'It's nice,' Alex said carefully. 'Seeing Matt and Claire so easy together.'

Patrick nodded.

'Are you like that with your ex? Friendly?'

Patrick twisted his mouth in an expression that could have been anger or pain. 'No.'

'I didn't mean to pry.'

Patrick glanced at Alex. 'Lindsay isn't a friendly person.' He turned back to the road.

'I think most people say that sort of thing about their exes.' Except Matt and Claire. 'It must have been a particularly amicable split,' Alex said. 'But Claire's sensible and resilient – she would have taken it well.'

Patrick threw her a glance that contained a question.

'Sorry,' Alex said. 'This is probably an inappropriate conversation.'

Patrick still didn't say anything. Still, deliberately, said nothing.

'What?'

Patrick stared straight ahead. 'Nothing.'

Alex frowned. 'Were you going to say something?'

Patrick turned to her slowly, then turned back to face the road. 'The air has a particularly bracing quality this far north, don't you think?'

25

Patrick slowed for a T-junction and turned left.

This wasn't fair. Patrick really hadn't been prepared for this conversation.

There was no way – *no way* – that Matt could have been the one to end it with Claire. There was punching above your weight, and *punching above your weight*. Claire was about seventeen fighting categories above Matt.

So Matt had lied. And this was a problem.

Because, if Alex worked that out and it caused problems this weekend, it would end up being Patrick's fault. Lately, with Claire, everything ended up being Patrick's fault.

It would be Patrick's fault even though Matt was the one who lied. And what was fair about *that*?

There was tension in Patrick's neck in anticipation of a conversation that hadn't happened yet. He rolled his shoulders back and forward a few times.

Already the weekend wasn't going how he'd planned. Claire was being short with him. It was like all the good-will tokens he should have had in credit for spending the weekend with her kid, rather than his, had already been used up. And that wasn't right. Because he should have had *a lot* of tokens for this.

And then there was Nicola and the stalking to consider. (No, not *stalking*. Unknown, well-intentioned proximity. Which was – objectively – completely different.)

Patrick turned to look at Alex. She appeared to be asleep in the passenger seat.

At least she wasn't talking any more.

Patrick felt his face redden at the thought of the race that morning. He was a fair man, and that *was* his fault. He might have started it off, but at least he hadn't been the one to kick a kid in the face. That gave him a small section of moral high ground, at least.

This weekend wasn't turning out as planned.

He still hadn't had a chance to tell Claire he'd signed up for the Ironman – and by 'chance', he meant 'spotted an opportunity to tell her when he knew she wouldn't get angry'. The longer he left it, the more of a deal it would be.

And the swimming pool that morning had been a disappointment.

He'd been expecting a place he could do length training. The brochure said there were ten different pools here, but that was stretching the truth. There were lots of mini pools, but they were landing pools for slides, or whirlpool baths, or lazy rivers that you had no chance of getting any crawl momentum up before crashing into an overweight woman wedged into a rubber tyre, loaded with jewellery and float-ing around with her eyes shut, like she had all day.

The main pool was even worse.

The only bit of pool you could actually swim in was tiny and irregularly sized, with edges too erratic to do tumble turns. It was designed to look like a jungle pool, in this place where creating a fake-jungle aesthetic was apparently more important than enabling guests to attempt their personal bests.

Even worse, a horn-signalled wave machine went off every fifteen minutes – which wouldn't have been too bad in itself, offering a little variety and extra resistance to Patrick's swim, if it hadn't meant hordes of people thundering into the pool, thrusting aloft toddlers in armbands.

Patrick changed gears.

This weekend wasn't what he'd been hoping for at all.

26

They bought what they needed at the supermarket, and Alex pretended to be asleep again on the car journey back.

Patrick clearly had a different view of how Matt and Claire's relationship had ended than she did. That's why he wasn't going there in conversation. Maybe Claire had told him a different story?

Because that kind of thing happened.

Alex wasn't judging Claire. It was natural and everyone did it, *et cetera*, and this was the twenty-first century and people should make the choices that felt right for them, *et cetera*, and there was no absolute right and wrong in how people ran their relationships, *et cetera*, and who was she to judge?

Alex could keep going all day, if necessary, with the other caveats and *et ceteras* that she actually, *genuinely* believed in. And that would all be very well.

Assuming it was Claire who'd lied. Not Matt.

Because Matt had definitely told Alex *he* was the one who'd left *Claire*, not the other way round. That was one of the many things she'd learnt on that third date in the cinema.

She'd learnt that Matt was a *half-salt, half-sweet* man, and that he often missed his mouth with the popcorn when he was concentrating, leaving a semicircle of kernels in the carpet round his seat.

She'd learnt that, in his words, Matt 'didn't do' subtitles.

She'd learnt that he had a love-hate relationship with 3D because 'it's just too fucking real', that he was extremely flinchy, and jerked his head backwards at the most predict-able of shocks.

She'd learnt that he didn't always do up his shoelaces, 'because he was only going to have to undo them again at some point anyway'.

She'd learnt that Matt liked to sit on the end of an aisle, because he always bought the largest drink they sold in the cinema.

And she'd learnt that Matt had ended his marriage to Claire. That was her lasting take-away from the evening.

Alex learnt that 'it wasn't working out' and Matt had 'realised what needed to be done, however sad'. That 'it was better for Scarlett if she didn't have her parents fighting' and 'no kid should grow up in a house where their parents don't love each other any more'.

But Alex was, now, starting to wonder if – actually – it was Claire who had left Matt.

And he might not have lied, of course. It still might have been Claire who'd lied to Patrick, or it may have felt like a mutual decision: they might both have both felt the cracks forming and it just happened that Matt was the one who confronted the conflict head on and took the bull by the horns and ended it.

Which would be fine, which would be reassuring. Which would be an interpretation of the facts that Alex could deal with – with one caveat.

It would have been fine, assuming Matt had *ever* shown in their relationship, *just once*, that he was the kind of person to anticipate change and confront conflict and take the bull by the horns.

Just once.

There were some absolute truths in Alex's life that she couldn't ignore.

She felt Patrick glance at her, but she kept her face neutral. Patrick looked back to the road ahead.

If Matt had lied to her, it could only be an ego thing. Matt trying to present himself as an unreturned, aspirational product of a man: a product still kept at full price and in the original packaging.

If it was that, she got it. But that didn't make it OK.

Alex knew she could never have a relationship like her parents': a relationship in which every item of clothing her mum bought was described as 'a steal, reduced to a fiver in the sale'. A relationship in which her dad still smoked thirty years after giving up, but only once a week, when her mum was at her evening pottery classes.

Alex watched Patrick change gears.

She took a breath. 'Don't you think it's a strange thing for us to be doing? This trip?'

Patrick shrugged.

'But don't you?'

'Ask your boyfriend.'

'Yes, but you know Matt – he'll go along with anything. It was Claire's suggestion.'

Patrick drove under the hedgehog sign into the holiday park. 'It was Matt's idea.'

'It wasn't.'

Patrick glanced at Alex, then back at the road. 'Claire definitely told me it was Matt's idea.'

Alex gripped the edge of the passenger seat. They rounded the corner towards their lodge.

'Shit!'

At Patrick's shout, Alex lurched upright.

Patrick jerked his foot onto the brakes; the tyres screeched.

Alex felt the unmistakable bump of an impact as the car shuddered to a stop.

*Post-shooting interview. Nicola Trevor, 43. Happy Forest
  guest.*
Face-to-face. Happy Forest lodge.

Do you know any more? Is he doing OK?
    Stable is good. Though Sheila at the entrance hut told
me that already. She's been coming to see me with updates, which is thoughtful.
    Awful, awful. And I feel bad we're still here, trying to
enjoy ourselves, but we're paid up till Boxing Day and it's
not like there's anything we can do, is there?
    The girls won't be able to tell you anything. And Emily,
the younger one, is terrified of the police after a pair of them
came to her school to scare the kids about the long arm of
the law.
    Sophia did go to a burlesque class yesterday, yes. And
when I heard the receptionist saying there had been an
incident and no one would be there to pick up Scarlett, I
took Scarlett back to our lodge to wait for her grandparents.
They only picked her up half an hour ago.
    Scarlett seemed fine. Why are you asking all this, anyway?
    But what a silly thing to think! It was an accident.
    Is that why you're here? But that's awful! Of course it was
an accident.
    I did see some tension in that lodge, but it was only
because Alex was drunk and kept saying pointed things.
There was no harm done, and I'm sure she was fine in the
morning.

It was just the drink talking. I don't know her, but I'm sure that was it.

I'd never met any of them before the trip. Well, except Patrick, but I hadn't seen him for twenty years!

Sheila said what?

But – that's not true.

He must have recognised me before, maybe. Maybe when we were queuing to get our keys. But—

No, he didn't say. I swear he didn't recognise me till the business with the pheasant.

I'm not sure how I feel about what you're telling me.

Is this why Sheila keeps coming round to see me?

27

'It was just there, in the middle of the road!' Patrick whirled round to look out of the back window. 'Looking at me, not moving – just standing there, waiting to be hit!'

Alex followed him out of the car, both leaving their doors open.

Patrick ran his hands over his scalp. He held his hands behind his head and stared forward, like a footballer who'd missed a penalty.

'The stupid, stupid thing,' Patrick said.

Alex looked at the pheasant. It lay in the middle of the road, lying straight on its back. It was stretched out, looking more relaxed than it should in the circumstances. In a tiny movement, its long, reed-like tail flapped gently against the tarmac. Its eyes were open.

Patrick rubbed his eyebrow in agitation. 'Do we move it to the side of the road?'

'It's alive. And it's suffering,' Alex said.

Patrick pulled the sleeves of his sweatshirt over his hands.

Alex looked at Patrick – at his puffed up chest, at the outrage and bravado and fear, and a pumping concoction of she-didn't-know-what-else in there. At the stretched sleeves. 'Are you going to do anything?'

But Patrick didn't move.

The pheasant's tail gave another soft flap.

Come on, Patrick.

But Patrick still didn't move.

Alex couldn't just leave it there, in that condition, while Patrick made up his mind. It wasn't fair to the animal.

She knelt gently by the unmoving pheasant, ignoring the dampness of the tarmac.

'Hi,' she said softly to the pheasant. Its tail flapped minutely.

Alex reached forward. She curled her hands round the pheasant's neck and felt the moist softness of the feathers in her palms.

She hesitated for a second then gripped the neck. She wrenched her hands in opposite directions.

Alex heard the crack and felt the velvety neck break between her hands.

Alex let the bird go. Gently, she laid it on the tarmac. She sat back on her heels, looking at the dead bird. A tiredness washed over her.

Behind Alex, a scream rang out.

Alex whipped her head round to look.

The family from the lodge next door with the red Corsa were all out in the front garden: the grandma, the mum and two kids. All looking at Alex. At Alex, with the dead pheasant in front of her.

But the scream hadn't come from that angle.

Alex looked further round.

Claire and Matt stood with Scarlett on the doorstep of

their own lodge. Claire had one hand over Scarlett's eyes, and was trying and failing to bustle Scarlett inside.

'She murdered that bird!'

Alex ran towards Scarlett. 'That's not what happened!'

'She's a murderer!'

'No! I can explain, Scarlett! It was the right thing to do. The pheasant had to die!'

Scarlett screamed again. 'Posey!' She thrashed wildly with her arms. 'Run away, as fast as you can! Save yourself!'

With a look of apology to Alex, Claire wrestled Scarlett through the front door. *I'll sort it*, Claire mouthed.

Alex walked towards Matt; they stared at each other. Alex looked down at the dead pheasant.

Alex brushed the dirt from the knees of her jeans.

Patrick cleared his throat. 'Well. Thanks for that.' He glanced up at the family in the next lodge and back to Alex.

'Yeah,' Alex said.

Matt put his hand on Alex's shoulder. 'Well done. I'm proud of you.'

Alex didn't answer. She walked into the house, leaving the pheasant in the road.

She walked straight past the lounge, towards her bedroom. She shut the door, but she could still hear Scarlett's juddering sobs from the bedroom upstairs.

Alex sank onto the bed.

She'd never wanted a drink more in her life.

28

Patrick stood in the road, looking at the dead bird. It looked so small and harmless.

He'd hit that bird and then stood there, just *stood there*, and let Alex finish it off.

'What do we do with the body?' Matt said.

Patrick still had Scarlett's cries of *murderer* in his head. 'Don't call it a body.'

His only consolation was that it wasn't him that Scarlett saw wringing the pheasant's neck. That would have made the next few weeks a nightmare.

It was too late to change the past, but the experience left him feeling unmanned. Outmanned. Like he needed to wring a bird's neck, too, to balance the world again.

And now Nicola Garcia – *lovely Nicola Garcia* – was walking towards him, her hands jammed in the pockets of her jeans, an expression of polite sympathy on her face.

This wasn't how he wanted to see her again. Not that he had planned a particular meeting, but it definitely was one where he made an impressive entrance, not one where he'd just accidentally maimed an animal and then stood by and let the nearest woman finish it off.

'Are you OK?' Nicola looked from Patrick to Matt. 'I wanted to tell you, I was standing at the window and it just ran straight out.' She looked back to Patrick. 'You had no chance of stopping.'

'Pheasants.' Matt gave her a smile. 'They've got no brains at all, they're just vegetables with wings.' He turned to Patrick. 'What do you think? Shall we take this back for the pot? Claire will know how to pluck it from her days on the farm.'

Patrick thought of Scarlett. 'Better not.' He turned towards Nicola, trying to think what to say.

He put his hands in his pocket, mirroring Nicola's stance. He rocked forward onto the balls of his feet and back again.

No words would come.

Over her jeans, Nicola wore a long fluffy waistcoat-thing that stopped mid-thigh; it bulked her up, putting Patrick in mind of a matronly farmer's wife. *It's funny*, Patrick thought. *If I hadn't known she was the most beautiful thing who'd ever walked the earth, I almost wouldn't know it from looking at her.*

'I'm Matt,' Matt said. 'I hope your kids aren't too upset about seeing that.'

Nicola smiled. 'Nicola. And they seem fine, which is a bit worrying. So God knows what they see at school.'

'I would have killed it myself,' Patrick said, 'but Alex reacted so quickly.'

He paused. He'd regretted what he'd done, getting the lodge next door to Nicola, but now she was here right in front of him and—

'I'm Patrick. Patrick – Asher.' Too late. He'd done it.

Nicola smiled with a friendly acknowledgment.

Patrick looked down. He scuffed one shoe against the other.

He glanced at Matt. He didn't want Matt there, but Patrick knew he wouldn't get a better chance.

Patrick screwed up his eyes as if peering at Nicola. 'Nicola . . . Garcia, isn't it?'

Nicola tipped her head to one side and studied him. Her face wasn't unfriendly. 'I'm sorry, but—'

'Patrick Asher.' He didn't need to hear how she didn't remember him. 'St Swithin's Comprehensive? GCSE Drama?'

Nicola's brow shifted; her expression opened up. 'Wow!' She gave a genuine laugh. 'I can't believe you recognised me! I'm Nicola Trevor now, nobody's called me Garcia in years.'

'You look just the same.'

She batted his arm with the back of her hand. 'I do not.'

'She does.' Patrick turned to Matt. 'Though we barely saw her at school. She kept getting sent home for the length of her skirt.'

'Too short or too long?' Matt asked with a grin.

Nicola grinned back. 'Depended on the day. Railing against the system every which way. Girl power.' She shook her head with a smile. 'I'm a mum now, of course.'

'Me too.'

Matt laughed at that.

'You know what I mean,' Patrick added.

'St Swithin's comp. Well, well.' Nicola's voice was lower than he remembered, crinkled by cigarettes and time. There was a joy implicit in her laugh that had never been there at fifteen. 'Time flies. Those are my two girls you saw. Sophia and Emily. Eleven and nine.'

'I've got a girl and a boy, fourteen and thirteen. Amber

and Jack. Though they aren't here, they're with their mother. I'm here with my partner's family.' He glanced at Matt. 'Not him, I'm not with him. My *girlfriend's* family.'

Nicola shook her head. 'Please don't tell me how long it's been since St Swithin's.' She stood back, as if taking Patrick in. Patrick stood up a little straighter. 'How lovely to see you! There's something about seeing old friends, isn't there?'

Patrick grinned back. *Friends.*

Patrick realised Matt was still there, grinning away with them. 'Small world.'

Nicola turned to Matt. 'Do you know about his star turn in *Hamlet?*'

Patrick smiled boyishly. Nicola had remembered something about him. (Admittedly, she hadn't remembered much – he didn't have a real part, he was just a random mute courtier at the back of the stage. But she'd remembered he was *in* the play and that's what mattered.)

'Did he have hair at school?' Matt said to Nicola. 'Or was he always a slap-head?'

Nicola smiled. 'He had hair. Lots of hair.'

Matt nodded. 'You should come over with the family, Nicola. Fill us in on all the Patrick childhood goss. I think he's got a free slot on his clipboard if you fancy a drink with us tomorrow night?'

Patrick tensed, on so many levels.

Nicola nodded. 'We'd like that.'

Matt grinned at her. 'Great. We'll get the eggnog brewing or something. You can tell us all about what kind of loser Patrick was at school. I bet he wrapped his text books in wallpaper and always got his homework in on time.'

Nicola laughed.

Patrick felt his grin stiffen on his face.

Matt nodded to the pheasant. 'I suppose we should move this.' He looked at Nicola. 'Unless you want it? A bit of a wash and some plucking and it'll be sound.'

'Not for us. But thanks.'

'Leave it, Matt. I'll deal with it,' Patrick said quickly.

Nicola gave a wave. Patrick saw that familiar crinkle of her nose as she smiled. She turned back to her own lodge.

Patrick watched her walk away. 'Nicola Garcia, right next door.' He turned to Matt. 'She was really popular at school. One of the cool girls. Wore great big hoop earrings.'

Matt grinned at him. 'You can knock one out to that memory later.'

Patrick tutted.

'What?'

'No need to be crass.'

'Pat.' Matt touched Patrick on the arm. 'I was just dicking about.'

'I've got a fourteen-year-old daughter, Matt.'

Matt held his hands up. 'I *said* sorry. You've made it sound bad and I didn't mean it like that.'

Patrick leaned down and picked up the pheasant.

The two walked to the recycling area by the side of the lodge. Matt lifted the lid of the grey bin and gestured to Patrick. 'Go ahead.'

'Wrong bin. Open the green one.'

'Pheasants can be recycled?'

'It's food,' Patrick said. 'It can go in with garden waste.'

Matt put his head to one side. 'Pheasants can be recycled. Who knew?'

He opened the green bin lid, and Patrick shoved the dead bird inside.

When Patrick had been fourteen, he'd observed Nicola mutely from afar. (It hit Patrick that his technique with girls hadn't got any more sophisticated in the last thirty years.)

Nicola wasn't the only one Patrick noticed. He observed all of the earring girls, and that was easy to do all at once because they were always together: standing thick in an intimidating throng in the playground or canteen.

But Nicola caught his attention most of all. She was shorter than the others, using her low centre of gravity to propel her along in a bouncing swagger. Her lips were perma-tinged synthetic red from those lollipops she sucked at every break.

It was the reason he'd taken drama: to meet girls like that. Yet it had turned out to be an unsuccessful strategy. *Everyone pair up*, Mrs Hunter said at the beginning of every class. And, however much Patrick had inched his way in the direction of the earring girls, somehow he would end up paired with the skinny Goth boy who hummed to himself.

Patrick spoke to Nicola once, at Steven Andrews' house party.

Steven Andrews had only been at St Swithin's for three weeks. He had been expelled from somewhere else (for some reason about which the rumours flew), giving him a certain insta-cachet.

Steven had sat next to Patrick in the first geography class and Patrick had lent him a biro. Three biros, in fact – one at the start of every lesson. But that was OK. Patrick was a boy who travelled with spare stationery.

That third week as they packed up their books, Steven turned to Patrick. 'I've got a free house this weekend, if you want to come? Tell your mates. My parents are at the cottage.'

Patrick didn't know what 'at the cottage' meant, but it didn't matter right now.

Patrick hoped Steven couldn't tell how fast his heart was going. That this was the first house party anyone outside the computer club had ever invited him to. And even Patrick knew that computer club parties didn't count.

The night of the party, Patrick put on his best Iron Maiden T-shirt and headed to Steven's house, clutching the four-pack of cider his dad had thrust onto him un-requested. Reflecting now, Patrick's dad was clearly also delighted his son was going to a non-computer club party.

On arrival, Patrick hid two cans of cider in Steven's garage, within the drum of the washing machine. Patrick took the other two cans with him, through to the lounge.

He stood in the lounge, leaning against the piano with deliberate nonchalance, drinking his cider and watching other people chat and laugh. He looked from group to group, listening to the conversations.

'Have you seen Paula?'

'She's gone upstairs with Shakey.'

'Let's give them five minutes then pile in when he's got his knob out.'

After some more standing and watching, Patrick headed back to the garage. He got his last two cans of cider out of the washing machine.

He was manoeuvring himself carefully past a clutch of bicycles when Nicola Garcia opened the door.

Nicola gave him a breezy smile and stepped inside the garage. 'Hi.'

Patrick coughed. 'Hi.'

Nicola's lips were a different kind of red than usual. A thicker red: coloured by lipstick, not lollies. 'Having a good time?'

Patrick smiled.

Nicola shut the garage door behind her. 'I'm looking for more alcohol. Apparently people have been hiding theirs in here.'

After a beat, Patrick held out the two cans in his hand. 'I've found these.'

'Nice.'

Patrick detached a can from the plastic loop and held it out to Nicola. 'I'm sure I can find more.'

'Great!' Nicola smiled at him. 'Thanks.' She took the can. 'Hey, it's cold and everything!'

Patrick glowed. He'd had stored the ciders in the freezer at home until they were deeply chilled. He'd anticipated the lack of fridge space or ice, but he'd never hoped to dream such planning would impress a girl like Nicola.

He watched Nicola put the can to her lips. She took a swig and wiped her mouth with the back of her hand. In the half-light of the garage, drinking from that can of Strongbow, Nicola's cheeks puffed out cherubically.

Patrick looked down at the piece of looped plastic in his hand that had previously held the four cans together. He pulled on one plastic circle until it spilt. He turned the plastic by ninety degrees and pulled on the next circle.

'What are you doing?' There was a lilting laugh in Nicola's voice.

'You have to do it. This plastic can strangle seabirds.'

'That's good of you.'

'Would you like to come to the cinema with me some time, Nicola?' The words were out there before he could stop them.

Nicola blinked at him.

'I'm sorry,' Patrick mumbled.

Nicola gave him a smile – a smile that was much too kind. 'I go out with Adam Camberwell.'

Patrick crunched his toes up in his shoes.

Nicola patted Patrick's arm. 'Adam's the hardest lad in the fifth year.'

Patrick flushed. He didn't know how you got that title: whether it was some kind of committee-bestowed thing, or whether it lasted after you left school. But it was an absolute: Patrick knew that.

'He's getting his provisional licence in September,' Nicola continued.

'I'm sorry.' Patrick knew, in that moment, he would never drink cider again. 'Please don't tell Adam. I meant no disrespect.'

Nicola laughed. 'Disrespect!'

'Is he here tonight? Will he kick my head in?'

Nicola looked at him, pity in her smile. 'He wouldn't come to a fourth-year party. I'm meeting him in the park afterwards.' She touched Patrick's arm and gave a tilt of her head. 'Don't worry, I won't tell him. Your head's safe for now.' She gestured with her cider hand. 'But thanks for this. I owe you.'

She walked away, sipping her cider.

Patrick stared at the dead bird in the dustbin, its body bent in the middle where he'd shoved it round the bin bags. Patrick adjusted the body so the bird was straight. He shut the bin lid carefully and followed Matt back inside.

Patrick thought of Nicola in her lodge, wearing her farmer's wife waistcoat. Still beautiful, of course. But now, more attainable. Something had see-sawed in the last twenty-five years and boys like Adam Camberwell were in prison now (probably), and girls like Nicola looked at men like Patrick differently.

On reflection, Patrick remembered reading an article in the local paper about the charity Adam Camberwell had set up with the profits from his property empire in the Canaries. But that was the exception that proved the rule.

Patrick put his hand on the door handle of the lodge. He stopped.

He hadn't even told Nicola he was a barrister. And he hadn't mentioned the Ironman.

The thought soothed him a little.

Next time. He'd tell her next time.

29

'She's a murderer!' Scarlett shouted.

Mum and Dad stood blocking her exit, trapping her inside the bedroom, both trying to hold onto her. But Scarlett didn't want to be held. She kept pushing them away.

This was their fault. They'd invited Alex here, hadn't they?

Across the room, Posey paced up and down, up and down. He kept pulling his ears down and letting them flip up again.

'Scarlett, let me explain,' Matt says.

'I want to go home.'

Mum and Dad looked at each other. 'Please no! This is our special holiday.'

'Then get her out of here.'

'That bird was already hurt,' Mum said. 'Alex didn't kill it on purpose, she killed it to put it out of its misery. Because it was in pain and dying. Do you understand?'

Posey bumped down onto the floor in his angry pose. 'It just *happened* to be in pain and dying, did it? That's what *she* says.'

'That's what *she* says,' Scarlett said. 'You trust the word of a killer?'

'She was being kind to the pheasant,' Dad said.

'Kind!' Posey jumped up and started pacing again.

'Shall we have some more of that advent calendar now?' Dad said, hope in his voice.

Posey turned and paced again. '*As if* we could think about chocolate at a time like this.'

'Why do you want me to like Alex?' Scarlett said. 'Can't you see she's awful?'

Claire and Matt looked at each other helplessly.

'Posey said he knew she was a murderer all along. I said I didn't believe him, but Posey insisted. And he was right!'

'I don't think Posey's really helping this situation,' Dad said carefully.

'Don't you be horrible to Posey!'

Mum put her hands on Scarlett's shoulders. 'Maybe Posey should take a breath and calm down. Let's all do something fun. Do you want to give me a piggyback?'

Scarlett panted for air. 'No! Just leave me alone!'

She couldn't breathe. Her tummy was going weird from seeing Mum and Dad comfort her together.

But she couldn't trust them. She knew she couldn't trust them – especially when they were trying to comfort her together.

That was why she had Posey now.

Three years before, Scarlett sat cross-legged on the bed after tea, resting her foil picture in her lap. She concentrated hard, scraping at the picture with the tool in her hand, following the outlines. When you scratched the black topping off, it left foil shining brightly beneath, and made a beautiful picture.

There was a knock on the door.

Scarlett knew, from the number of footsteps, that it was both Mum and Dad outside. Scarlett didn't want them to come in. There had been lots of whispering downstairs lately, rather than fighting. It should have been a good thing, but she didn't like it. So she kept working on her picture.

The foil picture was of a peacock, and Scarlett had worked very hard at following the feather lines. She didn't always manage to get the lines exactly right, but it was good enough. You could definitely tell it was a peacock. A good peacock.

Mum and Dad came into the room together. Dad shut the door softly behind them. The two stood there, just by the door, not coming further in the room.

Mum stared at Scarlett. Dad looked at the floor.

Scarlett put her scraping tool down on the bedside table. It rolled a little, and she put a hand on it to make it still.

Mum glanced at Dad and back at Scarlett. 'We need to speak to you about something important.'

Scarlett put her foil picture down. She pulled her pillow up the bed and placed it on her lap, squeezing it to her body.

Mum looked at Dad again. When he didn't say anything, Mum added, 'It's something sad.'

Dad kept staring at the carpet.

Mum sighed. 'You'll have noticed things have been a bit difficult round here lately. Mummy and Daddy have been shouting at each other more than they want to. We've been making each other unhappy.'

Scarlett saw the foil scraper had left little bits of black on the bedside table, making the white wood dirty. She dabbed carefully at the black bits with her finger, lifting them up.

'And we have to think what's best for you. What kind of home we want you to grow up in. So we need you to be brave while we tell you something.' Mum took another deep breath. 'Daddy's moving out. He's going to live somewhere else.'

Scarlett rubbed her finger and thumb against an empty sweet wrapper, trying to scrape all the black bits off her skin.

'Do you understand what that means?' Mum said. 'We will still be a family, a loving family, all supporting each other. Just a different kind of family. One who don't all live in the same house.' Mum looked to Dad. 'Matt.'

Dad didn't say anything. Something about his face made Scarlett hug the pillow again.

'Am I really doing all the talking, Matt?'

Mum turned to face Scarlett again, but Scarlett said fiercely, 'Don't say anything.' It was important, she knew, that Mum stopped talking.

The bedroom door opened again.

Mum and Dad didn't turn round to face the door. They stayed looking at Scarlett, their faces serious.

But Scarlett stared at the door. And she knew what was coming, right away, before she saw it.

A head appeared round the doorway. A human-sized purple head, with big pointy ears.

Scarlett shrieked. She let the pillow drop into her lap.

Mum and Dad both jerked their heads back in surprise.

Posey flapped one ear at Scarlett in a casual hello. 'Anyone miss me?'

Scarlett clapped her hands together with happiness. She shrieked again.

'Are you OK, Scarlett?'

Posey grinned at Scarlett. 'Howdy. That's Chinese for "Hello".'

'I know it must be hard to take in.'

Scarlett stared at Posey. He was so much bigger than Scarlett remembered. He was the same size as Scarlett now – bigger if you counted the long ears, though Scarlett wasn't sure where you measured a rabbit from – but it was definitely *him*. He had the same purple fur, the same patches faded in the places where Scarlett used to hold him. He had the same white round patch on his tummy. The same white pom-pom tail, the same red tag that said *Made in China*.

'Your Daddy has some things to say to you too. We both want you to know how much we love you. And how nothing will change that ever.'

Scarlett clapped her hands together. 'I thought Dad left you in that red car in Tenerife!'

Posey shook his head. 'He didn't leave me. I went back home for a holiday. To China.' Posey flicked the *Made in China* tag on his bum. 'Got to catch up with the old gang once in a while.'

'Without saying goodbye?'

'I always come back. Don't I?'

'I thought you'd gone forever.'

'Scarlett? Scarlett, what's going on?'

Posey looked at Mum. He stood on the bed then sat down next to Scarlett, who crossed her legs, facing Mum and Dad.

'Scarlett?'

Posey nodded towards Mum. 'She's talking to you.'

Scarlett looked at Posey. Posey nodded again. Scarlett turned slowly back to face her mum and dad.

'We're so sorry about this, Scarlett.' Mum pushed her fringe out of her eyes. 'We both love you so much. We will always put you first. But we're going to live in separate houses from now on.'

Scarlett felt one of Posey's hand-paws slip into her palm. The paw was almost too big to hold. It felt like a towel, warm from being in the airing cupboard.

'We will always love each other,' Dad said, 'because we made you together. And you are the best thing that ever happened to us.'

Scarlett squeezed Posey's paw tightly.

'You and I will stay living here. And Daddy will only be at Grandma Janet's. That's not far away.'

'I'll always be at the end of the phone. You can call me any time. Call me, and I'll come straight o-ver.'

Dad's voice went funny on that last word. He turned around to look at the wall by the door, at Scarlett's drawing of *The Little Mermaid*. Dad looked at the drawing hard.

'Just leave me here with Posey,' Scarlett said. 'Both of you. Go away.'

Posey squeezed Scarlett's hand.

Mum glanced at Dad. 'Posey's here? Now?'

'He's come back. From China.'

Daddy scratched his neck. 'I thought we left him in Tenerife.'

'He went to China. On holiday. And now he's come back.'

Mum and Dad looked at each other again.

'So can you both leave us, please. I want to speak to Posey.'

To show she meant it, Scarlett lifted her bum up, turning away. She set herself back down on the bed, facing Posey.

'We'll just leave you a minute then, Scarlett,' Dad said. 'Then we'll be back to check on you.' He paused. 'Come on, Claire. It's what she wants.'

Scarlett heard the door click softly shut behind them.

Posey gave a slow wink. 'So, do I look different?'

'You're taller. But you look thin.' Scarlett poked Posey in the belly, checking his stuffing. 'I hope you've been eating five-a-day in China.'

'Of course I have!'

'And been brushing your teeth?'

'Twice. Every day.'

'Promise?'

Posey pulled back his lips so Scarlett could look at his teeth. 'Promise.'

Scarlett had never seen Posey's long bunny teeth before. 'They look clean,' she said. 'I'm proud of you.'

There was a knock on the door.

Posey frowned. 'Shall we let them come back in?'

Scarlett glared at her. 'Let's just be the two of us a bit longer. Tell me about what you got up to in China. Are there castles there?'

'Yep.'

'And unicorns?'

'Loads of unicorns.' Posey stretched back on the bed, lying down. He put a hand-paw under his head. 'You use unicorns there like buses. You just hop on when—'

There was another knock at the door.

Posey looked at Scarlett. He raised where his brows would be.

Scarlett stared firmly at Posey. 'It's rude to interrupt. They're being rude. You keep telling me about China.'

With one paw, Posey pulled a long ear back in thought. 'OK. They eat corn cakes for breakfast and—'

There was another knock at the door. 'Scarlett?'

'Ignore them,' Scarlett said firmly. 'And don't worry, Posey, I'll look after us. Just promise you won't ever – *ever* – go on holiday without me again.'

30

Alex had a shower, hoping the sound of the rushing water would drown out Scarlett's sobbing from the room above.

It had worked – for about five minutes there. But Scarlett had stamina, so she was still going when Alex switched the water off.

Alex's skin still smelled of chlorine, two showers later.

Now back in the lounge, she listened to Scarlett whimper upstairs. Alex could hear Matt's voice, trying to soothe her.

Claire padded down the stairs and hugged Alex tightly. 'Don't worry about Scarlett.' A lock of Alex's sodden hair slapped onto Claire's cheek. Claire didn't push the hair away. 'She'll come round.'

Alex held onto Claire. She inched her nose closer to Claire's neck, detecting a trace of perfume.

'You smell nice,' Alex said.

'Back in a min.' Claire jogged up the stairs.

Alex sank onto the sofa, alone in the lounge. She pulled her shirt dress down to cover her knees. Her hair felt clammy, a clump of seaweed trailing against her face. She felt a cold trickle down her back.

She listened to the humming half-whispers of Claire and Matt reassuring Scarlett.

Alex sat back and closed her eyes. She pictured the perfume bottle Matt had bought her last Christmas. A clear bottle, with a waisted shape and a decorative lid-flower.

Alex inhaled deeply again, trying to conjure up a hint of Claire's perfume. But now she could only smell the tartness of her own shampoo, and a trace of underlying fridge odour.

She thought of Matt and Claire in Scarlett's bedroom, trying to stem the flow of tears.

Alex looked to the front door. Patrick was still outside doing – well, whatever it was that Patrick did.

Alex stood up and moved to the bottom of the stairs.

She paused, one hand on the banister, then padded softly upstairs.

The landing of the top floor of the lodge was dark, with a pointed roof, the ceiling too low to stand upright. The landing smelt even more of indoor wood than her bedroom did. It smelt like a sauna.

Alex looked to the three doors around her: one closed, two open. From behind the closed door she could hear the muffled sound of Matt's voice, then another muffled reply from Claire.

Alex looked to the first open door. She strode through the doorway before she could think about what she was doing.

The room was a bathroom, larger than Alex's en suite but still not big enough for comfort. She looked around at the toiletries in the room.

On the side of the bath stood a shampoo bottle with a picture of a cartoon apple, the bottle promising *no more tears.* An electric Tigger toothbrush stood on the sink frame, next to a vertical tube of Hello Kitty toothpaste.

Alex left the bathroom. She paused, looking at the last door.

She listened. There was still no sound of movement in the rest of the lodge.

With gentle steps, Alex padded through the final doorway. She looked at the suitcases piled up in the corner of the room, at the discarded jeans on the bed, the embroidery on the back pocket: jeans Alex knew Claire had been wearing earlier that day.

Alex pulled her shirt dress down a little further. After a brief pause, she padded through to the en suite.

There were two washbags open on the counter: one navy, one floral. Alex leaned over the floral bag and picked out the bottle on the top.

It was the same clear, waisted bottle, topped with the same decorative flower. This bottle was nearly empty.

Alex looked up from the bottle, to the image of herself in the mirror.

The woman in the mirror looked back at Alex, unmoving, the shoulders of her shirt dress discoloured by water. Her hair, also darkened by water, hung down the side of her face, leaving her cheekbones exposed and gaunt.

Alex watched a single droplet of water trickle down her face. The droplet hung, suspended, from her chin, before releasing its hold and dripping onto the floor.

Alex heard a door open.

'I won't be long.' Claire's voice wafted in, terrifyingly audible. 'I'll go and check what time we're doing golf. He can't still be dealing with that bird.'

Alex didn't hear Matt's reply, but Claire added, 'I think it's at six. I'm going to stay behind and do dinner.'

Alex heard footsteps on the landing, then down the stairs.

After a beat, she placed the bottle back in the washbag. She turned to leave the room but knocked a tube of toothpaste into the sink.

She placed the toothpaste back in its original position. She waited.

When she couldn't hear anything outside, she padded softly across the bedroom carpet to the doorway.

Across the corridor, Scarlett's bedroom door opened. Matt spoke into the room. 'Salted caramel or strawberry cream?'

'Strawberry,' Scarlett said in a mucus-y voice.

Matt turned and saw Alex. His eyebrows moved minutely together.

'I was just seeing if Claire had a hairdryer.' Alex closed the door behind her. 'I didn't want to disturb you all, I didn't think Scarlett would want me to come in. Should I go in and talk to her?'

'I wouldn't. She's still a bit upset.' Matt studied Alex for a minute. 'Don't we have a hairdryer downstairs?'

'A rubbish one. I wanted to see if Claire had brought her own.'

'And had she?'

Alex paused. 'I couldn't see one. I wasn't exactly going to go through her suitcase.'

Matt stared at her some more. 'Good. I'm pleased you wouldn't have gone through her suitcase. Particularly when Claire's just downstairs and you could have asked her.'

Alex looked down. She turned her ring slowly round her finger. 'Our room hairdryer will be fine, I'm sure. You did tell Scarlett, didn't you? Why I did it?'

'Of course,' Matt said shortly.

Quietly, they walked down the stairs towards the lounge.

31

'Alex!' On the crazy golf course, Patrick waved his club in her direction. 'It's your go.'

Alex didn't even practise her swing. She just stepped forward and hit the ball towards the windmill, like the whole experience was nothing to do with her.

Even though she was only two feet from the hole at the bottom of the windmill, she missed. The ball hit the wood with a thud. It rebounded slowly back towards Alex.

Patrick was ahead of all of the others by fourteen strokes at the moment, yet this game was still not as much fun as it should have been.

On the walk to the golf course, Scarlett had stopped and stared at the single feather in the middle of the road – a feather left behind after Patrick had moved the pheasant.

Scarlett had looked at the feather for a long time. Finally, she unzipped her anorak pocket and stashed the feather away before zipping the pocket carefully back up.

Now, when Alex took a step towards her, Scarlett took a step back.

When Alex asked if she wanted an ice cream (a shameless

effort, Patrick thought), Scarlett had, for the first time he could remember, refused.

Patrick was impressed by Scarlett's self-discipline and commitment to her cause. Not for the first time, he thought that Scarlett reminded him more of himself than his own kids did.

He watched her march to the edge of the crazy golf course. 'Where are you going, darling?'

'Me and Posey need to stand over here and talk about something important.'

'Righto,' Patrick said cheerfully.

He watched Scarlett continue her one-sided conversation at the edge of the green.

'I'm sure you'll be safe,' Scarlett whispered firmly to the air. 'It's birds she kills. Not rabbits.' She paused. 'You're right, Posey. *So far*, anyway.'

Alex looked up at Matt. But he turned away, crouching down to tie his shoelace.

Scarlett was still talking. 'I'll protect you, Posey. Just make sure you don't get too close. Safety first.'

Patrick turned to Matt, waiting for him to say something to Scarlett. But Matt just shook his foot out, straightening his jeans, and stood over his golf ball.

Matt swung his club now but, Patrick decided, not in a good way. Not like he was trying to practise. Just like he was killing time.

It was Patrick's turn to take a shot. He wondered whether, if he didn't take his shot, any of them would even notice. Or whether they'd all just stand there, lost in their own thoughts, listening to Scarlett badmouth Alex.

He waited. *One second. Two seconds. Three seconds.* He'd

got to twelve by the time Matt looked up.

'You're up, Tiger Woods.'

Tiger Woods. Even that was annoying. It would have been OK, if it wasn't for the fact Matt had called him that before they'd even started to play. Giving Patrick the kudos in advance, before he'd even seen Patrick's well-honed, Saturday-morning-finessed swing. Which devalued the compliment to nothing.

Patrick widened his stance. He studied the wooden obstacle ahead: the target painted with a clown's mouth, a hole between the teeth to aim for. It was a few metres between him and the mouth, over semi-rough terrain. If Patrick missed his shot, the ball would go down one of the slopes either side and roll right back to the beginning of the hole.

But Patrick wouldn't miss.

He took a careful practice swing. He steadied himself and took the shot.

The golf ball bounced over the grass and swept cleanly through the clown's mouth, not even touching the sides.

Patrick placed the base of his club on the green. He leaned forward on the club so it supported his weight.

'Well done,' Matt said eventually.

Patrick leaned down to pick up his ball; he placed it at the start of the next hole. He pulled the score sheet and tiny pencil from his pocket and marked his number of strokes. They were at hole number eight, and no one had matched his score once yet.

'Nice shot,' Alex said. It was an autopilot comment, no real admiration behind it.

'See that leaf, Scarlett?' Matt pointed at a leaf on the

green. 'I'm going to see if I can roll my ball over it on the way past.'

'But it's not on the way past!' Patrick couldn't help himself. 'It's in the opposite direction!'

Matt aimed his ball for the leaf. The ball missed it and rolled slowly past, away from the hole.

Matt wrinkled his nose at Scarlett. 'I'll get it next time.'

Patrick put the paper and pencil back in his pocket. He looked up to the heavens and shut his eyes for a second, before opening them again, and turning back to look at the game.

Post-shooting interview. Keeley Pope, 25. Happy Forest
   activity coordinator.
Face-to-face. Happy Forest activity centre.

I wondered when you'd come and see me! Come through to the back. Scandal!

   I said to the others, it's like we're in an episode of Ex on the Beach. *You wouldn't believe how many people came in this evening who weren't rostered on.*

   Oh, come on, it's no accident! When you found out they were messy exes, surely you worked that out?

   They were arguing all over the place. Like in Ex on the Beach *again. But Sheila said she's told you that already.*

   Yes, I'll look at your pictures.

   I met that woman, the dark-haired woman. Alex Mount. The shooter. Is she a Taurus?

   It just seems a very Taurus thing to do. Bull-headed. And I can say that because I am one.

   I met her when she came to take her daughter for the dance class. She was all flustered, you could tell the holiday was going wrong, even before she shot the guy.

   Just . . . out of breath. Panicky. Intense. It makes me feel a bit queasy now, when I think of it. How much that mum wanted to get her seven-year-old into a burlesque class.

   Yes, burlesque dancing. You know, classy old-school dancing with chairs and high kicks? I teach it myself sometimes. I always say it should be for older kids only, but when I peeked into the room, that little girl was getting the routine down pat, slow-squatting to the floor with the best of them.

No, the woman was definitely the girl's mum.

She wasn't the mum? But then why would she say she was? Do you think she kidnapped the kid or something? Is that why she looked so intense and out of breath?

I think she must be mental now. I mean, shooting some-one, I get how that could happen. But lying about being the kid's mum?

Maybe she wasn't a Taurus after all. That's not a very Taurus thing to do. We Taureans are straight up and honest.

No, I didn't meet any of the others. They look very seri-ous in those pictures, don't they? Security pictures are the worst.

Gemini, I'm thinking now. Split personality.

32

Back at the lodge, Alex reached round Claire to get a can of lemonade from the fridge. 'It's a shame you didn't come to golf.'

Claire leaned to the side to make space for Alex. She continued chopping onions. 'I wanted to get on with cooking.'

Alex slumped against the unit behind her. 'I feel like you're doing everything here! Please say you haven't changed your cooking plans because of the fish thing.'

'It's not a problem.' Claire flicked her gaze at Alex, chopping all the while. 'Besides, it's been a long day, what with Scarlett and the pheasant thing.' Claire indicated her wine glass on the side. 'I like getting drunk when I'm cooking. There's something about getting drunk on your own that feels good, isn't there?'

'Yes.' Alex kept her voice light. 'It felt great, as I remember.'

'Oh.' Claire stopped chopping. 'Sorry.'

'It's fine.'

'So, did you have fun at golf?'

Alex looked at Claire's glass and looked quickly away. 'Lovely, thanks.' She leaned round Claire again to get a tumbler from the cupboard. 'Can I do anything?'

'You just relax and put your feet up. Did Scarlett behave?'

Alex opened her can. 'Good as gold.'

Claire grinned. 'See. They can't hold a grudge for long at that age.'

Alex wondered if she should have told Claire how Scarlett really was. *No, she didn't behave. She kept conversing with her imaginary friend about Alex the Animal Killer.* But Alex would have no chance with Scarlett after that. No one liked a grass. Prison sensibilities were instinctive, even at seven.

Alex looked over at the non-kitchen part of the main room. Matt sat across the dining table from Scarlett, the two playing a hand-slapping game. Matt wouldn't let Scarlett win, and every new loss made her squeal with excitement.

'Fancy going for a walk, Matt?' Alex asked.

'All right.' Matt started to get up.

'Posey and I would like you to play another game after this, Dad,' Scarlett said.

Matt hovered for a second, half in, half out of the chair. He sat back down. 'As long as Posey doesn't cheat. I don't trust rabbits. They're notorious card sharks. Never play with a rabbit who's wearing sleeves.' He looked at Alex. 'After this, if that's OK?'

Alex turned to Scarlett. 'Do you know the joke about why you shouldn't play cards in the jungle?'

Scarlett kept looking at Matt. 'Posey wants to play Happy Families.'

Matt gave Alex a shrug of apology. He looked back to Scarlett. 'Posey has good taste. But let's both keep an eye on that rabbit, before he bankrupts us with his fast moves.'

Across the room, Patrick picked up his phone and dialled a number. 'Lindsay.'

Alex looked around; her gaze landed on *Ulysses*. She pulled the book towards her without enthusiasm.

Patrick faced out of the window into the blackness beyond. 'Are they there?' His voice sounded formal, like he was making an appointment with his MP. 'I've tried their mobiles. There's no answer. Again.'

Patrick strode across the room. He did a dramatic about-turn and strode back to where he was. He waved his hand in front of his face in a jerky movement. 'Just get them to call me. Please.'

Patrick jammed the phone back in his pocket. He hitched up the knees of his trousers and sank on the sofa opposite Alex, legs wide apart, radiating energy. He picked up his laptop and started jabbing at the keyboard with excessive force.

Alex felt her eyes watering from the onions Claire was chopping, making it hard for her to read. She watched Matt head into the bathroom. There was a wall between the two rooms and Matt had shut the door, but Alex could still audibly follow every stage of his piss: the waterfall, the petering, the drips, the flush.

Matt came back into the main room and smiled at Alex.

She smiled back.

Would it have been too much to have stayed in a place where they could get more than four metres away from each other?

'Patrick?' Claire said.

Patrick continued looking at his laptop screen.

Claire put her knife down on the kitchen counter. 'Patrick.'

No response.

Claire walked over to the sofa and stood over him. 'Patrick.'

Patrick flinched. He pulled the keyboard screen towards him. 'I hate it when you creep up on me.'

'I didn't creep! You just weren't listening to me when I was trying to get your attention. I don't understand how you can get so entranced by Facebook anyway, it's all fluff.' She waved at the screen. 'Who's that?'

'She's someone I used to be at school with. She's in the lodge next door, a complete coincidence. Matt and I met her earlier. Matt's invited her for a drink tomorrow.'

'How funny! Were you friends at school?'

'She was in my drama class.' Patrick paused. 'She was one of the popular girls, we didn't really move in the same circles.'

Matt snorted. 'She wasn't in the model aeroplane club, then?'

Patrick deliberately kept his gaze on Claire. 'What did you want me for?'

Claire paused. 'It's gone.' She walked back to the kitchen area. She took a swig of her wine and restarted her chopping.

'I remember the popular girls at school.' Matt grinned at Patrick and perched on the edge of the dining table with a seriousness that suggested he had much to impart on the topic. 'Gemma Cooper, she was the main one.' He flicked his head back, tossing his hair off his face. 'Her brother played for the Forest youth team. Walshy got off with her once, on the memorial bench in the park. We could none of us believe it.'

Claire laughed. 'You watched?'

'Course we watched! For a bit, anyway. It was an event!' Matt turned to Alex. 'Can you believe Walshy got off with the popular girl at school? He had all the chat back then. He didn't just get off with her, either. He also got' – he glanced at Scarlett – 'never mind.'

When Scarlett looked away, Matt mouthed *blow job*.

Patrick slammed his laptop shut with a bang.

'Not that we watched that bit. Looking back, I can't understand the attraction. She had a dodgy perm. And a big hair bump on the top of her head, thick with hairspray.' Matt shook his head. 'Gemma Cooper. Not thought about her in years. I'll have to mention her to Walshy, though it will probably only make him depressed. To think how far he's fallen.'

Later, they all sat round the dining room table.

Alex ate a forkful of pasta. 'Lovely, Claire. You're a very good cook.'

Claire gave a friendly wave of dismissal. 'It's just pasta.'

Alex stabbed another pasta twirl. 'With a sauce made from scratch, though.'

Matt grinned at Alex. 'I tell you something, Claire. She's a good cook in the main, but she's rubbish at puddings. She always makes them with too much fruit. I mean, where's the pudding in that? Where's all the sticky toffee and chocolate fondant?'

Alex put her knife and fork down.

Matt bent his head down, still chewing his pasta.

'I think you meant to say "Alex", Matt,' Patrick said. 'Not "Claire".'

Matt stopped eating. 'What?'

'You called Alex "Claire".'

'Did I?' Matt made eye contact with Alex. 'Really?'

'Yep,' Alex said.

'It must be because you're both here.'

'OK,' Alex said.

'Like when you get off the phone from your brother and you call me "Simon".'

'I know. It's fine.'

'Everyone does it. My mum even calls me "Karen" when my sister's been over.'

Alex's phone rang and she looked at the screen. 'It's Ruby.' She tried not to look like she was getting up too keenly. 'I'll take this outside.'

She hurried out of the lodge and answered the call.

'How's it going?' Ruby asked.

Alex walked quickly, wanting to get well away from the lodge. 'You win.'

'I win?'

'This trip's awful.'

'Oh, Al. Don't say I win!' Ruby sighed. 'How is it awful?'

'Oh, let me count the ways.' Alex bumped down on a bench opposite the lake. 'So, firstly, Scarlett hates me because I killed a pheasant.'

'Right.' Ruby paused. 'In anger, or . . .?'

'Patrick ran it over. He was just looking at the poor thing afterwards, hesitating like a squeamish kid at what he had to do. And the pheasant was in pain.'

'And you stepped in. Good for you.'

Alex looked at the surface of the lake. How could everything be so calm round here when she felt like *this*? 'Patrick resents me for it, I can tell. That man's a nightmare, Rubes. He keeps trying to compete with me. It's like ... everything's a chance to prove he's good enough. To some-one, *anyone*. He's *mental*.'

'He sounds like my stepdad. We just let him win at everything for an easy life.'

'I tried that when we were racing down the river ride, but it was impossible. How do you get to the age of forty-three without understanding the simplest fluid dynamics?'

There was a pause. 'You were racing him back?'

Alex coughed. 'A little bit. Maybe. I stopped as soon as I realised what was going on. After—'

'After?'

'Nothing.'

There was another pause. Alex looked down at her shoes.

'So what about Claire?' Ruby spoke more slowly than usual, like she was taking extra care with her words. 'What's she like?'

'She's just perfect. So wonderful and thoughtful.' Alex didn't need to take care with her words. The right words were *there*, all bunched up and ready to crash out. 'She loves cooking, it's just so fucking relaxing, apparently. And she put the milk in a jug on the table at breakfast. A *jug*.'

There was a pause. 'Right.'

'I mean, who uses a jug? I thought that was just some-thing people did only on telly. See? Perfect. She made non-alcoholic cocktails so I didn't feel left out. She's so fucking *nice*.'

'Is that sarcasm?'

'No! That's the worst thing about it! She's like, way too nice, always smiling and being so reasonable. She even bought me a spa voucher.'

'Really? You've met this woman before, right?'

'And she stayed back from family golf today because Matt told her I don't like fish and she'd prepared this massive fish meal and she had to make pasta instead – but not from a sauce, no-o-o, she chopped garlic and everything – and I just feel like she's the grown up and I should be sitting at the child's table with Scarlett and Posey, you know?'

'Right.' There was that care in Ruby's voice again. 'Take a step back for me. Who's Posey?'

'Scarlett's imaginary rabbit.'

There was silence on the other end of the phone.

'I must have told you about him,' Alex said.

'I think I would have remembered.'

'Posey hates me. He keeps making snide comments, saying I'm a pheasant-murderer. And he called me fat.'

Silence again. 'Right. And you know he says these things . . . how?'

Alex scuffed her feet impatiently along the path. 'By how Scarlett reacts.'

'You're not fat.'

'Well, obviously, and I'm not a murderer either. But Scarlett acts like she's the one trying to reason with him, telling him they don't know I'm definitely a murderer and I might be safe around rabbits because there's no proof I'm not and—'

'Come home. *Please* come home, Al. I'll ditch my folks and you can be with me and Kevin. I'll let you feed him his special Christmas sausages and everything.'

Alex didn't normally enjoy spending time with Ruby's flatulent dachshund, but even that sounded like a good option right then.

'I can't,' Alex said finally.

'Why not?'

'Because if I flounce out in a huff, it'll be worse next time I see them all.'

'Oh, Al.'

'And the worst thing, Rubes? Every day, I feel even more like I want a drink.'

'You've done so well. You can't have a drink because of *this* car crash of a holiday.'

Alex didn't say anything.

'I hope Matt's giving you a ton of grateful neck massages. He knows he has the most patient girlfriend in the world, right?'

Alex didn't reply.

'Al?'

Alex still didn't answer.

'Al? Is Matt being a knob?'

Alex scraped her foot along the path again. 'He's been to this forest place before. With Claire and Scarlett. He suggested the place to Claire. And . . . he didn't tell me that till we got here.'

Ruby let out a whoosh of air. 'Fucking hell, Al.'

'He didn't lie about it either. He just . . . didn't mention it.'

'I can see why you're a bit . . . fraught.'

'It *is* fair I'm a little pissed off about it, right? I've thought about it a lot, and it *feels* like it's fair.'

'You know I like Matt, but . . . thoughtless is *not* the

word. What a dick. Come home, Al, and speak to Matt later. You don't have to put up with this shit.'

'Look, I've got to go.' Alex clicked her phone off. She couldn't stand the sound of Ruby's sympathy. It was so much harder to hear than her sarcasm.

Alex sat on the bench for a while longer. She knew she should head back to the lodge, but couldn't quite bring herself to do it.

The worst thing was, she hadn't even told Ruby her other fear. That the whole thing might have been Matt's idea – and, if it was, that he'd lied to her again and again.

But she couldn't tell Ruby that. Because she didn't want to hear someone else reacting on the outside like she was reacting inside, right now.

She knew, once she said it out loud, that would definitely make it real.

33

Patrick had been disappointed to find out they weren't having fish for tea after all. But he didn't say anything because he was polite like that.

It was because of Alex, of course. And now Alex had taken a call during the meal and had been half an hour already which, considering all the effort Claire had put into making a back-up meal, was really rude.

Once they'd cleared the dinner table, Patrick sat back round it with Scarlett, Claire and Matt.

Scarlett offered round pieces of her advent calendar, but Patrick declined. He had a few months before his Ironman, but he still had to be careful. Patrick opened the Monopoly box and started counting out the money. He always liked to be Banker. It felt right that way.

Scarlett put two counters on the board. 'Posey likes to be the iron.'

'We're not playing with Posey, Scarlett.' Claire took a decisive swig of wine. 'Not tonight. It's family time.'

'But Posey loves Monopoly. He'll get upset.'

'I said no,' Claire said quietly. 'Put Posey to bed, please.'

Scarlett narrowed her eyes.

Patrick watched with distaste as Matt stuffed two advent chocolates into his mouth at once.

'Or how about,' Matt spoke thickly through the chocolate, 'Posey and Scarlett play together on the same team? You can still be the iron, together?'

Claire shook her head at Matt. But she didn't tell him off for undermining her, Patrick noticed.

Scarlett gave Matt a nod and turned to the side. 'You can sit back down, Posey.'

She pulled out a chair and tucked it back under the table – a chair which, presumably, had a rabbit in it.

The front door slammed and Alex walked back in. She looked cold.

Patrick couldn't help noticing that, on seeing Alex, Scarlett immediately stopped offering round chocolates and, instead, hid her advent calendar under the table.

'Everything all right?' Matt asked Alex.

'Fine.' Alex slid back into what had become her usual chair. 'It was just Ruby wanting to chat. You know how she bangs on. Are we playing Monopoly?'

Patrick handed Alex her money. 'I'm Banker.'

Alex rubbed her arms briskly to warm them up. 'OK. I haven't played for thirty years. But bring it on.'

Matt turned to Scarlett. 'Have you got any more of those chocolates, chicken?'

Scarlett shook her head.

An hour into the game and Patrick had managed to pick up two stations, plus the Electric Company, and one of the three green streets (which were his favourite).

Bingo! – he'd just landed on *another* green street. Two out of three. He could feel it now. The game going his way.

Patrick picked up the green card and placed it in front of him. He fanned out his money, ready to pay for the property.

He was conscious Alex was watching him. She'd been distracted at first, reading through the Monopoly rules and studying all the cards, but now she seemed to be paying attention to the game.

'You're buying Regent Street as well?'

Something in Alex's voice – an incredulity – made Patrick pause.

'You know the greens are the worst value on the board, right?'

Patrick jiggled his legs under the table. He looked down at his money again. He re-counted out three orange notes and, with a flourish of his hand to show it was the correct money, placed the notes in the bank.

'I'm just trying to help,' Alex said.

Patrick licked his lips. 'Why do you think they're the worst on the board?'

Alex indicated the Monopoly rules next to her. 'I've just done a quick analysis of the board and house prices. It looks like all the streets on the first half of a side can't possibly be as good value as the streets on the second half. And the green ones seem to have the worst buy-to-rent ratio of all, and they're expensive, so from a cash flow perspective . . .'

Alex stopped talking.

Patrick looked down at his two beautiful green cards, Regent Street and Bond Street. He straightened the cards on the table, so the edges lined up neatly.

'I was just . . . trying to help you win.'

Patrick didn't say anything.

'So, tell me,' Alex gave a try-hard smile. 'When's that Ironman thing again?'

Damn it!

Patrick glanced at Claire. 'April.'

Claire stared at Patrick, expressionless.

'What's Ironman?' Matt asked. 'Is it like a marathon?'

Patrick glanced at Claire and back. What choice did he have? 'It's a 2.4-mile swim, then a 112-mile bike ride, *then* a marathon.'

Claire said nothing.

'All in the same day?' Matt said. 'No way.'

'I can't believe you've booked an Ironman,' Alex said. 'It's impressive. Like an impressive punishment.'

Claire didn't look at Patrick. 'Booked?'

Helplessly, Patrick turned to Alex. 'It's a bucket list thing.'

Matt leaned back in his chair. 'Easier to swim with dolphins.'

'I think that's the point, Matt,' Alex said.

Matt leaned further back. He held onto the table, lifting the front two chair legs off the ground. 'Pat's gonna be a bloody *Ironman!*'

Patrick flinched.

'Can we get on with the game, please?' Scarlett said. 'Posey's not enjoying it. He's not feeling comfortable. What's that?' She looked at the air and nodded. 'Posey really wants us to be on our own.' She pushed her chair out. ''Scuse us. We're going to the bedroom.'

Matt watched her leave. 'Scarlett's got a bee in her bonnet about something.'

'It's me,' Alex said.

'Let's just leave her to calm down for a bit,' Claire said.

'While Scarlett's up there, I'll just go for a quick walk and a smoke.' Matt rubbed his hands together. 'I rolled up earlier. Fancy joining, Claire?'

'Smoke?' Patrick said. 'As in . . . cigarettes?'

'*Quite* like cigarettes,' Matt said with a smile. 'Fancy joining?'

Patrick coughed. 'No, thank you.'

Claire got up. 'Just a quick one then.' She turned to Patrick. 'Can you ring us if Scarlett comes back?'

Patrick just stared at her. He couldn't quite believe it.

Claire was about to *do drugs*. On holiday with *her daughter*.

'You coming for a walk, Al?' Matt asked.

Alex gave a tight smile. 'I might read in the bedroom for the rest of the night.' She picked *Ulysses* off the table next to her. 'I'm really into my book.'

'What's it about?' Matt asked.

Alex looked down at the book. She gave a little laugh. 'What's it *not* about?'

Claire and Matt put on coats and shut the front door behind them. Alex slipped into the bedroom and shut her door too.

Patrick was left looking down at the half-finished game of Monopoly – the game he'd apparently been playing wrong, all these years.

Two hours later, in the bedroom, Patrick rolled off Claire.

Claire leapt out of bed without speaking and headed into the bathroom.

Patrick lay on his back. He tucked his hands under his head.

That hadn't gone well tonight.

He'd made it to the end, of course, but when Patrick had realised he was losing Claire's attention, he'd pulled out all the stops, done his best *throw-her-around-a-bit* routine she used to enjoy, hoisting himself up on one hand athletically, straining with the effort.

In the bathroom, the automatic extractor fan whirred. Patrick listened to the rise and fall of the whirr, noticing how the fan worked harder at some points than others.

Someone needed to take a look at that motor.

Patrick lifted his head. He plumped up his pillow and lay back down. He hadn't brought his A-game to the sex tonight – it was hard, with all the frostiness after the Ironman thing, and with the others in the house.

But then, he'd never been completely able to relax when having sex with Claire – or anyone, if he was really honest. He was there, in the moment, but he was also across the room, watching. Monitoring the activity from a distance.

She's looking thoughtful – what's she thinking?

That's an odd grunt you just made, Patrick.

She's frowning at me, am I making a strange face?

If I stretch a little further it will accentuate my abs.

It was even worse when Lindsay got diagnosed with endometriosis. Patrick deliberately hadn't asked her too much about the physicality of the illness, knowing the effect it was likely to have on him. He'd just sympathised and tried to forget what she was telling him, and agreed with Lindsay to try for children immediately. But it had been a problem to concentrate that night, Patrick being distracted by the knowledge of – *things* – beneath. He tried not to think of the scan she'd shown him – *this is where the connective tissues are stuck to the wall of the bowel.* However vague Patrick kept his knowledge of her condition, every time he got intimate with her the word hissed from somewhere within. *Endometriosis. Endometriosis.*

Patrick watched films and heard conversations in bars; he knew not everyone felt like this. That there was a more hedonistic, Neanderthal kind of man who just got lost in the moment, grunting his way back to the Ice Age.

Not Patrick.

Still, it had become a *thing* when he got together with Claire that they were always going to make an effort, and weren't going to slip into being one of those couples who never had sex. But it was starting to feel less and less natural, like they'd made a rule and they had to stick to it regardless.

Claire opened the en suite door. She switched the bathroom light off and the erratic whirr of the extractor fan stopped. She padded across the room and slipped into bed.

'Claire.' Patrick knew his voice sounded formal for a conversation in the dark.

'Patrick.'

'Would you ever want to get married again?'

He felt movement from the other side of the mattress. He heard slithering as Claire pulled herself up into a sitting position.

After a minute she said, 'I don't know.'

Patrick stared into the blackness, waiting.

'We've been there, done that, haven't we?' He felt her hand give his chest a pat. 'Night.'

There was movement and more slithering of sheets. Claire lay back down and arranged the bedding around her.

Patrick felt the patch of his chest where she'd patted it.

He'd been aware of the warmth for a second, but now he was more aware of the absence of that warmth.

He took a long swallow. 'Claire?'

'Patrick.'

'I'm definitely going to do that Ironman in April.'

'I'm going to sleep now.'

Patrick touched the flatness of his stomach in a self-soothing gesture. Claire didn't say anything else, so Patrick turned over and closed his eyes.

He lay there and waited for sleep to come.

34

The creaking noise from upstairs stopped.

Alex lay there under the covers in the dark, listening to the soft, rhythmic snufting from the bed next to her – a snufting accompanied by the occasional loud click.

The first night she slept with Matt, she'd found the click disconcerting. In Alex's experience, a lot of things clicked – but not faces. Faces didn't click.

When she'd asked Matt about it the next morning, he had laughed.

'I should have warned you. I broke my nose as a child and there's a flap of skin or gristle – something – where it shouldn't be.' He lifted his chin so Alex could look up his nostrils. 'See?'

By now, Alex was used to that click. When she couldn't sleep, she found herself actively listening for it. She wondered if she could ever sleep next to anyone else happily. Someone who didn't click.

But she hadn't thought she'd need to. She'd thought that she and Matt were it: final. *The End:* scroll credits.

It occurred to Alex now that she knew nothing about

relationships. Because how could she? She'd split up with everyone she'd ever dated.

Even when she'd been going out with her early-years, VHS boyfriends, they had a spangly, futuristic air about them in the period before they became obsolete.

Could Matt be another VHS boyfriend after all?

Snuft. Snuft. Snuft. Click.

Alex had read that the biggest indicator of a successful relationship was meant to be how you felt about the other person's smell. And she liked Matt's smell: all biscuits and wool on top, an undercurrent of something sour in a good way. A sourness that made her rest her head on his chest and breathe him in.

Yet Matt thought Claire smelled like *home*. Even though Matt lived at Alex's house now. Their house, in fact.

OK, so they hadn't bought it together. But the place was rammed with Matt's junk: vinyl and shoes and faddy skateboard equipment everywhere – so if it didn't feel like *home* to him by now, he'd better bloody well act more polite, like an actual guest.

Alex gave a huffy turn, inadvertently disrupting her warmth seals. She reworked the duvet around her, tucking the edges under her so the cold gusts of air couldn't reach.

The night rumbled on.

Snuft. Snuft. Snuft. Click.

Post-shooting interview. Ruby Brown, 36. Friend of
  shooter.
Telephone.

Hello, Alex's phone?

  *She's gone out to get some milk. I'm trying to distract
her with tasks, she's been so jittery since she got back.
But then – she has shot someone. Bless her and her shit
coordination.*

  *Yeah, she skids around our lab like she's on roller skates.
They never should have let her near a bow and arrow, I'd
barely trust her with a knife and fork.*

  Ruby. We're lab buddies.

  *At her house in Nottingham. She didn't want to stay up
there, for obvious reasons. It's no skin off my nose, leaving
my family at Christmas. I've got Kevin with me – that's my
fat dachshund – so my real family's here. Kevin's way more
appreciative of my company, and he doesn't have a crying
fit if the sprouts are ready a different time from the gravy.*

  *Check out your sexist assumptions, Grandpa. It's my
stepdad who does the cooking.*

  *If you must know, Alex and Matt get on really well, but
he thinks the world's all candyfloss and rollercoasters, and
he'd like to teach the world to sing, and Alex goes along
with his stupid ideas too much. This weekend, for example.
What a terrible thought that was.*

  *I don't mean the accident, I mean the whole trip. You
know, she even made a Christmas cake? Alex? And she*

went to a spa, which, if you knew her, would blow your mind.

No, you've got that wrong. Alex doesn't drink.

She didn't tell me that.

I'm just disappointed for her. She's been doing really well this last year.

I'm sure she wouldn't have drunk before doing archery. Alex is clumsy, but she's very responsible. Pays her credit card off each month, always properly marks up the lab equipment.

A burlesque class? What a ridiculous suggestion. No way.

I think you're getting Alex mixed up with someone else.

I'm telling you, you're wrong. There is no way – no way – Alex would take a seven-year-old to a burlesque class.

||||||||||||||||||||||||||||||||||||||||||||||||||||||||||||||||||||||||||||||||||||||||||||||

Extract from the Happy Forest brochure:
There's so much to explore at the Happy Forest. Why not take one of our tranquil nature walks? Or set sail on our custom-built grand lake? In our acres of private woodland, your imagination will roam as free as our wildlife.

And it's not just for children here – there are plenty of activities for grown-ups too. If you're in need of a little pampering, our spa has several treatment areas and a relaxation lounge with twenty different immersion rooms.

We also have an on-site pub, the Five Bells, complete with seven pool tables. So why not relax and have a few drinks? Remember, in our car-free village, no one ever needs to drive home!

||||||||||||||||||||||||||||||||||||||||||||||||||||||||||||||||||||||||||||||||||||||||||||||

35

Saturday 23 December

Day 3

Alex felt her happy pocket of warmth being disturbed. She clutched fruitlessly at the duvet as it was wrenched from her grasp. A gust of freezing air hit her stomach. Her pyjama top had ridden up in the night, and most of the material was now wedged in a lump in her armpit.

Matt clambered inelegantly across from his own twin bed onto hers. He got under Alex's duvet, tucking himself in a zigzag behind her. 'Morning.'

Alex felt her thighs goose-pimpling. 'Delicate.'

'Always.'

Matt squeezed in further, while Alex gripped the duvet corner more tightly.

'How are you?' Matt said into Alex's hair.

'Asleep.' But Alex softened herself into Matt's body, feeling the warmth.

'I've been lying here thinking. Shall we do something on our own this morning? Hire a boat on the lake, just the two of us? We can recreate that scene from *Titanic*. Arms out. You can be King of the World, if you want.'

Alex turned her head to look at Matt. She held herself slightly away, so as not to hit him with her morning breath. 'I'd like that.'

'Then we can take Scarlett out for lunch,' Matt said. 'I'll get Scarlett to be nice to you, I promise. And I'll tell her she's got to leave Posey in a burrow somewhere. That rabbit can be a cold piece of work sometimes.'

Alex turned her head round, *Exorcist*-style, stretching as far as her neck would allow. She kissed Matt softly on the cheek.

Matt rowed the oars with an excessively splashy motion, making the occasional mock-manly grunt, while Alex took in the scene around them.

The lake was small, decorated with signs and barriers. Canoes and dinghies littered the lake, and kids in helmets and life jackets shrieked all around. A rotten-vegetable-and-plastic smell hovered over the lake surface in a pungent, almost-visible cloud.

'It's OK for you, sitting there like Cleopatra.' Matt pulled on the oars. 'I don't know how Patrick can be arsed doing rowing at the gym. Are we there yet?'

Alex looked around. They were about as far as they could be from land without actually heading back in.

Matt rested the oars back on their hooks. He stood up in a careful semi-squat, arms out. He took a tentative step forward and bumped himself down on the seat opposite Alex.

They both watched a moorhen float past.

Matt looked over Alex's shoulder at something in the semi-distance. 'Look at Patrick, legs pumping away like he's running from the Gestapo. No, don't look – you'll only encourage him.'

'You've got a lot to say about him, haven't you?'

Matt gave Alex a serious look. 'I just wish he and Claire were better suited.' He looked into Alex's eyes. 'I want her to be happy.'

Alex twisted her gloved hands together in her lap. 'You don't think she is?'

'Patrick won't make her happy.'

'You never know what's going on in other people's relationships.' And, she reflected archly, in your own.

'Claire can't be herself around him,' Matt said. 'I'm watching her, and she's being all considered and careful. She can't just dick about.'

'Maybe she's grown up since you were together. Not necessarily a bad thing.'

'Maybe.' Matt shifted in his seat, turning to face Alex head on. Alex put her hands on the side of the boat, steadying it. 'But you know what I found out yesterday? She's told him she's only slept with a handful of people!'

Alex tucked a piece of hair behind her ear in a careful movement.

Matt snorted. 'God knows how many people she's slept with, but she never did like to end an evening alone back in the day. Not when she was single.'

Alex created an image in her head: Claire as Jessica Rabbit, leaning on a grand piano, swaying her hips and singing. Alex conjured in her mind the red dress. The smoky bar.

'How would you even know how many people Claire's slept with?' Alex said.

'We were mates at uni, before we were anything else. We only started going out a few years later.' Matt rested his hands on the oars. 'Besides, we talked openly about things, like you're meant to. What kind of relationship is it if you can't tell people the truth? I mean, you know everything about me.'

'I do,' Alex said hollowly.

'The driving ban.'

'Yep.'

'You even know my meditation mantra after I went on that wank course.'

'I'm definitely not meant to know that.'

'The time I shat myself in that bar after too much coke.'

'I know a little too much about some things.'

'See? That's how things should be. You know all that, and you still love me.'

The boat gently rotated. The glare from the low winter sun dazzled Alex. She put a hand up to her eyes to shade them. 'You don't like Patrick, do you?' She squinted to make out Matt's face. 'I thought you liked everyone.'

Matt sighed. 'He's fine. He's harmless. I don't like to think he's going to be the man in the house while Scarlett's growing up.' He leaned forward. 'All his "Don't shout in the street" and "What will the neighbours think?" Implying the most important thing is that Scarlett goes out dressed *appropriately* and keeps her virginity till she's twenty-five.'

'Has he said that?' Alex said.

'He doesn't need to. I can tell. God knows what he says about me. "Your dad with his hair." "Think he could lift this tree?" "Think he could run a marathon?" "He's never run a marathon in his life."'

Alex rubbed his leg. 'You can balance it out. You'll be a good role model for Scarlett at weekends.' Her voice became tentative as she pictured Matt making a bong out of an apple. 'And Claire's definitely got her head screwed on,' she added, with more certainty.

'I just hope Claire ends it with him. Soon.'

Alex looked down. She brushed her hand along the side of the boat, sticking on a splinter. 'I thought you wanted her to be happy?'

'She'll never be happy with him.'

Alex picked at the splinter with her thumbnail. 'Have you discussed this with her?'

'She's said a few things.'

Alex picked too hard at the wood; the splinter went under her nail. She made to yelp but stopped herself. Matt didn't notice.

Alex pulled a tissue out of her jacket pocket and wrapped it round her thumb. 'When did Claire say these things?'

'When you two were at the shops yesterday.'

'Wasn't Scarlett there?'

Matt stood up. 'We chatted a little when Scarlett was upstairs.' He put his hands on each boat edge and deliberately rocked the boat.

Alex put her hands on the edges of the boat to steady herself. 'Hey!'

Matt grinned and sat back down.

Alex shaded her eyes again. 'Did you and Claire talk about us?'

'A little bit.'

Alex couldn't see Matt's face because of the sun in her eyes. 'What did you say?'

223

Matt squeezed her arm. 'What do you think?'

Alex gave a wan smile.

'Now' – Matt looked around him – 'I think we can both agree this boat trip was not worth twenty-two quid. Shall we head back to land and get a beer?'

Alex looked around at the boats and canoes brimming with life-jacketed children. An empty Quavers packet floated past the boat. 'I think I've seen everything I need to see.'

Matt rowed back towards the jetty. He strained with the oars, his movements slower and less splashy now.

Alex smiled at Matt. He smiled back as he pulled on the oars.

Alex and Matt walked back from the lake together.

Alex shoved her hands into her jean pockets. She tried to take a deep breath, but something was blocking her chest. She could only breathe in halfway.

'Patrick didn't look happy that Claire went for a smoke with you last night,' Alex said.

'I don't know what he has such a beef about, it was only a bit of puff.' Matt kicked up mud with his wellies. 'Claire sometimes smoked when we were together. Not towards the end, but I think that was probably her trying to make a point. Everything was a symbol of something at that time.'

Alex felt like her chest was bursting. 'Matt.' She couldn't hold it in any more. 'You know you just said we have no secrets from each other. Can I ask you something?'

Matt linked his gloved hand with one of hers. 'Shoot.'

'You told me that when you and Claire split up, you left Claire.'

Matt let go of Alex's hand.

'Did you tell me the truth?'

Matt looked down at his glove. He pulled it off with excessive care, one finger at a time. 'Where's that come from?'

'I don't think that's what really happened. I think *she* left *you*.'

Alex put a hand on Matt's arm. He didn't look at her, just kept on walking.

'It's OK. Just tell me,' she said gently.

Matt stuffed both his gloves into one coat pocket. He held his neck taut, looking straight ahead.

He spun round to face Alex. 'Why can't you just leave things?'

Matt gestured at her in a swatting motion. Alex was shocked to see his hands trembling.

'We've had a nice morning on the lake, I'm being all supportive that my daughter hates you, recognising that this isn't an easy weekend for you, and then you come up with *this*.' There was a look on his face Alex didn't recognise. She felt the need for an extra coat. 'Have I ever given you any reason not to trust me?'

'It's playing on my mind. You know what I'm like, if I don't understand something I think and think and—'

'You *think and think*.' Sarcasm made Matt's voice thick. 'Why would you dream of thinking that this is any of your *fucking business*?'

Alex took an involuntary step back. 'Because you've just said, five minutes ago, that we don't have any secrets from each other!'

'*My* secrets? What were you doing in Claire's bedroom yesterday?'

'I was looking for a hairdryer!'

'Were you? Because you looked like you were doing something shifty.'

Alex didn't answer that.

'And do you go through my messages and emails too? Have I got you wrong all this time? Have you just been acting nice and normal?'

'I'm not like that, Matt!' Alex made herself lower her voice. 'You're being unfair. And I learnt this stuff on this stupid weekend that you made me come on.'

'That again. Back to that again.'

Alex tried to keep her voice tremor-free. 'On the boat, you said how honest you are with me, that I know everything about you. So how do you think I feel that I don't think you've been honest with me?'

Matt didn't say anything.

'And I'm confused about whose idea this weekend was.'

When he didn't respond, Alex twisted her gloved hands together.

'You said you'd been split up for nearly a year before we got together, but now people have said things that suggest that isn't true, and you hadn't told me you'd been here before, and—'

Alex stopped, silenced by the hostility of Matt's gaze.

He put his hands on his hips. 'So Alex is confused. We can't have that. What exactly do you want to know, Alex?'

Alex looked at the mud on her shoes.

'I tell you everything. Every fucking thing. But you can't leave me with one corner of privacy. Just one little bit of my life you don't know everything about.'

Alex reached for his arm. 'That's not it.'

Matt shook her hand off. He took a breath. 'Yes, Claire left me. So thanks for pointing that out.'

Alex bit her lip.

'And yes, I turned into Walshy for a while, and couldn't get out of bed or see the point of anything. I sorted myself out eventually, but I was still a mess. I couldn't believe I'd fucked everything up and I wasn't going to be able to live with my own daughter.'

Alex reached out again. 'Matt.'

Matt took a step back and Alex's hand slid off his arm. 'What else? What else do you want to know?'

'Nothing. Please.'

'You want to know that I lied to you about how long me and Claire had been split up when you and me got together? That we'd only just split up, and I was still trying to win her back when I was on dates with you?'

Alex felt a new emptiness within.

'Happy now? Is this what you want to hear? That I got together with you straight away after Claire dumped me, and I was still trying to get her back?'

'You were a mess when we met?'

'I fucking was. But that was ages ago.' Matt threw his arms out wide. 'Look at me now!'

Some children wearing mittens walked past. They turned to stare at Matt.

'Look at me now!' Matt shouted again. 'I'm so fucking happy now! So fucking happy!'

Matt moved to storm off; he stopped and turned. 'And yes, this weekend was my suggestion. I wanted to spend Christmas with Scarlett without leaving Claire out. And I didn't tell you because I didn't want you to burst my bubble and tell me why it wasn't a good idea, what with all your *fucking* common sense.'

Matt re-stormed off. He went properly this time, striding across the grass towards the lodge.

Alex watched him go. She noticed something fall to the floor from his pocket: a black shape.

'Matt!' she shouted. He didn't turn round.

Alex followed him at a distance and picked up the item: a glove. She stroked it gently.

Alex felt a buzz in her pocket. She reached for her phone.

Ruby. *Are you feeling any better today? Have you spoken to Matt?*

Alex put her phone back in her pocket. She ignored the next buzz. She walked slowly back towards the lodge, Matt's glove screwed up in the palm of one hand.

36

Patrick vaulted a low fence. He landed, steadied himself, and sprinted round the lake.

He ran into a cloud of what looked like blackish pigeons. (Blackbirds? He'd never really got the measure of nature.)

Patrick ran faster, enthused by his power. He could shift a whole *flock*.

In the middle of the lake, Alex and Matt floated on a boat, both leaning forward so their heads were close together, looking serious. The oars were unused, still in their holsters. These people weren't even *trying*.

Patrick kept on running.

Claire should cut him some slack. He was doing a favour for her, coming here. Not that she acted like it, but he was. He missed his Amber and Jack more than ever at this time of year.

Alex had really landed him in it with the Ironman thing. It was his fault: he should have told her it was a secret, but he didn't want to expose any imperfections in his and Claire's relationship.

Patrick ran across the crazy golf course and vaulted over a plastic toadstool obstacle.

But maybe he'd landed Matt in with Alex too. Because Matt must have told her a lie about how Claire and he had split up.

Patrick had felt sorry for Matt back then. In fact, he still did when he thought about it now, because how Matt behaved back then was one of the few things about Matt that Patrick really *got*. Matt did all the cliché loser stuff that – if Patrick was honest with himself – he'd felt like doing himself when Lindsay left, but knew he had to rise above if he wanted to keep any self-respect at all.

Two years before, Patrick had been asleep in Claire's house. He had woken up with a sense of sudden urgency. There was a noise downstairs.

He sat up quickly. 'Are we being burgled?'

Claire sat up slowly. She didn't reply.

Even in his hazy post-sleep fug, Patrick scanned the room for something he could use as a weapon. He rejected the rollalong suitcase (too big), the pair of shoes (too small), the bedside lamp (too flimsy).

There was the noise again. Banging on the door. *Thud, thud, thud.*

Patrick glanced at his phone on the bedside table. He pressed the button and the screen lit up. After 1 a.m. – and on a school night.

Patrick turned towards Claire. 'Don't answer it. He can't keep doing this.'

Claire looked at the curtains, her gaze vague and thoughtful. Her silky nightshirt slipped off one shoulder, revealing her soft throat in a way that made Patrick gasp at his closeness to that uncovered skin. It was still so new.

He was here, in Claire Petersen's bed, with the actual Claire Petersen right next to him.

A blueish light flashed on Claire's bedside table. Though her mobile was on silent, the screen showed who was ringing. *Matt Cutler.*

Patrick felt a flush of pleasure at the full-name title in Claire's phone. He knew it was probably because Claire's phone was linked to her online contacts book and that had filled the surname in automatically, but he was still pleased he was *Matt Cutler* in Claire's phone.

He hoped he wasn't himself labelled in Claire's phone as *Patrick Asher.* It was suddenly incredibly important that, in Claire's phone, he was just *Patrick.*

Claire picked up the phone. 'I'm coming down, Matt. Stop banging. You'll wake Scarlett.' She placed the phone back on the bedside table.

She leaned to the side, swinging her legs out of bed and standing up in a one-move gesture that made Patrick's heart ache with the elegance of it. This woman was perfect. Actually, genuinely *perfect.*

She leaned over him and pressed her palm into his thigh; she squeezed reassuringly. 'Back in five,' she whispered.

Her nightshirt was so short and silky, it rose up as she walked out of the room, to the extent Patrick was convinced he could see a hint of pubic hair. He had to stop himself saying, *Are you sure you don't want a dressing gown?*

Patrick heard Claire step down the stairs.

He looked to his bedside table – to the curved lamp that Matt must have switched on a thousand times.

Patrick pulled his knees up to his chest in the darkness.

He heard Claire pull the chain off the door and turn the key.

Then she was speaking, in a low voice. 'You can't do this. Think of Scarlett.'

'Just ten minutes. Let me in for ten minutes. Please. I need to talk.' Matt was trying to keep his voice quiet, but there was no mistaking the high, pleading nature of it.

'Matt, I can't. You know I can't. It won't help anything. I will come and see you at the weekend.'

'Are you on your own?'

'It doesn't matter. Go home and sleep it off.'

'Please tell me.'

Patrick was sure Claire must smell of sex. Matt must be really drunk if he couldn't tell that.

'Yes, I'm alone. But it doesn't matter. I'm going to phone Walshy if you don't go away. Make him come and pick you up for your own good. But don't make me do this, you're breaking my heart. I can't believe you're still doing this.'

'Just ten minutes, Claire. Please. Just give me a chance to explain. I'll be different. I'll be what you want.'

'If Scarlett wakes up, she'll get confused. Don't make this any harder on her, Matt. Please.'

After a moment, the door shut quietly and Patrick heard the chain slide across. He heard Claire step up the stairs. He didn't see her come into the room, but felt the mattress angle downwards. Claire slipped into bed beside him.

Patrick reached for her hand; it was cold. It sat limply in his as he squeezed it.

'You OK?' Patrick asked.

'I'd hoped he'd stopped.'

'I'll go round tomorrow,' Patrick said. 'Tell him he has

to stop it. He shouldn't still be doing this after six months.'

'You won't go round,' Claire said, with a firmness Patrick didn't recognise. 'That's the worst thing you could do. We just have to leave it. Until he gets his head round it.'

Patrick's stomach felt sloshy and uncertain as he ran past Santa's grotto. He sped up.

He couldn't run for more than two hours today. He had to pick Scarlett up from Fluffy the Squirrel's Woodland Winter Wonderland (whatever the hell that was) before Claire was back from the spa.

'Patrick!'

Patrick slowed and turned.

Nicola jogged up to him, holding a sequinned child's jumper in one hand. 'Do you mind me interrupting you?'

'Not at all.'

'It's Christmas. You're being way too healthy running.'

'You were sporty at school.'

She laughed. 'At school. It was quite a while ago.'

'I still remember seeing the name Nicola Garcia on the list of the captains of the netball team.'

'That was Nicola Garcia. I'm Nicola Trevor now.'

'But your husband's not here?'

Nicola turned to look behind her. 'Hurry up, kids!' she shouted.

She turned back to Patrick. 'He died. When the kids were tiny.'

Patrick licked his lips. 'I'm so sorry.' He wanted to lean forward and stroke her soft hair. Her farmer's wife cardigan swamped her now-tragic figure.

'It was a long time ago,' she said. 'But Nicola Garcia

is long gone. Nicola Trevor hasn't captained any netball teams.' Nicola sighed and shook her head. 'She wouldn't know how.'

'I bet you would. You're still in very good shape.'

She smiled. Was that a hint of red in her cheeks? 'Thank you. And so are you. It's very impressive at this time of year.'

'I have to exercise. Next year, I'm doing—'

'Mum!'

Nicola paused. After a second, she looked over Patrick's shoulder. 'Don't tell me, you want your jumper back. That took all of three minutes.'

Patrick smiled at Nicola's two daughters, who had appeared behind her.

He looked at his watch. 'I'm sorry to be rude. I've got to pick up my stepdaughter.'

He stopped himself before he said where he had to pick her up from. He refused to say Fluffy the Squirrel's Woodland Winter Wonderland in front of Nicola.

'Of course,' Nicola said.

They looked at each other for a moment longer.

'I'd better be off.' Patrick turned and continued his run.

He wondered how much Nicola had hurried to catch up with him and, more importantly, why.

Patrick leaned on the wall of the lodge, pulling a leg out behind him and lifting his heel to his buttock, stretching his hamstring. He'd picked up Scarlett at the end of his run, before he'd been able to do a proper warm-down, so he was making up for it now.

Fluffy the Squirrel's Woodland Winter Wonderland had turned out to be another singing and dancing thing with adults in fancy dress. When Scarlett came out, she'd said, 'Me and Posey are too old for this kids' stuff.'

Patrick stretched his hamstring further. He wondered how many eggs he could eat without Claire criticising him for being selfish with his protein requirements.

He should have bought more eggs when he was at the supermarket. But he hadn't realised how many Matt and Alex would eat. He hadn't thought they'd be egg people.

Matt headed down the road towards Patrick. Matt walked quickly, head down, hands shoved in his pockets, like the teenager he still was, in some ways.

Patrick wiped his brow with the back of his hand. 'Good boat trip?'

Matt looked up, noticing Patrick for the first time.

'I saw you two on the lake,' Patrick added. 'Just floating there.'

Matt gave a nod. He stalked past Patrick and into the lodge.

Patrick let go of his foot and placed it on the ground. He lifted his other foot and brought it up in an echo of his original pose, stretching his other hamstring. The outside of his leg had the coldness of a cadaver.

He felt the bite of the muscle as it stretched. The stretch hurt, but it was a good hurt. A wholesome, winter's hurt.

Matt's voice carried to him from inside the lodge. 'Shall we go for lunch, Scarlett?'

'Just the three of us?' Scarlett asked.

There was a pause. 'Alex isn't coming.'

'I meant Posey.'

Matt laughed, the sound with more of an edge than

usual. 'What are his table manners like? I hope he doesn't eat with his paws.'

'You know he uses his spoon, Dad. You've eaten with him loads of times. And he never talks with his mouth full.'

'You can bring him along then.'

'And he doesn't put his elbows on the table either.'

Matt laughed again. 'Who taught you that rubbish? Farm Grandma?'

'Patrick says it's not polite.'

'That kind of knowledge will stand you in good stead if you ever dine with an earl. Shall we go? You can even eat with your elbows on the table. I won't tell Patrick.'

Patrick frowned. He stretched his hamstring further, trying to relax into the burn, like his yoga teacher told him.

Patrick heard the zipping and rustling of coats and wellies. Matt and Scarlett headed out of the front door.

'Come here.' Matt wedged a woolly hat on Scarlett's head.

Matt looked at Patrick. 'You staying around the house?'

Patrick placed his foot back down on the patio. 'Yep. Then there's no need to lock up.' He linked his fingers at the base of his spine. He pushed his arms out and felt the stretch across his shoulders.

Scarlett turned to Matt. 'Posey says he wants pizza.'

Matt sighed. 'That rabbit is a megalomaniac. God save us all if he develops any political ambitions. Pizza it is.'

Patrick wondered how Matt had the energy to keep humouring Scarlett. But he remembered his own son, Jack, had become particularly attached to one blanket and had, over time, started referring to it as 'Clive'. But that was only for a brief period, and at least the blanket hadn't stuck around long enough to develop actual opinions.

Patrick felt a pull in his stomach. If he brought Clive up with Jack now, would Jack even remember? Or would he look at Patrick with disgust for bringing it up?

He hoped he'd been as tolerant with Clive as Matt was with Posey.

Matt chatted amiably to Scarlett as the two set off down the road. 'There's a joke about a rabbit ordering bar food.' Matt adjusted Scarlett's hat. 'Toasted sandwiches. Do you know it?'

Scarlett readjusted her hat. 'No.'

Matt paused. 'Do you know what myxomatosis is?'

Scarlett shrugged.

Matt gave her plait an affectionate tug. 'I'll give it a few years.'

The two walked together towards the park centre. Scarlett took a little skip every fourth step.

Matt didn't have a clue.

Sometimes, Matt treated Scarlett like she was a toddler, but then – *megalomaniac*. And *myxomatosis*.

It wasn't Matt's fault. When Claire left Matt, she took away his experience of early parenthood. And now Patrick got to live with Scarlett instead.

Did Matt resent Patrick for that on the inside? And if not, why not?

He definitely, *definitely* should. It was only fair.

Alex appeared down the road, dawdling. Patrick did a dramatic lunge. He sank forward into a deep stretch, lifting his arms a little from his sides to keep himself from wobbling.

When Alex reached him, Patrick stretched into a lunge

on the other side. 'Matt and Scarlett have gone to the pizza place.'

'Thanks.'

Patrick put his hands on his outstretched knee. 'You could probably catch them if you scurry.'

Alex said nothing for a minute. 'Where's Claire?'

'She's at the spa.' Patrick looked at his watch; the movement made him wobble and he put a hand on the wall to right himself. 'In fact, aren't you due there now? I booked you in for two p.m.'

'The spa. How could I forget? Which direction is it in?'

Patrick pointed.

'Thanks.'

Alex trudged off in the direction Patrick had pointed.

Patrick stepped his front leg back. He sank into a lunge on the opposite leg again. 'Alex?'

She turned.

'If you're having a spa you'll need a swimming costume.'

Alex lifted her chin. She headed back into the lodge.

A minute later, she re-emerged, plastic bag in hand. 'See you in a bit.'

'Can I ask you a serious question?' Patrick said in a rush.

Alex turned to look at him.

'Does Matt mind that I get to live with Scarlett? Is he jealous of me? Angry on the inside?'

Alex paused. 'Matt doesn't get angry.'

'Never?'

She paused. 'Never.'

Alex set off walking, her plastic swimming bag flapping against her leg.

*Post-shooting interview. Claire Petersen, 39. Witness to
    the shooting.*
Telephone.

Still at the hospital.

*It's fine, we can talk now. I know they say you're not
meant to use phones in hospitals, but it's got nothing to do
with the machines. People love rules, and it's so stupid. I
make a point of using my phone at petrol stations.*

*I've already told you everything I know. I'm surprised you
haven't got better things to do tonight. Aren't there loads of
burglaries on Christmas Eve, or is that just what the papers
say?*

*I don't remember any arguments this weekend, but
there may have been some. We're a family, on holiday, at
Christmas.*

We get on fine. Alex is a good friend in her own right.

*Yes, the four of us were at the archery, I told you that.
And Alex wasn't at the training beforehand because she
took Scarlett to her dance class.*

Yes, burlesque class.

*I was fine with it. Kids are kids, they experiment all the
time, and they don't know something's sexual unless you
tell them. And why would you tell that to a seven-year-old?*

*Alex and Scarlett had just been for ice cream. It's good
for Scarlett to get to know Alex as a person, these things
can be hard for the stepmum. Patrick's kids barely ac-
knowledge me, though that's their mum's fault entirely.*

My parents' phone number? Why?

I don't want you speaking to Scarlett. She wasn't even there. She's distressed enough.

If you really need to speak to her, get a warrant or something.

I'm not being unreasonable. But let's be clear – I'm not going to let you upset my daughter any more today, just because some bored staff have been gossiping in a holiday park.

37

'The changing room's that way.' The receptionist beamed at Alex, her cheeks bunching. Her face was heavily contoured with make-up, the hills and valleys drawn out with a map-maker's precision. 'You can pick up a robe and slippers on the way past.'

Alex didn't move straight away. She watched people amble past at quarter-speed, all wearing matching teddy-bear-plush robes and complimentary slippers. After a moment, she pushed open the door to the changing room.

'Alex!' Claire waved to her from a fluffy dry corner of the room, the area segmented from the rest of the wet room by what looked like a wall of towels. Claire stood blow-drying her hair, white-blonde streaks sheeting out behind her as she moved the hairdryer round.

Alex took a breath. She raised her hand in a wave and made herself smile.

Claire was clothed, ready to leave, her foundation on and eyes outlined with liquid liner.

'Fancy grabbing some lunch in the spa restaurant before you start?' Claire had to shout to be heard over the hairdryer. 'Or are you itching to get going?'

'Do we have to wear dressing gowns to eat?'

Claire laughed. 'I don't think they force you.' She switched the hairdryer off and rested it in its holster.

Alex looked around. 'Seeing all those people walking so slowly in dressing gowns, I think I'm in the dementia wing of a nursing home.' She looked around at the button-backed furniture, at the hand cream and complimentary single-use razors. 'A nursing home for the super-rich.'

'You've *really* never been to a spa before?'

'I've *really* never been to a spa before.'

'Amazing. But then, I've never been to a festival.'

'Neither have I,' Alex admitted. She wondered what she'd been doing with the decades.

'I've always wanted to do a festival.' Claire shook out her hair. 'Will I do?'

Alex looked at Claire's minimal make-up, at her tight jeans and plain T-shirt, her messily dried hair falling in casual waves.

'You'll do,' Alex said finally. 'You look great.'

Claire ate a forkful of salad and smiled at Alex.

Alex crossed her arms over her chest. She smiled at Claire.

Claire pushed her plate away. She stretched her arms above her head and turned her neck from one side to the other. 'It's like my shoulders have melted. I've got a whole other person's shoulders. A teenager's shoulders.'

As Claire stretched, Alex noticed the definition in her biceps.

'You have great muscle tone, you know.'

'Oh, Al!' Claire laughed and shook her head. 'You say

that to me, yet my daughter calls you *heavy*. You're a good sport.'

'Don't worry.' Of all the things Scarlett had said to Alex, that was the one that bothered her least. 'I've never understood why people give that kind of thing a second thought.'

'Do you mean that?'

Alex frowned. 'Why wouldn't I mean it?'

Claire laughed. 'I really like you, Al. You're so refreshing. I think it's very good for Scarlett to be around you.'

Alex felt a little patronised, but she smiled back all the same. Claire wasn't patronising in other ways – she had never asked whether Alex wanted kids. Why she didn't have kids already. Whether she'd ever tried to have kids. Whether Alex and Matt had talked about having kids.

Damn it. Claire was so hard to dislike.

'You know, I wasn't so sure this thing was a good idea when Matt suggested it,' Claire said. 'But I'm pleased we did it now.'

Alex looked down immediately. She grabbed the edge of the tablecloth and straightened it in front of her.

'We get on so well. We're one happy little blended family, aren't we?' Claire continued. 'Though not on the other side – Patrick's ex Lindsay is a right cow. She'd better watch herself or I will gladly blend her head in a food processor.'

'What's wrong with Lindsay?'

'Where do I start? She tells the kids I'm a bitch.'

'How do you know?'

'I can tell.'

Alex dabbed her napkin against her mouth. 'And are you?'

'Am I what?'

Alex placed her napkin carefully on her lap. 'A bitch.'

Claire smiled. 'Only when necessary. Only to people who deserve it.'

Alex studied Claire. 'Do you remember when we first met? In that restaurant? I thought you were so pretty.'

Claire pushed Alex's arm in a *get away* gesture. 'I thought you looked too good for that clown.'

'I hardly knew Matt back then. It was only our second date. Things happened so quickly. You know' – Alex licked her lips – 'I never even saw Matt's flat. When we first got together. He just moved in with me straight away.'

'Ha! That's because he wasn't living in a flat. He did a Walshy and moved back in with his mum. Did he pretend he had a flat?'

Alex looked down at her napkin.

'I got that impression.' But then – had Matt actually lied? Or had Alex just made assumptions based on gaps in conversation? Alex longed to be back in her lab, where she could study empirical evidence, rather than working with these unsatisfactory hypotheses. She wanted to go back in time and digitally record and categorise *every single conversation* she'd ever had with Matt.

Claire shook her head. 'That man. Honestly. The truth is nothing to him. It means *nothing*.'

Alex kept staring at her lap, looking at her pristine napkin. 'So he just went from your house' – (*Home*, she thought) – 'to his childhood bedroom to living with me?'

'His mum must have been relieved when he moved into yours. She hated having him under her feet. I think it was having Scarlett stay over all the time, as much as anything. Exhausting, at her time of life.'

Alex realised she was gripping the tablecloth; she relaxed her hands. 'Poor Janet.'

'Poor Janet indeed.'

Alex had too many thoughts cramming in at once. She picked up her knife and fork and tried to eat again. 'How are you finding this weekend so far? Is it what you were expecting?'

Claire gave a brisk nod. 'It's great.'

'Matt said you thought it would be good for you and Patrick to get away.'

Was that what he said? Alex wondered. What did he say? And what did I hear? And are the two even the same thing?

Claire raised an eyebrow. 'Matt has a big mouth.'

'I didn't mean to pry.' Alex looked down at her lap. 'So what book did you bring with you? For family reading time?'

'I didn't bring one. I relax much more by cooking.'

'But you told everyone to bring a book.'

Claire shrugged. 'I didn't mean me. I prefer cooking.'

This woman was unreadable. Was it deliberate? Or did she just change, from one day to the next? Or did she make rules and then think they didn't apply to her?

'But Matt says you don't watch telly,' Alex said. 'Or read newspapers or do social media.'

Claire smiled. 'It's not a point of principle or anything, I'm not *that* unbearable. I just don't get round to those things.'

Alex tried to imagine how watching telly could be something you didn't get round to. 'But how does that even *work*?'

Claire shrugged. 'I'm busy with my job and Scarlett. With my free time, I just prefer to *do* stuff. You know?'

Alex didn't know. 'But what about here? The spa? That's the opposite of doing stuff.'

'That's different.' Claire grinned. 'Because that's doing something, even if you're doing nothing. See what I mean?'

'No,' Alex said honestly.

'It makes sense to me.'

'OK.'

'Are you relaxing here, anyway?' Claire asked. 'Is the forest air doing you good?' When Alex didn't reply, she added, 'Be honest. We're friends now.'

Alex put her knife and fork down. 'I'm finding things difficult with Scarlett. She hates me.'

Claire did a sympathetic head tilt. 'She doesn't hate you.'

'It *looks* like she hates me. She *acts* like she hates me.'

'The thing is, with kids – you just have to let them get over things in their own time.'

'But you did tell her that I was doing the merciful thing? She knows I don't go around killing animals for fun?'

Claire smiled. 'Of course.'

The lasagne Alex had eaten had been hot at the time, but it now sat cold in her stomach. She wanted to believe Claire. She *really* wanted to.

Claire looked at her watch. 'I told Patrick I'd be back an hour ago. I'd better make a move.'

She opened her handbag and threw some cash on the table. Too much, Alex noted.

Alex went to protest, but Claire waved her away. 'It's fine. I'm so pleased we had this chance to catch up, the two of us.'

'Before you go . . .'

Claire waited, open-faced, for Alex to finish her sentence.

'I really like your perfume.' Alex dug her fingernails into her napkin. 'Where did you get it?'

'How funny you should ask.' Claire grinned. 'Matt got it for me one Christmas. He has great taste all round.' She gave Alex a wave. 'Enjoy the spa!'

'I will,' Alex said. 'Thanks.'

Claire stood up to leave. 'Make sure you do the salt inhalation room,' she said. 'That's my absolute favourite. You can get super-cosy – it has blankets and everything.'

An hour later, Alex grabbed a plastic cup from the water station near the reception desk. She poured some water and took a sip.

It turned out spas weren't her thing. As she'd always known.

Being always right, Alex reflected, was usually more of a comfort than it felt like this weekend.

Alex crunched her cup in her hand and threw it in the bin. She took off her dressing gown, hooked it on the wall next to the nearest experience room, and went inside.

She sat on the stone bench in a steam room. This one was subtly different from the others because the air carried a hint of lemon, like someone had recently gone round with a cloth and a Flash kitchen spray.

Alex had discovered that the steam rooms were the best. They weren't too uncomfortably hot, and the air was helpfully opaque so you didn't have to look at anyone else.

The worst room here was the sensory experience room. Alex had sat there in the dark while multiple screens flashed up pictures of woodland scenes, sound-tracked by perky music that would have felt more appropriate for a Tex-Mex restaurant. She'd listened to the cod-Santana guitar and watched the woodland pictures scroll: autumn leaves, frosty mountains, a shifty-looking badger.

She didn't get it.

Alex swung her feet up onto the bench in the Flash Lemon steam room and lay down, stretching her arms above her head.

She'd just wanted Matt to tell her the truth. To make things clean.

Alex had never romanticised her relationships. She didn't believe in *the one*, well aware of the statistical discrepancy of there being only one *one*, and that person happening to be about the same age and social background, and living within five miles of your home. She didn't believe in love at first sight beginnings, or sunbathed, camera-panning-out endings. But there was a difference between being level-headed and rational, and being with a man who wanted to be with someone else.

Alex felt a cold gust across her back as the door opened. Two women entered the room and one sat on the bench next to Alex. She heard the wet squelch of thighs hitting stone, a fleshy vacuum formed and released in a second.

'The thing is,' the squelching woman said, 'it's all very well getting the dress made a size too small, but what if she doesn't lose the weight? Because she's troughing like a beast.'

'She can't diet at Christmas though. It's impossible.'

'She's only got six weeks. She's signed a contract with the

shop. She has to pay another three hundred pounds if she needs it altered.'

Alex listened to the chatter for a while, distracted from her depressing internal thoughts by these depressing exterior ones. Only when a man came in, sat down and started slapping himself theatrically, sending perspiration flying, did Alex slip quietly out of the room and into the salt inhalation room.

Alex got onto a bed and under a blanket. She shuffled up the bed so her head was under what looked like a shampoo-and-set helmet at the end.

She turned her head to the side and saw the man next to her was leaning up on his elbows, scrolling through his phone under the helmet. Doing his emails, Alex could see.

In spite of her mood, Alex smiled. Maybe she wasn't the only person here who wasn't good at spas.

In the main ambling area, Alex gravitated towards a display with tubes of bubbling water and piles of herbs in bowls.

She read the sub-heading. *Our botanicals. The restorative properties of the natural world.*

Next to Alex, a woman leaned over some lavender; she picked up a handful and sniffed it. She didn't notice her towelling robe inching undone. Crinkled cleavage peeked further over the top of her swimming costume.

Alex read the description above the bowl.

Research shows that the essential oil of lavender reduces anxiety, insomnia, depression and restlessness. Try our lavender experience room for the ultimate life-lift.

Alex sighed. 'What do they take us for?'

The woman looked at Alex; she moved a fraction away.

Alex poured some more water into a cup. She tossed it back and threw the plastic cup into the bin. She wondered how long she had to stay here to get Claire's money's worth. But then she thought about the lodge.

About Patrick, lunging low in his short shorts. About Claire cooking constantly, not needing any *help*. About Scarlett and all her one-way conversations.

About Matt, and the look on his face that morning as he shouted at her.

Alex decided to try the lavender room, after all.

Alex was unable to help mentally dragging her own past into a bright, clinical light. An unflattering light, the kind that showed the lesions and imperfections.

Alex and Matt's second date had been a daytime meal at an Italian restaurant in the city centre. Alex had got to the restaurant to find Matt with his phone out on the table.

Matt saw her look at the phone. 'I'm not planning to tweet the whole time – I've not turned into a complete cunt.' He kissed Alex on the cheek, smelling faintly of toothpaste.

Alex looked at her watch as she slid in to the booth. Two p.m. Had Matt only just got up?

'It's just that Claire – my ex – might phone. She might have to take her dad into hospital for tests, and want me to take Scarlett. I'm sorry in advance if I have to mess you about.'

'Is he OK? Claire's dad?'

'They're not sure. Some heart irregularity. He's a beast of a man, like the giant from the sweetcorn ads. He's going to outlive all of us.' Matt looked down at the table. 'I didn't want to cancel because I wanted to see you. If it ruins our date, I'll make it up to you.'

'You've got to do what you've got to do. There'll be other times, right?'

Matt grinned. 'Right.'

And when Matt's phone rang as they were finishing the main course, Alex didn't even mind. She liked this guy. He was decent and wanted to do his ex a favour when her dad was ill. How could she mind?

Matt gave Alex a smile of apology. He pushed his plate away and answered the phone. 'Hi, Claire.'

He listened.

'OK,' Matt said. 'Now?'

Pause.

'Ah, the thing is – I'm just in town. In Piccolos on the high street. I've had a drink, so could you bring Scarlett here?'

Pause.

'Yeah, but we both know I'm not as perfectly organised as you.'

Pause.

'Great, we'll stay here. Claire, I hope it's not weird but' – Matt smiled at Alex – 'I'm on a date.'

Pause.

'Yeah, we're all grown ups, right?'

Pause.

'OK, see you in ten.'

Matt clicked the phone off and placed it back on the table.

He leaned towards Alex. 'How do you feel about hanging out with a five-year-old in the park this afternoon? I'll shout you a ninety-nine – raspberry sauce and everything.'

Ten minutes later Claire bustled up to the table in a flurry of quick steps. She exuded friendly competence and, in her heeled boots and belted trench coat, looked more groomed than Alex expected Matt's ex-wife to be.

'Hi, hi.' Claire gave Matt a quick kiss on the cheek before turning to Alex. 'I'm sorry to ruin your dinner. And I'm sorry you have to meet me right now. I promise I'm not as much of a cow as he says.'

'He's only said good things,' Alex said. 'I hope your dad's OK.'

'Thanks.' Claire jerked her head towards Matt. 'Matthew's a good man, but don't let him get away with too much.'

'Claire!' Matt turned to Alex. 'I'm a catch, Alex, don't listen to her.' He looked around. 'Where's Scarlett, anyway?'

'I left her with the maître d'. In case you didn't want her to meet your new girlfriend yet.' She turned to Alex. 'But I mean absolutely nothing by that, if you know what I mean? Literally – nothing. I have zero thoughts about it.'

'It's fine.'

Claire gave a wave. 'Lovely to meet you, Alex. Enjoy your day.' Alex watched her hurry away.

That afternoon, Alex had been impressed by Claire. And impressed by Matt, by proxy. Alex enjoyed playing the reasonable grown up. She felt the role suited her.

The thing was – the reason why this was going round her head now, in this lavender spa room – was that she'd assumed Claire's father's hospital appointment was a last-minute thing. An emergency.

It was only later on she'd found out it was a routine

appointment, planned way ahead, and Matt had arranged this date on the same day anyway.

Even knowing that detail, back then, Alex hadn't thought anything of it.

But now . . . now, she was thinking about it.

The fabric of Alex's life was ruching up all round her, and she didn't know which strands to pull to make it neat again.

Post-shooting interview. Alex Mount, 37. Shooter.
Telephone.
Hello. Now's fine.

There was no point everyone hanging around the hospital,
so I came home. My friend Ruby's here, looking after me.
Though her dog's here too, and it's annoying, it barks at
every noise from the back garden. Like it could catch a
squirrel on its stumpy little legs, its belly practically scrapes
on the carpet. It's a superhero in its own mind, that dog. It's
spoilt. Ruby treats it like her baby, she—
     Of course I'm not nervous.
     It was an accident. I've never even held a bow before. I
couldn't have shot him if I'd tried.
     It all happened so quickly. He was standing next to the
target, pointing out where to aim. I pulled the string thing
back, seeing how the bow felt in my hands, and I released
the arrow accidentally. I hit him, I panicked, I called for an
ambulance. That's it.
     I didn't realise I was meant to stay on the line after calling
999. I must have put the phone on mute rather than switch-
ing it off. I was distressed, my hands were shaking.
     A finger guard?
     I'm just thinking.
     No, I didn't use a finger guard. I didn't know there were
any.
     They probably didn't mention it because I wasn't even
meant to be shooting. Just holding the bow.

Scarlett wasn't there because she wanted to do a dance class instead.

I only knew it was a class, I didn't know what type of dance. I'm not up on stuff like that. I was more of a tree-climbing kid, out on my bike all day until dark.

No, no arguments. We all got along famously, the whole trip.

We hadn't been drinking. At least – not before the archery.

I had given up, but not for special occasions. And it's Christmas, for God's sake!

You're right. I am upset.

Yes, and I feel guilty.

Because it was an accident, but it was still my fault. He's in a lot of pain and his shoulder will never be the same. Everyone keeps saying it's not my fault, but it is. If I hadn't been there, it wouldn't have happened.

38

Patrick had been trying to do something nice – that was all. Trying to do the right thing.

Yet here was Matt, shouting at him. Right here in the pub.

But maybe the tension had started before they set off walking here. When Patrick had seen Scarlett eating a piece of toast in the lane, and said, 'Scarlett, darling, you've just had your lunch. You're not to eat toast in the street, it's bad manners.'

Scarlett had looked around in an exaggerated gesture. And Patrick had followed her gaze to see Matt standing a few metres behind her, looking at Patrick with a thoughtful expression and – Patrick noticed, incredulous – also eating toast in the street.

Patrick had quickly changed the subject.

But it had been fine when they were walking here with Scarlett and Claire. And Matt had been fine when they'd got here and put the pound coins down on the pool table in reservation. He'd even been fine two minutes ago, when they'd found the chalk and chosen their cues.

But now they were buying drinks, and Matt was raising

his voice to a level louder than Patrick had ever heard it before.

'Leave it, Patrick, just once. For me. *Please.*'

Patrick looked from Matt to Claire and back. 'What's your problem?'

'You and Claire have paid for everything this weekend. The holiday. All the food. Me and Alex haven't paid for anything.' Matt picked the packet of kettle chips off the bar and ran his fingers along one edge. 'It's four drinks and a packet of crisps, for God's sake.'

Patrick looked down at his wallet. 'But I've got my money out now.'

Matt threw the packet of crisps down. The packet spun across the bar towards the teenage barman in his apron-fronted uniform. 'Patrick, stop being such a bellend!'

The barman raised his eyebrows slightly.

Claire glanced at Scarlett, who was waiting at the pool table. Claire pulled Matt to the side so that Scarlett couldn't hear their conversation. 'What's wrong with you today?'

'He's being a bellend, Claire. You *know* he's being a bellend.'

'But is that really helpful to say? In front of your daughter?'

Matt swatted his hand. 'She doesn't know what it means.'

'You want her repeating it at school? Playing hopscotch and saying to her pals "You're the bellend now"?'

The barman studied the glassware on the high shelf with excessive interest.

Patrick flashed the barman a smile. 'Sorry.'

'Don't apologise for me.' Matt turned from Patrick to the barman. 'Sorry, mate. But don't you think he's being a twat?'

The barman looked behind him. 'I just need to . . .'

Matt got his wallet out and paid for the drinks. He reached for his beer and sank half of it; he placed it back on the bar. He pressed his lips together, squashing his beer moustache to nothing.

'Let's just try to have fun, shall we?' Claire said.

Matt gave a sharp nod. He reached for the crisps and pulled the packet open. The movement was too hard: the bag ripped, the force scattering crisps across the bar and the carpet.

Patrick grinned. 'Now who's the bellend?'

'I'm sick of this.' Matt drained his pint and headed for the pub doors.

'Matt!' Claire shouted after him.

Claire turned to Patrick. 'Now what?'

Patrick shrugged and looked away. Claire had that expression on her face she used when she'd opened the egg box to realise there was only one egg left.

'I don't know *what's* got into him.' Patrick shook his head. He looked at Scarlett. 'Shall we rack up? Let's see if you can remember the order of the balls like I taught you.'

Patrick pushed the coin in the slot. He felt the balls rumble and heard them clatter through the table's tunnels.

Scarlett arranged the triangle on the felt. She placed the balls inside the triangle with careful precision.

There was a gust of chilled air as the front doors opened again.

Matt strode up to the pool table and looked Patrick in the eye. 'I'm sorry I insulted you.'

'No problem.' Patrick handed him a cue.

Matt lowered his voice to a whisper. 'I was being a knob.' He turned to Scarlett and spoke at a normal volume. 'I was being silly, Scarlett. Ignore me. It's all over now.'

'All forgotten. Now' – Patrick gestured to the pool table – 'hasn't Scarlett done a good job?'

Matt forced a smile at Scarlett. 'She has.'

'I taught her to rack them up like that. Some people just throw the balls in every which way, but it's important to get them right.'

Matt nodded.

Patrick tapped the end of his cue on the floor. 'So what should we do about teams?'

39

Back in the house, Scarlett and Posey lay on the bed, huddled over the iPad that Mum had still forgotten to take back. Mum wasn't herself this weekend, and that was a good thing. Scarlett and Posey kept the iPad under the bed now, and it was better this way.

Scarlett opened the iPad's search window.

'Two *l*s?' Scarlett asked.

'I think so,' Posey said.

Scarlett typed the words in. She pressed *search*.

> **Bellend**
> 'bɛl ˌɛnd/
> *noun BRITISH vulgar slang*
> *noun:* **bellend**; *plural noun:* **bellends**; *noun:*
> **bellend**; *plural noun:* **bellends**
> *1. the glans of the penis*
> *2. an annoying or contemptible person. 'He is
> a total bellend and should step down as soon as
> possible.'*

Scarlett and Posey looked up *glans*. Then they looked up *contemptible*.

Scarlett pressed the iPad *off* button.

'I'm not sure your daddy likes Patrick very much,' Posey said.

Scarlett put the iPad back under the bed. 'No.'

Posey jumped off the bed. 'Alex will be back soon. We have to get her out of here.' He started walking across the room. 'We have to protect ourselves.'

Scarlett rolled onto her back. She put her hands under her head. 'But what do we do?'

Posey turned and paced the other way. 'I've thought about it, and we've got to get your mum and dad back together. Then he won't need Alex around any more.'

Scarlett frowned. 'But what do we do about Patrick, if Mum and Dad get back together? Can he stay?'

Posey stopped pacing to think. 'Does Patrick's old wife have a new boyfriend?'

'I don't think so.'

'Then Patrick can go back to his old wife.'

'Clever. You're good at this.'

'But your mum and dad will need help to realise they want to get back together.' Posey started pacing again. 'What do they like doing together? What's their favourite joint thing? Colouring in? Jigsaws? Ponies?'

'No.' Scarlett looked around the room for ideas, at her toys and games and clothes.

Then she remembered.

'Singing,' Scarlett said. 'They never got cross with each other when they were doing karaoke. They laughed a lot.'

Posey nodded. His long purple ears jiggled with the movement. 'Then let's make sure we get them doing some singing. What was their favourite song?'

40

In the late afternoon, Alex left the spa and let herself back into the lodge.

In the living area, she saw the lounge had been rearranged. The coffee table and chairs were now at the side of the room, leaving a bare space of carpet in the middle of the floor.

Matt was stretched out under the TV, his rear sticking out towards the door.

'Having a good time under there?' Alex tried to make her voice light. 'That isn't your best angle.'

Matt looked round. The two made a second of eye contact before he turned back to doing something under the TV.

Alex threw her bag of wet spa things onto the dining table. She got her swimming costume out of the bag and stretched it out on the dining room radiator.

She looked round at the others. Patrick was sitting on the sofa with Scarlett on his lap. Claire was doing something in the kitchen.

Claire smiled at Alex. 'How good was that? Are you converted to the spa cause?'

Alex pushed a lock of hair from her eye. 'I've completely relaxed.' She turned to look at Scarlett. 'Thank you so much, Scarlett.'

Scarlett gave Alex a formal nod.

Matt reversed out from under the TV. 'I've sorted it. Loose connection.' He padded backwards and stood up with old-man slowness.

Alex looked at Patrick, surprised that something needed fixing, yet it was Matt who was doing it. Patrick wasn't trying to take over, or even flapping around him.

In the kitchen, Claire put her knife down. She took another swig of her drink. 'You're our hero, Matt.'

Matt kissed his biceps in mock-manly pride.

There was too much irony in this place, Alex decided. Could anyone here form an authentic response to anything if they tried?

She turned to look at Patrick; she started. Patrick was staring pointedly at her. He'd clearly been waiting for her to turn round.

The two shared a long moment of eye contact.

Alex looked around at the empty wine bottles scattered round the kitchen. 'Looks like I've missed a fun afternoon.'

'It's Christmas,' Matt said in a tight voice.

Alex put her hands up, palms outward. 'I wasn't judging.'

Matt picked up the TV remote and pressed some buttons. Alex looked at the black, whirring console on the floor, at the microphones on the table.

'You said there'd be no karaoke, Matt.' She meant it as a joke, yet it sounded like a criticism.

Matt put the TV remote down on the coffee table. He picked up his wine glass and drank the last gulp.

He turned to Alex. 'Scarlett wanted us to sing. And this is her weekend. What can I say?' He looked Alex straight in the eyes. 'I lied to you. I'm a liar.'

Alex reached out to touch Matt's arm, but Matt pushed past her into the kitchen without stopping.

Alex brought her hand back to her centre. She wrapped it round her middle in a self-hug.

Matt came back into the lounge with his wine glass refilled. 'I've got the machine working again.' He crouched in front of Scarlett. 'You're up. What song do you want?'

Scarlett glanced at Alex and back to Matt. She squidged herself round, twisting in the chair. 'You first.'

Matt raised his eyebrows. 'You don't want to start?'

Scarlett shook her head firmly. She poked Matt in the side. 'You and Mum do the song about how you met. With the man with the make-up. Show Alex.'

Patrick looked up; he gave Alex another pointed look.

Alex shook her head minutely in incomprehension.

'She means the Human League.' Matt turned to Claire. 'Come on, mate. Assume the position.' He picked up both microphones and held one out to Claire. He looked at Patrick. 'Sorry, Pat. Must be getting a little tedious.'

Patrick said nothing.

Claire took the microphone and gave a stagey shake of her hair. She stood with Matt in the centre of the lounge, waiting while Matt pressed some buttons on the console remote.

Alex looked at Patrick. 'Do you do karaoke?'

Patrick blinked at her. 'Sometimes.'

Matt put the console remote down. 'You're up next then, mate.'

'I'm afraid I'm not in the right frame of mind.' Patrick's voice was tightly polite.

On the TV, the video started. The iconic synth chords of the Human League's 'Don't You Want Me' kicked in.

Scarlett sank down to watch, cross-legged on the floor. 'Sing your special first line. And do the dance, Daddy.'

Matt winked at her. He twizzled the microphone in the air on its cable with mock professionalism.

The words came on the screen in blue lettering and Matt began to sing.

'We were dancing to Stone Roses on "A Pound A Pint" night'

'Those aren't the right words.' Alex gestured at the screen. 'It should be a waitress and a cocktail bar.'

'In the student u-nion'

Scarlett turned to Alex. 'It's their special first line.' Alex found the sharpness in Scarlett's voice disquieting. 'Because they first met when they were dancing.'

Alex scratched her cheek roughly. 'But that doesn't even scan.'

Matt ignored Alex and turned to look at the screen. He sang the proper words of the song now, his voice clear and crisp. He was able to hit deeper notes than Alex expected.

As Matt sang, Alex turned to look at Claire. She had her eyes shut and was moving her head from side to side, waiting for her turn. She banged her hand against her thigh coquettishly, like she was playing a tambourine.

Matt locked his gaze with Claire's as he sang. It was

theatre; it was ironic. Alex knew that, of course.

'Don't—'

Matt got to the deepest part.

'Don't you want me . . .'

Alex gripped her hands into fists.

'Daddy's a good singer,' Scarlett said, her head tipped to one side.

'Yes,' Alex said quietly.

Matt stretched his arms above his head as he sang. His T-shirt lifted up and Alex saw the faint line of hair that ran down from his navel to the top of his belt.

As they reached the chorus, Claire gave a cough; she put her mic to her lips. She narrowed her eyes in a parody of seriousness and strutted towards Matt.

'Don't you want me . . .'

Claire sang 'baby' directly into Matt's face, eyes screwed up. Matt sang right back at her. They must have been able to feel the warmth of each other's breath on their faces.

'Don't you want me . . .'

As Alex watched Claire and Matt over-egg the *oh-oh-oh-oh*, she realised this wasn't a normal karaoke performance. It was a well-practiced routine. It was a chunk of history, playing out in front of her.

Chorus finished, Matt spun in a circle on the spot; he untangled himself from his cable.

Claire pointed her finger at Matt and waggled it in a flirty *no* gesture.

'We were dancing to Stone Roses on "A Pound A Pint" night
In the student u-nion.'

'Still doesn't scan,' Alex said, quietly. 'Or rhyme.'

Claire smiled at Alex in acknowledgement and turned back to the screen. She wasn't a good singer – she kept missing notes. But she performed with an ironic confidence.

While she sang her verse, Matt pulled out all the moves next to her. He span in a circle and pointed his finger. He stepped over the cable so he didn't get tangled.

Matt and Claire reached the next chorus and the two pushed their backs against each other, Abba-style.

'Don't you want me . . .'

Alex took a step backwards from the lounge. And another.

Claire did a big spin. She shimmied forward with her chest and back again.

Alex turned to look at Patrick. He was watching the singers too, his gaze unmoving. He smiled a fixed, deliberate smile.

For a second, Alex felt euphorically, dizzily vindicated. She *knew* this weekend was weird.

Patrick stood up. He sidled slowly towards Alex, not taking his gaze off the singers.

Matt and Claire leaned their faces in towards each other, raising the volume for the final chorus.

Alex sensed Patrick next to her. The two standing close and focused, like they were watching a game on a football terrace.

The song finished. Scarlett clapped her hands together with excitement. She raised her eyebrow at Alex in a smug challenge.

Or did she?

No, she didn't. She couldn't have.

Alex picked up her mobile phone and placed it in her pocket. She turned towards her bedroom.

She changed direction and headed for the kitchen. She selected the largest wine glass from the cupboard.

In full view of the others, Alex chose a fresh wine bottle, uncorked it, and poured herself a glass of red wine. Without looking back, she picked up the glass and bottle and walked through the lounge towards the bedroom.

The only sound in the lounge now was the whirr of the disc as it spun in the karaoke console.

The last thing Alex heard, before she shut the door on the grotesqueness in the lounge, was Scarlett saying 'Now do the song from *Grease*.'

Then: '. . .Why's no one saying anything?'

41

Patrick watched as Matt and Claire stared at each other, mics slack in their hands.

'Matt?' Claire said the name like it was layered with questions.

Matt stayed looking at the screen and pressing his remote, watching song after song flick past. 'She's an adult. She can do what she wants.'

'Are you not going to go after her?' Claire asked. 'Don't be' – she glanced at Scarlett and lowered her voice – 'an arsehole.'

Matt shrugged. 'It's just booze. It's not going to kill her.' He turned to Scarlett and leaned down. 'Have we got time for one more song before we go and see Santa?'

After a few beats, he picked up the remote. He flicked through the songs on the karaoke console.

Patrick watched as Matt murdered an Elvis song, missing high notes all over the place. Matt wasn't a terrible singer, but Patrick had never understood why karaoke was so popular with people who weren't great at singing. He felt embarrassed for Claire every time her voice got to a screechy part – his stomach actually tensed on her behalf.

Patrick watched Matt sing and knew he should be angry with him. Matt was trying to seduce his girlfriend and Patrick was right here. But it was such a pathetic attempt. No decent woman would be won round by *singing*.

It was hideous, of course, how today was going. Excruciating. But it was worse for Alex than him. Humiliating.

It was obvious. Matt wanted Claire. How could he not? But Patrick, for once, couldn't even get angry with Matt. He was with this man's ex-wife; he couldn't be surprised that Matt was still trying to get her back. While Matt and Claire had already split up when Patrick came along, which meant Patrick and Matt had never been in direct competition; indirectly, it was a different story. Indirectly, Patrick had won this competition as surely as if he'd killed Matt in a duel with long-snouted pistols.

Patrick was a fair man. And Patrick could live with it, as long as Claire didn't respond. As long as Claire didn't want Matt back.

And Claire didn't. She definitely didn't.

When Matt finished his song, Scarlett tugged at his sleeve. 'Let's go to Santa now.'

Patrick studied Scarlett's face, all light with excitement.

Patrick remembered that look. He'd seen it when he took his own daughter to Santa's grotto in the out-of-town shopping centre six years ago. It had been worth all the traffic, and that row with that man about the parking space, and the fact he had to pay that arse-scratching elf *fifteen quid*, when he saw Amber's face as she sat on the knee of that Santa.

Patrick sat down, suddenly winded. 'You go without me

to Santa.' He tried to steady his voice. 'I'll stay here and check on Alex.'

Scarlett smiled at him. 'OK. Just Mum, Dad and me.' She skipped to the door.

'Come with us, Pat.' Matt's voice was sharper than usual. 'She can do what she wants.'

'No.' Claire's voice was firm. 'We'll go tomorrow morning, all together. I'm not leaving Alex here feeling rubbish. I'll rebook the session. Let's just have a few more songs then some tea and she can join us when she's feeling better.'

Patrick got his phone out. He found the video of Amber and the shoddy Santa.

He muted his phone and pressed *play*.

He watched.

The too-short trousers. The cigarette-stripped, raspy 'Ho Ho Hos'. The look of awe on Amber's face, just how he remembered it.

Patrick touched his hand to his stomach. *Exactly* how he'd remembered it.

The awe. The magic. The glance at Patrick. Their perfect shared second when, though Amber was still on Santa's lap, it was just the two of them in the world.

Patrick shut the phone off and threw it down beside him onto the sofa.

42

Alex looked at Matt's phone sat on the side table in the bedroom. She knew his passcode. But . . . no. Alex would not be that person.

Alex looked at the bottle on her bedside table, at the inch of wine left in it. She looked away.

She definitely wasn't going to drink that last inch tonight.

Alex re-entered the main room when she knew the karaoke had finished. Claire was placing plates of salad and sliced meats onto the dining room table. She gave Alex a quick smile and returned her gaze to her task, giving it an unnecessary level of concentration.

Matt, Patrick and Scarlett sat cross-legged on the floor of the lounge. Matt and Patrick held fans of cards in front of them, while Scarlett had laid her playing cards on the floor. She picked the cards up to look at them, one at a time.

Matt raised his head from his cards. He gave Alex a long glance. Alex stared right back at him.

'Can you grab the waters for the table, Al?' Claire's voice was nonchalant.

Alex didn't look at Claire. 'No problem.'

Patrick turned to Scarlett. 'Have you got Mr Bun the Baker's son?'

Alex filled five glasses with water and carried the first two through to the dining area. She passed Claire at the table and felt something – a gentle squeeze of her elbow.

'We cancelled Santa. It wouldn't be the same without you.'

'Right.'

'We've rebooked for tomorrow morning.'

Alex didn't say anything.

'I'm sorry,' Claire whispered. 'It was just meant to be fun.' She held Alex's arm. 'Me and Matt can be idiots sometimes. We just both get quite into karaoke.'

'I overreacted.' Alex moved forward so Claire's hand dropped away from her arm. 'It's fine.'

'It's just something we used to do. We didn't mean to act like dicks.'

Alex wished Claire wasn't whispering so loudly. Matt stared at Claire with a disappointed expression, like Claire had nothing to apologise for.

Matt blinked and turned back to Patrick. 'Fishmonger's wife.'

Patrick handed him the card.

Claire brightened her voice. 'Food's up.'

Alex put her hand on a dining chair to pull it out. She paused.

When she'd first left the bedroom, she'd had no intention of staying for food: she'd been planning just to show she was OK, then make her excuses and retreat to the bedroom. But her hunger was immediate, her stomach bleating. And Matt was wafting coldness in her direction.

She needed to change the expression on Matt's face. To any other expression, except that one that was there now.

Alex found herself pulling out the chair and taking a seat at the dinner table.

Matt arranged three long-stemmed glasses on the table and filled them with wine. He placed one in front of Claire and another in front of Patrick; he took a sip from the third.

'Matt?'

Matt turned to look at Alex with deliberate slowness.

'There's four adults here.' Alex gave a polite smile. 'We need four wine glasses. Not three.'

Matt paused. He went back into the kitchen and opened the cupboard.

'But where are my manners? Unless we need five, of course.' Alex turned to Scarlett. 'Does Posey need a wine glass? I don't know how old he is.'

Scarlett gave her head a tiny shake.

Matt banged a glass onto the table in front of Alex. He filled the glass slowly with wine, looking Alex in the eyes the whole time.

Alex smiled. 'Thank you.' She swigged the wine and placed the glass back down, careful not to spill it. She looked at Scarlett. 'So no wine for Posey. But he'll need carrots.'

She leapt up from her chair and got a carrot from the fridge. She put the carrot on the plate and placed it in front of the empty sixth chair, next to Scarlett.

'Does he need it peeling?' Alex asked.

Scarlett gave another small shake of the head.

Alex slapped her hand against her head. 'I know what we've not had. Christmas cake.' She jumped up again and fetched the cake tin and breadboard from the kitchen. She unwrapped the Christmas cake she'd made, and placed it on the breadboard with a knife.

The cake looked jaded after the journey in the car. The Christmas tree decoration on the middle of the cake leaned at thirty-degrees to the snow.

Alex didn't straighten the tree. She cut firmly into the icing. 'Who's for cake?'

'We're eating our main course, Alex.' Matt edged his voice with formality.

Alex put the knife down. 'Of course, darling.'

There was silence again.

'We're all so quiet!' Alex leaned over the table and plucked a slice of ham from the plate in the centre. She folded the slice and shoved it, whole, into her mouth. She looked round the table, from one person to the next. 'But we're having a lovely family tea time. All here together, our happy blended family. So what shall we talk about?'

Claire and Matt both reached for food. Patrick looked at Alex with an expression she couldn't read, but which pissed her off anyway.

'Anyone else hear pipes in the night?' Alex peeled another slice of ham off the stack. 'Just a kind of rhythmic pounding as the heating goes off around bedtime.' She shoved the ham in her mouth, staring at Patrick the whole time. 'Maybe you guys can't hear it. Maybe it's just because the noise is above us and noise travels down. Did you hear the noise? Patrick?'

Patrick shook his head.

'Strange.' Alex took a gulp of wine and wiped her mouth

with the back of her hand. 'I wonder what it was: one of life's little mysteries.' She looked from Patrick to Claire and back. 'I wonder if I'll hear that noise tonight. I'll be listening.'

43

At the dinner table, Posey turned to Scarlett. 'What's going on?'

'I don't know,' Scarlett whispered.

'I didn't even want a carrot. Why does Alex keep talking to me? And pretending I've talked back?'

'I think she must be tired.' That's what Mum always said when Auntie Katie got like this, that 'Katie was tired'. 'Tired' meant drunk – Scarlett couldn't believe anyone was fooled by that – but apparently it was politer not to say so.

'I'm not eating that carrot.' Posey pointed at the plate Alex had brought. 'The scientist might have poisoned it. And what does she mean about the noise from the pipes in the night?'

'Shush, Posey.' Scarlett flapped a hand at him. 'I'm trying to listen.'

'I asked you what you thought of the pipes, Patrick,' Alex said. 'Surely you have an opinion on those?'

Patrick looked down at the roll he'd buttered. He cleared his throat. 'I've found much of the infrastructure of the lodge substandard.'

Alex laughed. 'I love the way you talk, *Pat.*' She shoved another whole piece of ham into her mouth.

Dad concentrated hard on picking up breadcrumbs from the table.

'I don't understand what Patrick just said. And he's shaking the table,' Posey said. 'With his knee.'

'I know,' Scarlett said. 'Shush.'

'Let's do hopes and dreams then.' Alex looked from one person to another. 'What are your hopes and dreams. Anyone?'

The room was silent. An animal shrieked outside.

'Nobody?' Alex turned to the chair where Posey sat. 'Posey, get us started. Are you happy? What do you want out of life?'

Posey sat completely still.

Alex nodded. 'A mate, that's important. A supportive mate.' She gave another nod. 'A safe burrow and food? I know where you're coming from. But I wonder – is that *enough*? Will you feel *truly fulfilled*?'

Posey reached out to hold Scarlett's hand.

Scarlett turned to Dad for help, but Dad was stabbing hard at a piece of lettuce. He shoved it into his mouth in a way that showed he was angry.

Dad was hardly ever in a bad mood. Dad must be 'tired' too.

'Look!' Posey's voice was panicked. 'She's about to do it again.' He gripped Scarlett's hand tighter. 'She's about to *talk to me!*'

'Security *is* important – true.' Alex gave Posey an understanding smile. 'I understand why you wouldn't want things going all *Watership Down*.'

Posey frowned. 'Watership what?'

'Yes, I can see why that film would stick with you. How did watching it feel for you? Like a horror film? Or a documentary?'

Dad pushed his chair back with a screech. He picked up his plate and walked to the kitchen.

Alex narrowed her eyes. 'You washing up, Matt? Without being asked?'

Dad didn't turn round.

'You're such a good man. I'm so *lucky*. Lucky, lucky, *lucky*.'

Dad flourished the plate at Alex in a grand theatrical gesture. 'And so am I!'

Alex gave a wide smile. 'Fill me up, would you, darling?'

'Alex talks posher now she's got tired,' Posey said. 'She sounds like she's in *Downton Abbey*.'

Without looking at Alex, Dad filled her glass, then his own.

'And look,' Posey pointed to where Patrick was shifting in his seat, 'Patrick looks like he's sat on a hedgehog.'

Alex turned to Scarlett. 'What about you, Scarlett? What do you want to be when you grow up?'

'Uh-oh,' Posey said. 'Squeeze my paw.'

'An astronaut?' Alex continued. 'A lawyer? A postman?'

Scarlett put her fork down. 'A hairdresser,' she said. 'Or a vet.'

Posey dropped Scarlett's hand. 'Why did you answer?' he hissed.

Scarlett shrugged.

Posey folded his arms.

Alex raised her glass to Scarlett. 'Great choices.' She

took another swig. 'Different academic requirements, but great choices. Why a vet?'

'I like animals.'

'But *she* likes killing them,' Posey hissed.

Scarlett flapped a hand at Posey. 'Shush.'

'Was that *shush* at me?' Alex said.

'No. At Posey.'

Alex nodded. 'Well, that's the thing. You're used to dealing with animals, what with Posey.'

'Dealing with?' Posey turned to Scarlett. 'What does *that* mean?'

'It's a complex business, dealing with animals,' Alex glanced at Patrick. 'If you're a vet, you'll have to put animals down for their own good. Like I did with that pheasant yesterday, after Patrick mowed it down in the car.'

There was a silence.

'Patrick ran over the pheasant?' Posey said. 'On purpose?'

'You did know Patrick ran it over, didn't you?' Alex said. 'You had been *told*?'

Alex looked down at the table.

'Sorry, Scarlett.' Alex placed her fork down in a careful gesture. Her cheeks went pinker. 'That was rude of me. You'd make a great vet. Or hairdresser. You don't need to decide now and whatever you do, you'll be great at it. You know how I know that? Because you're switched on. You don't suffer fools.' Alex leaned towards Scarlett and grabbed her hands. 'You've got *gumption*.'

Patrick looked at Dad like he was trying to say something with his eyes.

Dad took a long, slow sip of wine.

'You know what gumption is?' Alex asked, still holding

Scarlett's hands. 'It means you know your own mind. You won't let anyone take the mick out of you. Not like me – I'm a *fucking doormat*. Now.' Alex beamed around the room. 'Who's for Christmas cake? Anyone?'

'I like her more for saying "fucking" in front of us,' Posey said. 'Like we're grown-ups.'

'Me too,' Scarlett said.

Patrick looked at Scarlett then back to Alex. 'Do you think you need a lie-down?'

'Do I?' Alex glared at him. 'What do you think? Do I need a lie-down?'

Patrick cleared his throat. 'I'm just thinking of you. How you'll feel in the morning.'

'How sweet. But how will you feel in the morning, Patrick? Exhausted? Refreshed?'

'I—'

'What if the pipes keep you up tonight? So loud. So rhythmic.'

Claire turned to Matt. 'So, are you two still thinking of moving house? What are you looking for in a new place, is it extra space or a location thing? Have you seen anywhere you like?'

There was a knock on the front door of the lodge. Alex jumped up to answer it.

She opened the door to a group of carol singers dressed as elves, wearing green outfits with red hats and stripy tights.

Without saying a word, the elves launched into 'O Little Town of Bethlehem'. An old man at the front held out a money bucket with writing on it.

Alex turned to the others with a beam. 'More singing!'

Scarlett turned back to watch the singers. Carol-singing elves, *here*, at *her* lodge.

She felt Posey's paw slip into her hand. 'They're good singers. They're not as good as your choir though.'

'I know,' Scarlett said.

'Your choir are brilliant.'

'I know,' Scarlett said again.

She turned to say thank you to Patrick for arranging the singers, but he was whispering with Mum and Dad at the table now Alex was at the door. Scarlett couldn't hear what they were whispering about because of the loud elf singing.

The elves finished their song. The group in the lodge clapped, Alex most of all.

'That's your bedtime cue, Scarlett,' Claire said softly.

Scarlett didn't even argue. She stood up. 'Night-night.'

She skipped up the stairs without a word.

'I tell you what,' Posey whispered, following Scarlett upstairs. 'When your dad moves back in I'm going to smash that karaoke machine. All this singing's doing my head in.'

Scarlett frowned at Posey as she opened the bedroom door.

'Now, let's clean our teeth and get under the duvet.' Posey crawled under the bed, his cotton tail bobbing. 'Then we need to find that film Alex talked about. *Watership Down*. That meant something.' He pointed at the iPad and looked at Scarlett in a question.

Scarlett nodded.

Scarlett and Posey cleaned their teeth in the bathroom. Scarlett closed the bedroom door after them and got in bed.

She leaned down under the bed and brought up the iPad. She placed it on her lap. 'We're not really allowed to do this, you know.'

Posey snuggled into her. 'But you know your mum's Netflix password, right?'

44

Patrick watched Scarlett go upstairs, confused. What, no complaints? No 'Ten minutes more', or 'Can I take the iPad with me?'

Alex clapped her hands. 'That carol singing was wonderful.' She waved the man with the bucket into the lodge. 'I haven't got any money on me. Matt, have you got some?'

Matt got his wallet out of his back pocket. He put a ten-pound note in the man's bucket.

'We've got Christmas cake as well,' Alex said to the bucket man, 'if you're interested?'

Patrick was surprised to find himself feeling sorry for Matt.

'Oh, no.' The man rubbed his stomach. 'I've had a bellyful of Christmas cake.'

After the thank yous and Happy Christmases, Alex shut the door after him.

'Thanks, Matt,' Claire said, sitting back down at the table. 'Generous.'

'Matt's extremely generous.' Alex turned to Claire. 'Admittedly, he hasn't offered me any money for rent since he moved into my house nearly two years ago, but that's

285

an oversight, probably. And you know that trust fund his parents pay into for when Scarlett's eighteen?' Alex gave an expansive wave of her arm. 'Matt has lent the capital to Walshy. How thoughtful is that?'

Matt turned to Claire. 'It's not like that.'

Alex took a long sip of wine. 'And the one thing we know about Walshy is he's a safe bet for a return.'

Claire and Matt stared at each other.

Claire put her wine glass down. 'Please say you didn't.'

Matt put his hands palm down on the table. 'Mate, I will pay that money back whatever happens – it's on me, I promise. Walshy was just in debt to a payday loan company at a ridiculous APR and getting himself deeper in debt. It was just a cash-flow thing.'

Claire licked her lips.

'I promise, don't worry.' Claire didn't respond, Matt added, 'Don't stress.' Then, 'Don't stress,' again.

Claire had her gaze fixed on Matt. 'This isn't over.' Again, Patrick almost felt sorry for him. 'I'm not talking about this now,' Claire said, 'but we will definitely – *definitely* – be talking about this tomorrow.'

The doorbell rang again.

Patrick beat Alex to the door this time. Nicola stood on the threshold, wearing a segmented top that shimmered like the scales of a fish. She held out a bottle of wine. 'Is now a good time for that drink?' Goose pimples sprang up on her arms. 'I can come back another time.'

'Of course!' Alex shouted. She made a wafting *come in* gesture. 'Now's perfect. What are you drinking?'

Nicola smiled at Alex and looked at the table. 'Red wine's good.'

Alex went to fetch another glass from the kitchen.

'Nicola.' Nicola reached out her hand to Claire. 'I went to school with Patrick.'

Claire focused her gaze on Nicola. 'I couldn't believe it when I heard, it's such a coincidence. Lovely to meet you. I'm Claire.'

Nicola took the glass of wine Alex handed to her and sat at the table. 'Kids in bed?'

'Kid. Just one,' Claire said. 'Scarlett. And yes.'

'Cool.' Nicola looked around at the others. 'I'm just trying to work out the dynamic' – she wafted an arm – 'here.'

Alex beamed at her. 'We're one big happy family. Let me explain. I'm with Matt and he used to be married to Claire.' She gestured with her arm at each person in turn. 'Claire's now with Patrick, and we don't know each other at all, and we've all come on holiday together to a small lodge with shared air in the middle of nowhere. That's not strange, is it?'

Nicola smiled back. 'It's a great thing to do.'

Alex gulped her wine. 'So it is. Pass me the bottle, would you, darling?'

After a beat, Matt passed the red wine bottle over to Alex.

'Patrick's ex-wife isn't here, sadly.' Alex concentrated hard on the bottle as she poured. 'They don't get on.'

Patrick turned to Nicola. He shrugged helplessly.

Nicola gave him a sympathetic smile. 'I've never had to do the "ex" thing. Can't be easy.'

Alex made a *piffle* dismissal gesture with an arm. She knocked her glass an inch along the table. The glass wobbled; she steadied it.

Patrick continued to beam at Nicola, with a smile that was feeling falser by the second.

Alex leaned towards Nicola. 'So what was Pat like at school?'

'Um . . .' Nicola looked at Patrick and back. 'Nice. Quiet. Studious.'

'I'm not surprised,' Alex said. 'He's still serious. He knows about interest rates and – what is it Matt? Con-so-lid-at-ed' – Alex enunciated the word carefully – 'debt obligations.'

Matt slammed his hands down on the table. He walked into the bathroom without a word.

Patrick frowned at Alex. 'I don't really know a lot about that stuff. I know a bit about sub-prime mortgages and the crash but—'

Alex interrupted him. 'Do you play the cello?'

'No.'

Alex waved a hand and turned back to Nicola. 'Was he good with the ladies at school? A charmer?'

Nicola smiled. 'You'd have to ask him that.'

'No,' Patrick said shortly. 'I was a geek.'

'We moved in different circles.' Nicola gave Patrick a warm smile. 'He was a top-set boy, whereas I was usually bunking off, smoking and doing my nail varnish at the top gate. We only crossed over in drama class.'

'School. So long ago.' Alex sat back in her chair. 'All that mattered was sex. I lost my virginity to a guy I didn't know the surname of, in the botanical gardens in the park. I was fifteen. I remember being surprised it was pretty unspectacular, I could mainly feel the twigs cutting into my bum.' She turned to Patrick. 'What do you think about that, Pat?'

Patrick took a large sip of wine. 'Each to their own.' He looked at Nicola. She stared at the table now, lips pressed together, playing with her necklace. She wasn't smiling any more.

The room was silent, apart from the waterfall sound of Matt pissing in the bathroom.

Matt flushed the toilet and re-entered the lounge.

Alex turned on him. 'You were even younger when you lost your virginity, weren't you, darling? Fourteen, wasn't it? Behind the waltzers at the fair?'

'You have the red teeth of an old lush, Alex.' Matt's voice was even. 'You look like a pissed-up vampire. Maybe best to *shut – the – fuck – up.*'

'Someone else go now.' When no one spoke, Alex sighed. 'I'm just trying to have some fun.' She looked around at the others. 'OK, then. How many people have we all slept with? Me' – she leant her head to the side – 'probably fifteen. But that's an estimate, there's a twenty per cent tolerance on each side.'

'Alex,' Matt kept his voice low. 'Grow up.'

Alex turned to Patrick. 'Do you think that's a little? A lot?' Alex twisted towards Claire. 'What do you think? Too many? Too few? How would you judge me on that?'

Nicola drained the rest of her wine.

'Go to bed.' Matt's voice was quiet, firm.

Patrick turned to Nicola. 'Another drink?'

Nicola stood up. 'I told my mum I'd only be five minutes.'

Patrick looked from Nicola's fish-scale party top to the bottle of wine she'd brought. 'Of course.'

Alex kept her gaze on Claire. 'Because some people lie about that kind of thing. Don't you think it's sad if someone has to hide their past? You wouldn't lie about that kind of thing, would you, Claire?'

Claire held her gaze. 'Do we need to have a chat outside, Alex?' She stood up. 'Shall we?'

Patrick pushed his chair back. 'I'll walk you home, Nicola.'

'It's not far.'

'Such a gentleman, Pat,' Alex said. 'A chivalrous man from a different age.'

Nicola stood up, a carefully polite smile fixed on her face. Patrick ushered her towards the door of the lodge.

'Do you want some Christmas cake before you go, Nicola?' Alex shouted.

Nicola gave a kind smile. 'I don't really like it. But thanks.'

'No,' Alex said thoughtfully. She picked up the knife. 'No one really likes it.'

Alex plunged the knife into the centre of the cake with both hands. She left the knife there, its handle sticking up.

Nobody moved.

Matt pushed his chair back. 'Alex. Everyone has been trying to spare your blushes but you've now officially shown everyone what an awful drunk you are, including the nice lady next door who you've *never met before*.'

Patrick and Nicola hurried out of the lodge and into the cold. Even with the door shut behind them, they could still hear Matt's raised voice.

'Go to bed before you embarrass yourself even more, and hope to God at least one person here is still speaking to you in the morning.'

*

Patrick and Nicola crunched wordlessly across the frozen grass to Nicola's lodge.

Patrick shoved his hands into his jean pockets. 'I should explain.'

'No need. It's fine.'

'Alex doesn't drink usually.'

'A holiday like this always has bust-up potential. Any family weekend, really. My kids have been at each other since we arrived, it's quite straining to the nerves. But they've gone to bed now.' Nicola gave him a little smile. 'Do you want to come inside?'

There was a bang of a door behind Patrick. He looked back at his own lodge: Matt strode across the grass towards the lake, coat on, head down.

Patrick looked at Nicola. She was so small. So delicate. 'I probably should get back to Claire. Try to clear up this mess.'

Nicola put her arms across her chest and rubbed her goose-pimpled arms. Patrick tried not to notice her nipples, hard with cold and visible against the fish-scale top.

'You probably should just go inside, Nicola.' Patrick held eye contact. 'Have a nice evening. I'm sorry.'

'Not your fault.' Nicola gave Patrick one last achingly vulnerable smile and retreated into the lodge, shutting the door quietly behind her.

Patrick walked away from the lodge, not looking back. He knew the door to another world had closed, never to open again.

45

Scarlett watched the end credits travel down the iPad screen.

Scarlett held Posey's paw as the two lay together under the duvet. Posey squeezed Scarlett's hand. Scarlett didn't squeeze back.

They stared at the screen again.

When the credits stopped, the two sat there in silence. Scarlett pulled the bedding closer round her. She was trying not to cry again.

Posey started to speak. 'That was . . .'

'Some of those rabbits were *awful*.'

Posey said nothing. He looked scared, like there might be a ghost in the bed. He looked how Scarlett felt.

'I thought I knew all about rabbits,' Scarlett said.

'So did I,' Posey said.

Scarlett pulled her hand out of Posey's paw. 'They turned on each other. All that *blood*.'

Scarlett wanted Posey to say it had all been a mistake.

But he didn't. 'Maybe . . . maybe we don't know as much about rabbits as we thought we did.'

Scarlett thought about this. She stared straight ahead.

Eventually, she said, 'Would you mind getting out of my bed?'

Posey pulled back the duvet and got up. He placed the duvet carefully back round Scarlett.

He stood across the room, by the door, watching her. 'I'm sorry.'

Scarlett said nothing.

'We ... rabbits must get in bad moods sometimes. I didn't know, honestly. I'm as surprised as you are.'

Scarlett pulled her knees up to her chest. She wrapped her arms around her knees.

'Are you scared of me after watching that?' Posey asked.

Scarlett squeezed her knees in tighter. 'A little bit. Yes.'

'I don't think I'd ever do anything like that. Not the ... you know. Turning on other rabbits.'

'Please stop talking.'

They sat there for a moment longer.

'Do you want me to go back to the airing cupboard now?' Posey asked.

'Yes, please,' Scarlett whispered.

46

Alex squeezed herself more tightly into her curled-up position on her side. She tucked the duvet under her chin.

She had expected to be able to get to sleep quickly, with the effects of the evening's ethanol acting on her medulla. The quality of the sleep itself would drop because – of course – the alcohol would suppress the production of vasopressin. But getting to sleep should be fine.

Instead, she'd lain here for an hour, thinking about what she'd said. Her thoughts kept returning to the inch of wine, still left in the bottle on the bedside table.

Alex leapt out of bed, grabbed the bottle and headed for the en suite. She poured the wine down the sink and placed the bottle on the side of the bath.

She got back into bed.

Once Matt had left the house, Alex's bluster snuffed out in an instant. Matt slammed the door and something within her crumpled, leaving just self-disgust to balloon within, filling her mouth and throat.

Alex stared at the table. 'I'm sorry.'

'Maybe you need some sleep,' Claire said.

Patrick quietly let himself back into the house.

Alex put her hands over her face. 'I'm sorry,' she repeated, voice muffled.

'Alex,' Claire said. 'However bad that was – and it was pretty bad – it was just us. You're drunk, we've all done it. Nobody's died.'

'There's no point discussing it when you're in this state.' Patrick's voice was much harsher. 'Just go to bed.'

Waiting for Matt to return, Alex had cleaned her teeth; she'd taken her make-up off. She'd got into her pyjamas. She'd even *flossed*.

And she'd lain here ever since, curled up, occasionally turning her open mouth into the pillow, thinking about what she'd said, muffling herself too late.

After drinking so much, she should be benefitting from increased dopamine levels right now. It didn't feel like it though.

Alex curled her hands into fists. She dug her nails into her palms till it hurt.

Her heart was beating too quickly. That would be a result of anxiety, causing increased intensity of the neurons in the locus coeruleus. Norepinephrine would be acting on her heart, and on her blood vessels and respiratory centres.

Alex turned over in bed.

The alcohol must have an effect on her medulla soon.

The bedroom door creaked open; Alex woke with a start.

She forced herself to sit straight up, despite the pressure in her head. 'Matt.'

She had no clue how long she'd been asleep. Minutes? Hours?

'I'm only coming to get my duvet.' Matt's voice was

businesslike in the darkness. 'I'll sleep on the sofa.'

'But' – the dryness of Alex's mouth made her voice click as she spoke – 'what will they think? If they find you there?'

'They will think I can't bear to be in the same room as you. And they would be accurate.'

Alex felt a chill spread across her chest. She pulled her duvet up further.

'You care about that now, Alex? What people think?' Matt's voice was quiet. 'Because if you think the others haven't noticed something's wrong then you've lost it even more than I thought.'

Alex's eyes acclimatised and she saw Matt's shape across the semi-darkness. A rigid shape, striding towards his side of the bed in jerky movements.

'I threw some of the wine away. I didn't drink it all.'

'Go to sleep, Alex.' Alex wondered if Matt's voice had ever been as heavy with dismissal as it was now.

He pulled at his single duvet but it didn't move from the bed, a part of it trapped underneath Alex.

'After Claire was so nice to you.' Matt gave the duvet a vicious tug. Alex jerked to the side and the duvet flew out from underneath her. 'And this is how you treat her.'

Alex grabbed the corner of the duvet to stop Matt pulling it free; she clutched it tightly. 'Saint perfect fucking Claire.'

'Oh, OK. So that's how it is. That's nice.'

'I'm bored of kneeling at the altar of Saint Claire.'

'And when were you kneeling tonight? Tell me. Was it when you were asking her how many people she'd slept with, in front of Patrick?' Matt pulled at the duvet but Alex wouldn't release the corner she was holding. 'Or when you said you could hear them having sex?'

'I didn't *say*, I just implied—'

'Or when you told her about Walshy having Scarlett's money? And – *by the way* – thanks for that. Darling.'

Matt tugged the duvet harder; it jerked out of Alex's hands.

She grabbed for the duvet but Matt whisked it away with a bullfighter's flourish.

Alex rested her back against the headboard, defeated. 'If you feel like that about Claire, you might as well remarry her. Go to Paris and renew your vows.'

'Tonight, I'd kill to marry Claire again.' Matt pulled the duvet along the floor behind him. 'Just to get away from you.'

Matt opened the door. Light from the hallway filled the room long enough for Alex to see the sneer on his face. 'Go to sleep, you *nasty* lush.'

Matt slammed the door and was gone.

Alex blinked in the fresh darkness. She shuffled down the bed till she was under the duvet, the pressure in her head building. Knowing she had the whole night ahead to obsess about the coldness on Matt's face; hours to wonder whether he would ever look at her again without that scornful expression, or whether he would hold it there for eternity and keep it there, just for her.

47

Patrick heard the front door open and close while Claire was in the bathroom, cleaning her teeth.

Claire padded back into the bedroom.

Patrick put down his phone. 'Matt's back in the lodge.'

Claire switched off the main light. 'That's good.' She slipped under the covers. 'I pictured him sitting by the lake, shivering, wondering how long he had to stay out to prove he was still angry.' She gave a snort. 'He must have decided it was too cold not to forgive Alex.'

'He hasn't forgiven her. At least, he hasn't gone into their bedroom. He's put the telly on in the lounge. He's watching an old episode of '*Allo 'Allo*.'

Claire picked up her phone and set the alarm. 'Let's go home tomorrow. Tonight tells me this was clearly a mistake.'

Home. Patrick thought of his kids. That there would be prearranged plans, excuses, awkward phone calls. The evidence of his family's ambivalence to him would be right in his face, and being home at Christmas would make it all so much worse.

'But what about Scarlett?' Patrick said.

'I suppose you're right. Let's see what it's like in the

298

morning, but we don't have to stay. No one can make you stay for the rest of your holiday.'

'Did you two argue like that? Like Matt and Alex did tonight?'

Claire rolled onto her side, facing away from him. 'Everyone rows.'

'Alex is a loose cannon.'

'She's not herself. This holiday's making her crazy.'

Patrick wished Claire would look at him. 'I still don't understand some of the stuff she was talking about.'

Claire yawned loudly, not bothering to cover it. 'She was hammered, Patrick. It's not meant to make sense.'

'But I'm not surprised this weekend's sent Alex loopy,' Patrick said to the back of Claire's head. 'She's scared.'

Finally, Claire rolled over to look at him. 'Why?'

'It's obvious. Matt wants you back.'

'Ridiculous.'

'Alex sees it.'

'And he adores Alex. He's just frothing with her today because she got pissed up and super-mouthy.'

'He was crushed when the two of you split up.'

'Old news. Dead and buried.'

'You'd never get back with him, would you?'

Claire yawned again. Patrick still wished she'd yawn more quietly. More nicely.

'Please, Claire. I want to hear you say it. I *need* to.'

A sigh. 'Of course I'm not going to get back with him. No.'

'Are you sure?'

'What's going on between us has nothing to do with Matt.'

Patrick sat up straighter.

'Pat.' Even Claire was at it now. 'Getting back with Matt would never be on the cards. Never, ever, *ever*. Maybe if we hadn't had Scarlett, if we'd had a simpler life, we would have made it work. But it doesn't matter that we get on now, because it didn't work when we had to function together. It's that simple.'

'But what did you mean by "what's going on with us"?'

Claire turned back to face the wall. 'Figure of speech.'

'Claire—'

'I'm tired. It's been a long day and I'm too exhausted to talk. I'm going to sleep. OK? *Please*.'

Patrick stared at the back of her head, taking in the kink in her hair from where she'd tied it up in a hairband.

'Night,' Claire said into the wall.

Patrick reached out and stroked Claire's arm. 'Night.'

When she didn't say anything else, he said, 'I love you.'

Claire leaned an arm back and patted Patrick on the hip. 'Night.' She took her arm away and shuffled an inch towards the wall.

Patrick continued to stroke her arm. He breathed in the scent of her neck. The mixture of familiar smells. The almond oil shampoo she bulk-bought off the internet. Her perfume. Even the faint, chemical tang of her contact lens solution. Claire's signature smell.

Within seconds, Claire's breathing deepened and she started making a whooshing sound with her mouth: Claire's pre-sleep countdown indicator. She would be dreaming soon.

But what do you dream of, Claire? Patrick stared the question into her hair.

Post-shooting interview. Sophia Trevor, 11. Happy Forest guest.
Face-to-face. Happy Forest lodge.

Mum, I can't think properly with you here. You'll try to do the talking for me.

You will, you know you will.

Thank you. And close the door behind you, please.

Mum fusses. She thinks I should be upset, but I didn't even know him. She likes having things to worry about, and if she can't find anything then she makes something up. It's hard for me because I'm the oldest and doing everything first, Emily gets away with murder. Mum lets her do loads of stuff she wouldn't let me do when I was nine. We have the same bedtime now, how's that right?

Yes, I saw the little girl in the dance class. When the dance lady came and said her parents were delayed, Mum wanted to wait with her. We hung around for half an hour and got crisps and drinks from the vending machine, then the dance lady told Mum it would be longer. So we took the girl back to our lodge till her gran turned up.

It was a great class. If I get a chair I can show you.

Oh, OK.

I'd never met any of them before the trip, just round the holiday park. The problem with Mum is she likes everyone. It can make going anywhere slow. Aldi, Morrisons, Tesco, she knows them at every checkout.

I didn't see the people next door much. Mum wanted me

to go round and play with the little girl, but I'm eleven, so why would I want to? Emily's bad enough. And there was singing from their lodge. Grown ups singing old songs. What's that about? I said to Mum, 'I'm definitely not singing, they can't make me.' And Emily wouldn't go then, either, because Emily's a sheep and does what I do.

So Mum gave up in the end and said we could stay with Grandma. Mum put on her best top, the silvery one she was saving for Christmas Day. Grandma noticed Mum's special top too, she gave Mum a look. Mum said she'd run out of clean tops. Grandma said 'People who play with fire get burnt.' Mum turned to me and said Grandma was going quietly senile.

Half an hour, maybe? An hour? Not long. We played one game of chase the ace. Which I won.

The man from her school, Patrick, walked her back and they stood talking outside for a bit. He fancies her.

It's obvious, if you have eyes.

Mum encourages him, but it's not her fault. She's lonely. I want Mum to meet someone, but someone better than him. Though he did have a good car, until he squashed a pheasant with it.

Just ran it over in the street. So now the car has a pheasant's life splatted all over it. Even though you can't see it, you know it's there.

I didn't like him. He talked to Mum in a special voice, like he had a script. He barely looked at us, which was fine by me. He wore shorts, even though it's December, and he was always stretching. Like – big stretching.

Mum didn't even know him at school. She said seeing someone from school made her feel young, so I told her, 'You're not young, so it should make you feel old, if anything.'

I've definitely never met him before. And Mum only met him again when we came out of the lodge after he'd squashed the pheasant.

He said that to the lady behind the desk? But that's a lie!

I knew it. He's properly creepy. I bet he'd stalked her here from Facebook. What did Mum say when you told her that?

Mum's too nice.

She was telling you the truth. I know when she's lying. She lied about wearing her best top, her other clothes weren't all dirty. She lied about Santa's grotto being full, she just didn't want to spend the money. But she was surprised when she saw the man next door.

Poor Mum. She always gets the weirdos. I didn't really feel sorry for him anyway, but now I think he actually deserved to get shot, after all.

It's only fair. And he ran over that pheasant and what goes around, comes around.

||||||||||||||||||||||||||||||||||||||||||||||||||||||||||||||||||||||||||||||||||||||||||||||||

Extract from the Happy Forest brochure:
In December, the Happy Forest turns into a Winter Wonderland. Give your little ones the Christmas gift of seeing Santa and his elves in his award-winning grotto.

Or why not learn a new skill with the help of our experienced archery hosts? If that's not your thing, we have dance classes suitable for all the family!

||||||||||||||||||||||||||||||||||||||||||||||||||||||||||||||||||||||||||||||||||||||||||||||||

48

Sunday 24 December
Christmas Eve

Day 4

No no no no no! Alex woke in an explosion of nerves.

She pushed herself up from the bed, despite the ache in her head and her kaleidoscoping vision. She pulled her duvet round her shoulders and adjusted her pyjama bottoms, pulling them higher up her hips.

She took a breath and opened the bedroom door.

Matt sat on the sofa in the lounge, his arm round Scarlett, the two watching cartoons on the television. Matt had spread his single duvet across their knees like a blanket.

Alex took a step forward.

Matt didn't take his eyes off the telly. 'Morning.'

Alex faltered, her duvet-cape sagging around her. 'Morning.'

'And how are you today?'

'I've been – better.'

'Are you not well?' Matt still didn't look at her.

'I appear to have picked up some kind of virus.'

'How odd. Maybe you'd better go back to bed.' Matt

squeezed Scarlett's shoulder and took his arm away. 'Back in a bit, chicken.'

He got up and walked past Alex into the bedroom. Alex followed him in.

She shut the door after them. 'I'm sorry, I'm sorry, I'm sorry, I'm sorry.'

'You were a fucking *nightmare*.'

Alex sat on the bed. She leaned sideways dramatically, till she fell onto the bed. She closed her eyes, then opened them slightly, peeking up at him.

Matt remained standing, looking down at her. 'A horrible lush.'

'I missed your clicky nose. I couldn't sleep without that click.'

'Fucking awful screechy banshee. I was like *where's my nice girlfriend gone? And who put this troll in her place?* You'd better apologise to Claire.'

Alex gave a small wail.

'What was that?'

'Me remembering things. Details.'

Matt sat down on the bed. 'Serves you right.'

'You were horrible too.' Alex took a peek at Matt from under her lowered eyelids. 'Hurtful.'

'Who are you to judge?' Matt's tone was harsh, yet he took her hand between the two of his. 'I'm surprised you've got any memory of it at all.'

'I remember.'

Matt looked down at her hand. He brushed his thumb over her knuckles. 'How is your hangover, really? It must be bad.'

'I'm on pins. I've got cold waves washing up and down

my back. I'm dizzy and it hurts to look up. I'm struggling to stand. Or even sit. Have you got any sunglasses with you?'

'It's December. And you deserve the pain for being a cunt.'

'The singing upset me.'

Matt continued stroking her hand with his thumb.

'You seemed so happy together, you and Claire.'

'Don't be stupid. Is that what all this was about?'

Alex squeezed her eyes shut. 'Did you really still want to be with her when we got together?'

'Is that a real question?'

'Yes.'

Alex listened to the sound of Matt breathing. When he spoke again, his voice was serious.

'OK. At first, I did, yes. But then – pretty soon – no. Then definitely, absolutely no way. I got together with you before I was completely over Claire. But that doesn't change anything. I really liked you, from day one. I just had some shit to get over.'

Alex nodded into the pillow.

Matt squeezed her hand. 'I was trying to upset you yesterday. Because you were being so awful.'

Alex closed her eyes against the pillow. 'Can I ask you one more thing?'

A rotting smell reflected back at Alex from the pillow. She inched her face backwards.

'Just one more?'

'I promise. Then I'll put the crazy in a box forever.'

'OK.'

'Claire is wearing the same perfume you bought me last Christmas.'

Matt paused. 'I bought it for her.'

'Did you buy it for me because you wanted me to smell like Claire?'

Matt straightened up instantly. 'No!' He opened his eyes wide. 'Al, of course not. Why would you ever think that?'

Alex stared at him.

Matt pushed his hair back from his eyes. 'Al. I bought that perfume because it smelled nice in the shop, and I didn't know what to get Claire for Christmas and I'd left it too late. So I bought two bottles, and I spent enough in the chemists to get a free electric razor, not that that was why. I was getting you some other stuff as well, so I didn't think it would matter that I got you one present that was the same.'

'But you told me you didn't get her anything.'

'I said that because I just didn't want to tell you that I bought her the same thing as you. That I'm *that* kind of thoughtless dick.' Matt stroked her hand again. 'But you're a nasty lush, so we're even.'

Alex heard a sound like raised voices. She strained to listen. 'Can you hear that? Is it Claire and Patrick upstairs? Are they arguing now?'

Matt tilted his head to one side, listening.

There was a soft knock on the bedroom door.

'Dad?' Scarlett's voice wobbled with fear.

'What is it, chicken?'

'There's a spider.'

Alex felt Matt's hand tense.

'It ran under the sofa, Dad. It's as big as a door handle.'

Matt glanced at Alex, then quickly away. 'I'm not dressed.'

Alex opened one eye. She looked the fully clothed Matt up and down.

'Is your Mum not there?' Matt said carefully. 'Or Patrick? I'm sure they're up. I can hear voices.'

'They haven't come downstairs yet.'

Matt took a deep breath. He stood up slowly. 'Then I guess I'm coming, darling.'

Matt turned to Alex. 'I'd better go, I suppose.'

Alex smiled despite her pain. 'Do you want me to do it?'

'I want Scarlett to respect me. As a protector.'

'Give me a shout if you need me.'

'You think that will make up for last night?'

'A little. Maybe.' Alex gave him a tiny smile. 'If it's a big spider, it might.'

A minute later, Matt was back. 'You're up. It's massive, as big as a carthorse. It's got hooves and everything.'

Alex pushed herself up from the bed.

'You're the designated animal murderer anyway, after pheasantgate,' Matt said.

'You need to learn how to ask for a favour,' Alex said.

Alex entered the lounge. She was about to say something to Scarlett about the night before, but Scarlett just pointed at the sofa.

'It's under there.'

Alex got on her hands and knees slowly, trying to control the dizziness. She looked under the sofa and found a reasonably sized house spider.

She caught the spider between her hands. 'Can you open the front door so I can put it out?'

'Aren't you going to kill it? Dad always kills them.'

Alex felt the scrabbling of the spider's legs on her palms. 'Why would I kill it? It's done me no harm.'

Scarlett stared at Alex.

'You all right?' Alex said.

'You need to take it far away. Don't just put it right outside the door.'

'I will.'

Alex didn't want to put the spider down for fear she wouldn't catch it again, so she walked up the front path without putting shoes on, the cold gravel stinging her feet with every step. She took the spider across the road and set it down carefully by the lake.

She looked back at the house and was surprised to see Scarlett watching her carefully from the window.

Alex went back into the bedroom and shut the door behind her. She flopped back on top of the duvet.

'It wasn't *exactly* a monster,' she said.

Matt hitched his shoulders in a mock-shudder. 'I can still see it. I feel it like it's walking up and down my spine. I need a shower. Don't touch me. I'm jumpy.'

'Are we OK?' Alex said.

Matt brushed her hair out of her face. 'You were really nasty.'

'But I removed the spider.'

'Yes. Yes, you did.'

'Does Scarlett hate me? Even more than she did already?'

'I expect so.' Matt nodded. 'Probably. And if she doesn't, she should.' Matt turned to the doorway and called out. 'Scarlett?'

After a moment, Scarlett appeared in the doorway.

Matt patted the bed. 'Come in here and talk to us.'

Scarlett sat down where he indicated.

Matt smiled at her. 'Alex has got a virus. She wasn't very well last night.'

Scarlett studied Alex, unblinking. 'She was tired, Dad. She was drunk.'

A fresh wave of cold washed down Alex's spine.

Matt raised his eyebrows. 'She was, Scar. She was.'

'You know she doesn't like being called Scar. Because of the bad lion in *The Lion King*. Stop shortening people's names.' Alex made herself sit up. 'I'm sorry, Scarlett. If I said anything that upset you. Or Posey. I was sad about something and I wasn't thinking.'

Scarlett studied Alex for a minute longer. She turned to Matt. 'You were tired last night too.'

'I was.' Matt sank onto the bed next to Scarlett and stroked her hair. 'I know it hasn't been perfect here. But it's been so nice to have everyone I care about around me.'

Scarlett looked at her feet. She kicked the air limply.

Matt glanced at Alex then back to Scarlett. 'You know Posey's your best friend? Well, Alex is mine.'

Alex reached down for Matt's hand. She squeezed it.

'And I need you to tell Posey to be nicer to her. Because Posey can be quite cutting.'

Alex leaned an inch towards Scarlett. 'I'm sorry I tried to feed Posey a carrot.'

Scarlett looked down at the bed.

'Are you OK?' Matt asked.

'Posey and me had an argument last night,' Scarlett said. 'He wasn't there when I went to look for him in the airing cupboard this morning.'

'What was the argument about?' Matt asked.

Scarlett shook her head. 'It's private.'

'I'm sorry to hear you argued,' Matt said. 'Sometimes, after a row, guys just need a little space.'

'Do you forgive me?' Alex asked Scarlett. 'For what I said when I was drunk?'

Scarlett turned to Alex. 'Can I ask you something?'

'Of course.'

'You're a scientist.'

Alex nodded.

'And that means you cut up rabbits. For fun.'

Alex blinked. 'No. No, it doesn't.'

Matt laughed. 'Is that what you think? Alex doesn't cut up rabbits for fun, or for anything else. She's not *that* kind of scientist. There are different kinds.'

Scarlett peered at Alex. 'Then what kind is she?'

Alex turned to Matt. 'This'll be interesting.'

'She' – Matt cleared his throat – 'works in the university. Something to do with cells. And diabetes.'

'Go on, tell Scarlett more,' Alex said.

Matt gave Alex a pleading look. He turned back to Scarlett. 'She does experiments on cells taken from humans during surgery. Humans that are alive, and have agreed to it, and they're under anaesthetic.' He turned to Alex. 'Is that close enough?'

'Close-ish.'

Scarlett looked like she was processing this information.

'Anything else you want to know?' Alex asked.

Scarlett narrowed her eyes. 'What other animals have you killed? Don't leave any out. Posey is quite scared of you because you're a scientist. And he's a rabbit.'

'Animals I've killed? In my whole life?'

'Yes.'

'You don't have to answer,' Matt said quickly.

'I don't mind.' Alex thought. 'Well, I killed that pheasant, as you know. I think that's the biggest animal I've killed.'

Scarlett nodded.

'And I've twice stepped on a frog, by accident. And loads of snails too, I don't know how many. I don't always look where I'm going.'

Scarlett looked like she was processing this.

'And I went fishing once, with my dad, but then I didn't actually catch anything.'

'Eating fish is disgusting,' Scarlett said.

Alex nodded. 'I agree. Completely. It should be banned.'

'Yes,' Scarlett said.

Alex thought again. 'I can't think of anything else I've killed.'

'And you don't kill spiders.'

'There's no need. Oh . . . I've just remembered, I destroyed a wasp's nest once. So that's thousands of wasps.'

'But that's wasps,' Scarlett said. 'They're evil. They don't count.'

Alex shrugged.

'So you don't kill animals.'

'No. Though I should add, for completeness, primate tissue samples are particularly useful when—'

'I think you've answered Scarlett's question, don't you?' Matt looked at his watch deliberately. 'We're going to have to leave in a bit. To go and see Santa.'

Alex glanced at Matt. 'I don't think I'm well enough to see Santa this morning. Not yet.'

Matt turned to Scarlett. 'How about we go and see Santa with your mum, and then Alex takes you to the ice cream hut afterwards? Hopefully her virus will be better by then. I know Alex wants to buy you an ice cream sundae.'

Alex sensed the morning-after fug around her. She covered her mouth with her hand and pulled her pyjama top further down. 'I'll shower first, of course.'

'What about you?' Scarlett asked Matt. 'And Mum? What will you do?'

Matt stood up. 'I can always go skateboarding.'

Alex rolled her eyes and Matt gave her a soft punch in the gut.

He turned back to Scarlett. 'I'll chat with your mum about a few things – about you, probably. That's what me and your mum normally talk about. You, all day and all night, and we never get bored.' He turned to Alex. 'Do you mind?'

Alex gave a small smile. 'Of course not. Not *now*.'

Scarlett looked up from her feet. She stared at Alex for a minute, holding her head to one side.

'I will let you buy me an ice cream today.'

Alex gave a tiny nod. 'Thank you.'

49

At 4 a.m., Patrick had had enough. He tried to shake Claire awake but she just mumbled into the pillow.

'Just go back to sleep. Everything will look different in the morning.' That's what she said. Like he was *a child*.

'I can't sleep.'

'Go for a run or something.'

'It's pitch black outside.'

She didn't answer. She'd given him enough of her time, it seemed.

Patrick waited for morning, his legs jiggling on the mattress, his mind churning on a repetitive loop.

She'd never encouraged him to go for a run before. *Never*.

At 5 a.m., Patrick did press-ups on the landing.

At 6 a.m., he crept downstairs and grabbed Scarlett's *Frozen* pad from the TV table, along with her pencil with an unidentified fluffy animal that swung from the top as he wrote.

Patrick wrote and wrote till the pencil was blunt. Six sides of paper.

Dearest Claire,

I've been lying here thinking about how much you mean to me, and I'm not sure I tell you enough. So here we go.

I love the little things about you. I love how you sleep with an arm over your face, lifting up the front of your nose like a piglet's. Do you know you do that? It's gorgeous.

I love how your hair overlaps everywhere in the morning. I love how you eat cereal so delicately.

I even love how you just tuck your shoelaces into your trainers without tying the laces up, although I know I've said in the past that it could make you trip.

I love how you make that snorting sound when you laugh really hard. (That's another pig reference, I see that now. But Claire – lovely Claire – please don't read too much into this.)

I love that you have such a naturally tiny waist and runners' legs, even though you never do any exercise.

I love your stir fries. I love your sea bass. In fact, I love all the food you cook, and how good you are naturally at creating balanced nutritional ratios.

I love that you cook for me. I love how you make me feel loved. The first time I met you, you said to that receptionist, 'Just think: whatever, Arseface,' and I thought – yes! That's a woman I want on my side.

I love how generous you are. I love how kindly you laugh when someone makes a joke that isn't funny, just to make them feel better.

I love what a good mother you are to Scarlett. I love how you always want good things for my kids,

*even though they call you the Blandwitch. (If I've not
mentioned that before, please pretend I didn't mention
it. Please don't let this ruin my love letter. It's because of
something to do with sandwiches that happened the first
time you met them – I don't understand the reference
properly, but I know they don't mean it. They're just
young and under the spell of a certain unhelpful influence
who I'm not going to taint this letter by mentioning.)*

*I love how you're so certain about things, how you
always know what you think on every subject at that
point in time. Yet I love that you are so changeable and
I can't always predict what you think about something,
even though sometimes it can look like I'm quite frus-
trated about that. Deep down, I love it.*

*I am so proud of you when anyone mentions you at
work. I want to shout out, 'The solicitor, Claire Petersen?
Isn't she wonderful?'*

*I am your ever-willing servant. I will protect you
from earthquakes and volcanos if I can. I'll be like your
human shield. Your very loving human shield.*

I love you, Claire.
Kind regards,
Patrick

At the first sign of Claire stirring, Patrick leapt up and
pulled the curtains open.

Claire squeezed her eyes shut and jerked onto her front.
'Christ, Patrick,' she said face-first into her pillow.

Patrick held out the letter. 'I've written you a letter.'

Claire didn't move.

'Don't you want it?'

'I have literally just woken up. You *watched me* wake up.'

Patrick's letter-arm sagged.

'And I don't want to talk about this any more.'

All the fear of the previous night came rushing back. 'What did you mean last night, "What's going on with us"?'

Claire shuffled up the bed, onto her elbows. 'Not now. We're on Scarlett's holiday.'

'We *will* have this conversation, Claire. And we will have it now. I've been waiting all night.'

Claire sat up and pushed her hair out of her face. 'Please calm down. We've got to go to Santa.'

'I haven't slept because of what you said.'

Claire pushed the duvet aside and stood up.

'I know you were just trying to hurt me,' Patrick said. 'I know it.'

Claire headed into the en suite. Patrick clenched and unclenched his hands.

Everything was on her terms, all the time.

He listened for movement in the en suite. Eventually, the toilet flushed. Then the tap ran.

Claire re-entered the room; Patrick leapt up.

'Have you seen the iPad?' Claire scanned the room. 'I haven't seen it for a while.'

'The iPad? We need to *talk*, Claire.'

She held up a hand. 'Let's not talk now. It's Scarlett's special weekend.'

Patrick gestured with his bundle of papers. 'You need to read my letter, at least.'

Claire looked at the bundle. She didn't reach to take it.

'And what did Alex mean when she asked you how many people you'd slept with?'

The question had hooked itself into his consciousness at threeish, that morning. It had dangled there in his mind ever since, turning slowly.

Claire closed her eyes. 'Alex was just stirring.'

'But stirring what? What exactly was she stirring?'

'Nothing.'

'You can't stir nothing. You need something to stir. A pot. A soup.' Patrick knew his voice sounded uncertain. 'A stew.'

'She was drunk and spouting shit.'

'Everyone knows what's going on except me, Claire. I deserve to be treated with respect.'

Claire scratched the side of her mouth, studying him.

Eventually, she said, 'OK.'

Patrick nodded in satisfaction. 'OK.'

'Matt must have told Alex how many people I've slept with.'

Patrick thought. He raised his shoulders in a question.

Claire sighed, like she was having to dumb things down for a child. Patrick tensed his hands again.

'And I've slept with a lot more people than I told you I had. A lot more. I lied because I knew you wouldn't like it, not because I'm ashamed.'

Patrick knew he was at a fork in the conversation, with two different roads unfurling in front of him. She'd lied to him then told Matt the truth, the two cosying up together, laughing at stupid old gullible *Pat*.

He chose the simplest road because his brain was full. 'How many people?'

Claire closed her eyes. 'I don't know.'

'Twenty?'

Claire shrugged.

Patrick felt himself frown. 'Fifty? A hundred?'

'I told you, I don't know. I didn't count.'

This was incredible. *Incredible.* Patrick sank down onto the bed. He put his face in his hands.

There was a knock at the door.

Claire jumped up. She strode across the room and opened the door.

Matt stood there, wallet in hand. He nodded at Patrick and turned to Claire. 'Did you say we've got Santa at ten, mate? We need to be off.'

'Sorry. I'll throw some jeans on and be down.'

'No worries.' He looked past Claire to Patrick. 'Morning, Pat.'

Patrick looked at Claire, in the short Smirnoff T-shirt she slept in, the one that only just covered her pants. But he couldn't complain. Matt had seen it all before, he supposed.

Everyone in the world had seen it all before.

'Listen' – Matt stepped into the room – 'I'm sorry about last night. Alex is mortified, she'll be avoiding you the rest of the weekend. She's going to skip Santa this morning to nurse her head and have a good long word with herself.' He looked behind him and back; he lowered his voice. 'Sorry you had to be there for our pissed-up drama. But we're good now.'

Claire waved his words away.

'And I promise I'll get Scarlett's money back, mate. There is no way I'd let Walshy keep it. Ever, ever, ever. I'd put the money in myself if he didn't pay it back. But he will. And I'm charging interest for Scarlett, a better rate than the bank would give her. She's a baby loan shark, she just doesn't know it.'

'I'm not going to ruin Scarlett's weekend,' Claire said. 'But we are going to talk about this again. And you are going to fix this, as soon as you get home, I don't care if you have to remortgage Alex's house.'

'I'll never do it again,' Matt said. 'And I bet Alex feels terrible for worrying you.'

'No, Matt,' Claire said. 'This particular one is not about Alex. *You* should feel terrible about this one.'

Patrick sat back against the headboard. He couldn't believe this.

Alex and Matt were OK? *After all that last night?* After Alex had made such a fool of herself, spouting bitterness and stirring up trouble? Driving *lovely Nicola Garcia* away?

Matt tipped his head and some hair fell into his eyes. Patrick wanted to lean over, grab a clump of that hair and rip it right out.

Matt didn't deserve that hairline. He hadn't worked for it.

'You all right, Pat? You look a bit red in the face.'

'Press-ups.' Patrick noticed he still had the letter in his hand; he jerked his hand behind his back. 'I've been doing press-ups.'

'I'll get Scarlett into her coat and boots.' Matt left the room. 'See you downstairs, amigos.'

Claire shut the door behind Matt with what looked like reluctance.

That burned afresh. 'I'm humiliated, darling.'

'And I'm sorry to hear it.'

Claire picked yesterday's jeans up off the floor and pulled them on over yesterday's pants.

'*You've* humiliated me,' Patrick clarified.

Claire narrowed her eyes. 'How?'

Patrick faltered. 'What do you mean, how?'

Claire pulled off her T-shirt. She grabbed a bra and fastened it behind her back. 'Why, precisely, are you humiliated?'

'You've lost me.'

Claire sighed with exaggerated patience. 'Are you humiliated because I've slept with lots of men, or because I lied to you about it when I told Matt the truth?'

Claire pulled on a fresh T-shirt.

Patrick coughed nervously.

There was some kind of test going on. There was a pass and a fail option. Or maybe two fail options – or multiple ways to fail, like one of Scarlett's mazes with a handful of dead ends and only one right trail.

Claire ran a brush through her hair, studying Patrick as she waited.

'I can't believe you'd do that to me. That you'd tell him. You and him just laughing at me about how gullible old Patrick is.'

'Alex has got a lot more to be embarrassed about than you have this morning.'

Patrick waved a hand.

'And Matt's not exactly my favourite person,' Claire fastened her hair in a band, 'what with the money thing, and the fact he shared our private conversation with Alex. So let's just write it all off as a bad night.'

'I'm a laughing stock.'

Claire pulled a ball of socks from the suitcase.

It was like any compassion she'd ever had was gone, and there was now just this stranger standing in front of him, pulling her socks on in jerky movements. Patrick hadn't known that you could put socks on dismissively. But you could.

Patrick cleared his throat. 'What else have you told Matt? What else do they know that you laugh about? My foreplay rituals? The pouch of fat in my tail area? What my sex-face looks like?'

'You come out of last night smelling of roses, Pat. You're the only one who does.'

'It's Pat-*rick*!' Patrick sprang up from the bed. 'It's fuck-ing Pat-*rick*! You know that!'

Claire grabbed her handbag. 'I don't have time for this. We have to get to Santa.'

'I can't face them.'

'Then don't come.'

'Just like that?'

'Just like that.'

'Fine, I didn't want to go to see Santa anyway. Not with you.' Patrick took a step towards Claire. 'Do you know who I want to go and see Santa with? With my own kids. But I can't. Because I'm here with you.'

Claire opened the door. 'I don't think they'd want to go and see Santa. What with them being teenagers.'

'Don't patronise me, Claire!'

'I'm going to see Santa. You sort yourself out. Go for a *run*. Then, when you've remembered how to behave like a grown up, you can join us at archery.'

'Stop saying "run" like that.'

Claire hitched her handbag onto her shoulder.

'I can't face them downstairs. With them knowing this about you. Laughing at me.'

'They've got bigger fish to fry.'

Patrick shrugged.

'You'll ruin Scarlett's Christmas. Is that what you want?'

'How is this all my fault? How is everyone else in the wrong and this is my fault?'

Claire opened the door. 'It's not all your fault, of course not.'

But, still, she went.

50

In the queue for Santa's grotto, Mum handed the twenty-pound note to the elf. She turned to Scarlett. 'How cool is this?'

The elf put Mum's money in a pocket he carried on the front of him, where a kangaroo carries its joey. He rustled in the pocket and gave Mum a pound coin back.

Mum looked at the coin. She didn't take it. 'That it?'

The elf nodded. 'Merry Christmas.'

'Merry Christmas to you too,' Mum said, sounding like she meant something else. She turned to Dad. 'Rinsed again. They see us coming.'

Dad smiled at Scarlett. 'Do you want us to come in to see Santa with you? Or do you want to go in alone?'

'Alone,' Scarlett said. 'I hardly ever do things alone.'

Dad beamed at her.

Scarlett knew she should be enjoying this morning. She was here with Mum and Dad, just the three of them, just like it used to be. And Mum and Dad weren't talking about whose turn it was to wash up, or who parked the car so badly that it got scraped on the street, or why Mum had 'had it up to here', or why Dad was 'sick of this crap', so it was much better than the old days Scarlett remembered.

But Posey had gone missing. And that made Scarlett scared. And upset. And relieved. And angry.

Had Posey taken himself away to protect Scarlett in case he hurt her, like in the vampire books Charlie the babysitter was always talking about?

Because Scarlett knew Posey was scared too. It was bad enough for her to watch the film, but he was a *rabbit*. And some of what those rabbits did . . .

Scarlett couldn't bear to think about it.

But Posey had never done anything like that, not that Scarlett could remember. Scarlett didn't think he was that kind of rabbit. The worst Posey had ever done was to be childish and refuse to go somewhere, to sit down on the floor with a bump and say 'no', because he was scared. And if Posey refused, sometimes that meant Scarlett didn't have to go to the place either. So Scarlett didn't even mind Posey's moods, a lot of the time.

Still, in another way, it was quite nice not having Posey around.

On the walk here, Mum and Dad had taken one hand each. They tried to swing Scarlett between them, like when she was a little kid.

'No chance,' Mum said, puffing like she was out of breath, trying to lift Scarlett's feet off the floor.

Scarlett gripped higher up Mum and Dad's arms, near their elbows.

'Ow!' Mum said. 'You're too big!'

'This is a proper workout. You're getting big and heavy, Scarlett,' Dad said. 'Who ate all the pies?'

Mum narrowed her eyes at Dad. 'You think that's helpful?'

She went on to say some other stuff about 'self-esteem' and 'irresponsible' that Scarlett couldn't follow because sometimes Mum used long words and talked quickly when she was angry.

But it was nice to hold both their hands, even though Scarlett was a little old for it. And it was good that she didn't have to stop, to check Posey didn't mind being left out.

Scarlett wondered if she should get used to spending more time with other people and less with Posey. She hadn't always felt brave on her own, and she felt braver when she looked after Posey. But, today – today she wasn't sure what she felt.

She didn't want Posey to go. Not like this. Not because of *Watership Down*. Because Scarlett was certain now, while standing in this queue, that Posey wasn't a *Watership Down* kind of rabbit. Posey had his faults, but they weren't hurting others, or using his teeth to kill other rabbits in fields and hedgerows.

The elf with the kangaroo pocket bent a fat finger towards Scarlett. 'Next up!'

Mum gave Scarlett a little push towards the elf.

The elf led Scarlett by the hand into Santa's grotto – to the fake Santa, who Scarlett pretended was the real Santa, for her parents.

Posey would really have liked seeing fake Santa. Scarlett wouldn't have even told him the Santa was fake.

Fake Santa beamed at Scarlett. 'Hello, little girl!'

Scarlett smiled her best excited smile back as she walked to take her seat.

51

Patrick ran and ran, past the lake, past the ice cream hut, past the crazy golf course. He ran into the woods and past the exit sign.

You are now leaving the Happy Forest Holiday Park. Thanks for coming – we'd love to see you again soon!

He had to get away from this place.

The world was conspiring against him. Take just now, when he'd gone for a run to get away from them all, running without a plan in a random direction through the forest and yet had *accidentally passed* the three of them going into Santa's grotto. *That* was the kind of luck he was having. He'd had to see Claire, Matt and Scarlett, all laughing together, like they were a family unit. Like they were all having a great old time. Like Patrick had never existed.

Patrick ran even faster after that. He couldn't stop to talk and he couldn't look at Matt's smug face. He just had to . . . not be here. He needed to run and run and run, until he forgot. Until he ran it all better.

He saw Nicola and her family walking together through

the park, her kids playing on their phones as they walked. She looked up in his direction, but Patrick didn't even falter.

Now, he needed to run.

Patrick sprinted down the single-track road he and Alex had taken towards the supermarket, barely even looking out for traffic, just focusing straight ahead, pumping his legs hard, running like there was something sharp-clawed chasing him.

He had lost her.

He'd seen the signs. The contempt in Claire's eyes. The unwillingness to talk about anything. She didn't need to talk because she'd already decided. She hadn't even read the letter: she'd treated it like an irritant, not like a carefully worded expression of love.

It was Matt: it must be. Matt had ruined everything. He wanted Claire and, inexplicably, Claire wanted him too. He'd won her back, after all, with his skateboarding and his teenage hair and his stupid singing.

And it had to be about Matt: there was nothing else. Claire couldn't just not want to be with him, not after last time. It couldn't be like Lindsay all over again. That would be too cruel.

Matt had manipulated this whole holiday situation to this end. It had never been about having a holiday with Scarlett: it had been about winning Claire back. Alex was just a distraction.

Alex had been right to be worried, all along. And Patrick hadn't been: that was the irony. Because he *trusted* Claire.

After all he'd done for her.

All that time he'd spent with Scarlett, reading all her

bedtime stories, doing his best farmyard impressions for *Hairy Maclary from Donaldson's Dairy*.

He'd put the time in. He deserved to be happy. He deserved to be respected. He'd *earned* the right to stay in this family.

Claire couldn't do this to him. She couldn't.

Patrick tripped on a loose branch; he went sprawling. 'Shit!'

He rolled onto his back and sat up, panting. He blinked liquid out of his left eye and wiped his eyebrow with the back of his hand.

Patrick blinked again but the liquid kept coming. A mix of blood and sweat, roughened with specks of gravel.

Patrick held his hand over his eyebrow, pressing the skin to stop the blood flow. He sat there, holding his eye, panting. His body temperature was dropping by the second, the cold biting his legs.

Patrick shivered.

The rain started up, a trickle at first, the drops increasing to big splatters.

He pressed his eyebrow harder now. But however much he put pressure there, the tears still pricked his eyes.

The rain came down in a deluge now.

Sitting in the middle of the lane, Patrick put his bleeding head in his hands and started to cry.

Post-shooting interview. Matt Cutler, 38. Witness.
Face-to-face. Happy Forest lodge.

Hi.

I sighed because it's been a long day. I've come back to pack our stuff, then I'm going back to the hospital. You're here about the shooting, I'm guessing?

Yeah, sorry about that. Had my phone on silent.

No, I switch the vibrate setting off. I like to look at my phone when I feel like it, not when it tells me to.

Well you've got hold of me now, so that's something. How did you know I was back?

Yes, Sheila's very helpful.

I can't tell you anything the others haven't. Alex didn't have any training, and she can be a clumsy fucker. She picked up a bow and shot him by accident. Alex and Patrick got on fine, and there's no reason she would want to shoot him. Which is, I think, what you're getting at.

Yeah, we had a couple of arguments.

They were probably embarrassed to say. Only silly ones, nothing major.

I don't remember one about crisps, but you're right, that is about our level.

Sorry, but I'm not one of life's listeners. I'm 'spectacularly vague', according to Alex.

But Scarlett wasn't even there for the archery.

You should have asked Claire if you wanted to speak to her. She's in proper charge of Scarlett, if you get what I mean. But if you must speak to her, she's at her grandparents'.

Here. Take the number off my phone. But I'm trusting you not to upset Scarlett. She likes Patrick, and this has been tough enough on her already.

52

When Alex heard everyone return from seeing Santa, she approached Scarlett tentatively, bracing herself to be rebuffed by the rabbit. The rabbit must hold a grudge from last night.

Yet neither Scarlett nor Posey protested. Scarlett shrugged her coat back on and waited by the front door, blinking at Alex with all-knowing eyes.

And when Alex set the ice cream sundaes down on the table, Scarlett actually said, 'Thank you.'

Even better, while eating, they had some direct question-and-answer conversations of the proper call-and-response format.

Alex took a spoon of her sundae, tasting the over-sweetness of the salted caramel. 'Did you have fun with Santa?'

Scarlett shrugged.

'Your dad said the man gave you some Percy Pigs.'

Scarlett scraped the side of her sundae glass with her long spoon.

Someone set off a firework on the lake. Alex jerked back dramatically, as she had to any sudden noises or motion all day. She'd forgotten what it was like to have a hangover.

Alex tried again. 'Did Santa tell you what you were getting for Christmas?'

'He wasn't the real Santa. His beard wasn't real.' Scarlett raised her gaze slowly to look at Alex. 'But he said we looked like a very happy family.'

'That's nice.'

Scarlett moved the liquid round with her spoon.

'Are you OK, Scarlett?'

'Posey's gone.'

'Oh.' Alex wasn't sure of the right reaction. 'That's a – shame?'

'It's because of you.'

'OK?' Alex kept her voice neutral.

'Because you mentioned the film *Watership Down*.'

Alex put her spoon down.

'We didn't know what it was, so we watched it last night on the iPad.'

'Oh God, no!' Alex felt the pressure in her sinuses; she held the bridge of her nose. 'I didn't mean for you to watch that. It's a horrible film.'

With her fist, Scarlett wiped some ice cream off the tablecloth. 'And Posey got scared of himself. Because he didn't know the bad things about rabbits before watching that.'

Alex had her head in her hands. 'Scarlett, I am a *terrible* stepmum. I'm so sorry.'

'But you got rid of the spider for me.'

Alex lifted her head a little. 'You're right, I got rid of the spider.'

'And you didn't kill it.'

'I didn't kill it.'

'Which proved Posey was wrong. About the scientist thing.'

'It was Posey who wasn't sure about me?'

'He was scared of you. That's why he was so mean. He was the one who suggested Mum and Dad did karaoke so they'd get back together. He was trying to protect me from you.'

Alex nodded.

'He said when you were gone, Patrick could go back to his old wife and leave me with Mum and Dad.'

'I think ... I think what Posey doesn't understand is that Patrick probably doesn't want to go back to his old wife.'

'It sounded like a good idea when Posey said it.'

Alex held Scarlett's gaze deliberately. 'Do you miss it? It just being you and your parents? It's OK to say that, you know.'

Scarlett looked down at her ice cream. It was pooling into a sludgy liquid at the bottom of the glass.

'Because you know they won't live together again,' Alex said, gently. 'Don't you? That they're happier living apart?' She watched Scarlett put a half-hearted spoonful of melted ice cream into her mouth. 'Do you understand? I'm sorry. It must be sad. For you. It must be normal though. Loads of families like that at school, I bet?'

Scarlett pushed her sundae glass away.

'What about your friends? They can't all live with both their mums and dads?'

'Erin doesn't live with her dad.'

'Is Erin a friend of yours?'

'Sometimes. When she's not being an idiot.'

Alex thought of Ruby. *Yes.* 'But Erin must have fun with her dad when she sees him.'

'He's in a prison. He robbed a post office.'

'Did he really?' Alex would have to ask Claire more about Erin's dad. 'What about your other friends?'

'Stan's dad doesn't live with them. He fights pirates.'

Alex gave a polite smile.

'Not cartoon pirates.' There was that familiar look of scorn. 'Real, modern pirates. On boats on the other side of the world.'

Alex stopped smiling. 'Oh.'

'Stan says his mum likes it when he's away with the pirates. She's more shouty when his dad's at home. Bangs doors more.'

Alex pushed her melting ice cream away. 'What can I do, Scarlett? To make it better for you?'

Scarlett shrugged again. She'd got that shrugging gene from her dad, Alex thought. The gene would be super-dominant down the paternal line.

'Don't buy me clothes any more. For presents.'

Alex laughed in surprise. 'OK.'

'Clothes aren't presents.'

'OK. Noted.' Alex remembered something. She stopped laughing. 'I—' She stopped. Would a spoiler alert make it better or worse? 'Doesn't matter.'

The two stared at each other.

'Do you want another ice cream before we walk over to archery? Or a Coke?'

'I'm not allowed Coke.'

'I won't tell anyone if you don't.'

'I don't want it. It rots your teeth.'

Alex held her hands up, palms facing Scarlett.

Scarlett pushed her sundae glass away. 'You never have good toys at your house. It's boring. Where do you keep all your toys?'

'I have lots of jigsaws. Made of sustainable cardboard.'

'Jigsaws don't count.'

'Clothes aren't presents and jigsaws aren't toys.' Alex gave a firm nod. 'This has been useful. Because I don't always know what to do, because I don't have kids of my own. Which is why I need you to help me.' She leaned further across the table, resting her elbows. 'So how about you tell me what counts as a toy, and I'll see what I can do for next time you visit.'

53

When Patrick got back to the lodge, it was like the row with Claire had never happened. But not in a good way.

Claire barely looked up as he shut the front door behind him. She was tidying the kitchen in that overeager way she did: scrubbing the surfaces down with a cloth like she was doing an important thing, using the activity to completely shut him out, but in a way that meant he couldn't complain. She must have noticed the cuts on his face, but she didn't care enough to ask.

Matt had his feet up on the sofa and was swiping at his phone with a restless finger. 'All right, Pat.' He peered at Patrick's face, clearly about to ask about the cuts, before changing his mind. 'How was your run?'

Patrick studied Matt for any significant signs of new knowledge. Claire had better not have told him. It was none of Matt's business.

But when Patrick didn't answer, Matt just looked back down and swiped at his phone again.

Patrick poured a glass of water. He drained it. 'Where are the others?'

'Alex took Scarlett for ice cream.' Claire slammed the dishwasher shut. 'They're meeting us at the archery in half an hour.'

Patrick poured another glass of water. 'I'll grab a quick shower.'

When no one responded, Patrick headed up the stairs.

She'd better – *better* – not have told Matt.

'You handle the arrow like so.'

The teenage instructor held the tension of the archer pose, holding his bow and arrow aloft as he demonstrated how to use the finger guard. His voice was too know-all for Patrick's taste – he was the kind of lad that other people liked but Patrick didn't trust. He always associated that level of confidence with a disruptive influence.

And how young this boy Alfie was. How many opportunities he still had.

Patrick nodded, not sure what he was nodding at but knowing this Alfie wouldn't move on without seeing acknowledgement. Matt and Claire did the same.

Patrick let his mind drift over the events of the morning as the instructor went through his script.

Alfie looked at his watch. 'I really should wait for the other two. But they're late. And I've got a driving lesson.'

'We're good to go. Have you got a health and safety waiver form?' Claire winked at him. 'I'll sign it, then you've done your bit. Honestly.' She gave him her full-beam lawyer's smile. 'I've done loads of shooting, I'm practically Robin Hood. I can teach the other two.'

Patrick was going to say something about rules being

there for a reason and that it was important to honour the integrity of the forms but he stopped himself. This kind of law-following anti-cool might be one of the reasons Claire was leaving him.

Uncool. Just for trying to keep them all *alive*.

Matt reached forward towards their box of equipment. Patrick picked it up and hitched it onto his hip before Matt could grab anything.

'Here,' Matt held his hand out, 'let me take some of that stuff.'

'No need.' Patrick inched the box away from Matt. 'I've got it.'

'The bows, at least. That box will be an arse to carry with bows sticking out of the top.'

'I'm fine.'

Matt shrugged. He set off walking with Claire.

Patrick followed Claire and Matt to the archery field with some difficulty, repositioning the box on his hip continuously, shifting the weight across his aching arms.

He listened as Matt and Claire chatted on about nothing. Matt had his hands thrust deep in his pockets.

Had Claire and Matt even noticed that Patrick wasn't saying anything? Did they not notice, or not care? Or both?

When they reached the field, Matt unlocked the gate and held it open for the other two.

Patrick followed Matt and Claire up to the shooting area. A row of circular, primary-coloured targets greeted them, the targets set out on stands. Lines on the ground indicated shooting positions.

Patrick half placed, half dropped the box on the grass. He stretched his arms out with difficulty, muscles throbbing with the pain of release.

'Nice to have the range to ourselves.' Matt took his wallet and keys out of his pockets and threw them onto the grass. 'Result.'

Claire looked around the field, hands on hips. 'People are scared of a bit of rain.'

Patrick looked up at the steel grey clouds around them, clouds that turned to charcoal directly overhead. A single fat drip of water hit him in the eye.

Patrick blinked, blinded for a second. He was surprised how much the drop smarted.

He waited to feel more drops of rain, but they didn't come. Just that one single spot, right in his eye.

'Have you really done this before, mate?' Matt asked. 'Or did you just say that so we didn't have to have an instructor?'

Claire crouched down at the box. 'Grew up on a farm, Matt, far from a town.' She sorted through the equipment on the box, moving bows and quivers of arrows. 'As you know. Not much to do.'

Matt kicked carelessly at a clod of earth, appearing not to care he was showering his keys and wallet with soil. 'What a waste, when you could have been using that time to chat to the Countess. You could have practised walking with a book on your head, or learnt which side of the cup to drink from.'

'Your jokes haven't changed in ten years, Matt. Leave my mum alone.'

Patrick put his hands on his hips and looked up. He

wanted to bellow into the heavens. He didn't even exist now. They were continuing their relationship right in front of him. Patrick had just been a tiny blip – a blip they couldn't even *see* any more.

Matt looked at the equipment box. 'Shall we get started, or do we wait for Scarlett and Alex?'

Claire took the bows out of the box and laid them on the grass. 'We might as well have a practice.'

She dug further into the box. 'Finger guards.'

Claire pulled out a piece of misshapen black leather. She slipped it onto her hand and wiggled her hand in front of her, studying it like she owned a new ring. 'We didn't have these on the farm. Just ripped our fingers to shreds. I probably don't have any fingerprints left.'

Claire took out a quiver of arrows. She loaded her bow and stretched her arm back. She pointed at the nearest target and held her position, arm straining.

'Go on then, Katniss,' Matt said. 'Show us what you're made of.'

Claire moved her arm an inch, training the bow on the target. 'Don't watch.'

She adjusted her aim minutely and released the arrow. The arrow flew across the field and lodged itself in the large white circle on the edge of the board with a solid *thunk*.

Claire lowered the bow. 'Out of practice.'

'You hit the board,' Matt said. 'That's better than we'll do. Right, Pat?'

Patrick picked up a bow and arrow. He stood in front of a target next to Claire's. He took an arrow from the quiver and placed it into the bow.

'There's finger guards, Patrick.'

344

She didn't get to tell him what to do any more. 'I don't need a finger guard.'

Claire rolled her eyes. Actually *rolled her eyes*. At Matt.

'Whoa, Pat.' Matt raised his hands and held his palms up towards Patrick. 'Can you point that somewhere else, please?'

Patrick looked down at his hands. It seemed he was holding the bow up in Matt's direction, like he was aiming it.

Patrick lowered the bow.

'Did you not listen to that instructor banging on about health and safety?' Claire shook her head at Patrick. 'He might have been about twelve, but he talked sense. Don't ever point the bow at a person, even if it's not loaded. Good shooting habits are important.'

Patrick wanted to argue, but he couldn't. 'Sorry.'

'Christ, Patrick.' Claire turned away and concentrated on her target. 'Scarlett will be here soon.'

Patrick turned back to his target. He stretched his arm back again and felt the strain in it, the muscles weak from carrying the box. He aimed at the target and released the arrow. The arrow bounced off the corner of the board; it twanged into the grass.

Matt laughed. 'I bet you couldn't do that again if you tried.' He picked up his own bow and arrow.

Claire took another shot at her target. This time, she hit the red inner ring.

She gave a satisfied nod. 'Getting my eye in.'

Patrick walked to his target. He picked up his fallen arrow and examined it closely. It looked OK. He reloaded the bow.

He heard Matt's voice behind him. 'Arrow OK, Pat?'

Patrick scowled.

'A bad workman always blames his tools.'

Patrick spun round to face Matt and his *fucking grin*.

'Hey.' Matt frowned. 'Stop pointing that at me!'

Patrick looked down, not understanding what Matt meant. He looked at the angle of his bow and realised he'd lifted it without noticing.

Matt must have actually thought, for a second, that Patrick might shoot him. How ridiculous this man was.

Patrick lowered his bow. 'Don't be silly.'

'Patrick, you're all het up. Calm yourself down and stop being an idiot.'

'An idiot, Claire?' He swung his bow round to face her. 'Is that what I'm being?'

'Stop pointing that at people!' Claire was shouting too. 'That thing's dangerous.'

'Since when do you care about safety? You're always telling me I'm too uptight. "Patrick, no one wears a bike helmet to go to the corner shop." "It doesn't matter that I've left the hairdryer plugged in." "We don't need coasters."' Patrick had raised his voice to a mimsy one, in an impression of a Claire. It sounded nothing like her.

'Stop pointing that *actual weapon* at people.'

'Then why are you pointing yours at me?'

Claire looked down at her bow. 'Because you're scaring me!'

Patrick turned his head towards Matt. Matt was glancing between Claire and Patrick, shifting his weight between his feet.

'She's leaving me. Did she tell you that? She probably did in a nice cosy chat this morning when you all went to see Santa. Did she tell you how she can't wait to be rid of me after this weekend? The relief she's going to feel when she finally gets me off her plate?'

Matt frowned. 'Pat, please. You're really upset. Put down the bow and arrow and let's talk.'

'An idiot!' Patrick shook his head. 'I've been everything you wanted, Claire. I've not even seen my own kids over Christmas. And this is how you repay me. By leaving me for *him*!'

Patrick swung his bow round towards Matt.

Matt dropped his bow and arrow; they clattered together onto the grass. He put his hands up. 'You've got it wrong, mate. And you wouldn't shoot me, you're not that kind of guy. You're a good guy, Pat – you're not yourself this morning. Let's get off and let me buy you a beer.'

Patrick felt the wind whip across his neck. He locked his legs in position.

Matt paused. 'But if you won't stop pointing that bow at me, I'm going to have to point mine at you.'

Matt waited. He picked up his bow and slid the arrow into place. He waited again.

Patrick didn't move, apart from the small vibration of the tension in his body.

With obvious reluctance, Matt raised his bow and arrow and pointed them at Patrick.

Patrick panted; he tried to get his breath back. He didn't lower his bow, despite the pain in his arm.

Across the field, a bird squawked. Another bird chirped in response.

The three of them stood still in the field, pointing their shaking weapons at each other, silent.

54

Alex and Scarlett wandered away from the ice cream hut in an amiable quiet. The pressure on Alex's sinuses was growing. This was either an extreme hangover or a thunderstorm was coming. Or both.

Spots of drizzle settled on Alex's eyelashes momentarily. 'We need to cross this road.' She gestured with her hand. 'Then the archery field should be coming on the right. Your mum and dad will be there already. Hopefully, they've saved some arrows for us, hey?'

A stench of manure wafted over. Scarlett wrinkled her nose.

Alex smiled in acknowledgement. 'The countryside. It's magical.'

'It smells.'

'It really does.'

The two ambled across the road towards the archery field. Over the wind's constant roar, Alex thought she heard a shout in the distance. Excitement, probably.

A sign in front of the field showed a picture of an arrow spearing the centre of a target. *Archery Arena. Guests should follow health and safety guidelines. Children should be supervised at all times. Enter at your own risk.*

The field was surrounded by a thick bramble hedge, the hedge tidy and recently cut. Still, it was taller than Scarlett.

Alex walked towards the entrance gate and looked into the field beyond. She faltered.

She saw Matt, Patrick and Claire across the field, behind a row of circular targets. The three stood in a near-equilateral triangle, bows poised, pointing arrows at each other in a woodland Mexican stand-off.

Patrick had his back to Alex. He shouted something to Claire, whirling his attention from Matt to her, yet he kept his bow trained firmly on Matt. The other two had their bows pointed at Patrick.

Alex couldn't hear the angry discussion going on, but she could see the fear on Matt's face. The redness of the skin at the back of Patrick's neck. The wobble of Patrick's bow as he gestured furiously.

Alex put her hand on Scarlett's shoulder. 'Stop a second.'

Scarlett looked up. 'What?' She gave no indication she was able to see what was going on in the field.

Alex consciously straightened her face, still staring ahead. She looked at Matt's panicked face, at the arrow pointing at him. The balance of her body was wrong now, like there wasn't enough weight in her legs to keep her upright. She couldn't really be here, now, like this. She couldn't really be seeing what she was seeing.

Matt glanced away from Patrick, towards Claire. In that second, he noticed Alex. The two made distant eye contact.

Alex reached down to pat Scarlett's hair in a gesture to Matt.

Matt widened his eyes. He jerked his bow in a sharp

movement and Alex knew what he meant. *Get her away from here.*

'Is Posey waiting for me here? Can you see?'

'No one's here.' Alex moved her hand to Scarlett's shoulder. 'The archery's been cancelled.' She kept her gaze on the figures in the field. 'Because of the rain.'

Matt looked at Alex for a moment longer, then snapped his gaze back to focus on Patrick.

'It's hardly raining at all,' Scarlett said. 'I'm not wet. And Posey might come here to find me.'

'It'll make the equipment slippery. And dangerous.' Alex heard her voice wobble. 'Come on, let's find something better to do.'

Patrick pulled his arrow arm back, raising his bow higher. In response, Matt stepped back. He gave his head a tiny shake, his gaze not leaving Patrick's face.

'It'll be dark later.' Scarlett's voice crept up to a whine.

'No arguments, missy. We'll come back tomorrow. Let's find a fun indoor activity instead, hey? You can do anything you want.'

Slowly, Alex turned to face the road. She made herself take a step away from the field, then another step.

One by one, she increased the speed of her steps, until she was striding away, Scarlett trailing behind.

Before they turned the corner out of sight, Alex took one final glance into the field.

Patrick, Claire and Matt stood there still in their triangle, bows lifted, tired arms wobbling.

Alex made herself look away. She focused her gaze straight ahead and ushered Scarlett towards the sports complex.

*

Alex strode up to the young woman behind the counter. The woman beamed at Alex, her teeth spectral-white and framed by a vibrant coral lipstick, making her mouth hyper-real.

Everything was hyper-real now. The world was showing itself to Alex with its protective sleeve removed.

'Hi.' Alex tried to regulate the pitch of her voice. 'I've got to be somewhere, and I need to leave my daughter here. Now. What activities are there for her to do?'

The receptionist looked down at her screen. 'There are places left at a dance class that's about to begin. It's a two-hour session.'

Alex pulled her purse out of her handbag. 'Great.'

The receptionist peered down at Scarlett. 'It's Intro to Burlesque.'

'Perfect.' Alex slapped a twenty-pound note onto the counter. 'Her name's Scarlett Cutler and we're in lodge 219.'

'It's aimed at pre-teens.'

'She's got strong thighs, she gives loads of piggybacks. Besides, you're never too young for burlesque.'

'Well,' the woman said, 'if we have parental permission . . .'

'You do.'

Alex crouched to face Scarlett. 'There's a dance class now. Follow the nice lady. I'll go and see what' – a lightness overwhelmed her; she put her hand to the floor to keep her balance – 'your mum and dad are up to.' She stood up. 'Is that OK, Scarlett? You'll stay here?'

The sensation of lightness in her body wouldn't go away. Alex leaned back against the reception desk.

'What kind of dancing?' Scarlett asked.

'Grown up dancing, you'll love it. Your dad will come and pick you up after, you can show him your moves.' Alex forced a smile. 'He'll be so proud.'

Scarlett didn't say anything.

Alex squeezed Scarlett's shoulder. 'Have fun.'

Alex turned towards the door. She made herself walk out of the sports centre and amble towards the archery field with determined nonchalance. She rounded the corner, speeding up as she went.

By the time she was over the road, Alex was sprinting. She tore towards the archery field, arms and legs pumping, running as fast as she could.

55

'She's with me!' Patrick knew he was sending out spittle as he shouted, but he couldn't stop. 'She wanted to be with me instead of you. I won!'

Matt blinked at Patrick, his face neutral.

Patrick knew it should have felt good to be telling Matt this. So why did Patrick feel like he wanted to cry?

Patrick tried to control the wobble of his bow. 'I won!'

Matt didn't look in Claire's direction. Instead, he kept his bow pointed at Patrick, the arrow lifted but steady. 'You won.'

'And now,' Patrick hated the wobble in his voice, 'it's like I never existed.'

'You exist, mate.' Matt's voice was quiet, a new patience in his tone. 'You definitely exist.'

Patrick raged afresh. Matt had a weapon pointed at him, and *he was tolerating Patrick.*

'Well you can't get back with Claire if I shoot you. You know what, Matt?' Patrick's tiredness made him struggle with his aim. The point of his arrow was all over the place now, dipping, swooping. His arms were aching, shaking with exertion. 'I'm going to shoot you. Right now. And I can shoot, by the way.' He turned his head towards Claire. 'See, I did have those archery lessons before I came. I had them when I said I was golfing with Joel.'

Claire stared at him for a moment.

'And Nicola Garcia came on to me last night. I dreamed of her for a decade. Yet I said no, Claire. Because of *you*. Because I love *you*.'

'Pat, calm down,' Matt said. 'Please.'

Patrick swung his gaze back round to Matt. 'My name's not fucking Pat! It's *Patrick*!'

'I was trying to be friendly. Sorry, Patrick, mate, I won't—'

'You don't deserve someone like Claire! You've never tried for anything in your life. You can't even get my name right.'

'It's Patrick. I've got it, it's Patrick. I won't forget again, so we're all good here.'

'Patrick,' Claire shouted. 'Don't fire at Matt. You'll only miss.'

Matt shot Claire a look. 'In what way was that helpful?'

Claire jerked her bow at Matt in a *hang on* gesture. She turned back to Patrick. 'And if you shoot him, then I'll shoot you. I'll shoot you so fast, your head will spin.'

'I told you, Claire, I had archery lessons. So if I shoot him, I'll hit. I did homework for this weekend.' Patrick turned back to Matt. 'You think you deserve Claire, but I bet you didn't put any homework in for this weekend. Did you? Did you do homework?'

'No,' Matt said.

'I work so hard, and yet you win. *You win.* How's that fair? Tell me how that's fair.'

'You really need to calm down, mate.' There was a crack in Matt's voice for the first time. 'You've got it all wrong, and this isn't even you. You're a good man.'

'I'm angry.'

'I can see that. Let's all just take a moment.'

That tolerance again. Infuriating. 'You're so fucking lucky. This is all the wrong way round. Yet here we are! You're so lucky.'

'I don't feel that lucky right now. Not with a madman – no offence – aiming an arrow at my face.'

'Shoot him, Matt, before he shoots you!'

'Claire, you're *really* not helping. And he's not going to shoot me. He's not that kind of guy.'

Patrick baulked. 'I bloody am that kind of guy.' He refreshed the lift of his bow.

'Shoot him, Matt!'

Matt lowered his bow, he looked at Claire. 'If you're so keen, why do I have to be the one to shoot him? You've got a bow.' Matt glanced back at Patrick. 'But no one's going to shoot anyone today, so let's all just relax.'

'I'm going to do it!' Patrick's bow shook. 'Before you try to take me down.'

'No one's going to take you down, mate. No one even wants to. You're the one who keeps banging on about shooting people.'

When Patrick didn't say anything, Matt raised his bow again slowly.

'I'm going to do it.' Patrick's arrow dipped; he lifted his bow higher. 'Right now.'

Matt shook his head in disbelief.

Patrick took aim.

An explosion of pain flared in his shoulder. He staggered backwards. *Fire! Fire!*

Across the field, Matt dropped his bow and arrow onto the grass. Patrick looked at Matt, then to the arrow, confused.

Patrick realised he was lying down. He was on the carpet, looking upwards.

No. 'Carpet' wasn't the word for this stuff. 'Grass'. 'Grass' was it.

He honestly had no idea was going on here.

'Claire, what have you done?' Matt's voice was barely audible over the siren noise in Patrick's head. 'He wouldn't have shot me, no way!'

Patrick looked down at his chest. He saw the wood thing sticking out of *him*, the redness blooming through his coat. The redness coming from inside *him*.

Oh, Christ.

'He was going to shoot.' Claire's voice was high-pitched in panic. 'I saved your life.'

'Fucking hell, Claire! I *told you* he wasn't going to shoot me.'

Patrick lifted his head an inch. 'To be fair,' his tongue felt like it overfilled his mouth, 'I was.'

He laid his head back down. Was he dying, was that why he said it? Was this how it felt, the need to set the record straight?

It was because he was a fair man, Patrick realised. A fair man.

'You weren't going to shoot me,' Matt said fervently. 'You never would have done.'

'I was.' Patrick licked his lips. 'And I would have got the shot bang on.'

'Oh, God.' Claire dropped her bow on the grass. 'What have I done? Is he all right?'

Patrick tried to generate wetness in his mouth so he could speak. 'I see stars, tunnels, everything.'

Claire knelt next to him. She held his hand.

'White lights, celestial choir, the lot.'

The siren roared continuously in Patrick's head. He felt a heaving pain in his shoulder and upper chest, an emptiness in his stomach and legs. He may not be seeing lights and choirs but he knew, with certainty, he was dying.

Patrick looked at the concern in Claire's eyes. 'You're not going to get together with him, are you, Claire? After I'm gone?'

Claire gave a firm shake of the head. 'No. And you're not going to die.'

'You've got it all wrong.' Matt knelt next to Patrick. 'I'm all about Alex, mate.'

'But you were going to leave me?' Patrick's voice was higher now, desperate. 'Claire? Weren't you? I wasn't wrong?'

Claire looked at Matt.

'He wants to know,' Matt said. 'He really wants to know.'

'Was I right?' Patrick's voice was pleading. 'I know I was right. I have to have been right. Or—'

'You're not dying.' Claire stared at Patrick, unblinking. 'But you're right. I was going to leave you.'

'Thank you!' Patrick said decisively.

Claire gave a slow nod. 'But not for Matt. That's so ridiculous.'

Patrick let his head rest down on the wet, cold grass.

It hit him that he was dying young, in his physical prime.

He pictured the throngs of people at his funeral. The flowers. The tears. His kids' tears. Their realisation they hadn't appreciated him enough when he was alive.

They'd immortalise Patrick. And this kind of thing would mess Lindsay up for a long time.

Patrick wondered if Nicola Garcia would go to the funeral.

He closed his eyes, and decided she probably would.

56

Alex reached the gate at the entrance to the archery field.

Over the hedge, she saw Matt and Claire kneeling on the grass next to the lying-down Patrick. Both were talking to him, over each other.

Patrick looked wonky. Broken. There was something sticking out of his shoulder, pointing at the sky.

Alex put her hands to her mouth. 'What have you done?'

Matt looked up and made eye contact with Alex. Claire jerked her head up.

Alex ran across the field, stumbling on clods of earth as she ran. 'Patrick! Are you OK?'

Matt took his coat off. He pressed it around the arrow wound. 'He's unconscious. Shock, probably, not blood loss. He's not dead.'

Alex knelt down and looked at Patrick. He looked peaceful. 'He looks dead.'

'He's dead,' Claire cried.

'Claire,' Matt's voice was patient, 'he's definitely not dead.'

'We should phone the police,' Alex said. 'The ambulance.'

Claire leapt up. 'And say what?'

The three looked at each other.

'Who did it?' Alex heard her voice getting higher.

Alex stared at Claire and Matt. Neither said anything.

'This isn't school, you know. Tell me.'

Still neither answered.

Alex took her phone out of her pocket. She pressed 999 and put the phone to her ear. She turned away from the others.

'He's been shot.' Alex's voice caught. 'Please help. We need an ambulance at the Happy Forest Holiday Park. Please hurry. We're in the archery field near Santa's grotto.'

After a minute's conversation with the operator, Alex put the phone on mute. She dropped it into the grass and turned back to Matt. 'They're fifteen minutes away. I stayed on the line with the phone on mute, so they can't call back.'

'We need to *think*,' Matt said. 'What to say.'

'Say the truth. Which one of you shot him?'

'Does it matter?' Matt's voice was shaky. 'And I know it sounds strange, but he's happier now. Really, Al. He was smiling.'

Claire nodded. 'He looked happier than I've seen him in ages.'

'He'll be fine when he wakes up,' Matt said.

Alex blinked at Matt. 'Matt, you can't spin this. You can't hide. This is *real life*. Who shot him?'

Claire and Matt looked at each other.

Matt turned to Alex. 'The thing is, we're both culpable, Al. We were both here.'

'That means it was Claire.' Alex turned to Claire. 'You're going to prison, Claire, I'm sorry. It can't be helped.'

'Shit,' Matt muttered. 'Sorry, mate.'

'We'll have to tell the police the truth,' Alex said. 'Patrick will tell the truth anyway, when he wakes up.'

'Claire didn't want to shoot him,' Matt said. 'She was protecting me. And Patrick might not grass her up. He'll know when he wakes up this was his fault. He admitted it. Practically.'

'I shot him.' Claire sank onto her knees on the grass. '*Shot him.* Oh, God. Who am I?'

Matt put his hand onto Claire's shoulder. 'Don't think about it now. We have to be practical.'

'He could *die*. He has *kids*.' Claire put her head in her hands. 'OK, they hate him, but still.'

'We don't have time for that now.' Matt's voice had taken on a parental sternness Alex didn't recognise. 'It happened, and he won't die. Pull yourself together.'

'I shot him.'

'That's not the story,' Matt said firmly. 'We need a new story.'

Alex raised her voice. 'The story is that *Claire shot him*!'

'That isn't what we're going to tell them. Claire might go to prison. Can you think what that would do to her? To *Scarlett*.' Matt turned to Claire. 'Sorry. I care about you too, obviously.'

Claire gave a wave of the hand.

'She won't go to prison if Patrick says it was an accident,' Alex said.

All three of them looked towards Patrick, to the contented half-smile on his face. He could have looked asleep, if it wasn't for the arrow sticking out of his shoulder, the redness blooming across his blanket-coat.

'I reckon Pat'll go along with it,' Matt said. 'Once he's calmed down.'

'If he tells the police it was deliberate, they won't believe me that it was an accident.' Claire kicked a clod of earth with her boot. 'They could get evidence to say he was pissing me off. I'd told my friends I was thinking of ending it even before this holiday. If you cover for me, you may get in trouble too. What if we all go to prison? Who'll look after Scarlett?'

Matt looked around. 'Where is she, anyway?'

'She's learning to pole dance.'

Matt snapped round to face Alex. 'What?'

'She'll be fine for an hour, it won't kill her.' Alex turned to Claire. 'Why did you shoot Patrick?'

'He was going to shoot Matt. He said so. Patrick knew I was going to leave him.' Claire shoved her hands in her pockets. 'He was furious. And he thought I was going to leave him for Matt, which is so ridiculous. I don't want Matt. No offence.'

Claire gave an apology head-tilt to Alex. As an afterthought, she gave another one to Matt.

'No offence taken,' Alex said.

'*A little bit* taken,' Matt said. 'If I'm allowed to have a view on this.'

'Sorry,' Claire said.

'We'll say I did it,' Matt said. 'An accident. It's less fishy if it's me. Claire knows how to shoot but I don't. And we just hope Patrick goes along with it when he wakes up. Which he will, I reckon. As long as he knows I'm not back with Claire.'

'But if we said it was you, they still might think you did

it on purpose,' Claire said. 'That you were jealous. And the barman might remember your argument at the pub. When you called Patrick a bellend.'

Alex looked at Matt. 'When was that?'

Matt shook his head. 'Can't be helped.'

'No,' Alex said. 'Claire's right. They'll say she's protecting you. As Scarlett's father.'

'Then what?' Matt said. 'What can we say?'

Alex knelt down by Patrick. 'That I was here.' Alex looked into Patrick's face. He did look remarkably peaceful. 'And I did it. Patrick was showing me how to shoot – he'd had a lesson, hadn't he? I've never held a bow before and I didn't attend the training. I can't be held responsible.'

Alex took a deep breath. She grabbed Claire's bow and touched it in several different places. She leaned over Patrick and touched the arrow pointing out of his shoulder. She circled the arrow with a hard fist.

Alex let go. She stood back and studied Patrick. She turned round to face Claire. 'What angle did you shoot him at? You and Matt show me how you were standing.'

Claire and Matt looked at each other. They took up their positions, Claire with an imaginary bow and arrow. Though there was no weight to lift, her arms shook.

'Is that right?' Alex asked.

'Right,' Claire said, her voice clipped.

'Right,' Matt said quietly.

'OK.'

Alex looked away, round the field. At the grass. At the hedges. At the normality. She shivered.

'What if Patrick doesn't back us up?' Matt said.

'Then it's our word against his,' Claire said.

They all stood in silence.

'Al.' Matt looked towards the lane. 'You took Scarlett to dance class before you came here. Everything happened the same. Except we were getting on well all weekend.' He looked at Claire. 'There was no tension. But everything else was exactly the same.'

'Right,' Claire said.

'Right,' Alex said, into the wind, which carried the sound of sirens.

Post-shooting interview. Scarlett Cutler, 7.
Telephone.

Dad said you might ring. Are you a detective?

*Of course I know about it. They're trying to protect me
because I'm a kid. But I know everything. I know how
Patrick got hurt. Alex shot him with a bow and arrow.*

*Sophia next door told me. Don't tell Mum, I don't want to
get Sophia in trouble. Is Alex in trouble? She only ever hurts
things by accident.*

Because I know everyone she's killed.

*One pheasant, two frogs, loads of snails and wasps.
But she takes spiders out of the house in her hands. I used
to think she wasn't a nice person, but that's because my
friend didn't like her.*

I don't want to talk about him now.

Yes, he was with us at the Happy Forest.

I said, I don't want to talk about him now.

*The adults didn't argue much. Though Dad did call
Patrick a bellend – which means a contemptible man
and the glans of the penis. But they were fine after that
and we all played pool. And there was that argument
after the karaoke, but that was Posey's fault. He started
it.*

Posey. My friend.

I don't know where he is. We've had an argument.

*It's Rabbit. He doesn't have a middle name. My middle
name is Chloe. Without any dots on the E, because*

Dad said he couldn't be bothered finding the dots on a keyboard.

No, an actual rabbit. He's purple and a hundred and forty centimetres tall, if you don't count his ears. He has a red tag on his bum that says Made in China.

OK. Goodbye.

If you do find Posey, tell him Scarlett said hi.

‖‖

Extract from the Happy Forest brochure:
After a few days in our peaceful woodland, you'll be truly relaxed.

We know that, once you've visited, you'll be keen to return, so please see our friendly reception team to discuss special discounts. We'd love to see you again!

The Happy Forest. Once experienced, never forgotten.

‖‖

57

Monday 25 December
Christmas Day

Day 5

The nurse stood back from the bed, appraising her expert repositioning of Patrick on his newly fluffed pillows.

Patrick rested back into the bed. He pulled on the shirt of his pyjamas, trying to dislodge the sharp packing creases. Claire had bought these pyjamas from the twenty-four-hour supermarket and they were creased and garish and too short at the ankle. But they'd do.

He pulled the neck of his pyjamas back and looked at the tube going into his chest.

'Can I get you anything else?'

'No thanks.' Patrick looked from the tube to the nurse and smiled. He found her briskness reassuring.

Patrick looked around the room. At the vases of orchids and peonies and the cards on the sideboard. At the box of single malt sent by his chambers.

How they had managed to get flowers and bottles sent on Christmas Day was beyond him. But they'd managed it anyway – at great expense, he was pleased to imagine.

The nurse followed his gaze. 'You must be a popular man.'

Patrick gave a generous smile. 'Thanks for everything you've done.' He pointed to a card on the sideboard, the card showing a picture of a bear with an injured paw. 'Could you pass me that before you leave?'

The nurse passed him the card and left the room.

Patrick sat with the card in his lap. He smoothed his thumb over the picture on the front.

He should be devastated about his shoulder. He knew that.

When Dr Uba came into the room after the operation, Patrick had indicated the tube in his chest. 'What's this for?'

'It's a chest drain,' Dr Uba said. 'You have a small pneumothorax – punctured lung – which we will continue to monitor.'

'A *small* punctured lung,' Patrick said.

'We'll arrange another X-ray for a couple of weeks' time. I need to tell you to expect restricted movement in the shoulder joint.'

'But I'm an athlete,' Patrick said dully.

Dr Uba said nothing.

'What about swimming?'

'Swimming will help recovery, at the right time.'

'I mean, I'm a competitive swimmer. I'm doing an Ironman in a few months.'

The doctor shook his head. 'I don't think you will be. I'm sorry. And I should tell you – the police have been trying to speak to you. I expect they'll be in shortly.'

Patrick found himself looking round at the flowers. The phone rang on the trolley next to him. He picked up the receiver.

'Dad?'

'Hi, Amber.' Patrick relaxed further into his now-wilting pillows.

'How's the shoulder?'

Patrick automatically turned to look at it, he felt a twinge of pain. He moved his head carefully till he was facing forward. 'It's not too bad.'

'I've convinced Mum to drive us up to see you after lunch. I've booked a hotel on her credit card. We've had a screaming row about it, but I deliberately got the room non-refundable. I told her, you're my dad and it's not fair, her keeping us from you when you're on your deathbed.'

Patrick grinned.

'Not that you're on your deathbed.'

'I know what you meant. How's your day going?'

'Day?'

'Your Christmas Day? Any nice presents?'

'Dad, how can I be thinking about that when you've been shot? I haven't opened any presents. I can't think of that stuff now.'

'Maybe you can bring them up here, then. Open them with me.'

'But I haven't got you anything, Dad.' Amber's voice was small. 'I didn't know what to get.'

'You're coming to see me, despite what your mother wants. And that's all the present I need.'

'I'm so sorry, Dad.'

'What for?'

He heard a little snuffle down the phone.

'Darling. It's fine. And I can't wait to see you later.'

After Patrick put the phone down, he looked down at the card in his hand. He opened the card and reread it.

> *I'm sorry, Patrick. I had no choice.*
> *Please don't speak to anyone about the accident till you've spoken to me. We've told everyone something very specific. It's complicated. But anything I did, I did for Scarlett.*
> *I'm sorry about your shoulder. And I'm definitely not getting back with Matt. I promise.*
> *I want the best for you in the future. I'm still very fond of you.*
> *Get well soon, and I'll be outside when you wake up.*
> *C x*

Patrick closed the card. He ran his thumb over the card's picture, the bear with the injured paw.

He closed his eyes and leaned further back into the pillows.

Post-shooting discussion. Sai Indra, 32. Detective Con-
   stable, North Yorkshire Police.
Face-to-face. Police station.

Morning, boss. I'm not sure sleeping on it helped.

   The whole set-up, for one. A holiday with ex-partners? And someone ends up shot?

   I was pretty cynical, even before I started this job. But, I admit, it doesn't help.

   You playing devil's advocate? I'm game.

   Firstly, Alex Mount lied about the arguments. They all lied. They want us to think they got on like a house on fire. And why would they do that if there was nothing to hide? Same with the drinking. Why cover that up unless they wanted us not to know something?

   They're all in on it, clearly.

   You're right – not all of them. I don't think Scarlett knows anything, though she's not exactly a reliable witness, what with the five-foot purple rabbits. And I don't think the Trevor family are in on it either.

   But if there's nothing to hide, why would Alex pretend to be Scarlett's mum to the receptionist? And why would they do archery without the child, when she was the whole reason they were there?

   Don't even get me started on the burlesque class. I agree with the friend – Ruby. There's no way Alex Mount would have taken a child to a burlesque class.

   I don't know what I mean, that's the problem.

Next point. Why would a sensible man stand in front of an archery target? And why would a sensible woman point a bow and arrow at him?

I think we have to assume they're sensible. A barrister and a research scientist, no criminal records, qualifications coming out of their ears. And what about the phone going silent after Alex Mount knew the ambulance was on its way?

I know it can happen, that your ear puts your phone on mute. But when you add it all up, there are far too many accidents here. I'd put money on Alex doing it deliberately because she didn't want to answer any more questions from the operator.

I know it doesn't sound like much.

OK, the cuts on his face? No one has explained that.

I know, I know. Another accident. It's going to be hard justifying we have any case at all, unless Patrick Asher says something to contradict them.

I'm ready to go to the hospital when you are.

58

Scarlett sat cross-legged on the rug in front of the telly in Grandma's lounge. She stared at the iPad that she'd propped against a chair leg.

She looked at the clock on the wall. Nearly seven minutes past eleven.

She stared back at the iPad's blank screen.

In her armchair, Grandma blew on her mug of tea. 'It'll be your father's fault they're running late.'

Scarlett took a peek at the pile of presents next to her. Looking at them gave her that itchy, squirmy feeling she got when she needed the loo badly.

She looked back at the screen. She'd memorised the presents by now anyway.

Grandma took a sip of tea. 'A watched pot never boils.'

Scarlett ignored her.

She knew that, next to her, there was one big box wrapped in paper covered in silver stars. There was one smaller box in reindeer paper. Next to these was one smaller present, squishy and flat, in grown up paper that looked like it was made out of paper bags.

Finally, the iPad lit up. Scarlett pressed the button to

answer even before the ringing started.

Mum and Dad's faces appeared on the screen. The white walls and posters behind them – *Do You Need a Flu Jab?* – showed they were still in the hospital canteen.

Scarlett waved.

'Merry Christmas!' Dad said.

'You don't have to say that every time we speak today.'

'I do, because it's a celebration.' Dad rubbed his hands. 'You ready to get fired in?'

Scarlett nodded. She slid the present with the silver star paper in front of the screen. She looked up in a question.

Mum nodded at her. 'Go for it. This one's from me and your dad.'

Scarlett pulled the paper off the present.

She sat completely still. She couldn't speak, just stared at the box.

Here it was, in real life. Like magic. Bryan the Lion's Jungle Palace.

'It's got the rope-vine working lifts and the mane hair salon and everything,' Dad said.

'But you said it was too expensive for Santa!'

Mum winked. 'What can I say? I got it wrong.'

'I think Santa came into money. He hit it big on the horses,' Dad said. 'Now, open the next one before we get kicked out for using a phone in hospital.'

Mum shot Dad a look. 'There is no way I'm missing this. Just *let them* try to make us to switch this off. Bring it on.'

Scarlett didn't want Mum to forget what they were here for, so she deliberately made lots of crinkling sounds as she pulled the squishy brown present towards the screen.

Dad tugged at an arm next to him – an arm Scarlett

hadn't noticed before. 'That present's from Alex.'

The arm became a body too, and Alex's face loomed onto the screen. She gave a shy wave.

Scarlett looked back at the present, suspicious now.

She moved the present between her hands, weighing it, feeling the squishiness of what was inside.

She didn't open the present. Instead, she looked back at Alex.

Alex's smile wobbled.

'Really?' Scarlett said.

Alex sighed. 'In my defence, can you remember we didn't actually have that conversation till yesterday? That I'd already bought your present?'

Scarlett shook her head to show disappointment.

Alex paused. 'Why don't you just leave it there, wrapped up, and I'll take it back and get something else.'

Scarlett sat straighter at that. 'Will you get the Bryan the Lion's Jungle Palace extension kit, so he's got somewhere to park his trailer?'

'That's not fair on Alex,' Mum said quickly. 'It's too expensive.'

Alex touched Mum's arm. 'Every lion needs somewhere to park his trailer.'

'Too soft,' Claire said. 'And you don't understand how the next conversation goes. Because Scarlett hasn't even *got* the lion's trailer.'

'Thanks, Alex,' Scarlett said simply.

Alex reversed out of shot again. 'You're welcome.'

Scarlett pushed the brown present away. She pulled the box with the reindeer wrapping closer. 'Who's this one from?'

'This one's from me and your dad too,' Mum said. 'Now hurry up and open it, because Patrick's allowed visitors in five minutes.'

Scarlett ripped the paper off the reindeer present.

She looked at the box and gave a gasp of surprise.

59

There was a knock at Patrick's door. 'Come in,' Patrick said.

Claire entered the room and pointed at the bed in a wordless question. Patrick gave a teenage shrug of *whatever*.

Claire sat on the bed, twisting to face him. 'I see they've brought you Christmas cake.'

Patrick looked at the plate of cake on the tray in front of him. He shrugged again.

'How are you?' Claire's voice was gentle.

'I've been shot in the shoulder. I have a punctured lung.'

'How does it feel?'

'Like I've been shot.'

'Right. Does that mean you want me to go away?'

Patrick said nothing.

'I just thought it would be good if we had a conversation. About us.'

'I thought we split up yesterday.'

'We didn't split up yesterday. We had a ... bit of a chat, but Alex and Matt were there, and there were ... other things going on. We didn't finish the conversation.'

'Nevertheless, I'd rather we didn't. Let's just leave it as it was.'

Claire put her hand on his leg. 'We have to talk about it.'

Patrick lifted her hand from his leg and placed it back on the bed. 'We don't, actually. As long as we're both clear, we don't have to say another word about it. That's what I'd prefer, and I'd like you to respect my wishes on this particular occasion, thank you.'

'But you understand I don't want to be together any more?'

'Of course. So – please, Claire – give an injured man a break after you shot him.'

Claire glanced at the door. 'I could go to prison, you know. If you said that to the police.'

'It was my fault you shot me. I'll tell them that when they ask me. They're coming here soon, apparently.'

Claire widened her eyes. 'Please don't say that.'

'I'll ask them if I can take your punishment. I'll protect you, despite everything.'

'I don't think that would work, so please can you just stick with the story.'

'I'm an honest man, Claire. I'm not a man to tell lies to the police.'

Claire glanced at the door again. 'It's Scarlett who will lose out if I go to prison or I get struck off. She loves you, you know. You can still see her, whatever's happened with the two of us. Even if you hate me.'

'*If* I lie to the police.'

'Either way. But, Patrick – please go with the Alex story. Everyone else will suffer if you don't.'

'However ashamed I am of my actions, I still have my integrity. It's all I have left now.'

Claire pushed herself up from the bed. 'It's not all you

have left! Don't be so melodramatic. You have *everything*.' Claire paced around the tiny room. 'Your kids have had a wake-up call, and you'll see more of them now, I know it. You've split up with a woman who doesn't love you enough and you're moving on to a better chapter in your life. Things are OK.'

Patrick looked down at his hands. *Things are OK.*

Could they be? Wasn't this the most humiliating thing that had ever happened to him? Claire leaving him like this? Patrick going – well, *angry*, and rampaging around with a bow and arrow? Being *shot*? No longer being able to do an Ironman?

It was the worst thing that could have happened.

And yet ... the sky hadn't crashed in.

And yet ... Claire was looking at him with more fondness in her eyes than she had in a long time.

'Just do me a favour, Patrick.'

Patrick was about to say he didn't feel like doing her a favour. He looked at the softness in Claire's eyes and stopped himself.

Claire sat down on the bed again. 'With the next woman you're with. Be the best man you can be, you know?' She took both Patrick's hands in hers. 'Don't twist yourself into someone you're not because you're worried things might go wrong.' Claire tried to catch his eye but Patrick looked deliberately away. 'Maybe, with the next one, just assume everything will go all right? That you're good enough?'

Patrick looked firmly at the drip next to him. 'You think there'll be a next one?'

'*Of course* there'll be a next one. You're handsome, clever and kind. But you and me don't fit together. I wasn't my

383

best self around you either. I made fun of your quirks, and lied to you about things I'm not even ashamed of, just for an easy life. That's not right. That was a warning sign that things were out of sync.'

Patrick looked down at his feet.

Claire squeezed his hand. 'What are you thinking? Do you hate me?'

Patrick didn't know. He had thoughts going round in his head, but none of them landed for quite long enough to process before another one came.

He had to say something.

'How many men *have* you slept with? Just out of interest?'

'Quite a few. A hundred maybe? I had some fun in my early twenties.' Claire laughed, then looked serious. 'You don't have to rush to move out. I don't want you thinking there's a chance we'll get back together, but if you can deal with it, and as long as Scarlett doesn't get distressed or confused, you can have our spare room as long as you want.'

'We'd have to move the clothes horse. And the exercise bike.'

'Yes. Yes, we would.'

'And your bank statements and tax records.'

'OK.'

'It couldn't be the ironing room any more. That wouldn't work for me.'

'Whatever you want. Just think about it. It's a relief that we're over—'

'A relief!'

'Because this has been coming for a while. But I don't hate you, that's what I'm trying to say. Even if I'm saying it badly.'

Patrick smoothed the bedding over his legs. 'What about you, Claire? Will there be a next one for you?'

Claire sighed. 'I don't want anyone right now. Maybe it'll be just me and Scarlett. She's already got good men in her life, with you and Matt. She doesn't need any more. And I'm not sure I need any more.'

'Not even to have sex with?'

Claire shrugged. 'You don't need to be in a relationship for that.'

Patrick wrinkled his nose. 'You do though.'

Claire smiled.

Patrick thought. It would be nice to have a partner who hadn't slept with a hundred men. Or roll her eyes at him. It would be nice to have a partner who needed him. Who maybe looked up to him a little?

And it would be nice to have a partner who hadn't actually *shot* him.

He had been trying so hard to keep Claire lately. And that didn't feel good. To feel like every conversation had to go perfectly, or someone else had the power to take everything away. Of course it had made him a bit . . . intense.

Maybe Claire was right. He wasn't going to tell her this, of course.

'You OK?' Claire asked.

Despite his intentions, Patrick found himself nodding.

60

In a chair outside Patrick's room, Alex looked at her watch. Next to her, Matt jiggled his feet on the floor, lifting his heels and setting them back down. Alex put a hand on his knee to stop him.

'Sorry. Excess energy.'

Alex took a deep breath. She'd driven back up to the hospital that morning and it was like she'd never been away: the smell of chemical cleaner hooked firmly into her nostrils, her backside moulded itself instantly back into the hard chair.

Matt's knees started jiggling again. Alex put her hand down to stop them.

Matt grinned sheepishly. 'Nervous. I wonder how it's going in there.'

'Claire's only been in there for a minute. They won't have got past "hello".'

A minute later, Alex turned to Matt. 'What do you think they're saying now?'

They strained to hear. The voices in the room sounded controlled and pleasant.

'I can't hear shouting or anything.'

'She's still leaving him, isn't she?' Alex asked Matt.

'Of course.'

'I thought he'd be shoutier.'

They listened some more.

'Maybe he's had some kind of stroke,' Matt said.

'What time did you tell your ex-in-laws we'd pick up Scarlett?'

'I said "afternoon". The good thing is their expectations of me are so low, they'd never expect me to be specific. There are advantages to people thinking you're shit.'

'Are they OK with having her?'

'Apart from being confused about why Scarlett keeps high-kicking and gyrating against chairs, they're fine.' Matt reached into his pocket and pulled out an envelope. 'Anyway. I've been waiting to give you this all weekend. Happy Christmas.'

'Your presents are back home.' Alex looked at the envelope. 'I didn't think you'd got me anything.'

'What a stupid thing to think.' But Matt's voice was gentle.

Alex took the envelope and eased the flap open. Self-conscious under Matt's gaze, she pulled out the piece of card from the envelope. It was a flyer for a boutique hotel in the Cotswolds.

'I've booked us in for a weekend in two weeks' time. I thought after this trip, you might want some proper time away to relax.'

Alex looked at the flyer. She eased her thumb over the stone walls of the cottage in the picture. 'When did you book it?'

'Four weeks ago. Right after you agreed to come here.'

Matt scratched at his chin, making his shaving rash worse. 'The bar has thirty-five different types of vodka, apparently. Now you're drinking again.'

'I'm not drinking again.'

'Thank fuck for that. Great, *great* decision.'

Alex gave a small smile.

Matt made his face deliberately blank. 'Of course, I wouldn't want us to go on holiday just the two of us, now I know how successful these big trips can be. So I've invited some other people. Your parents. Both my parents, despite the divorce. Our bosses.'

'Lovely.'

'That simpering newsreader whose voice gives you the creeps.'

Alex put the flyer back in the envelope and closed the flap. She kissed Matt softly on the cheek.

Nicola Trevor rounded the corner, her two girls trailing behind.

'Once we've done this,' Nicola said to the girls, 'we can have the chocolate fountain as a treat. If you're good.'

Nicola noticed Matt and Alex; she stopped. 'Hi there.'

Matt grinned at her. 'Happy Christmas.'

'Nicola.' Alex looked at the floor. 'I should apologise. Last time we saw each other ...'

'Don't worry about it,' Nicola said.

'I don't drink any more, you see,' Alex mumbled into the floor.

When Alex made herself look up again, Nicola gave her a smile. She looked from Alex to Matt. 'How's he doing?'

'He's OK,' Matt said. 'He's made of strong stuff, he's been a bit of an all-round hero.'

Nicola nodded.

'And it's so sad for him.' There was a naive look on Matt's face that Alex recognised. 'He was due to do an Ironman this year. He's practically superhuman, he can run like the wind and lift a truck. He's like Speedy Gonzales and Geoff Capes, rolled into one. But now he can't because of his shoulder.'

'An Ironman?' Nicola shook her head. 'Wow. He's driven, isn't he?'

Matt grinned at Nicola. 'He is.'

Alex squeezed his hand.

Down the corridor, Claire opened the door to Patrick's room. 'You can come in now.'

Claire glanced at Nicola, she gave a wide smile. 'Lovely to see you. He'll be pleased.' She turned to Matt. 'It's all fine.' She looked at Alex. 'We're good.'

'Really?' Alex said.

'Surprisingly, really.'

Alex looked at Matt. 'There's too many people. I'll wait out here.' She squeezed Matt's hand. 'But I'll be here when you get out.'

61

Matt crashed onto Patrick's bed with his usual force. 'How are you, Ironman?'

'I'm not going to be an Ironman now.'

Patrick noticed Matt's gaze flicked round the room. He usually made clear eye contact, but not with Patrick, not today. 'You'll always be an Ironman to me.'

Patrick peered closer to see whether Matt was joking, but his face was expressionless. There was no hint of humour in his eyes.

That gave Patrick the confidence to ask, 'I was wondering, Matt. Do you know if they've still got the arrow? Could you go back and ask?'

'The arrow?'

Patrick tapped his bandaged shoulder. '*My* arrow. It's a big deal to get shot.'

'It is,' Matt said. 'I'll ask, but I'm guessing the police have it.'

'I just think it might look good in a case on the mantelpiece. Of wherever I end up living.' He held Matt's gaze. 'Claire and I have split up.'

Matt nodded softly. 'Unlucky, mate.'

'Yeah, well,' Patrick said.

'She can be annoying though,' Matt added. 'So – swings and roundabouts.'

'Shall I leave?' Claire asked.

Patrick picked a grape from his side table and popped it casually in his mouth. 'Matt and I are finished with that topic now.'

'Yep, we're all done. Old news.' Matt took a grape too. 'I just hope you'll still hang out with Scarlett,' he said. 'She needs you to teach her all the stuff I don't know.'

Patrick considered this. 'She definitely does.'

A shadow fell across the doorway. 'Knock, knock.'

Nicola stood tentatively in the doorway, wearing her farmer's wife cardigan.

Patrick hauled himself upright and pulled his pyjama top straighter.

Nicola pushed a piece of hair out of her eyes. 'Are you receiving visitors? I can come back another time.'

'Of course. Thank you for coming.'

Nicola looked down at her hands. 'I wanted to bring something but – Christmas Day. Everywhere's shut.'

Matt tutted. 'No effort at all, Nicola. You could have got him firelighters from the garage.'

Nicola nodded. 'I could have, you're right. Sorry, Patrick.' She looked round the room. 'So many flowers in here! How did they get delivered at Christmas? You must mean a lot to people.'

Patrick controlled his smile as best he could. 'I'm lucky.'

Did he actually mean that? he wondered.

He thought he actually might. After all – he was a *survivor* now.

Nicola looked behind her, to the empty doorway. 'Kids,' she shouted. 'You coming in?'

Two girls peeked into the room and disappeared again.

Nicola turned back to Patrick. 'Matt told me you were going to do an Ironman. I bet you would have been brilliant. I'm so sorry.'

Patrick gave a brave smile. '"Life is what happens when you're making other plans." Was that John Lennon?'

'Are you going to sue the holiday park?' Nicola asked.

'We can't sue. Claire signed the waiver illegally.'

Claire was about to say something, but Patrick smiled to show he joking.

Claire stood up. 'I'm going to get a coffee. Coming, Matt?'

Matt stood up. 'Any orders from in here?'

'You could see if they've got any protein shakes?' Patrick asked. 'I feel a bit weak.'

Matt grinned. 'I'll see if they've got any spinach, like Popeye.'

Matt and Claire left the room.

'May I?' Nicola perched gently on the bed. Patrick felt the mattress compress as he rolled slightly towards her.

'I spotted you.' Patrick stared firmly at the bed. 'When we got to the holiday park. I wanted to get a chance to say hello and I didn't get one. I made a really quick – bad – decision.'

'I know.'

'I realised right after that it seemed a bit – stalky. That was never the intention. I'm quite a gentleman normally.'

'I'm pleased you asked for the lodge next door.'

Patrick dared to raise his gaze from the bed. Nicola was smiling at him.

'Claire and I have split up, you know. It's been on the cards for a while.'

Nicola gave a small nod. 'Matt told me.'

'Did he?'

'Yesterday. When he came to pick up Scarlett from the dance class. He wasn't gossiping.'

'It sounds like he was gossiping.'

'He wasn't.'

'I'm pleased I don't have to deal with that man any more.'

'He's not a bad guy.'

'No,' Patrick admitted. 'He isn't.' He looked to the doorway. 'Are your girls coming in? I'd like to meet them properly.'

'You sure?'

'Invite them in then. The more the merrier.'

Nicola stood up and strode to the door. 'Girls,' she shouted.

After a moment the girls appeared. Nicola ushered them inside.

Patrick smiled at them. 'Sophia and Emily, isn't it?'

Nicola flashed a beam at him.

Emily gave Patrick a shy look. Sophia stared at him with clear and open hostility.

Patrick met Sophia's gaze and raised an eyebrow. She glared.

Patrick smiled at her again.

Kids were kids, he supposed. But that was OK.

'Shall I take your phone number?' Patrick turned back to Nicola. 'So we can catch up – as old friends – sometime in Nottingham? Talk about old times?'

'I'd like that,' Nicola said.

Patrick beamed at her. It was too soon to be considering dating someone else, he knew that. And he didn't really want to be starting anything from Claire's spare room, with the tax records and exercise bike there or not. But he liked this woman. He'd take *a thousand* arrows for this woman.

'I'm so sorry about your shoulder,' Nicola said.

'Yeah.' Patrick licked his lips. 'Well.'

'You'll still be able to run though. So maybe you could do marathons instead of the Ironman? But, like – *loads* of marathons.'

'Yeah.' Patrick thought about this. 'Yeah. Maybe I will.'

Scarlett sat on the wall in the back garden at her grandparents' house.

This bit wasn't really a back garden – Scarlett could see milking machines in the yard – but she wasn't sure where the garden ended and the farm began. Patrick had once said about the farm that it was 'no place for children' – but really, with all the cows and geese and pigs, who else was it for? *Grown ups?*

Scarlett heard the squelch of Grandma's wellies on the mud as she came round the side of the milk shed. 'Scarlett!'

Scarlett watched Grandma approach. Her wellies were dirtier than Posey's boots. His boots were always clean – but that was because his boots weren't real. *Posey* wasn't real.

It was time to grow up. Like Sophia said: 'You can't be a little kid forever.'

Scarlett traced a silvery path on top of the wall next to her, tracing where a snail had gone before and left slime behind.

Scarlett hadn't told Sophia about Posey. Sophia had been talking about the vending machine outside the dance studio, telling her that little kids got flat drinks but you could have fizzy drinks when you're older. Still, when Sophia said it, Scarlett thought of Posey.

You can't be a little kid forever.

Scarlett knew it was true.

But, still. Scarlett hadn't seen Posey since he'd slunk off to the airing cupboard that night after *Watership Down*. His ears had drooped as he walked. He hadn't even looked back.

Grandma reached Scarlett, her wellies making sucking sounds in the mud. 'You doing all right out here?'

Scarlett nodded.

'Your father's phoned again. He's going to pick you up at some point today.' Grandma bumped down onto the wall next to Scarlett. 'That was as much information as I could get out of him. You know what your father's like.'

'Why do you say "father" like that?'

'Like what?'

'Like it's got loads of other words in there as well.'

Grandma gave a bright smile. 'I don't know what you're talking about.'

Scarlett traced the snail's journey with a finger again. 'Did Dad say if they've seen Patrick yet?'

'Yes. He's recovering well from his fall, apparently. And he's in high spirits, so that's a relief.'

'He didn't fall. He got shot with an arrow. By Alex.'

Grandma kept her smile stiff. She stared into the cow field. 'How do you know that?'

Scarlett shrugged.

'Are you OK? You know it was an accident?'

Scarlett shrugged again.

Grandma kept staring into the field. 'So. Apparently, this Alex lady is coming with Dad to pick you up. Whenever that ends up being. It's not like we have animals to feed, or meals to cook, or anything.'

'Right.'

Grandma looked at Scarlett out of the side of her eye. 'Do we like Alex?'

'We?'

'You.'

Scarlett thought about this. 'Yes. We do now.'

'That's good.'

'She needs to buy better toys for her house. But she knows that now.'

Grandma squeezed Scarlett's shoulder. 'I'm going back inside. Shout if you need me.'

Scarlett traced the snail's trail on the wall. She heard the sound of boots on the path again.

'Do you want me to come in, Grandma?'

When Grandma didn't reply, Scarlett looked up.

Posey stood on the path in front of Scarlett. 'Howdy.'

Scarlett felt her heart beat faster.

Posey nodded at her feet. 'Nice gear.'

Scarlett looked down at her moonboots. 'They're almost the same as yours.'

'They're better. They're gold. Gold is better than silver.'

Scarlett looked down at her feet. 'They get dirtier than yours.'

Posey shrugged. 'That's just how it goes.'

'I also got Bryan the Lion's Jungle Palace.'

Posey whistled his approval. 'So Santa *could* afford it!'

Scarlett nodded.

'Do you want to show me your new dance? From your dance class?'

'I haven't got a chair here. I'd need a chair.'

'Shame,' Posey said. 'I bet you were really good at it.'

'I was.'

Posey sat on the wall next to Scarlett. 'I came to say goodbye. I'm off on another trip.' Posey flicked the red tag on his bum. 'I'm going back to China.'

Scarlett looked at his tag and back to his face. 'Will you be long?'

'It's a big country. And I know everyone there, so I might be a while.'

'Will you live in a castle?'

Posey shrugged. 'Probably. There are a lot of cool castles there, but I haven't decided which one yet. I just want to do my own thing for a bit, you know?'

There was neighing in the distance. Scarlett heard the sound of hooves cantering across the ground.

'I'll help you pack.' Scarlett reached down to the floor and picked up some leaves, which became twenty-pound notes in her hand. She held the notes out to Posey. 'You'll need some money for your trip!'

Posey gave a kind smile. 'We don't use money in China.'

Scarlett let her hand drop. 'I don't know much about China.'

'I can see that. Maybe I'll tell you all about it sometime.'

Scarlett thought about this. 'You might come back?'

'If you want me to.'

The sound of hooves on the ground was getting louder. Closer.

Posey didn't seem to notice. 'And I could come back for special occasions. I could come back to celebrate your big one-oh. Or I could be your date for your school prom.'

'Yes,' Scarlett said. 'I'd like that.'

'Anyway.' Posey looked over his shoulder and back to Scarlett. 'Gotta run.' He indicated behind him with his thumb. 'That's my unicorn.'

A unicorn galloped round the corner. It came to a stop beside Posey with a neigh, shaking its rainbow mane.

Scarlett gasped.

Posey tapped the unicorn's saddle. 'Good girl.'

Posey attached metal things to each of the unicorn's feet, testing each one carefully. The unicorn lifted up each hoof after Posey had finished, studying it, before placing the hoof back down again.

When Posey had done all four, the unicorn gave a soft huff of approval.

Posey pulled on the side of the saddle to check it was on properly. He put a boot in one of the stirrups and lifted himself up and over the unicorn, setting himself back down, straddling it.

Scarlett put her hand over her eyes to shade them from the sun.

Posey smiled at her. He pulled on a lever at the side of the unicorn, like Patrick used to start the lawnmower. The metal things on the unicorn's hooves started shaking and spluttering.

And then Posey and the unicorn weren't on the path any more. They were moving up, straight up, into the sky. Flames shot out from the unicorn's hooves, red and gold and yellow streams firing brightly from its rocket-feet.

Scarlett watched, her hand over her eyes.

Posey and the unicorn went higher and higher. Posey

pulled on the reins and the unicorn did a fancy turn in the sky.

Scarlett gave a clap of delight.

Posey leaned back and raised the reins. He gave Scarlett a salute.

Scarlett stood as straight up as she could. She saluted Posey back, hard.

Posey and the unicorn started moving forward now, stiffly, like a horse on a merry-go-round. They rode through the sky, over the trees, over the farm buildings and past the fields.

Scarlett chased after them, though they were getting further and further away.

When they were nearly out of sight, Scarlett slowed and stopped. She waved furiously with both arms, trying not to cry. 'Say hi to everyone in China for me!' she shouted.

She didn't know if Posey had heard, but he waved anyway. Eventually Posey and the unicorn became just a speck in the sky.

Scarlett put her hand to her chest, panting. She knew the fast beat of her heart was because she'd been running in wellies, but she felt something else as well. Her throat filled with feelings, choking her a little.

Scarlett watched the speck in the sky turn to nothing. She screwed up her eyes anyway, searching the horizon. There was nothing to see.

Eventually, she stopped shading her eyes. She stopped searching the sky.

This time, finally and forever, Posey had gone.

Post-shooting interview. Patrick Asher, 43. Shooting
victim.
Face-to-face. St. Thomas' Hospital.

OK, thank you. Comfortable. Probably because of all the drugs. They work wonders, don't they? I've never done drugs before, I should have tried them sooner.

That was a joke, officers. I'm in quite a jolly mood.

I've dodged a bullet, haven't I? This is my It's a Wonderful Life *moment. Yesterday could have been it – my time, up. I saw a white light. I saw my funeral in my head – the flowers, the people. Then, next minute, I was waking up here, with everything mainly intact and everyone crowding round me.*

Claire and Scarlett were here, obviously, and Matt and Alex. My kids are coming this afternoon. Their mum's bringing them, even though she's meant to be doing Christmas dinner. Lindsay hates it when her plans are messed about, but the kids were desperate to come and see me, so what could she do? Those pigs in blankets just have to wait.

My parents can't travel but they've been on the phone non-stop. And I hear Nicola Trevor is coming back this afternoon. So that's nice.

I've not seen her since school. Complete coincidence.

I can see that would have been confusing. We were in the lodge next door because I stood behind her in the queue for reception, thinking I recognise this woman. It was only after she left that I realised who it was. So I had to ask the receptionist to put us together, didn't I? I couldn't spend the weekend looking for Nicola round the holiday park. How did you know that, anyway?

Does Claire know?

Right.

It's just . . . a little awkward. How embarrassing.

Did Matt ask you about the arrow? My arrow?

I understand not right now. But I'd like it as a souvenir eventually, if possible.

Yes, I've forgiven Alex. She didn't mean to shoot me, did she?

It was the funniest thing. I was showing her how to load the bow, standing in front of the target, no thought of the danger. I know, it's crazy, not like me at all.

I'd had the training, yes. But I told Claire we shouldn't have signed the waiver when Alex hadn't. But Claire's so impulsive. She thinks rules are for wimps, and now look what's happened. Rules are there for a reason, that's what I always tell Claire. You need to control the fun, or it risks spilling into chaos. But she never listens to me, and now look where we are.

I was standing in front of the target, explaining to Alex how to shoot, and she was holding her bow, stretching her arm back like I told her. I didn't see what happened, but suddenly I was down, trying to work out why my shoulder was on fire.

Yes, really stupid. Not like me at all. But there we are.

I don't know where the other two were. I was concentrating on Alex. Not hard enough, clearly.

That was another joke.

I felt a searing pain. The other three rallied round me but I fell unconscious quickly.

I don't know what they talked about. I'm not aware of anything until I woke up with a drip in my arm.

Yes, we all got on famously, all trip. Barely a whisper of an argument.

Who said there was tension?

I can see why Nicola would have thought that, but it was just drunken high spirits. That's how we are – all private jokes. We probably take a bit of getting used to.

I can't think of anything else. I'm sorry we've wasted so much of your time over Christmas.

My face? I went for a run yesterday morning and I slipped on some loose gravel. I'd forgotten I had cuts and bruises, what with everything.

That's why you're asking these questions? How funny.

It's funny to me. You think Alex shot me deliberately? Please. Why would she?

It was just a nice, quiet holiday with our extended family. We're all reasonable people. The weekend was going fine. We were having a lovely time, no drama, no fights. We're all adults.

I just don't know why people find the concept so hard to understand.

Acknowledgements

This book would not be here without my fabulous agent, Caroline Hardman. Caroline, I am so grateful for your support and honesty, and so pleased to have you alongside me for this whole out-of-body experience. Thanks also to Thérèse Coen for your tireless enthusiasm on my behalf, and to the other brilliant people at Hardman & Swainson – I love being in such good hands and great company.

Thanks so much to Emad Akhtar for championing my writing, and for providing so much thoughtful insight and making me laugh in every interaction. Also thanks to Bethan Jones, Lauren Woosey, Laura Swainbank, Jen Breslin, and everyone else at Orion who has worked so expertly on my book and looked so patiently at my dog photos along the way.

Thanks to Andrea Walker and the team at Random House in the US, and to all the other overseas teams who are publishing this book: at Fleuve, AW Bruna, Euromedia, Aufbau, Mondadori, Evro Books, Znak, General Press and Hachette ANZ. (Also, to any other publishers who have taken it on since I wrote these acknowledgements in February 2018 – thanks on behalf of future me.)

Thanks to the Savvy Authors for all the fun, support and wise counsel. I dropped lucky the day I found you.

A different kind of thanks to the non-book people. To my friends who are competitive exercisers, or in blended families, or barristers or scientists: I'm going to start with an apology. Obviously you are nothing like these people. Eek.

Thanks to Andrew Bennett, Darren Birtwell, Craig Blyth, Miriam Bradley, Lorna Davies, Emma Duffy, Anthony Dutton, Dom Doughty, Ali Hogg, James Hogg, Aston Kelly, Amanda Moffat, Stu Moffat, Alison Peace, Claire Raffo, Kate Regan, Matt Regan, Chris Taft, Kate Taft and Jane Shlosberg. Also, to the poker boys, the Holmes Chapel-and-beyond crowd and my VM and EBS friends. Thanks to Mum, Dad, Tom, and all the Hulses, and to Ted and Linda.

Finally, to Fletch. For bringing the imagination, the comedy, and the geeky clumsiness on a daily basis. Thank you, most of all.